A BIRD OF SORROW

Visit us at www.boldstrokesbooks.com

By the Author

The Arravan Series

Nightshade

Blackstone

A Bird of Sorrow

King of Thieves

A BIRD OF SORROW

by

Shea Godfrey

2019

ISBN 13: 978-1-63555-009-2

This Trade Paperback Original Is Published By
Bold Strokes Books, Inc.
P.O. Box 249
Valley Falls, NY 12185

First Edition: May 2019

Credits
Editor: Ruth Sternglantz
Production Design: Susan Ramundo
Cover Design By Shea Godfrey

Acknowledgments

Thank you to my ever patient editor, Ruth Sternglantz. I appreciate all that you do.

Dedication

This book is dedicated to my mother, Joanie.

Thank you for gifting me with my first library card.

Thank you for every Saturday morning trip to the bookstore.

Thank you for always letting me get "just one more…"

Thank you for our long lunches, and Sunday mornings,
sitting on my bed and talking.

Thank you for always believing.

For your kindness and your strength.
For your generosity and your fierceness.

Thank you for being you.

Thank you for your friendship.

I love you as big as the sky.

The Panther and the Lark
Lilith Bellaq

From the land of burning sands as black as night,
Grow the Dark Ridge Mountains from the bones of the earth.
A Lark whispers of love and lifts high in flight,
For no less than a throne her heart will prove its worth.
Hooded, she soars beneath a guise of peace,
Her heart tethered in bells and heavy sorrow's shade.
In a land of rivers and green a Prince offers release,
But dreams of riches and gold upon a throne of jade.
A royal daughter who stands within the shadow of a crown,
The Golden Panther in name is the woman who waits.
Beneath the moonlight, with a kiss, a thread is unbound,
The Lark speaks of love amidst the Loom of fate.
For lost lovers who dream, a thousand years was too long,
For the Golden Panther alone, the Lark sings out her song.

Callous princes and kings begin their deadly dance,
When no price is paid for the promise of a throne.
Two women shall stand and seize their chance,
The heart wages its war for the kiss of love alone.
One bloodline is broken, while yet another revealed,
The first battle is fought where deception abounds.
The Panther's sword, for her love, becomes Arravan's shield,
The Lark's majik, for honor, once lost is thus found.
A duel to the death as rumors of war take wing,
A vile prince is laid low as another ascends.
A love declared is challenged despite the oath of a king,
With a treasonous arrow their dream of peace ends.
A jilted groom breaks all faith with a murderous gaze,
Chasing the Panther and the Lark into the heart of a maze.

...to be continued

CHAPTER ONE

Autumn 1032, the Year of Attia's Spear
The Lanark River Estate
North of Ballentrae, Arravan

It was the celebration of the autumn moon and Jessa, the Princess of Lyoness and lover of Darrius Durand, had never before encountered such a good-natured and straightforward event. The main barn of the Lanark River Estate had been transformed in a rather spectacular manner, the wood floor swept clean, the boards smooth and polished with not a wayward nail or peg. The doors and windows had been thrown open for days, and the air was heavy with the scent of pine and roasted meats, the odor of spices and baked apples layered beneath the heartier aroma of mustard seeds crushed with wine and onion.

Small bronze lanterns hung throughout the barn, and their golden light filled the structure with a welcomed warmth. One of Darry's Boys, Lucien Martins, played the fiddle upon a small dais, accompanied by the daughter of Raymon Kenna. The Seneschal of the estate stood beside a table laden with sweets and sugared fruits as the delicate sound of his daughter's flute moved beneath the strings. He had been speaking with Theroux Cain for days about the horses Darry wished to purchase, and no doubt their conversation continued. Emmalyn's first husband, Lanark's former owner, had long dreamt of running a stable of prized steeds, and that dream was now shared by many at Lanark.

Jessa's gaze found Darrius with little trouble, and her emotions intensified as Darry stepped about Bentley and Etienne in search of a goblet. The former Princess of Arravan, and the now unofficial captain of Darry's Boys, always seemed at home no matter the circumstances. The soldiers who followed her without question were not only Darry's brothers in arms, but her brothers in spirit, as well. A family that had accepted Jessa into their ranks without hesitation.

Their flight from Blackstone Keep, the official seat of power in Arravan and home to the Durand royal family, was still fresh in her mind, though four months had passed since that dark night. That the Crown Prince of Arravan had sought to murder his own sister was still a shock to her. She was not unwise to the ways of a royal son, for her own brothers represented the worst in men, at least from what she had seen thus far. The sons of Durand were of a different sort, however, and it continued to haunt her thoughts. Prince Malcolm had murdered his own advisor that night, and implicated both Bentley Greeves and Etienne Blue, two of Darry's most trusted friends, in the bargain. It was an unholy mess of power and greed, with pieces moved upon a board that stretched beyond the borders of two countries. *And we are right in the thick of it*, Jessa thought as she watched the lamplight catch upon her wine.

King Bharjah, Jessa's own father, had been assassinated, which had left her brothers entangled in a civil war that was destined to pull her country apart at the seams. Arravan was on the brink of war, not only with Lyoness, but the Fakir of the Kistanbal Mountains. Her grandmother and teacher in all things, Lady Radha, had left her for the journey home, and Jessa's own majik had blossomed beneath the weight of her need for it. The world had opened to her in all its unexpected glory and darkness, just as Radha had promised it would. *Not so long ago, actually, beneath a spring moon. And we will have to face it all, at some point.*

Jessa turned her left hand over and moved her fingers, rubbing her thumb against them. She could still remember her panic when Etienne had stumbled through the door of Sebastian's Tower with Darry in his arms. Her hands had been bathed in blood, and at times, Jessa could still feel its heat upon her skin.

"Stop."

Jessa smiled but did not look up.

"How am I to woo my lady on this fine autumn eve, if she is caught within memories that darken her heart against my words?" Darry asked in a sultry voice.

Jessa felt the heat of her lover's body as Darry stepped closer.

"There is no poem, nor song sweet enough, that might charm your clever thoughts from the endless tide of strategies and countermoves that wash ashore. I cannot compete."

Jessa lifted her face at that, wanting to laugh.

Darry's eyes were bright with both humor and love. She was lean and powerful in her dark coat and red silk tunic, her black trousers tucked in her polished boots. Her hair fell about her shoulders and down her back, the main weight of her golden curls tied with a scarlet ribbon between her shoulder blades. Jessa understood that, as a warrior, Darry no longer needed a weapon—she *was* the weapon. And yet, there was an undeniable softness and warmth to her steel, and a taste unlike any other enticement in the world. It was a taste that Jessa ached for at any given moment.

"You have no competition and you know this, *Akasha*."

Darry surveyed the room. "I would not dare entertain such an arrogant idea, my love," she said beneath the music. "I am not worthy of so fine a woman as you. That is what I know."

Jessa's thoughts caught upon the words, surprised.

"Though I will say, now that I have you?" The quiet nature of Darry's expression softened with the arrival of a smooth playfulness Jessa recognized. It made her heart quicken. "You shall not be going anywhere without me, anytime soon."

Jessa's smile returned as Darry set her goblet on the table beside them. She took Jessa's, as well, and then held out her hand. "I would dance with you, my sweet Jess. As we should have danced in the Great Hall, not so long ago upon Solstice Eve."

Jessa slipped her hand in Darry's and the warmth of her lover's touch spread beneath her skin and pushed its way along her arm. She could feel her blood rise and a blush heat the skin of her neck.

Jessa followed her onto the center of the floor and Darry spun upon the toes of her boots. Jessa caught her breath as she was pulled close, and she let her gaze drift along the curve of Darry's mouth and the shape of her nose. Darry's eyes were filled with fire, the deep blue of the sea beside the intense green of the forest.

The music faded into silence and Jessa's knees were oddly weak. She felt as she had the night of her welcoming fete at Blackstone Keep, at the mercy of her heart and not knowing what to do about it. The Mohn-Drom had been danced and she had fallen in love.

Darry's expression was filled with mischief. "Don't worry," she whispered. "I'm saving the Mohn-Drom for later."

Jessa's heart thrummed in her chest and then she laughed happily as the odd spell was broken. She stepped close, took Darry's face in her hands, and kissed her soundly. She tasted of Darry's tongue for a brief instant and then Darry took her hand. Darry found Lucien, who waited for his cue upon the small dais. "The Amandeese, Master Martins, if you would, please."

"Aye, Cap'n," Lucien responded with a grin.

Jessa remembered all too vividly their first dance as she stepped close and turned her head to the side. Her left hand was raised high in Darry's right, and just as before, the touch at Jessa's waist burned through her dress as if it was not even there, and then the music played.

They stepped into the opening turn and Jessa found Darry's eyes. Their thighs pressed close as they moved, so much closer than before, with Darry's left arm against the side of her breast. It was wonderfully intimate and familiar, so different than that afternoon in the solar all those months ago. Darry led with a sleek confidence that had been lacking in their first dance, and Jessa understood this time the true majik of Darry's attention.

Darry stepped away and Jessa lifted her arm high, Darry's touch like a flame across the skin of her palm as she spun beneath Jessa's outstretched arm, once, twice, and then she was close once more.

Darry's right leg was deep between her own as they turned and then twirled through the last sequence of steps. She fell into her lover's strength quite willingly, and without the shyness that had once been her closest companion. The last steps were upon them before she knew it and the quick step turning passed away as they spun as one through the finish.

They stood before all of their friends, their new family, and it did nothing to temper Jessa's passion in the sudden silence. Darry's lips were so close, and the scent of her skin overwhelmed Jessa's senses, musk and the sea impossibly entwined.

"Are you going to kiss me?" Darry asked in a whisper.

"I might," Jessa responded, her desire awake and alive in her belly.

Darry's full lips curled with a smile and Jessa lifted her eyes. "I think you should."

"So do I," Jessa agreed as her left hand found the back of Darry's neck and drew her down. She opened Darry's mouth and kissed her with passion, her hand fisting within Darry's hair. Darry bent her back in response, and she gave Jessa the kiss she so desperately wanted, passionate and hot-blooded with promise.

A riotous cheer went up and the fiddle burst forth with sound, a reel that sang out bold and fast beneath the high roof of the barn.

Jessa felt the lack of Darry's lips as Darry released her in a swirl of movement, and Tobe Giovanni, Matthias Brave, and Matty the Younger crowded close. Orlando Davignon reached out and took her hand. "Dance, my Lady?"

Jessa's eyes found Darry as Matthias said with conviction that he'd been promised the reel that very morning.

Darry returned her gaze, her eyes intense as she smiled in a most beautiful, open manner.

Jessa licked her lips for any last taste of her lover. "I love you," she said in a soft push of words.

Darry's expression deepened and her eyes flared, and then Bentley took hold of his dearest friend and danced her away before Jessa could speak against it.

"My Lady?" Matthias demanded. "Tell him."

Jessa laughed. "I believe I promised Matty."

The younger man laughed happily and let out a whoop as Orlando grabbed Matthias by the collar. "Dance with me, you handsome fool."

Matthias slid in close as he took Orlando by the waist. "You're such a tart."

"I have a nice ass, too."

Matthias flashed a subtle and yet somehow wicked smile. "You do, actually, it's true."

"What about me?" Tobe called as they spun away from him.

Jessa found Matty the Younger, suddenly quiet and still as he considered his unexpected victory. "Do you know the reel, Matty?"

The young man stared at her offered hand and his face was red as he looked up.

Jessa stepped closer and took his elbow. "Then I will teach you. They'll never know."

"I didn't expect to be chosen," Matty replied, startled.

Jessa pulled the young man with her as she stepped onto the open floor. She caught sight of Darry as Bentley and her lover spun smoothly near the dais. Jessa smiled as Matty took her by the waist with an uncertain touch. "Neither did I," she admitted.

Chapter Two

Autumn 1032, the Year of Attia's Spear
Lokey, Arravan

"Do you think it will work?" Emmalyn, the eldest daughter of the Durand family, studied each of her younger brothers in turn.

Jacob's expression was uncertain. "I don't—"

"I don't give a whore's cock whether it will work or not," Wyatt Durand said as he moved from the shadows and into the firelight. He was nearly six and a half feet tall, with the broadest shoulders Emmalyn had seen upon any Durand, even her uncle Sullidan. His formal uniform was cut close about his chest, and his white tunic was bright beneath it. His sword belt caught the light from the fire, as did his blue eyes beneath his tightly cut curls of black hair. He had shaved that afternoon, but the light caught upon a fresh dusting of beard growth and turned it gold. "I will fucking beat it out of him in front of the entire rotting court." He glared at Jacob, frustrated. "These bloody games will get us nowhere!"

"Please, Wyatt." Emmalyn's voice was quiet and calm. "Keep your voice down."

"Why?" he demanded, leaning back at the waist. "Because of his spies?"

Jacob sighed and sank farther into his chair. "Yes."

"Aren't *you* supposed to be the bloody Prince of Spies?"

The silence was thick within the room and then Jacob rose up, his chair shoved back with such violence that it tipped over with a clatter.

"Listen, you bloody oaf." Jacob's right hand stabbed against Wyatt's chest, but Wyatt's feet did not move. "If this is the truth, and Gamar help me, I know that it is, then Malcolm has done murder... aside from trying to kill his own *sister*, a daughter of the blood. Do you think he will confess that information just because you knock his nose to the side in front of the ladies? He is playing a game deeper than any I have seen, and if Jessa was right, his assassin has killed a *king*. And that assassin was my man, an honorable man who sacrificed his life for his family."

That Malcolm had coerced a man into murder by threatening the lives of children had changed the game and sent them all tumbling into an ethical and moral darkness they might never escape from.

"And where is his family?" Jacob continued. "They are not where I last left them, I can tell you that much. Five young girls and their mothers fled from the only homes they have known, and their fathers, caught in the turning and forced to entrust their children to the son of their country's greatest enemy. And where did *that* get them?"

Jacob took a small step closer, looking up. His anger was on display and it was a rare thing. "Into the mouth of a hell I had promised to save them from, that's where it got them. Until we find them, Wyatt, we can do nothing without *proof*, or the heirs of Almahdi de Ghalib will haunt us for the rest of our days."

Emmalyn could see that Wyatt took Jacob's warning to heart. It dampened the fire of his anger in a way that Emmalyn had not seen from him before. When he had gone north five years ago for the Greymear border and Senegal, he had been a hotheaded young man with confidence and charm to spare. Emmalyn could see that while he still possessed those traits in abundance, he had grown in both subtlety and compassion. His temper was much the same, although that, too, had changed into something more measured and somewhat mysterious in its presentation.

He had been home for over a month, and he had returned to a house in turmoil, embroiled in scandal and on its heels. He had been informed of Darry's absence from Blackstone, but he had borne the news with a quiet, frustrated expression and not much else. It had been a true surprise to both Malcolm and their parents that his reaction had been so hardened.

Emmalyn had Royce to thank for that. Her lover's secret trip to Kastamon City in order to meet with Wyatt, before the Seventh crossed the Armasha River for the last leg of their journey home, had been the key to everything. Royce had delivered Emmalyn's letter with no one the wiser, and Emmalyn knew that Wyatt had wept when he read it.

"But she is truly well now, isn't she?" Wyatt asked in a worried, almost defeated voice. "She is fully recovered from whatever he did to her, isn't she? Telling me she is well is not good enough. You must tell me where they are, Jacob, please. Don't make me keep asking."

Emmalyn met Jacob's gaze. Jacob stepped to the side and said, "Then you must ask our sister. Even I don't know where they are." Jacob gave her a grudging smile. "She takes my missives and they end up where they end up."

Emmalyn lifted her eyes to Wyatt's. "No."

"That isn't fair and you know it, Em."

"Perhaps not. But what will you do if I tell you?"

Wyatt considered the question. "I would find some way to see her, and let her know that she's not alone in this." Wyatt's handsome expression was filled with tender emotion. "I would…I would kiss the hand of her beloved."

Emmalyn's heart gave a tug at his words, and she recognized the wonder in his tone. "She is not alone, and she is recovered from her wounds. She has Jessa, and she has the Wild Bastards."

Wyatt blinked and then his brow went up. "The Wild Bastards? When did *that* happen?"

"When Darry's Boys rode through a cyclone that tore half the barracks to the ground, sucked the stones from the mortar of the solar walls, and then disappeared into a magical garden never to be seen again," Emmalyn said with a sly grin. "It's too dangerous, Wyatt, and I will not allow it. She is well, and she is not alone. You have my oath on it."

Wyatt stared at her and Emmalyn tilted her head to the side, ever so slightly.

"Yes, my Lady."

"Father excludes Mal from what he can, but if it is known that the succession is in jeopardy, a schism will break the court. With Father's impending war against the Fakir but a careless word away from spilling into Lyoness instead, on the backs of a screaming Arravan horde, he can only do so much without pitting himself against his firstborn son for all the world to see. Malcolm's following among the young lords on the council has become too great."

Emmalyn pushed from her chair and smoothed at her skirt as she stood before her brothers.

"Find Almahdi de Ghalib's family, Jacob, and see if you can find a reliable spy in the Salish home. I've not forgotten Melora's treachery against Darry, and with Marteen dead, she may have become more of a confidante to Mal than she wished to be. Though how that may end when the truth of what happened that night is finally revealed, I have no idea. Malcolm's tale of Bentley seeking revenge for Darry's downfall may make sense to those who know him by reputation alone, but the scene and the circumstances of the crime are a lie in the worst way, and everyone sees it. And they see it without having the information that we do."

Emmalyn's eyes drifted to the flames in the fireplace as she remembered how Etienne Blue had refused to leave her side during the Siege of the Great Hall. When the Sahwello had broken past the wall of tables, he had stepped in front of her and stood his ground. *I won't leave you*, he had said, and he hadn't.

"I will speak to Lord Greeves myself, on Etienne Blue's behalf," she added as she turned from the fire. "That he has no one to stand for him, as Bentley does, is its own injustice. Treemont Greeves will listen, and I'll not have the crimes of another fall onto Etienne alone, for the sole reason that he lacks a rightful name. I think Malcolm is finding the Greeves family more powerful than he had imagined they were."

Jacob nodded. "I agree, on all of it, Emma."

"And let us not forget the weakest link in Malcolm's chain."

"I'll see to that one." Wyatt's tone was dark as he acknowledged her words. "It shouldn't take much to woo him over."

"No," Emmalyn countered. "Leave Captain Jefs alone. Your sudden attention will raise suspicion, if not with Jefs, then most certainly with Mal. He is the man who supports Mal's story of what happened that night. He is either under his thumb, as Lord de Ghalib was, or a partner in whatever Mal is planning. Either way, he'll be closely watched."

Wyatt frowned. "Then what in all seven hells am I supposed to do?"

"Become a charming new member of Malcolm's circle," Emmalyn answered with ease. "Avoid any talk of Darry. Your affection for her is a well-known fact, and he'll not forget that. Don't overdo things, but side with him against Father when you see the advantage. Take him drinking at Madame Dubassant's and pay for his pleasure. Throw your arm about his shoulders when he becomes frustrated, and then, when the moment is right? Share with him your belief that Lyoness will be ripe for the picking. When the bloodletting between Jessa's brothers comes to an end, any soldier with an eye for such things will know it for the truth. Invite him into the inner circle of the Seventh, which he has always looked upon with great desire."

Wyatt's shoulders fell somewhat.

"Ask him for his advice on matters of war."

Wyatt's expression contorted. "Gamar's *balls*, Emmalyn."

Emmalyn couldn't help but smile. "Wyatt, you are the only man Malcolm has ever openly admired. That is a weapon entirely too useful to leave rusting by the side of the road, merely because it is heavy. We have no choice but to seek justice, not only for Darry, but for Marteen Salish. We have Bentley's account of what happened from Nina, and Jessa's word, as well. Do you have faith in Darry's honor?"

"More than my own," Wyatt replied with a slight grin.

"Then you must give Jessa's words the same weight you would give Darry's." A lift of her eyebrow silenced any further comment. "And I don't care if Marteen *was* a toad, as Darry was wont to call him. Murder is a crime that demands justice, and I will not stand by and watch the throne of Arravan be sullied, nor turned into a game piece for Malcolm to gamble with."

"I'm with you, Emma, but you're not letting me use my best weapon. Intrigue is a blade I might open my own throat with, and we all know it."

"Then improve your skills as quickly as you can," Emmalyn advised. "Because I assure you this is Darry's best hope, and ours, as well."

Wyatt sighed and his face cleared somewhat. "What was Bentley Greeves doing in Nina's bedchamber, anyway?" He gave a smile. "I thought our little water rat was going to marry Hammond Marsh."

"She still is, as far as I know."

Wyatt's blue eyes gave a playful flash. "Cousin Nina is all grown up."

"Stow that in your pocket, *little* brother," Emmalyn warned. "Hammond is lovely, but he's a complete bore and we all know it. Nina will follow her heart, and you will both be nothing but supportive of her, and you will defend her honor to the last if it comes to that. Bentley Greeves may have the reputation of a cad, but he is one of the most honorable and trustworthy men I have ever met. I'm not surprised that he's not met his match until now."

Wyatt set a hand upon his brother's shoulder and looked at her, his scrutiny as keen as she had ever seen it. "Are you still unbeaten at Kings and Jackals, sister?"

"She is," Jacob answered for her. "And so what now?"

"Now we attend the autumn moon celebration. Alisha and Nina can only keep the wolves at bay for so long, before our absence is noted." She looked to Wyatt. "And make sure that you dance with your queen, or I shall tan your tall and pretty hide for all the Seventh to see."

Wyatt's expression softened. "Yes, my Lady."

Emmalyn turned with a swirl of her silken skirt and walked away from them. When she reached the door, Wyatt's voice stopped her.

"We should talk soon, Emma, about Mother's place in all of this. We've not spoken of her yet, and I think it's time we did."

Emmalyn felt the cool iron of the door handle against her palm. "She mourns the loss of a second child…" The words burned through her chest and she let them light her way. *And she will lose another before this is over, one way or another.* "Darry shall not return to us, unless it is to kill Malcolm. And so I believe she's not likely to ever return." Emmalyn closed her eyes against what she knew to be true. "Mother will come to us when she is ready."

Chapter Three

Jessa followed Darry down the shadowed hallway, a single lamp left lit by the top of the stairs. They had danced and they had eaten. They had laughed and played games of chance, and they had told stories. And then they had danced some more, leaving an empty cask of spring wine in their wake. Her feet had never been so sore, but she had one last dance left, and the music of its beat sang within her veins as she tightened her fingers about Darry's. She had never danced the Mohn-Drom with another, but she was about to, and she had been ready since Darry had first spun out the intricate steps upon the polished floor of the Great Hall.

Darry opened the door, and Jessa moved smoothly as she twirled into their room. Darry closed the door behind them and then followed, close at Jessa's hip. She caught Jessa by the waist and Jessa swayed and bent away from her, smiling at the certain strength that pulled her back. They turned across the floor in a glide of close steps.

Jessa felt the hands low upon her hips, and the press of Darry's body, her powerful thighs and the smooth, defined muscles of her upper body. Jessa pushed back, the pulse between her legs pounding well beyond her memory of the bodhran's beat. Darry's left hand was possessive as she cupped Jessa's breast, Jessa's hardened nipple caught beneath Darry's thumb. Jessa kissed her and Darry lifted her from the floor as their tongues met, Jessa grasping Darry's curls and pulling the ribbon free.

Jessa's mouth opened fully and she moaned, her body demanding more. "I don't..." Darry turned them toward the bed and Jessa's feet touched the floor. Jessa began to undo the buttons at her waist. "I don't think you're meant to finish this *fikloche* dance."

Darry stepped back and yanked her jacket off, her hands moving down the buttons of her tunic an instant later. Jessa took advantage, her hands gliding upon Darry's exposed skin and over her heavy scars. The scar upon her ribs from the Siege of the Great Hall, and the lighter one beneath that, the cut to repair the damage her duel with Joaquin had caused. Her touch was fervent upon the dark tissue below Darry's left collarbone, a constant reminder that their love held a price in blood. She closed her hands upon Darry's breasts and leaned in. Darry kissed her again, naked from the waist up as the remaining buttons at the back of Jessa's dress opened beneath the subtle skill of Darry's fingers.

Jessa pulled free of the bodice and pressed her breasts against Darry's.

"I love you," Darry said in a strained voice. Her different-colored eyes were on the edge of wild, and yet they held a keen awareness that tipped Jessa's world.

Jessa's hands slid upward until she held Darry's face. Her mouth brushed against Darry's as she spoke. "You are the sweetest thing I have ever tasted, *Akasha*." Jessa kissed her deeply, a hard quiver of pleasure sliding along the flesh between her legs. She wondered if she would spend her spirit upon a kiss. It would not be the first time she had done so, nor the last, her heart wagered.

Darry's hands pulled at Jessa's skirt and the fabric rustled as Jessa pushed completely free of her remaining clothes. The buttons of Darry's trousers popped open beneath Jessa's fingers, and she slipped her hand beneath the soft material of Darry's breeches as well. She felt briefly of the heat and then slid her hand free, moving her nails along the tight skin in a teasing manner. She licked her lips as Darry's abdomen jerked in reaction. "Kiss me, *Akasha*."

A smooth whoosh of air rushed along Jessa's skin as she fell.

The bed caught her with softness and Darry moved between her legs, Jessa's hands sliding about Darry's ribs, and then lower, grasping at her buttocks as the firm muscles pushed smoothly. Darry's mouth opened Jessa's, and Jessa felt the fierce rise of her pleasure, pulling her hands back as Darry slipped her arm between them.

Jessa was lost at the first passionate caress upon her sex, her hips thrusting in reaction as she tried to breathe within the depths of their kiss. Darry's fingers circled and stroked her flesh with ever increasing speed, and Jessa fell from the edge as she spent in a wave of heat, the fullness of Darry's fingers slipping within her body. She cried out, her hands pulling at Darry's shoulders as her head pushed into the soft covers of their bed. Her flesh seized and convulsed with the purest of pleasures, Darry's left hand closing in Jessa's hair. Darry turned Jessa's head as Jessa spent beneath her, her open mouth tasting of Jessa's neck. The bite caused a sharp burst of pleasure to blossom atop the first, and Jessa's cry moved along her throat in a decadent manner, never released, as the muscles of her neck strained beneath her satisfaction.

Jessa's hands moved weakly in Darry's hair as her body jerked and then shuddered into that profound place beyond the intensity of her bliss. Darry's touch gentled in a slow manner and Jessa opened her eyes, her heartbeat still wild as her hands tightened in Darry's hair. Darry's fingers slipped free of her flesh but did not leave as Darry shifted her weight.

"*Akasha...*" Jessa whispered with love and closed her legs upon Darry's hand.

Jessa took hold of Darry's face and lifted it to her own.

She stared into Darry's eyes while she caught her breath, and she remembered the midnight streets of Karballa, where she had worn her loneliness like a second cloak beneath the protection offered by the Veil of Shadows.

Her steps had been silent amidst the people, and she remembered having no fear as she moved through the darkness. She remembered the sea of voices, and the music of stray laughter somewhere in the distance. She remembered the heat, and the sound of music, as if from a dream as it drifted above the rooftops. Lovers glimpsed through a window, their passion shared as their bodies moved beneath the cries of pleasure given and received. Things she had long understood would never be hers.

Jessa grabbed Darry by the shoulders and pushed away from the bed, rolling them over.

She straddled her lover and kissed her, breathing in Darry's scent, tasting her, savoring and living their love. She reached beneath

Darry's clothes and stroked her, Darry's hands taking hold of Jessa's thighs in a rough manner. Jessa's tongue stretched and searched, her heart dazed by the silken, swollen touch of Darry's need. She let her fingers play and tease, and then like a hunter, she demanded her price.

It was always this, this wonder that filled her soul when Darry was beneath her touch, the certain knowledge that Darry loved her regardless of what the Great Loom might want. That she had found so much passion in a life that had always promised so little of such things. It was as intoxicating as any other joy they experienced together.

Jessa could feel it in Darry's flesh and she freed her lover's mouth, pressing her face against the heat of Darry's cheek. She closed her eyes and bit her lip at Darry's rough, aching cry, Darry's legs tightening as her hips lifted from the bed in a rush of spirit.

"What is this?" Jessa asked as she ate another piece of blackened meat.

"It's rabbit."

Jessa licked her fingers as she leaned back between Darry's legs, at her leisure against the warmth of Darry's naked body. They were covered by the sheet and light blanket of their bed, the plate balanced between Jessa's chest and raised knees. The lamp upon the bedside table had been lit, and its light was filled with warmth. "It does not taste like rabbit."

"There is a sauce of sweet peppers and spices, and then it's baked."

Jessa leaned to the side and smiled back at her lover. Darry accepted the piece of meat she offered with a slow, playful mouth.

"It's very good," Darry agreed. "Give me your fingers."

Jessa's eyes closed slightly and her lips parted in a heady wave of desire as Darry sucked the sauce from her fingers, one at a time. Her stomach flipped in a slow manner and she felt it deep within her thighs. "Your mouth might topple an entire kingdom, *Akasha*, if used in such a manner."

Darry's legs tightened their embrace. "Not when my feet hurt this much."

Jessa laughed and returned to their food. "The Mohn-Drom is the only dance that did not crush my toes."

Darry laughed with her. "Praise the gods."

"I will say, though, that never once did *you*, Darrius Lauranna, overstep your boundaries upon the dance floor." She ate another piece. "Nor did Arkady or Bentley, for that manner." Jessa stopped chewing and turned her head slightly. "Did you dance with Arkady?"

"I did not dance with Arkady, my love," Darry answered, and Jessa could hear the smile in her voice.

"A wise decision."

Jessa could feel Darry's face in the fullness of her hair, and then the warmth of Darry's breath along the side of her neck. The flesh between her legs clenched in reaction. "Do not be jealous, my Princess."

"This very bed, *Akasha*, is proof of how the Mohn-Drom is meant to end." The sudden, subtle push of the Vhaelin was in her blood and Jessa set the plate aside, sensing the panther's presence. "I could not take it," she confessed as she twisted about at the waist. "To see another person touch you so, I could not take it again."

Darry shifted them both in a quick movement and Jessa opened her legs. Their bodies came together and Jessa filled her hands with Darry's hair. "I will not ever leave you, sweet Jess. Not *ever*, I promise. Do you not understand that I am only here in this life for you and you alone?"

Jessa smoothed Darry's brow, easing the crease her passionate emotions had caused. It was a new expression for Darry, since her encounter with Malcolm. Darry had lost something that terrible night, some essential part of her carefree spirit. That lost innocence had been replaced with a dangerous ferocity and, oftentimes, a sadness that Jessa knew would always be there. "I have only just found you again, *Akasha*...For the rest of our lives, I will have only just found you."

Darry's hips thrust smoothly and Jessa caught her breath as her passion flared. Her nipples ached with the sweetest of pains, pressed beneath Darry's. "Then let us make the most of it." Darry kissed her and bit gently at Jessa's lower lip. "And feast while we may."

Jessa smiled as Darry moved down her body, Darry's lips burning a trail of intent. Darry's fingers traced along Jessa's swollen sex, flirting through her spirit before she parted Jessa's legs. Jessa reacted to the delicate touch and scattered the pillows in search of the carved spindles of the headboard.

Darry took hold of Jessa's hips in a decisive manner and pulled her closer before she kissed her belly, slowly, tasting of her skin so thoroughly that Jessa felt the delicious echo of Darry's lips within her legs. "The Kingdom of Lady Jessa," Darry said softly, and Jessa could hear the smile in her voice.

Jessa laughed in her throat and turned her face to the side, closing her eyes in pleasure. "Perhaps I should jus—" Darry kissed her sex, no longer teasing but decidedly certain of what she wanted. Jessa pulled against the headboard as she caught her breath. "*Surrender.*"

Darry walked through the throne room of Blackstone Keep, the light from the lamps above twisting in the hot breeze that washed through the chamber. The light slashed and cut across her vision and she narrowed her eyes against it. She moved with caution through the haze that floated just above the floor, a fog of warmth rolling over the worn stones.

She was dressed for battle, her heavy homespun blacks worn beneath her armor, the layered leather vented and shifting with her as she moved. The studs and buckles on the dark brown leather would flash into the shadows and she would have to turn her head against it. She flexed her fingers upon the grip of her sword.

"Is this better than a cell?"

Darry crouched and spun upon her toes, only to rise up in the heat and slash with the back edge of her blade. The heat parted upon her steel and she turned smoothly, her father's throne rising up on her left with an odd screech of sound. The ornamental leaves rattled and shook upon their branches until they broke free of their fasteners and clattered across the floor, disappearing.

"Do you think a cock for a tongue will please her?"

Darry whirled into the dance and the chamber filled with the unbroken sound of her sword. Her movements flowed like water, without a hitch or a stutter.

She slid to a stop as her weapon slashed downward, held beside the length of her right leg with a final ping of sound. She fell within a stillness she recognized and tried to focus. The heat swarmed about her boots and it was hard to breathe. She could feel the sweat slide down her back as the lamp above her went out beneath the whisper of her name.

The girl appeared from out of the mist and walked toward her. Her dress was a dark blue, a silk that shimmered and flowed until it stopped just below her knees. Thick black hair tumbled about her shoulders, blue ribbons caught in the curls.

Darry's heart hammered in her chest and she took a step, her sword falling lax at her side as she stood up straight and her shoulders eased. She recognized her mother's eyes in the child's face and a pang of sadness twisted through her heart.

"You came back," the girl said in a pleased voice. She lifted her hands, and the fragile, faded petals she held floated into the air upon a wave of indigo light. "These are for you."

Darry felt the arrow enter between her shoulders despite the armor she wore, the broad head ripping and pushing through her flesh. Her back bowed forward as the leather gave way between her breasts and the bolt tore free in a shower of blood. *Her sword clattered to the stones as she slammed to her knees, tipped to the side, and fell.*

Darry stumbled from their bed and dropped to her knees in reaction to the pain. It swarmed through her body, and she pulled her chin back as it threatened to split her skull. Her fingers dug into the rug, and the darkness behind her eyelids flared with a piercing light that tumbled away from her in a shower of stars.

The blood that fell between her hands soaked the rug. It was but a few drops at first, and then it was more, too much, and she knew it. Darry pushed to her feet and swayed as the room tipped, her blood hot as it filled her nose and slid over her lips. Her voice was strained. "*Jess...*"

She stepped to the end of the bed and pulled on her trousers, concentrating as she did each of the buttons. Her hands shook, and though she willed them to stop, they did not. She coughed in a rattling manner as she stepped back with her tunic and shrugged her shoulders into it. The birds of morning had begun to sing, though the sun had yet to crest the edge of the world. It was coming, though, and she could feel it as her heart took on a new beat, a faster beat, a more powerful beat.

She blinked and looked down as she pulled her touch along the skin of her stomach, her hand coming away rich with blood. Jessa's presence filled her body and she could smell her lover's flesh, the very essence and heat of her blood, as well as the sweet aroma of her sex. She turned in a stilted manner, unable to stop the release of strength that poured through her muscles.

She had not allowed her full *Cha-Diah* blood to come since the Sahwello had attacked, and so she let it, understanding that it was far too late anyway. She let go and a soft moan slipped along her throat. Her muscles shuddered with a bone-deep relief that was both wondrous and terrible at the same time. "Jessa."

"Darry," Jessa whispered, pulled from her sleep. Jessa blinked and took a deep breath through her nose as she stretched. The majik overwhelmed her senses in an instant, its pungent, ancient scent trampling over all else. She pushed up and twisted about, her eyes wide.

Darry stood near the bureau across the room, barefoot and half dressed, her dagger in hand. The curved blade caught the lamplight as it stretched away from the back of her hand. Her power rolled in waves, pouring over her shoulders in a cascade of soft, golden light, flecked through with a strange blue. Blood painted her lips and chin, curving its way between her breasts and over the muscles of her stomach.

Jessa moved with extreme caution as she pulled herself to the edge of the bed. She dropped her feet to the floor and pushed the covers aside with a slow, deliberate hand. "*Akasha*, come to me, please," she said softly, her mind searching instantly for the proper spell. She did not possess the proper runes, however, and she knew it. She did not even know what those runes might be. Darry's majik had overwhelmed her, and Jessa had no idea how she might stop it.

"*Don't...*" Darry's voice was a low growl of sound from deep within her body. "*Don't be afraid, Jess.*"

Jessa smiled as she stood up and reached out, the gesture measured and gentle. "I'm not," she lied. "My love…come to me now, all right? It will be all right." She took a careful step.

Darry turned, and Jessa jerked at the burst of movement, startled as Darry bolted onto the balcony, swung her legs over the railing, and disappeared into the darkness.

Jessa ran and slid to a stop against the railing, tipping past its safety for just an instant until she grabbed it with strong hands. The courtyard below her was empty, the trees caught in the fall of moonlight and shadows both. The hedges that were trimmed so neatly and the pathway which led to the front hall were eerily still and silent, and her gaze was pulled to the gates that had been left open. That way lay the gardens and the orchard, and beyond them both, the depths of the forest.

She pushed back and turned her right hand, her palm wet with blood from the rail.

She took a slow step back, and then another, the air before dawn cool against her naked body. A shiver moved along her spine, and she closed her eyes, her heart sinking like a stone as a sea of regret opened wide beneath her. She could hear Radha's voice in her head, rightfully harsh with disappointment. *How could you not have looked for the runes, you foolish child!*

Chapter Four

Darry moved through the heart of the Yellandale Forest faster than she had ever run before. Her feet barely seemed to touch the ground as the muscles of her legs surged with unrestrained power. The undergrowth, when caught underfoot, snapped and burst, thrown up in her wake. She glanced to her left and Hinsa kept pace farther up the rise, her sleek golden coat catching the late afternoon sun in dapples of brown that moved along her shoulders and back.

Little one! The stag...

Darry leaped the fallen oak smoothly and cleared the broken branches and rotting leaves with distance to spare. She looked to her right, to the ground some twenty feet below, the crumbling bluff covered with moss and scrub grass as it spilled downward in a sharp cut of rock.

The great stag tore through the growth beneath the bluff. Branches broke and the ground shook beneath his mighty hooves, showers of dirt exploding into the air as he ran. His coat was almost black, and Darry could smell the blood from the wound upon his hindquarters. His breath, came in great pain-filled snorts as he leaped. He was losing speed and, as a result, the distance he would need to survive.

They're coming!

Darry heard the howl and tightened the grip on her dagger, her hair wet with sweat as she glanced back. The heavy strands clung to her face and shoulders and held to her battered tunic. Her lungs burned with their pace, but it was good, and so the thought slipped away as quickly as it had come.

The wolves moved like ghosts, their silver and white coats weaving among the landscape like lightning that had fallen to the ground and never stopped. They were great beasts built for the hunt, clever and certain of their prey. The wolves were many and the stag was old—Darry knew it. He wore his years atop his head in a velvet laden crown unlike any she had ever seen. He was holy, and she could feel it.

The stag jumped, his massive rack of antlers reaching forward as he neared the wide stream. They were too heavy though and threw him off balance in his fatigue. Water splashed and he stumbled as he tried to turn, a wall of brambles and stone upon the opposite shore perhaps closer than he had gauged. He slid and fell, his legs flying to the side as his shoulder hit the ground with a great rumble of weight.

The wolves scrambled at the near edge of the water and came together as Hinsa turned down the rise. Darry lengthened her stride, cutting to the right. The pack broke apart and rushed the stream as the stag flailed and stumbled to his legs, lifting up from the mud and grit with a bellow of defiance.

Darry leaped from the bluff with a brutal push of muscle, Hinsa bounding beside her and soaring from the edge in a shower of rock and shale.

Darry felt the water and the mud as she entered the stream and her legs absorbed the shock, and then she felt the heat and claws of her enemy. The guttural sounds of anger ripped through her head as she drove to the far edge of the stream with a slash of her dagger.

The stag thundered and slammed his hooves beside her as Darry pulled her right shoulder close and turned her head with a cry of pain. She spun and splashed away as the stag speared her opponent and then heaved the wolf to the side. There was a high-pitched howl of pain amidst the breaking of bones and Darry was tangled anew in fur and the snapping of jaws. She took a blow to her right thigh and she brought her dagger underneath. The heat of blood spilled forth and the enormous weight of the wolf shifted in her arms and pulled her over.

Hinsa's scream echoed through her head and she called back. Pain shook through her left shoulder and down her back and she went under, trapped beneath the wolf and pushed to the bottom of the stream. She twisted and shoved with her legs as the rocks against her back rolled and shifted, allowing her to slip free.

She stood in a rush and threw her hair back as she filled her lungs with air. She took an awkward step to the side in the waist-high cold of the water. Hinsa screamed again and moved low upon the opposite shore, attentive as the remaining wolves bolted through the brush and long grass. Darry's right leg gave out when she took another step, and she stumbled through the water and went to her knees. The steady flow moved about her chest and she welcomed it.

The stag stomped along the sandy edge and then pushed into the steady spill with a toss of his mighty crown. Darry reached out, her dagger still in hand as she grabbed at his heavy coat. He pushed against her, gentle in his invitation.

❖

Jessa sat back in the saddle and pulled the reins. Vhaelin Star turned her head with a snort of defiance and high-stepped to the side before she obeyed. Jessa wore a homespun shirt and trousers tucked in her knee high boots, her hair tied back and out of the way. She was hot and dusty from the search, but her fear outweighed all other concerns. Bentley and Arkady Winnows rode through the trees and underbrush in the distance and she called out to them.

Bentley heeled his mount. "We lost the blood trail. There's no sign of her," he said as they entered the small clearing.

Jessa turned at the waist and peered into the forest they had yet to explore. It seemed endless, and it cut away at her hopes.

"It's getting dark, Jessa." Bentley's tone was not a happy one. "We must go back, at least to the meadow. Etienne and Tobe have set up camp."

"Please, my Lady," Arkady added.

The cedars and towering spruce trees tangled with mountain honeysuckle and fallen oaks that had crumbled into the undergrowth. Pines and spunwood trees and the heart of the Yellandale still lay before them. The far arc of the sun slashed through the leaves and slid along the high boughs, its golden light an unwelcome herald. Night would be there in but a few short hours, perhaps even sooner with the heaviness of the foliage above.

"No."

"Yes, Jessa, it's far too dangerous for—"

Jessa yanked upon the reins and Vhaelin Star wheeled to the left and reared back. Jessa threw the witchlight into the air where it shattered and spun into a flat, circular wave of light. It expanded outward with force and flowed into the surrounding forest with a low-pitched shudder of sound. Arkady's horse shied and bolted into the brush as the light poured over them and then rolled beyond, Arkady cursing as he fought to regain control.

Bentley's horse merely lowered her head into the long grass and sampled its taste.

"I thank you for the concern," Jessa stated simply. "But I do not need your protection."

"I know that," Bentley replied calmly as he brushed a smear of dirt from his sleeve. "But I do not let a friend ride into the unknown without being there to watch her back. Call it a habit, if you will."

Jessa eased back into her saddle at his words. If he were not such a man, Darrius would be dead and she knew it. "Your horse is either very old, Bentley, or the most well-trained animal I have ever seen."

"She's as blind as my old nursemaid was," Bentley said with affection.

"I should go on alone." Jessa's voice was tired and scared and she could hear it. "I think it might draw her out. I think she will come to me."

He swung his right leg over the neck of his horse and slid to the ground. "You're probably right," he agreed. "Leave a trail of your"—he wiggled his fingers at her—"parlor light trickery, so we can track you in the morning."

"I'll be fine, Bentley, I promise."

"Arkady and I will camp here and split the distance to the Lanark. The others have orders to stay put until dawn. Do you have enough water?"

Jessa was relieved by his words, though she didn't say it as she checked her saddlebags. "I have food and blankets, and two skins of water."

Bentley looked up as he neared. "Do you have a dagger?"

"In my bag."

"I will make you a belt for Winter Solstice, Princess. Your dagger will do you little good if you must stop and unpack before defending yourself. The first decent stream you come to, make camp. Do not cross until tomorrow. She'll need water at some point." He smiled beneath his mustache. "And the stars will sparkle in the current for you, like jewels in a crown of night."

Jessa found herself upon the receiving end of his infamous charm, and she felt herself blush regardless of everything. She leaned over in her saddle and touched his cheek. "I like things that sparkle."

"All the best girls do."

"I'll leave a trail for you."

Bentley stepped away. "I'd slap your horse's ass, but I imagine she'd pound me into the ground before I could appreciate the foolishness of this entire endeavor."

Jessa pulled the reins and Vhaelin Star backed away until they turned, and Jessa tapped her heels to the filly's ribs. Vhaelin Star high-stepped once more into the brush beyond the clearing and the trees closed in as they moved along the trail, their path darker than Jessa had expected. The wilds of the Yellandale swallowed them up rather easily, and Jessa clicked her tongue for a bit more speed despite the unknown terrain.

The forest was filled with life and more obscure than she had imagined. Small animals moved among the growth that covered the forest floor and high up in the trees, as well, and Jessa recognized only a half of what she had encountered thus far. The forest had become Hinsa's home since they had left the Green Hills behind, and it was a heady, magnificent place.

Jessa knew she had been a fool not to pursue Radha's scrolls with more vigor, as well as the many scrolls she had hastily taken from Sebastian's Tower. She had neglected her studies when her knowledge had been needed the most. The fear that Darry might not wish to come back after living in the depths of her majik was like a fresh wound, and it was a harsh one.

Their present life was an intoxicating thing for both of them, to be in a place of freedom where their responsibilities were only what they needed to be. For Darry especially, Jessa had realized early on. Not only had Darry needed time to heal, but to see Darry at her leisure with her friends and comrades was a joyful thing. Jessa had been easily lulled into the harmony their often aimless pursuits provided. They worked hard, for the estate was large, but for the first time in perhaps all of their lives, Darry's Boys' included, they were beholden to no one and duty bound only to each other and the well-being of their company. Darry had been most adamant that they rest while they had the chance.

Darry had released her majik in full during the attack by the Sahwello, after a lifetime of hiding and repressing her connection to Hinsa. The boundaries of her majik had expanded and changed in a drastic manner, and untapped depths of power had risen up to fill the void. That Darry's body might not be strong enough to contain and control her new power had never occurred to her. Jessa had spent very little time considering how those changes might affect Darry's abilities where her *Cha-Diah* powers were concerned, and the omission had been a dangerous one.

As Jessa traveled farther into the heart of the Yellandale and night fell, even her witchlight was not enough. She could see very little after the sun went down, and it was not a comfortable feeling. She was not an experienced tracker, nor a hunter, and she was bitterly amused by her lack of experience altogether. A lifetime of being a Princess of the Blood and sequestered behind the walls of the Jade Palace had yet to reveal any skill that would come in truly useful in the wild. She was learning though, and she had spent a great portion of her time since leaving Lyoness on the road and amongst those who would impart their knowledge when asked. When they happened upon a new game trail miles beyond the clearing, they followed it.

Radha's words continued to haunt her. *You must mind the strength and the nature of the animal that is within her, and have a care when her power is high. The panther is a wild creature, always remember that. Do not ever forget that, Jessa, or you might both regret it.*

Her throat was tight and she wiped at her tears with an angry hand as they dampened her cheeks. The realization that her knowledge did not match her power was a bitter taste upon her tongue that she could not wash away. She did not like regret in the least, and being lost within a strange forest in the dead of night did nothing to ease her remorse.

Vhaelin Star huffed and lifted her head, Jessa's dark thoughts pushed to the side as she pulled the reins back. She could hear a new and welcome sound in the darkness, and much to her relief, she recognized the flow of running water. Jessa clicked her tongue and gave the filly her freedom along the narrow trail.

Chapter Five

High King Owen Durand walked through the front room of his private chambers in Blackstone Keep and pushed the hood back from his cloak.

Autumn was upon them, and though it was not yet too cold, the dark cloak was long and light and it would provide him with the secrecy he desired. The guards that stood watch at the entrance to their private wing did so now with dogs, as well, and they did so in two-hour shifts. After the Sahwello attack, he refused to take any chances with Cecelia's life.

The Palace Guard had been decimated that night, but their numbers had come back strong, with an entire platoon of veteran soldiers from Alistair Lewellyn's command signing on. Cecelia's family was a force to be reckoned with, and in this instance, the Lewellyn crest with its motto of family and loyalty could not have been more accurate. It pleased him, as well, that men whose families Cecelia had known since she was a child were now a part of her daily life. It should not have taken an assassination attempt to provide such a simple comfort for his wife.

Blackstone Keep was filled to the rafters with guests, and he could not remember the last time so many relatives, both his own and Cecelia's, had been under his roof. They had planned on a huge celebration for Jacob and Alisha's Solstice wedding, but that had not come to pass as they had once imagined it. A quiet ceremony in the Queen's Garden had been held instead, and considering the circumstances, he had been most pleased with the outcome. The celebrations for Solstice had taken place as he promised they would, and the fortnight of festivities had included a special fete for Jacob and his new bride, which had sufficed.

The autumn moon celebration just the night before had been the liveliest in years, and though he had other things on his mind, he was relieved that Cecelia had seemed to enjoy the revels. No doubt the arrival of Wyatt and the Seventh, as well as the Fourth from Kastamon City but a week later, had played a part in that.

Malcolm had tended his flock of powerful young lords with skill and charm, and he had added to the list of names that might support his hopes and plans for the future. With those young men, however, the older generations had appeared, and Owen knew every rotting one of them. They had fought battles and waged war together, and they had wooed women looking for the one that might love them for the fools they were. Together they had shaped Arravan, and not a single one of them had forgotten it. Malcolm might be feeling his power at the moment, but there were twenty doting grandfathers he himself had added to his council, and every one of them could still pull a young man's heart out with their bare hands if they had to. Although the most relevant power they held was over the family purse strings.

The game was in play, and while he was close to completing his plans for the assault on the Fakir in their Kistanbal stronghold, his priorities had been drastically shifted by the death of Bharjah. His assassination had caused a wave of chaos in Lyoness as Jessa's brothers vied for the throne, despite Sylban-Tenna's declaration. Owen had not forgotten what Jessa had said, and he suspected that the real fighting would begin before Winter Solstice. The dance for allies and resources had gone on for months, and while there had been several minor battles, the true war for power was about to begin.

Darry and Jessa's disappearance had caused utter chaos, and Owen had known at once that it was the most dangerous situation of all.

Something dark and foul had happened that night, aside from the murder of Marteen Salish, and he was determined he would learn the fate of his youngest child. As a tactician he was well aware that Darry and Jessa's flight from Blackstone had not been an action born out of guilt or vengeance, but a retreat instead, and a rather magnificent one at that. It had been a defensive maneuver meant to ensure survival, and for Darry to take such a drastic measure instead of burying her dagger at Malcolm's feet, she must have been left with no other choice. If that had been his daughter's last, best hope, he would find out why, no matter what it might cost him.

If he was lucky, more than a few questions would be answered this night, and he wanted Cecelia to be there for whatever those answers might be. Darry's sudden disappearance was too much like a fatal loss, and the grief it was causing was a terribly familiar weight. And he could not deny that Jessa's absence from their lives had caused an additional sorrow that he could not seem to shake. He had let her down, his young queen, and it was a bitter failure.

He stepped through the archway into the bedroom and his eyes were drawn to the hearth.

Cecelia sat in her favorite chair and at her leisure, her dark gray dress one of her favorites when the weather was cool and her duties were light. Her eyes were closed, and there was a small book on her lap, the fingers of her left hand tucked between the pages.

He approached the chair beside hers.

"You're out and about very late, my love," Cecelia said before he could sit.

Owen smiled as he flipped the back of his cloak out and sat down, claiming the edge of the cushion.

"Should I be worried?"

Owen took note of the tease in her eyes, though it was not as filled with fire as it once was. "Only that I might get a cramp in my hip, and tumble down the back stairs into the kitchen."

Cecelia chuckled happily. "That's why I had the rail put there."

He blinked at her, surprised. "That was you?"

"Of course it was," she said with a sly grin. "The last thing you need with so many guests in attendance is to be carried from the kitchen in your nightclothes for trying to steal a pastry in the dead of night."

Owen's expression tightened. "If the pastry is in my own kitchen, I cannot be stealing it."

"Just so, then."

She looked at him with love and he felt their old life brush past him in the warmth of the flames from the hearth. He leaned his right elbow on his knee as he sat forward. "I swear upon my mother's bones, Cecelia Lewellyn, you are more beautiful to me at this moment than when I first saw you in your father's hall..." She was startled by his words. "There is no majik more powerful to me than your face beneath the light of an autumn fire. You make me as weak as a spindly legged lad."

She smiled and leaned her temple against the wing of her chair. "Keep talking like that, rich boy, and you won't need the fire to keep you warm tonight."

He felt the push of blood through his veins at her words.

She lifted her head away from the chair, a new spark in her eyes. "What have you been playing at, Owen?"

"I would like you to come with me. Are you up for a late-night walk?"

"And where would you take me?"

Owen considered avoiding the truth, but he had learned long ago that such diversions never worked as planned where Cecelia was concerned. "With all good luck, to Sebastian's Tower."

His answer took her completely by surprise.

He gathered his words and let them fall into place. "Jessa's majik is a thing to be wary of, to be sure. There are two men still in the infirmary, two men left out of fifty who've been injured trying to enter that bloody maze. Her spells are not unknown to the priests of Gamar, as you know, but there are significant differences—"

"In the runes," Cecelia agreed. He had her full attention and he was glad of it. "The shamans of the plains let their spells gather from the elements, and from the earth itself. It is a blending of wills, not an intrusion of one upon the other."

Owen nodded. "Precisely...and this has had me thinking, then, of a majik that at its roots may have a more familiar flavor to those damn weeds and—"

"Jezara!" Cecelia interrupted again as she sat forward.

Owen smiled. "Right again."

"*Owen.*"

"Do not run ahead, Cece," he warned her with some compassion. The emotion held by but a single word from her was overwhelming. It was the first he had seen of her true spirit since Darry and Jessa had disappeared. "Jezara's influence is not the same, and I have been warned of such. But I do think that I have found something no one else could have."

She waited.

"A year or two before my brother was to marry Luce Malakee, he fell in love with a young woman from Artanis. They had a secret affair, and from time to time, I helped them in keeping their love hidden, so they might meet undetected."

Cecelia seemed thrown by his words and the direction in which they had gone. "Luce Malakee," she said softly. "Blessed Gamar, I haven't thought of her in many years. We were good friends, once upon an age."

"Malcolm and this young woman had an affair for almost a year, and all things considered, it was a somewhat forbidden relationship on several levels."

"You never told me this," she replied, and he could hear the disbelief.

"Luce was your good friend, remember?" He leaned against the arm of his chair. "And that Malcolm would ask for my help with something so important to him…" Owen felt in that moment like the young man he had once been, always one stride behind his hero, and yet another behind the brother he loved. "He never needed me for too much."

Cecelia's eyes filled with feeling while the fire shifted and the night moved beyond the locked balcony doors. "Why was it forbidden?" she asked softly.

"Because she was to be a priestess of Jezara's temple." He made a face of disagreement. "And while Jezara most certainly does not forbid the pleasures of the flesh, she does forbid liaisons that might deter a rising acolyte from her devotions." He sat back a bit. "And this affair was most certainly that. When she was discovered by the High Priestess at the time, the Mistress Antonia, it was a great scandal in the ranks of Jezara's followers. She was made to choose between her devotion to Jezara and her love for my brother. It was a horrible situation and Malcolm pleaded with the Mistress on their behalf. But it did no good, and the girl was forced to choose which love she would follow.

"She was the daughter of a fisherman, one of the skiff trawlers of Artanis. In the end, she chose for herself what she thought to be best. She and Malcolm were allowed to meet one last time beneath the blessings of the goddess, and then their affair was over. He was to marry Luce the following year, but the Lowland War broke out. He did not live to see his heart full once more."

Cecelia's eyes were rich with emotion. "Owen."

"I know, I see it…At least Jezara offered freedom and power, and a multitude of pleasures that might fulfill a woman's desires. I offered but gold, and the weight of a shame Aiden was never meant to bear."

Cecelia sat forward and reached out to him. "That's not what I was going to say, my love." Her eyes were tender as he took her hand. "I'm sorry that you've carried this sadness alone, all of these years. Poor Malcolm."

Owen gave her fingers a squeeze before letting go. "He did not speak of what might have been said on their last night, but he seemed at peace with it, in all honesty. The point of their story, however, is how what happened then affects *our* story now."

"Which is what? How?"

"They would meet in Sebastian's Tower."

Cecelia stared at him.

Owen couldn't help but smile, feeling a bit roguish. "And when they were there, the maze itself would answer to her spells, at least somewhat, and protect them from any who might try to enter, even the gardeners."

Cecelia's eyes widened. "Who was she?"

"A better question would be, who she is *now*."

Cecelia's eyes were intense as she waited and her patience at his silence came to an end rather quickly. "Owen?"

"She is the Mistress Clare Bellaq," he answered, satisfied as he watched her reaction. "The High Priestess of Jezara's holy temple in Artanis."

Cecelia's expression turned to shock. "Gamar's rotting hounds!"

Owen laughed. "Indeed."

"But how does that help us?" Cecelia demanded as she sat forward in her chair. "I don't see how she—"

Owen held up his hand and she was instantly silent. "If I had remembered these things earlier today, while Grissom and I discussed promotions for the officers, it wouldn't help us in the least. But I did not. I thought of it when Jacob kissed Alisha in the wild heart of your garden, and sealed their pledge of marriage on Solstice Eve." Owen pushed up from his chair and looked down at his wife. He held out his hand. "Would you care to attend the midnight service with me at Gamar's Temple?"

Cecelia slipped her hand in his but did not stand.

He pulled her to her feet and she stepped readily into his arms, still holding her book and somewhat amazed as she looked up at him. "I hear that sometimes, you might run into an old friend."

CHAPTER SIX

The trees began to thin out and Jessa smiled as they moved into the long, heavy grass that lined the banks of a reasonably sized stream. She turned Vhaelin Star and they stopped in an easy manner. Jessa dismounted and gathered the reins, her legs stiff as she took the first few steps. Jessa patted Star in appreciation, and the filly snorted and gave a playful step as they walked to the stream. Jessa laughed quietly as her boots crunched upon the pebbles and grit near the edge, and Vhaelin Star stepped in the water and lowered her head.

Jessa listened to the night around them and her blood gave a small push of excitement. She could feel the majik around them, its low hum drifting beneath the spill of the stream and the calls of the night birds. It flowed within the cool breeze and wove through the sway of the grass. It was unwavering in its presence, and as she looked upstream and considered the movement of the water, she knew what must be done.

When Vhaelin Star had drunk her fill, she walked to the grass to eat, and Jessa let her. She went about setting their camp, finding a spot upon the edge of the grass and gathering rocks for the fire. She found wood and spoke the spell, a small flame smoldering in the dry leaves she had layered beneath her branches. She unsaddled Vhaelin Star and wiped her down, the soft rope she had serving as a halter with a few turns and a simple knot, the filly more than satisfied as she grazed. Jessa added more wood to the fire, shrugged into one of Darry's cropped jackets, and then sat down upon a blanket where she ate bread with honey and drank cool water from one of her skins.

She could feel the panther's presence as she sat cross-legged before the fire, but she let her mind drift, moving back along her own thread and finding what she needed among her memories.

Radha had stood on their long terrace in the Jade Palace, her face raised to the sun as she chanted the words of an ancient prayer. The words were a blessing among her people, one that Jessa's own mother had sung with reverence and worship in her youth, before she'd been stolen by Bharjah. It was a benediction for the Vhaelin and their many gifts, and though Radha's voice was not of the sweet nature that her daughter's had been, Jessa's was more than up to the task.

With the prayer clear in her mind and her course chosen, the Nightshade Lark found her place in the rhythms of the forest, and then she sang.

The notes were smooth and clear, and Jessa let them find their proper weight before she released them, for she had not sung in earnest since before she had left Lyoness. She had sung softly to Darry within the maze, and several times as they lay in each other's arms, but not as she did now, allowing the words their full due. Words of the sun and the grass beneath it. Words in praise of the rain that falls and the hawk that flies. Words for the rivers that flow, and the trees that sprawl through the earth. Jessa's voice opened in all its strength and rose pure into the night.

Her small fire reacted and the flames licked higher into the night, heavy and filled with their own voice as the wood moved and shifted within. Vhaelin Star lifted her head and moved a few steps closer with a shake of her mane. The long black hair fell along her face and down her powerful shoulders.

The Vhaelin rushed through her blood and she felt the runes, her prayer becoming a layered vessel of notes. Notes that caught on the wind and traveled beyond her camp, drifting in the darkness of the Yellandale. The stream tumbled and churned with her song, and as she let the final notes sink softly in offering, she could hear the water responding. Jessa reached out upon the strength of her gods, though she did not have far to travel.

The Nightshade Lark opened her eyes and looked beyond the flames.

Darry stood in the farthest reaches of the light, her tunic undone down the center of her body. The sheen of her skin flared with orange and gold from the flames, and her trousers hung low upon her narrow hips, torn along her right leg. Her hair fell about her face in dark curls, golden one moment and black the next as the fire moved and the light shifted.

"My mother told me a story once." Darry's voice was soothing in the darkness, and Jessa smiled. "Of a Shaman who tamed a wild bear instead of killing him, and he asked the bear to protect the children of his village."

Jessa set her right hand down and stood. She took a step, and then took it back as she remembered the last time she had approached her lover.

"He played the lute until the bear came to him…And the bear offered him fish from the river and berries from the bushes beyond his winter cave, so he would keep playing."

Jessa was finding it hard to catch her breath. "Lee-Otis was his name."

Darry had moved closer. "Yes."

"The Shaman, I mean." Jessa fought desperately for more words, but there was really only one. "*Akasha.*"

"I am not a bear."

Jessa smiled at Darry's statement and then licked her lips. She could taste Darry's majik, and though it was vivid and wild beyond her most reckless dreams, it was no longer untamed. "No, you're not."

Darry stood but a few feet away and Jessa could see the wounds on the right side of Darry's face beneath the fall of her hair. Jessa's heart caught at the gashes along Darry's jaw and down her neck. Darry's eyes were bright and filled with unexpected fear. "Are you afraid of me now?"

Jessa's arms were about Darry's neck, though she did not remember moving. Darry's arms were fierce about her ribs and Jessa turned her face, the smell of Darry's hair and skin wild and strong like the forest around them. Jessa held on as tightly as she could, her relief beyond all measure. She was in the safest place she had ever known.

The softness of Darry's lips touched the edge of hers and Jessa leaned back. She took Darry's face in her hands, and her touch was delicate as she pushed at Darry's hair. There were three distinct lacerations, the skin about the wounds slightly swollen and hot. They looked clean though, and Jessa could smell the yarrow root. They would need stitches and Jessa felt a hard push of concern, for she had no idea what else there might be. She would need plantain root, which she had, for a tea and a paste. *Perhaps you will not need stitches, my love.* She let her touch settle upon the side of Darry's neck.

"I can't control it." Darry's voice was rough, her eyes quiet in the firelight. "I'm sorry, Jessa. I've been trying."

"It's all right, my love." It was as she had thought, and Jessa felt certain now of the path her studies must take. "Hinsa has been sleeping for a very long time." Her hand slipped down and landed upon Darry's chest. "In here, yes?"

"Yes."

"I will not lie, *Akasha*…I know very little of *Cha-Diah* majik. But Radha's scrolls contain many ancient spells, and they have been passed down for a thousand years. I will find something that will help, I know it. We shall find a balance."

Darry's eyes brightened in the changing light and tears slid along her thick lashes before they fell. "She has words, Jess."

Jessa wiped gently at Darry's cheek. "Who has words, my love?"

"Hinsa," Darry answered, her voice thick with emotion. Her shoulders trembled and Jessa stepped closer. "It was…" Darry lowered her face. "For the first time, I heard her speak."

Jessa's eyes widened and her smile was instant. Jessa leaned under and kissed her with tenderness, drawing Darry's face into the firelight once more. Jessa pushed Darry's hair back before she turned in her arms.

Hinsa moved from the darkness farther up the riverbank, and Vhaelin Star chuffed and shook her head, looking to the trees. Hinsa approached slowly and then sat down in the long grass. Her head and shoulders peeked above the swaying tips and she leaned her head forward, smelling the air.

Darry leaned down a bit. "We have a gift for you."

Jessa was surprised by the words.

"But you must come with me."

"A gift?"

"Will you come with me?"

"Of course, *Akasha*, but should we not wait until morning? I have food and there is a warm fire. Come and sit with me."

"No," Darry whispered. "This gift will not wait until morning. You've made a safe camp for the fire, and Hinsa will watch over Vhaelin Star." Darry smiled a bit. "She likes her."

Jessa stepped back a little but she did not let go of her. "Then take me," Jessa replied with confidence. She had no idea what sort of gift it might be, but the look of unspoiled pleasure in Darry's eyes pleased her greatly. The expression deepened as Darry walked backward, her feet silent in the grass. She held Jessa's hand and pulled her after.

"You are going to walk into the stream," Jessa warned. Her love was safe and relatively unharmed, and the wilderness around them was old and new at the same time. There was a rush of anticipation in her blood. Darry stepped forward quickly, and before Jessa could argue, she was swept up in Darry's arms. She held on to Darry's shoulders and tried not to laugh at the surprise of it all. "What are you doing?"

Darry turned around as she carried her with ease. "Walking into the stream," she answered and stepped without pause into the rush of water.

Jessa smiled as she glanced down and saw the moonlight, and the stars, sparkle in the rush of the current. The crossing was quick, and when they were fully upon the opposite shore, Darry set her down, took her hand once more, and guided them toward the trees.

"My love, where are you taking me?" Jessa asked in a whisper as they moved through the wild grass and undergrowth. They walked for a short time among spruce, sagging saplings, and wildflowers, and Jessa tried to absorb the riot of life around her.

There were birch trees ahead, and Jessa stopped when Darry did.

"The birch tree grove, you must go there." Darry looked down into Jessa's eyes and her hair tumbled across her face, wild and free.

Jessa's brow rose in question. "Why?"

Darry's left hand was warm against Jessa's face. "I love you, Jessa. I have killed for you, and I would die for you. Without a thought I will do whatever is needed to protect you from anything or anyone that might wish you harm." Darry leaned down and kissed her, a truly splendid kiss that sent Jessa's heartbeat into a faster cadence. The panther was everywhere and the taste of Darry's mouth was exhilarating. Her words were even more so. "This moment is my gift to you…the only thing that might ever come close enough to showing you how I feel. The grove is a sacred place," she explained, her lips still close. "You will feel it as you approach."

"But I do not worship Gamar. You should come with me."

Darry grinned in the darkness. "It is not Gamar who lives there, my sweet Lark. It is the Vhaelin, and they wait for you."

Jessa was startled by the words and she turned. The birches swayed slightly, and the grass that led to the grove shifted in an easy manner. "But I don't…No, *Akasha*, I do not feel them."

"You will." Darry's hand moved in Jessa's hair and reclaimed her attention. "I asked him to bless you, and he spoke your name."

Jessa stared long into Darry's eyes.

"In my head, I heard your name. He knows your name."

Jessa took a deep breath and considered what she'd been told. "Who, *Akasha*? Who has spoken my name?"

"The totem of your gods."

Chapter Seven

Jessa moved through the grass among the liana vines that grew up from the soil. Thin willow trees reached up and then showered back down in long, flowing tendrils beside saplings that bent and turned as they drew her forward. The birch trees stacked back, and she could see, even in the darkness, the flow of their line as they curved away upon each side. The leaves spoke gently and she listened, trying to decipher what they told her.

It was not until she stopped at the edge of the birch trees that she felt it, and it pushed through her chest like a wave of heat from the sun. Her head tipped back and she closed her eyes beneath the touch of her gods.

"You know where you are..."

"Yes, she does."

"She looks different."

"Taller."

Jessa heard laughter in her head, playful and yet slightly discordant.

"What are you afraid of?"

"She's not afraid."

"She is."

"We heard you singing."

"Yes, we did."

"Come closer."

Jess let out a harsh breath and stumbled forward. She reached out for the nearest birch tree and used it to regain her balance, its bark bending beneath her hand. There were voices everywhere. They whispered in the veins of sap that ached and crawled through the trees, and the eager fingers of life that bloomed in the leaves and new branches. Stray words found their way into her thoughts as motes of dust and wayward leaves that drifted through the darkness.

The voices were both male and female, and an odd mixture of both, a tenor that spoke of neither but, instead, something so otherworldly and filled with dreams, it had no voice but the one in her head.

"The panther saved us."

"She did."

"The wolf was brave and strong. It is the way of things."

"The cat carries her prophecy well."

"She is unprepared."

"Perhaps."

"I said she is. You must help her or we shall all be lost."

"Like before."

"Like before, yes."

"Terrible."

"It was terrible, yes."

"You need our—"

"Stop," Jessa said simply, her voice raw beneath the sovereignty they held. Her whole body shook with it, a pulsation that filled every aspect of her being and threatened to rip her apart. It was too much and she had no protection against it. She called on all of her strength and still it was not enough, and so she called on Darry. "Please, stop."

She felt Darry's majik answer her call and race across the forest floor on subtle paws. She felt the power of the *Cha-Diah* support her weight, flesh and blood, muscle and bone. She felt their love, and it reached back through time, just as easily as it held power over the present.

Jessa took stock of her body, the feel of her clothes suddenly rough against her skin. She could feel her hair move about her shoulders and tickle her face, a breeze of its own. She opened her eyes and looked through the trees.

"Come closer."

"We would bless you."

"Yes, you will have need of it."

"She will."

"Come."

"Come to us—"

"—let us give you a gift."

"And one for the panther, as well."

"Yes, you're right. Earned in blood."

"Come to us."

Jessa let go of the birch tree and obeyed, her legs moving in a stilted manner as she fought to find the core of her strength, reaching for it, chasing it as she stepped through the last row of trees and entered the grove. The perfect circle of trees welcomed her, and she kept walking until she could take no more, and her eyes came up.

The stag stood in the fall of moonlight, a magnificent and giant beast. The points of his antlers were too thick and vast to be counted, though Jessa thought there might hundreds. He was stunning, and she stumbled at the sight of him and fell to her knees. Her fingers closed in the earth and the coolness of the dirt rose about her fingers as she bowed her head.

She had worshipped the Vhaelin from her first breath, she had always known it. She had felt them surround her and she had felt them abandon her. And yet always they had been there, the very essence of the world she moved through, as small as the smallest bird caught in a storm, and as brutal as the storm itself.

Jessa's body trembled as she wept, she couldn't stop it.

"Neela wept."

"Yes, those of your thread have wept before."

"What is her wish?"

"Ask her."

"Speak your desire if you wish, or do not if you—"

"Ah!"

They laughed and Jessa smiled through her tears at the joyous, perfect song that it was.

"Your heart is loud."

"It is not tired."

"Yes, it is certainly of use to you. We were not as cruel as you thought."

"No," Jessa offered in penitence. "No, I was wrong. Please forgive me."

"You are free to doubt, you are—"

"—always free."

"There is a wish there, I see it."

"Yes, we see it."

"I just…" Jessa's voice failed her. What could she say that did not seem petty and small?

"Look up, child!"

The command rang through Jessa's head and she let out a startled cry as she fell back upon her heels. The stag pushed forward with a powerful lunge, and Jessa's right arm came up to shield herself. She stared into his endless brown eyes, where the stars wheeled and spun into the vast distance of the night sky and perhaps even eternity itself held sway.

The stag leaned his head down and let out a scream, a mighty shudder moving along his neck and rolling through his shoulders. His body twisted to the side and then his hindquarters shook. A violent flash of light filled the grove, and Jessa turned away from it as she fell to the ground and tried to protect herself.

Silence filled the grove as the light passed over her and beyond, and slowly, Jessa opened her eyes and pushed up from the ground. Her arms shook as she turned upon her hip, afraid and yet unwilling to keep her eyes closed against what was to be the will of her gods.

The stag stepped back from her, proud and tall, his shadowy coat no longer dense and shaggy, nor matted with scars. Instead, it was fresh and beautiful, a light brown that was clean with the softness of youthful splendor. He lifted his head with a muted bark, and his magnificent rack of antlers caught in the light before he dropped his head forward and shook it.

The antlers of new bone growth trembled and fell free from his immense rack, clattering to the ground amidst a tumble of moss and ribbons of supple velvet hair. Beside them lay the dark coat that he had shed.

"Gifts that are fit for a High Priestess."

"Should she survive the Blood Fires."

"We can hope."

"Yes, we will hope for wisdom."
"And strength."
"Tell the panther we thank—"
"—her for the life of our talisman."
"Yes. Our old friend. He was tired."
"Our voice lives on."
"He loves her a little, now."
"He has kept the scars for her."

Jessa's gaze lifted from the untold bounty of their gifts as the stag turned and walked away. Jessa saw the faded remains of his wounds, three deep scars that trailed along the sleek power of his hindquarters, only to disappear into the shadows beneath his tail. Wounds that were not so unlike those that now adorned the soft skin of Darry's face. Wounds earned in a battle fought to save the talisman of her gods.

"Akasha," Jessa said in sudden understanding.

"Yes, not her gods."
"She thought only—"
"—of you."
"The Cha-Diah *majik is—"*
"—sweet, is it not?
"We remember its taste."

Jessa felt the warmth of their laughter move in her blood, her head tipping back as a push of air passed her lips. She fought to breathe properly as a wave of white-hot, pure desire blossomed in the pit of her stomach and flowed outward. Their remembrance of *Cha-Diah* passion was her reality, and she could not help but be affected.

"Her blood is not the blood—"
"—of the Fox People."
"There is terrible danger for her. Sorrow will come."
"Yes, a bird of sorrow will come for you both, if you're not careful."

Jessa fought to clear her thoughts of her unexpected need. Her skin was alive with it and her blood was thick with want. She felt Darry's body against her own, moving with sleek heat, moving with her as Darry's hand slipped between their joined bodies. She felt the heaviness of her own breasts, hard and aching for the touch of Darry's mouth. She shook her head and tried to break free. Their words would not let go. "Danger?"

There was more laughter.

"You may bless our grove."

"What…" Jessa licked her lips and swallowed. She closed her eyes and turned her face to the side, trying to concentrate. For the first time since she had come to Arravan and found Darry waiting, for the first time since she had found her heart and her love, she pushed Darry away. "What…what danger?"

"As you once did."

"Yes, call to her."

"Please…what danger is she in?" Jessa managed in a strained voice.

"Sorrow brings danger."

"Call to the panther."

"She waits beyond the trees, frightened for you."

"We give all blessings to—"

"—your union. The Loom shall remember."

Jessa let her power rise through her blood, even in the presence of her gods. She looked up, defiant, though it was only in defiance of their game, not her reverence for them. "None shall harm her—I will not allow it. Tell me now what you mean!"

There was gentle laughter.

"And do not forget her gift, by the river, where the—"

"—slain ones now sleep. Their ghosts will walk beside her, and offer protection. They respect the order of things. Always. We give them leave to—"

"—continue the hunt."

"Call to her."

Their words were plain, and yet a riddle, and she was certain they toyed with her. Radha had told her stories of such, and somehow, she knew she was caught in their challenge. Always there were riddles, like her beloved Radha, always moving a piece upon the board. Always a test of her skills. "Always a game in play," she whispered.

Jessa pressed her legs together and drew them close. It had merely been a prompting, their memories of *Cha-Diah* power that had fanned the flames of her own desire, a desire that was always so close to the surface. Radha had been right, for her love was separate and apart from their memories. Her passion for Darry was free from all meddling, free from prophecy and expectations. She had no defense against it, though. Within the grove, she had no defense against anything at all.

"We will leave you—"

"—to your devotions."

A soft, silken laugh tickled at the back of her skull, and she looked up as the stag neared the far edge of the trees. He turned and looked back at her, magnificent and silent in the fall of silver light. He was the most exquisite animal Jessa had ever seen, and her eyes skipped along his powerful shoulders, and farther still. The fresh scars upon his new coat fairly glowed in the light as he disappeared through the trees and into the darkness beyond.

Jessa gave in and closed her eyes. Her whisper caught upon the breeze. *"Akasha."*

Chapter Eight

The High King and Queen stood in the alcove beyond the main cathedral of Gamar's Holy Temple and waited upon the acolyte. Their arrival had been expected, and when they were led down a side corridor to the abbey of Gamar's chosen, Cecelia caught sight of Armistad Greyson among the midnight worshippers, and several of his men scattered about the worn oak benches. Owen's First Councillor and lifetime friend was most certainly aware of his duty. They were out of uniform as they said their prayers, but they were also alert and ready to defend them if danger should arise. Their posture could never be mistaken for the absentminded presence of the body during honest prayer, and from their discreet glances, they were well aware that their king and queen were present. The lack of Kingsmen or personal guards from the palace was noted by Cecelia and she did not question it.

She understood as they waited within the shadows and golden lamplight of the alcove, that what they were doing was dressed in the guise of normality. A midnight prayer and blessing at Gamar's Temple was not out of the ordinary for her, and to spying eyes it would be seen as such. Owen had seen to their security though, and he had done so with discretion and foresight.

The temple and its gray marble stones presented a different sort of character in the dead of night, and Cecelia had always enjoyed the mysteries that accompanied the shadows cast by the arches and carved spires of stone. It was a beautiful temple, and the shutters that held the night at bay were carved from the smoothest blackwood, an addition Cecelia had donated herself.

A hooded priest walked from the shadowed hallway which led to the abbey and bowed his head. "If you will follow me, please, Your Highness." He turned to her and she recognized him as a priest high up in the Order. "My Queen, High Priest Master Haba Una has asked to see you."

Owen took her hand in response and she followed close at her husband's side. They moved through several corridors and into the heart of the abbey, the acolytes they passed stopping in their duties and bowing their heads. They entered the private wing of living quarters, and after several turns the priest came to a stop before a familiar set of maple doors.

"Master Una," the priest bowed his head briefly while he grabbed the edges of his hood. He revealed his face and shaved head. "Master Una has taken a turn for the worse," he said in a soothing voice.

Cecelia was startled by the news. "I thought he was on the mend."

The priest's expression was filled with sadness and compassion both. "If you were not here now, my Queen, you would have received a summons by morning."

"The wasting tumors," Cecelia said, and a pang of fear cut deep. "They've returned."

"With a vengeance, my Queen. And I wish…I wish to prepare you. He is much changed, even in the few weeks since you saw him last."

"How long does he have?" Owen's hand tightened about her own in a gentle manner.

"His time here is now measured in days, perhaps hours."

Cecelia touched the priest's arm. "It will be all right…"

"Master Kaleb, my Queen."

Cecelia smiled a bit. "Of course, I'm sorry Master Kaleb. I remember you from the Solstice celebrations. Master Una has relied on you a great deal. He has great affection for you."

His eyes filled with emotion. "As I have for him." He turned to the double doors and opened them before he stepped to the side. "He waits for you both, with one of his healers. I will stay here and guard the doors. I will place the High Priest's seal upon it, and none shall enter until it is removed. Knock on the door, and I will speak the spell that releases the runes of the seal."

"Thank you, Master Kaleb," Owen said as Cecelia stepped through the doors. "You and I shall speak again, I'm sure."

Cecelia moved through the antechamber, walking about the center table and past the red-cushioned chairs that lined the walls. She passed beneath the arch and into Haba Una's chambers, her eyes sharp in the lamplight. She noted that the high up windows were open to the night air, though regardless of that, the room was thick with the smell of herbs and sickness. As Cecelia neared the bed, she could smell the impending death.

The healer beside the bed stood back, and it was a woman, the blue robes of her profession darker than usual in the light and haze of the lamps. Her hair was a rich brown and pulled back from her face, several pins in the thick strands. She appeared to be of a similar age to Cecelia, and when Cecelia met her eyes the woman did not look away, nor did she lower her gaze. She was quite beautiful, actually, with high cheekbones and a lovely mouth that begged for a smile. She stepped back from the bed and finally bowed her head in deference.

Master Haba Una, the High Priest of Gamar's Holy Order met her eyes as she neared. "My Lady," he said and smiled in a pale, gaunt face. "Come no closer, please."

Cecelia ignored him. "Do not be foolish, my old friend," she said in a gentle voice as she walked along the bed and then leaned down. She fixed the covers so they would not pull against him when she sat, and then she took her place beside him. She lifted one of his hands between her own. "My sweet Haba," she greeted and then was forced to stop for a moment. She swallowed upon a tight throat and reined in her shock and sorrow. It was plain to see that it would be the last time she spoke with her old friend. "You should have sent for me sooner."

Haba Una had always been old, even as a young man. He had been chosen by Gamar when but a boy, for his soul and his wisdom, even then, had been ancient. As he had risen through the ranks of priests and acolytes, there had been little question as to who he would eventually become. The fact that twice, while in the presence of others, Gamar had gifted him with his presence, was a surprise to no one who knew him.

"I have been excited to tell you..." He paused and his breathing was quite shallow. "Some things."

Cecelia smiled and buried her sorrow in a practiced manner. "I have much to tell you, as well, my old friend. But you first, if you please. Your stories are always so interesting. The doings at court cannot usually compare."

Haba's eyes were covered with a film of white, but she could see that he still had his sight. "Not as of late, perhaps."

Cecelia laughed quietly, but it was in earnest. "You do not lie, my friend, I am sorry to say. Court has become a blood sport."

His eyes closed and Cecelia sat with him. She held his hand, and after a time, she took the damp cloth from the bowl upon the bedside table and wrung it out before wiping at his forehead and cheeks. Her touch was gentle as she pushed aside the white wisps of his hair, and she could hear the singing of the acolytes through the windows. It was both soothing and somewhat otherworldly.

Haba opened his eyes with a start. "Cecelia?"

"Yes, Haba, I am here."

"I have been visited by my god, for a third time."

Cecelia's eyes widened. "Haba, that is wonderful!"

"You were there, that day, when Gamar took back his Holy Man."

Cecelia adjusted to the apparent change in subject with ease. "Yes," she replied. "Upon the steps of the temple, and on a day filled with sunshine. It was a sight to see." She leaned forward as if they shared a secret. "I shall never forget it, lightening and fire out of the clear blue, and that terrible crack of thunder echoing against the entrance and down the stairs."

"He came to me, just last night."

"The Holy Man?"

Haba licked his lips. "Yes."

Cecelia's brow went up and she set the cloth aside and took his hand once more. His voice had weakened further, and though she did not wish to tire him, he clearly had something to say. "Did he speak to you?"

Haba smiled weakly. "Yes. He brought…he brought a message."

Cecelia waited, and it was some time before he spoke again.

"For Darrius."

Cecelia's heart gave a painful thud of shock. "*Darry?*"

"Yes." Haba pulled his left arm from beneath the covers and his face showed the effort it took, the blankets shifting slowly. Cecelia sat back and her eyes went to his hand as he freed his arm and extended his fist, his entire body trembling. "Open my hand...please," he instructed her. "For I cannot."

Cecelia took his left hand in both of hers. His bones were light and felt brittle beneath his thin skin and she merely held his hand, afraid to exert any force upon his long and graceful fingers.

"Please," he said in a strained voice. "You will not hurt me." He took several breaths and turned his head to the right. His eyes searched the shadows. "Tell her."

The healer stepped forward upon silent feet. "He cannot open his hand," she told Cecelia in a lovely, almost curious voice. "It has been sealed by his god. I can see the runes. They are wrapped about his hand like a rope...but they have parted for your touch."

Cecelia stared at her for a long moment and then turned back to their joined hands. She felt nothing but the weight and fragile presence of his flesh and bones. She saw nothing but her own hands covering his.

"You will not hurt me, Cecelia," Haba repeated. "I promise you."

Cecelia pushed her thumb into the opening beside his, and his fist opened to her like a flower in bloom. There was a pop of silver light and Cecelia closed her eyes against it as it spread outward. She felt Owen's strong touch upon her back, but he did not pull her away as she opened her eyes.

A silver disc floated in the air above Master Una's palm, and it caught the light in a brilliant fashion. It was a coin, and it turned slowly in the air that washed through the room as Cecelia's eyes widened in recognition. She pulled back from it, and Owen's hands were upon her arms from behind, holding her strong as he stepped as close as he could.

It was a birthing day coin, and it was of the royal family, the Durand crest upon one side, and her daughter's name and childhood likeness raised upon the other as it slowly turned: *Darrius Lauranna Durand*. It had been minted by a master for the seventh anniversary of her birth, and it was made of Blue Vale silver and the purest of gold. The shine had long been worn away, but as it floated in the air above their hands, she recalled Darry's expression upon receiving it. And she remembered when Darry had given it away on the steps of Gamar's Temple, to the wild haired Holy Man who had no shoes. How she had spoken to him when no one else would, and held his hand while she did.

"Take it," Haba said, and his voice was but a whisper of what it had been. His expression was filled with relief, and a strange contentment. "I was to give it back to her," he explained, a slight smile playing upon his pale lips. "But I will not live to see that day."

Cecelia lowered Master Una's hand to the blankets and then reached up, her hand stopping just beyond the gently spinning coin. Her eyes met his.

"The Holy Man upon the stairs, that day," Haba said. "He was no Holy Man, my friend. It was Gamar himself." He cleared his throat and took a breath. "Always there, dancing. No one ever approached him, not even the priests. We would set out food and drink, but only upon the stairs. There was not a one of us who looked beyond his wild hair and filthy clothes, though we admired his devotion. For when other Holy Men would come and then travel on, only he stayed. There was not one person who was not frightened, at least in some way, by the terrible wildness of him."

Cecelia smiled briefly and her eyes filled with tears. "But not Darry." She took hold of the coin and the spell was broken, the weight of the silver and gold heavy in her hand.

"Tell my dear and glorious young friend..." Haba's eyes lifted and centered upon Owen, and even veiled behind the white gaze of his sickness, they seemed piercing. "Tell the daughter of your blood, the child who saw you at your worst and darkest..."

Cecelia felt Owen stiffen against her shoulder.

"The child who understood your grief for Jacey Rose and bears it at the center of her own heart, like a dagger that chases her still...Tell her that she was right, and I concede our debate." His eyes lowered to Cecelia. "She holds Gamar's favor, although I do not know how that shall play out for her."

"Probably in the midst of a great deal of mayhem." Cecelia was somewhat in shock but she kept her attention solely upon her friend.

"Yes," Haba agreed. "You're right, of course. I shall miss seeing that."

"She loved you."

"Yes...Tell her that I leave her my recipe for the black spice tea. I shall have it sealed and sent to Blackstone with my official missives. Please give it to her, and only her, when she returns."

Cecelia closed her hand about the wide coin and pulled it close to her breast, the heat of it pouring into her chest. She took Haba's hand with her left, applying only what force she needed. "I shall miss you, my friend, and I shall think of you often, upon your journeys."

Haba's eyes began to close. "Good-bye, my dear Cecelia," he replied, and his smile returned for an instant. "I'm rather frightened, actually." His eyes closed completely. "Faith only answers so many questions, you know."

Cecelia held his hand into the silence, and the room became thick with emotions she could not yet begin to sort out. The coin was smooth in her hand, and she held it tightly as the healer stepped close to the bed. Cecelia let go of Haba's hand but did not rise as the woman laid her touch upon Haba's balding head.

"He is sleeping, Your Grace," she said with compassion as she met Cecelia's eyes. "His time has not come just yet, but it will be here very soon. It was good that you came when you did. I'm not sure Gamar would've let him go, until he'd given over the talisman." The woman's blue eyes lifted and she looked beyond Cecelia. A knowing smile curved her full lips. "Hello, Owen."

"Hello, Clare."

Cecelia's interest turned into something else entirely when the High Priestess of Jezara's Holy Temple in Artanis returned her scrutiny.

Clare Bellaq smiled, a great deal of mischief and welcome in her gaze. "I have long wondered upon the woman who captured Owen's heart," she said with confidence, and some small bit of curiosity. "It did not surprise me to find that you have been a most treasured friend to Master Una, the kindest man I have ever known. He has shared with me your many conversations on faith, and let slip that it was you, my Queen, who paid in gold the price for Jezara's Library in Hockley. A rather substantial amount, I might add, that my Order could not afford." The High Priestess extended her hand and Cecelia took it, and held it tight. "Know now that you have an ally in me, and if I am as lucky as Master Una has been, a true friend, as well."

Cecelia smiled in surprise as the weight of her pending loss brought tears to her eyes. "No one was to know about the library," she replied, and her voice was rough. She cleared her throat and looked down at her sleeping friend. "I should've known better, I suppose," she whispered. "He's always loved a good secret."

Chapter Nine

Darry crouched upon the trunk of a fallen oak tree and waited, her arms braced straight out upon her knees. Her dagger was stabbed in the wood beside her, should she need it.

The circle of birch trees did not move in the breeze, and neither did the grass. She could not see beyond the layered ring of trees, and try as she might to find it, Jessa's scent was completely gone from the night air. It was merely the way it was, and she accepted her place within the bigger events at play, at least at first. When Jessa had disappeared into the grove, Darry had encouraged it. It was what she had fought for, both she and Hinsa. It was a prize worthy of their wounds.

As the minutes passed, however, the situation seemed more and more suspicious. She had lost track of time since she'd first felt anxious, and things had gone astray from that moment on.

She stared at a bush in the distance, heavy bunches of black berries pulling the thin, tangled branches toward the ground. They were not unlike her worries, which had grown fat with their own weight.

Her right hand came back and slid upon the skin of her upper chest until her scar was beneath her fingers. The tissue was heavy and tight, and in some quiet part of her soul, she could still feel the pressure of Malcolm's boot against her shoulder. The pain caused had been much deeper than even *he* had intended, and she was well aware of the pleasure that fact would bring him if he knew. She closed her eyes.

So now you will disappear into the night…We shall all grieve, of course, and there will be tears. Mother's heart will be broken, but she'll bear it, just as she did when Jacey Rose left us.

She had struggled with duty and honor her entire life. How to be a good daughter, how she might stay true to her nature and yet please those she loved the most. How to serve her family name and her respect for the legacy of those who came before. It was clear early on that the sword was her way to do that. No matter how much it went against tradition, and her father's wishes, it was the gift she had been given and she loved it. To throw that away, to deny it, would have been an affront to Gamar.

The High Priest Haba Una had told her to follow her path no matter where it led, and this would be all that Gamar could ever ask. *Be true, Darrius Lauranna, and Gamar shall bless you. There are so many who lose their way, but all he has ever asked of us was that we be true.*

They had argued over the years about what that meant, exactly. The High Priest would brew his black spice tea and they would debate until Haba laughed and ordered her to go home. *Be true to your best self then, Darrius, until we might agree.*

Her gift was the sword. Her gift was the grace of Honshi and the Dance of Steel. Her gift was Hinsa, and Hinsa had spoken. She had language and words, or at least, when lost to her deepest blood. Darry had finally had the chance to hear her. To have been denied such a thing because of caution, because of fear, it had been weak and…no, not weak. She had never been weak.

But she had always been frightened. She had been terrified they would kill Hinsa, or keep them apart in some way. That they would cage her, and one day, at some point, Hinsa would just disappear.

Your blood actually is diseased. You truly are a mongrel now, aren't you.

Hinsa would've been easy prey for Malcolm's men, if trapped somehow. Her fear had been well founded, though only hindsight gave her that knowledge. He would have mounted her head upon the wall of the King's Lodge in the Green Hills, and laughed when he looked at his trophy.

You're a backward cunt, and I am the Crown Prince of Arravan.

Darry's eyes narrowed into the darkness as Malcolm's voice drifted through her head.

Poised to take the throne.

His choice of words and his tone had been interesting now that she had some distance from that night. He had always had plans in motion, but now, they were spiraling about the throne of Arravan with a vengeance. They would be tightening, and the King's Council would begin to split, if it hadn't already. Killing Marteen had been a horrible mistake on his part, and she was still unsure of why he'd done it. Perhaps with Bentley and Etienne as unexpected witnesses to his treachery and treason, he felt he could no longer trust his advisor to keep quiet.

Then the joy shall be all mine, as she fights against me. Though either way, Darrius Lauranna Durand, I shall plant my heirs in her womb.

Jessa needed protection, and her Boys understood that almost as much as she did. Bentley and Etienne has heard Malcolm's threats, and no doubt they had shared with the others, at least in essence, what he had threatened. Jessa knew what Malcolm wanted, but she would argue that she needed no such safeguards, especially if they put others in danger. Darry understood the truth. Jessa was the key to Malcolm's grand schemes concerning Lyoness, which made her lover the most vulnerable of them all. Somehow it was the truth, and Darry had always known it.

She looked down at her feet, balanced so easily upon the fallen oak.

The Lanark River Estate had been a true gift to them all, and Darry felt a pang of sadness that Emmalyn could not share in its uncomplicated joys. Emmalyn had seen to their safety when they had been in dire need, and she had done so within hours of their escape into the maze. For her missives to have reached Ballentrae and be waiting for them, the house prepared and the Seneschal and his people at the ready, Emmalyn had acted with ruthless efficiency.

Emmalyn was on the move, and Darry could not think of a more dangerous opponent to have. Malcolm had challenged her once at Kings and Jackals, and when it was obvious he had no chance of winning, he had abandoned their game. When it was spoken of, he would boast of having allowed Emmalyn her victory. The lack of honor in such a small matter had always galled Darry, but Emmalyn would only smile. *Time will tell*, she had said.

Wyatt was home. He had to be. Her protector and defender in all things, her brother and boon companion. They had been robbed of their reunion, which they had planned even before his departure. They had promised themselves a stolen bottle of Artanis Gold from their father's private collection, and they would drink it while sitting upon the thrones of Arravan. And she had missed Jacob and Alisha's wedding.

Malcolm had backed her into a corner and she could feel it. Her blood pushed and screamed through her veins and she lifted her head back. A low growl of rage rolled along her throat and lifted quietly into the night as it moved through the trees. The noises around her ceased in reaction, the crickets and the night birds, and the frogs, as well. Only the breeze remained as it moved through the forest.

Darry looked toward the river and smiled a bit sheepishly. "Sorry."

She was tired beyond her capacity to measure it and she still had no answers, and so she closed her eyes. She could feel Jessa's body against her own, certain and safe and filled with such life. She felt herself drift in the sweetness, letting it soothe her blood as well as her troubled thoughts. Sleep was but a heartbeat away, and she fought against it, right up until she couldn't…

"I would hold my love beneath the skins, when the winter wind would scream beyond the walls of our tent. She would tangle me up and kiss me in her sleep."

Darry looked to the fallen birch among the undergrowth, less than ten feet away.

The scarred woman sat upon the bend of rotting wood, her body glowing with moonlight. Her figure caught at the hidden colors of the night, and they poured over her shoulders and fell from the tips of her heavy hair like rain.

"I cannot describe in words how I felt, only to say that in those moments her love made me feel like a god."

"I know this feeling," Darry whispered.

The scarred woman smiled in a tender manner. "I know you do, love."

"How am I to protect her?"

The scarred woman gestured to the grove. "This place, it bends things. The light and the colors. Time." Her expression held a touch of something close to disapproval. "The Great Loom is exposed here, like the moments between life and death. It's vulnerable. Everything here is on the edge of forever. Enoch use to say that the gods come here to play with men, like toys." Her eyes were intense and Darry felt a touch of unease at the raw power they held. "But they come here to worship, as well. To worship *us*, to worship men because they live with passion. A passion for life, and each other, that the gods have long since forgotten. If you can find the right thread?" She grabbed at the air, and the closing of her fist echoed in Darry's head. "You can ride it, and there is nothing they can do to stop you, because they are afraid."

"Afraid of what?" Darry felt like a child before the fire, listening to her grandmother Asa Lewellyn tell a tale of the Olden Men and their wars.

"Of being lost." The scarred woman smiled a mercenary sort of smile. "They have nothing to anchor them in time." The thick scar that ran down her face bent as her amber eye flared with light. She looked young with her enthusiasm, terribly young and alive. "But we have our blood."

"Why do I feel like you're telling me something important?" Darry asked, suddenly wary.

"Because the Loom is moving, and it will be a cruel change of seasons, not just a shift in the wind. And because time is not what people think it is."

Darry knew she was right. War was coming, and for Lyoness, it had already arrived.

"There are many groves like this, I have found, and though they are all different they are the same. Do you understand?"

"Like priests," Darry answered.

The scarred woman smiled again. "Yes. But not the Holy Men."

"No, they're different."

"The Vhaelin gods are almost as old as the Dog Star gods, who made the *Cha-Diah* people. No one knew who they were, either. Saving their totem, it was a thing of great respect."

"I respect their power, but I did it for her."

"I know."

"How am I to protect her?"

"You must leave her."

"I won't," Darry replied as her deep ache of peacefulness turned quickly into something else. "I will never leave her."

"Yes…when Sorrow comes for you, you must leave her."

Darry did not understand, but it didn't matter. "*No.*"

The scarred woman stood up in a smooth move and crossed the distance between them. With each step she took, the moon's light seemed to bend around her, just as she had said. She left shimmers of color in her footsteps through the grass, like lamp oil that had been spilled in pools of water.

When she stood close, she reached out and touched Darry's cheek. Darry felt the wave of light from the woman's hand slide down her neck in a supple manner. "If you would stay with her, then you must. Sorrow is the only weapon I have left with which to help you. That was my fault, and I'm sorry. When he comes for you, take his hand, or you will lose all that is yours. All that is good and clean and sweet. If you don't, you will lose everything…just as I did."

Darry frowned. "I don't understand."

"And you must remember whose blood runs in your veins, and return to it when it calls you home. Remember your blood."

Darry felt the full effects of the love in the woman's eyes, and it filled her bones with weight. "Are you going to make me climb that damn rock again?"

The scarred woman chuckled happily, the sound deep and rough. "You will have to. You forgot what I left for you."

It took her a moment, but Darry remembered her promised gift.

"You should wake up now, my daughter…She calls for you."

Darry opened her eyes with a start, still balanced upon the fallen oak. Her heart was beating fast, and she turned her head, her eyes intense upon the trees of the grove.

The name whispered through her thoughts and she pushed and leaped, on the run as she hit the ground. The saplings seemed to crowd her path, and as she neared the grove an unnatural wave of fear rolled over her like the incoming tide. Perhaps it was meant to warn her away, but she was more confused by its sudden presence than frightened. She knew only respect and curiosity for the Vhaelin. Darry ran through it and rushed past the ring of birch trees, four or five trees thick, and grown so close that it slowed her down before she burst through into the open grove.

Jessa sat in the center of the grass circle, leaning upon her left arm as if it were all she could do to stay upright. Her hair tumbled about her face and shoulders, the dark curls reaching toward the ground.

Darry ran and slid upon her knees as she approached, stopping before her lover. Her heart beat with an honest fear, a fear not born of spell or trickery. She could feel the power of the Vhaelin in the grove, and it swept against her skin in a swell of otherworldly presence that raised the hair upon her arms.

Darry touched Jessa's face, her fingers gentle upon the familiar feel of Jessa's cheek. She smelled of jasmine and pine and the sweet, enticing scent that was uniquely feminine to Darry's senses. "Jessa?"

Jessa smiled slowly, her expression filled with unexpected indulgence. Her eyes opened as her hands came forward, and the fullness of her touch slid along the muscles of Darry's stomach. The caress pulled the air from Darry's lungs as Jessa took hold of Darry's breasts in a covetous manner, turning her hands as her eyes lifted.

"I love you, *Akasha*."

Jessa rose onto her knees and kissed her, her mouth smooth and hungry as her arms went about Darry's back beneath her open shirt. Darry returned the embrace, lifting and pulling Jessa close. Jessa's mouth tasted like home, and her dark curls filled Darry's hand like the heavy waters of the Sellen Sea, alive against her skin and filled with mystery.

Darry fell beneath the influence of Jessa's tongue, their passion weaving a spell that called out to the tattered remains of her wildest blood.

Her left hand slid beneath Jessa's trousers and breeches and took hold of Jessa's buttocks, grasping at the smooth skin as they kissed. Darry moved against her once, and then again. Jessa's arms tightened and her mouth opened as her body pushed and reached in response.

Her intimate, unexpected cry as she released her spirit flipped Darry's heart and sent a shiver of pleasure along the flesh between her own legs.

Jessa rolled her shoulders and Darry felt the touch along her ribs, and then her neck. Jessa was careful about Darry's wounds, but she would not be denied until she held Darry's face. Jessa kissed her, wet and full with longing. "Don't," Jessa said, breathless. Her touch held the sort of possessiveness that thrilled Darry to her very bones. "Don't ever run from me, Darrius, please. You must stay close. You must try."

Jessa's eyes in the moonlight were a splendid sable violet, abundant with so many treasures. A sweetness and unguarded innocence that only Darry knew, as well as strength, and a hidden potential for rage and temper that few would expect. There was laughter, and tenderness, and a power that knew very few restraints unless imposed by Jessa herself. A dry wit laced with a lethal mockery that only appeared when Jessa was frustrated or challenged. Darry understood her sexual appetites, held just beneath the surface of her shy surprise at being loved. Her girlish love of simple joys remained intact alongside the pain of a life lived beneath the darkness of others. A darkness that should have made all such gifts impossible, though instead, it had given her the capacity for more than Darry could possibly fathom.

"*Akasha?*"

Darry's hand tightened in Jessa's hair and Jessa caught her breath as Darry pulled her head back, ever so slowly, to expose Jessa's throat. Jessa grabbed at Darry's shirt as Darry leaned in, and the material slid along Darry's back. Darry tasted the skin of her lover's neck, her teeth grazing along the tender flesh, the pounding rush of Jessa's blood just below the skin. So tenuous, all of it, so utterly vulnerable.

Darry closed her eyes and savored the intense tremor in Jessa's body.

Jessa let out a startled cry at the touch of her bite, and her hands dug at Darry's shoulders as she tried to pull closer. Darry sucked the flesh as her tongue replaced her teeth, and her left hand slipped between them. She undid the buttons of Jessa's shirt, slowly, blindly, unwilling to abandon her desire. She felt Jessa's nails upon the back of her neck, and Darry turned them both to the side, a rumble of hunger moving hard along her throat. The muscles in Jessa's legs let go instantly, and she tipped within Darry's arms as Darry opened her mouth upon Jessa's exposed breast.

Jessa's tremble had turned into something deeper and altogether more violent as Darry undid the buttons of Jessa's trousers, certain of what she would take and loving in what she would give. Her touch slid beneath her lover's clothes.

Darry felt little of the Vhaelin in that moment, but she felt the influence and sovereignty of her own blood as Jessa jerked in her arms and pulled at her. The grass enveloped them as they sank in its thickness and Darry kissed her.

Jessa pulled her mouth free. *"Salla."* Her shoulders shook as her emotions overwhelmed her. *"Salla tuah de Akasha..."*

Darry took her time as she removed her lover's clothing, Jessa's left hand refusing to let go of Darry's shirt. She was blatantly helpless against Darry's actions despite where they were, the temple of her own gods suddenly silent as Jessa gave herself over.

Darry took hold of Jessa's wrists and claimed her body, her hips pushing smoothly between Jessa's legs and pressing against her. She pinned Jessa's hands to the earth and looked down at her amidst the fall of her hair. Jessa returned her gaze, her eyes bright and full with tears. Darry leaned down, her lips but a breath away from Jessa's mouth. Her voice, when it came, was barely there at all. "My sweet Jessa...my love."

Jessa closed her eyes and Darry watched as her tears slipped free. They raced back along her temples, finding sanctuary in the darkness of her hair. Darry opened her hands and released Jessa's wrists. "Give me leave."

Jessa moaned and took hold of Darry's face as she pushed up to meet her.

Darry thrust against her as she pulled from their kiss, her lips finding Jessa's breast instead. Darry opened her mouth, her bite somewhat sharp before she smoothed the skin with her tongue and kissed it with her lips. Jessa moved beneath her, her breathing filled with excitement, her passion unrestrained as her fingers clawed at Darry's shoulders. Darry felt her own release rise and she let it, her hips pushing as she grabbed and pulled Jessa's left leg higher. Jessa cried out as Darry spent her spirit, the muscles of Darry's legs and buttocks pushing and stretching. The pleasure flowed through her sex, through her legs, through her whole body in such a wild rush that her blood changed beneath it.

There was a crack of sound and a flood of witchlight raced away from Jessa's body in a surge of power, rolling through the grove and shattering outward in a swell of intense golden light. The birch trees swayed as the growl left Darry's throat in a sharp burst, and she dragged her face between Jessa's breasts, biting and tasting, finding the hard and yet tender nipple of Jessa's left breast.

Jessa spoke in a raw, broken voice as Darry tasted her way down her lover's body, leaving her mark wherever it pleased her to do so. The words she spoke were unknown to Darry, but the sentiment was not.

When her mouth claimed the aroused, heated flesh of Jessa's sex, Darry finally understood her place in the Great Loom, and she bound their threads together as tightly as she knew how. She tasted of Jessa's spirit and kissed her sex, sucking the tenderness in her mouth. Her tongue craved her lover's flavor, and she savored deeply of her want with a fierceness that was the very essence of her wild heart. Jessa's body writhed beneath her touch, bathed in moonlight, as she cried out, the primal sounds Jessa made in the warm air of the grove an erotic prayer as unique as she was, free and pure. The sheen of exertion and pleasure upon the fullness of Jessa's breasts, her nipples raised and her back arched as she came with a wanton shout of pleasure, her offering of life to her gods.

Darry stripped her clothes and slipped between her lover's legs. Jessa moaned as she grabbed her and pulled her close, the scent and taste of Jessa's body sending Darry's passion into a renewed fever. Darry moved against her, their spirit mingling as Darry's lower body rolled in quick thrusts of need. Darry felt the warmth of Jessa's witchlight pass through her body once again, and it expanded outward as Jessa's legs wrapped about her thighs and tangled her up, her hands grasping at Darry's neck and hair as she pulled Darry's tongue into her mouth.

Chapter Ten

Jessa's gaze wandered through the trees as the runes moved smoothly in her thoughts, filled with persuasion.

She rode upon Vhaelin Star, wrapped in the sacred hide that the totem of her gods had gifted to her. It engulfed her body with room to spare, the hide tanned by her gods and laced with immeasurable power. Upon the soft underside, against her body, the runes had been burned upon the plush leather. They sang and whispered against her bones with a music she had never heard before, for they were the runes from Hinsa's portal.

Darry clicked her tongue softly as she walked beside Vhaelin Star along the path that would take them home, the filly as charmed by Darry's presence as she had always been.

Jessa looked at Darry's hair and tried to rein in the pull of her own majik, each strand of her lover's hair, each frayed braid amongst the rest calling out for Jessa to touch. The lacerations upon Darry's right cheek and jaw were bruised, but the flesh was clean and the skin was already healing. Jessa remembered their touch beneath her lips. She remembered everything and it wrenched at the small bit of strength she had left.

There were runes that spilled and slid along Darry's shoulders and caught the light, and Jessa narrowed her eyes against the flames and fullness of their presence. She heard the gentle laughter of her gods in her head and turned her face downward, trying to shield herself from the memory and command of their presence.

Vhaelin Star came to a gentle stop and Jessa opened her eyes as Darry's right hand slipped beneath the stag's hide and took hold of her own.

Akasha...

Darry flinched just a bit at the echo in her head, and Jessa adjusted the power of her spell. It was not one she liked to use, but she had little choice in the matter.

My sweet lover.

"Are you all right?" Darry's voice was painfully rough, but it was quiet in her throat.

Jessa tightened her grip upon Darry's hand. Darry's eyes were filled with an abundance of color, bright and splendid with love as well as worry. She could see the striations within each, and the darkness of her pupils seemed to swirl with bursts of sunlight.

You will lie with me and I shall hold you, and we will sleep for days, yes?

Darry smiled. "Yes, my love."

Are you in pain?

"A little."

Jessa looked up, feeling a shift in the air. She took stock of where they were. *Bentley and Arkady are beyond the next rise, I think*, she warned.

"Just Bentley." Darry glanced at the path and then returned to her with a slight grin. "He needs a bath."

Jessa leaned down despite that it caused the blood to rush in her ears. Her balance tipped to the side. Darry looked up at her, beautiful and wild and spent. Her shirt was still open and she bore the mark of Jessa's mouth upon her neck and breasts, and Jessa could still taste the lush, intoxicating flavor of her skin. Her trousers were ripped and they hung low upon her narrow hips. Darry's muscles were lax and her skin looked soft and pale with fatigue. It would take hours for Jessa to clear the tangles from her hair and undo the braids. The bruises from her battle at the stream were deep and stippled with blood, and Jessa could see in the sunlight that the lowest wound upon her jaw and neck would need additional attention.

She had never been more beautiful to Jessa, or more completely fragile and vulnerable to the world around them. Jessa felt the tears burn in her eyes.

Darry smiled and her dimple pressed in her left cheek. "I think you broke my tongue," she whispered and her eyes were bright.

Jessa laughed quietly and her tears slipped free.

"Perhaps we shouldn't visit their temple again, maybe…at least for a while."

Jessa had no words for what she felt. Not for the moment they were in, nor for what they had shared in the grove. "I think you might be right," she said softly, and a flash of pain moved in her head at having spoken aloud.

Darry was quiet and Jessa felt the profound echo of their passion sweep through her heart, its absolute dominion toppling the last remaining walls she had built. Even now, after all they had been through, stones had yet remained. Collapsing walls against fear and towers that tipped in the dead of night upon her uncertainties, they had held on, if only in shadow and crumbling ruin. Defenses she had constructed through the years and then fortified anew before traveling the road to Arravan. She felt the dust of what remained swept away, and her heart left clean and full with life. She had been so very certain of what her fate would be, and she had been so utterly wrong in all of it.

"Just a few more hours, Jess." Darry's expression was filled with tenderness. "We shall have a hot bath and a warm meal, and then we will sleep for days, just as you said."

Hinsa moved through the long grass beside the small trail, her low growl turning them both to the path ahead. Bentley Greeves topped the rise and stood at the top of the hill, surrounded by spunwood trees as their leaves flipped and turned in the breeze.

Jessa squeezed Darry's hand once more and felt a pull of desperation. They were no longer alone, and for an instant, it was a desolate feeling. *Akasha.*

Darry smiled up at her, her eyes bright and yet touched with sadness. "Me, too, my love."

Darry's hand slipped away and she stepped along the trail, patting Vhaelin Star's neck and taking up the reins once more. Jessa sat back and pulled the stag's coat more tightly about her shoulders in an act of protection.

Bentley had moved down the rise with a long stride, and as they walked toward him, Jessa could see that his eyes were keen and quick. As he approached, Darry pulled them to a halt and they waited.

Without a word Bentley walked up to Darry and hooked his right arm about her neck, his movements filled with care. Darry leaned against his chest and he held to her shoulders. His expression was curious and filled with questions. "My Lady Jessa," he said simply and gave her a caring smile. "It is very good to see you." He glanced down at his friend. "Both of you." He placed a kiss upon Darry's temple and then stepped back from her.

"We're very tired, Bentley," Darry replied. "Jessa has spoken to her gods, and…and we need to be home. It is good to see you, too, but things need to be quiet, I think, for a bit."

Bentley studied Darry with interest and then returned his gaze to Jessa. "Are you wounded, as well?" His question was touched with worry.

No, Bentley, just…

Bentley's eyes narrowed at her voice in his head, but he did not react as most others did, with fear or pain. It was curious, and strangely like him to be the exception, and so she smiled. She remembered then that he had could see through the Veil of Shadows with little difficulty.

"Just?" he asked softly.

By the stream, by the bend beneath the bluffs…my gods have left gifts for Darry, for saving their sacred totem. Might you retrieve them, and bring them home for her?

Bentley gave a nod. "Yes, I would be honored to do that, my Lady."

Thank you, my friend.

Bentley smiled at Darry. He looked as if he wanted to say many things, and that he had questions was obvious, but he chose the course that was best for his friend. "Off with what's left of your shirt, Cat," he said with some authority. Darry dropped the reins and obeyed him. Bentley undid the buttons of his tunic and pulled it free of his belted trousers with a roll of his broad shoulders. "Put this on, then."

Darry met his eyes. "You keep losing your shirts."

He watched as she shrugged into it, and then he stepped forward and did up the buttons for her. "Yes," he agreed simply, and his tone was kind. "Though perhaps this says more about you, Princess, than it does *me*. You always were a bit dodgy on your etiquette."

Darry laughed, the sound low and rough. Jessa's arms ached for her and it was a strange sadness in her muscles that would not abate. Just to hold her and know that Darry was safe, it was all she wanted. The Yellandale was glorious beneath the morning sun but decidedly harsh at the moment, and they needed respite.

"Take my Bella—she's over the rise and ready to go. I was about to come after you. Arkady went back to the river for supplies and horses. I'll wait here for him." He turned to Jessa. "We shall take care of things, my Lady, and see you at home." He grinned suddenly beneath his mustache and his eyes held a knowing glint that was not altogether discreet. "An autumn moon celebration to remember, yes?"

Jessa tried not to laugh as she looked down, closing her eyes against the ache that moved through her head. Even the blush he had caused brought discomfort. *Yes, I quite agree.*

Jessa sat naked upon the edge of their bed as the afternoon sun struggled to reach through the heavy drapes that had been drawn.

They had eaten warm buttered bread and hot vegetable stew in a beef gravy. It was quite possibly the best meal Jessa had ever eaten, and the cook, Lady Abagail, who was a plump woman filled with stories and recipes and easy laughter, had blushed when Jessa told her so. They had bathed, and Jessa had found her willpower even as Darry's had faltered.

Darry was covered in bruises and scrapes of all kinds, and there were claw marks upon her back as well, glancing blows she had won in her battle. Jessa had taken a line of stitches upon the underside of Darry's right jaw and down onto her neck, treating the tender skin with a salve of passionflower and yarrow root first. Darry had not flinched, nor had she reacted in any way that might cause Jessa alarm, though Jessa had asked Darry to close her eyes. The blue and green of Darry's gaze held an intensity that Jessa had been in no shape to endure for very long. Darry had smiled, kissed her, and obeyed. The taste of her full lips had almost stolen Jessa's tenuous strength all over again.

She let her fingers move through the clean softness of Darry's hair, the strands dark with damp upon her pillow. It had not taken her as long as she'd thought to comb them out and clear the braids, and she had sung softly, a song that was a favorite of the Dark Ridge tribes.

It felt good to sing. It felt good to use the gift her mother had given her. She had reclaimed it in the Yellandale night, by the light of a fire that had smelled of pine and oak, with the sound of the stream flowing nearby.

Darry's naked body was only partially covered by the sheet of their bed, and Jessa added to the inventory of scars that her lover wore. They were all hard-won, and not a single mark had been careless. Her touch hovered above the mark of the wolf, and she wondered how great the beast had been. The scars would announce Darry's strength in a bold manner few others could claim, and a mixture of pride and desire fluttered through her chest.

It would announce her lover as a warrior few would wish to engage, and she remembered the long, heavy scar that Neela's lover had worn upon the left side of her face.

Tannen Ahru, she thought, and her eyes found the hearth across the lengthy room.

The fire burned upon the grate and its light moved upon the stag's hide, rolled and waiting for her upon the divan. Beside it, her dusty saddlebags held both the ribbons of velvet hair and the antlers he had shed for her. They were tokens of magnificent power, and though her excitement at the spells she might now use was great, she also felt a good deal of apprehension. She had never known Radha to possess such tokens.

She could not yet contemplate the runes upon the hide. It was too much.

Darry's arms slipped about her waist and shoulders and Jessa let out a sigh of relief. Her muscles let go and her eyes fluttered shut as she was pulled across Darry's body. The softness of their bed greeted her like an old friend as the silk of the sheet drifted over them both.

"*Stop.*"

Jessa smiled at Darry's intimate whisper and pulled her down. Darry moved gently against her side and Jessa shifted, holding her lover in her arms as she had promised she would.

❖

Bentley turned the chair around, straddled it as he rested his arms upon its back, and let his eyes travel down the long table.

Darry's Boys had always been brothers, but as Kingsmen they had been comrades as well, and their unique style of fighting took their bonds of love into a unique space that Grissom Longshanks had never truly understood. On the battlefield they fought as a single man with a dozen swords, and they moved with a purpose so that each individual's skill might support the whole.

In life beyond the Kingsmen and Blackstone Keep, their brotherhood had only intensified, and he smiled at his chosen family as the afternoon sun poured into the dining hall. A hall in one of the buildings they had made with their own hands, of their own volition upon their own land. "You've all seen what we brought back?"

His brothers looked back at him and a murmur of assent moved down the table.

"Darry killed him with a dagger. The biggest wolf I've ever seen, by far."

"He had to have been at least fourteen stone," Orlando said. He was their best hunter, and he had seen more game than most of them. "I don't understand how the pelt came to be."

"Aye," Lucien added. "That's at least a fortnight of work there, and by a skilled tanner."

"It was a gift from the Vhaelin."

"Lady Jessa's gods?" Sybok asked as several men leaned back in surprise at Bentley's words. The young man's face was pale. "*Those* Vhaelin?"

"Aye, boy, those Vhaelin."

"All right..." Theroux spoke with a frown, his dusty blond hair pushed back from his brown eyes and hooked behind his ears. "But what does that mean?"

"It means," Bentley began and then stopped for a moment. "Listen…I believe in the trinity just like most of you. I worship Gamar, I fear Amar, and I cast my longing eyes upon the dangerous maids of Jezara." There was some laughter, but he had their attention. "But I know there are others out there, other gods with power and followers, and long histories. And I know that *none* of them are above meddling in the affairs of men."

"The Vhaelin like the forests and the plains, and the places where men don't go," Lucien said. "I guess we shouldn't be surprised they turned up in the Yellandale."

"Aye," Bentley agreed. "And I won't sit here and tell you that I understand such things, as to what the gods want or need, or why they choose to show up when they do. But we were all there when Gamar took his Holy Man from the steps of the great temple."

"I missed that," Lucien said with a rueful smile. "And Darry did, too."

Their expressions changed, as they each remembered the summer's eve when Gamar had come for one of his wild Holy Men, sweeping him up from the temple plaza in a blast of light and blue fire.

"But we saw the power of Lady Jessa's majik firsthand at the siege of the Great Hall, and in the courtyard, as well. It cannot be denied."

"We all believe, Bentley," Jemin responded in his crisp accent, "in the gods, and in the power of all sorts of majik, especially Lady Jessa's. And we all saw Hinsa's portal, we all walked the maze. We've all seen the runes at work one way or another. Where are you leading us?"

"Something is happening," Bentley answered quietly. "We've all been witness to more majik in the past half year than ever before. There is war in Lyoness, and soon, there'll be war in Arravan. Whether our friends ride for the Kistanbal Mountains or Karballa, I don't know. But the armies of Arravan will ride, make no doubt about it. War *is* coming." He sat back a little. "And so when I saw the wolf pelt, I thought…" Bentley tried to put his words into order.

"You thought what?" Tobe prompted in a kind voice.

"I thought…I thought that Jessa has twelve brothers."

"And we are twelve," Orlando said. "Though it will be eleven now, with Joaquin dead. You're not the first of us to see that."

"Aye," Matthias agreed. "All of it, it's like a great stew of trouble."

"Marteen murdered at the foot of the throne," Etienne said.

"And that fucking shriveled cock, Malcolm," Arkady added, his quiet voice touched with warning. "They aren't safe, not a one of them at Blackstone."

"And now the gods leave gifts," Matty the Younger said, looking a bit startled.

Bentley looked to the entrance at the opposite end of the room, and he sat a bit straighter in his chair. "*Hiyah*," he whispered.

Hinsa bent easily about the half-open door and padded into the hall, walking sleekly into the light as every man at the table followed Bentley's gaze.

She quickened her step for several strides and then leaped, landing upon the surface of the long table in an easy manner. Her fur was golden and flecked, and she bore several wounds upon her left side. They did not seem to trouble the great cat as she padded along the table. Her claws brushed softly upon the wood until she found the spot she wanted, lying down in a splash of sun as it spread across the oak planks.

"Gamar's balls," Etienne said with a smile.

"I think she doesn't like being left out of things." Arkady set his hand within a few inches of Hinsa's front paw, and the golden mountain panther craned her neck forward. She sprayed his hand with moisture as she sniffed.

"So no more sitting on our backsides, and eating Lady Abagail's berry pies," Lucien said, his eyes warm as he looked at Hinsa.

"It's time we made ourselves ready," Bentley agreed. "When Darry gives the word, she'll want to go. I'd like us to be ready before she asks us to please hurry up."

There was laughter.

Orlando's hazel eyes were bright as he looked down the table. "I'll see to the food stores we'll need, and Tobe and I will salt and smoke what we can. We should have plenty to travel on, no matter which direction we take."

"I'll speak with Master Kenna about the horses. We'll need twice the number we have now, and then we'll choose the best. I'll see to the wagons, as well," Theroux replied.

"I'll help with that," Jemin said.

"We need to see to the estate," Arkady added. "Matty and Sybok, you're with me. When you're not in the practice yard, we shall see to the needs of the staff and the estate itself. They've gotten used to our help. The stores must be full for winter—everything we can do to make things easier for our people here, needs to be done."

There was a pause and Orlando smiled. "We have a home now."

He was not the only one who enjoyed the words, and Matthias reached out with his left hand and brushed the backs of his fingers upon Orlando's clean-shaven cheek. "Aye," he said softly.

Bentley grinned. "We'll need armor, and plenty of it to go around. We have what we brought from Blackstone, but it's not much, and Darry's will have to be altered again. She's gotten leaner."

"And she keeps getting faster." Matty the Younger smiled.

Matthias set his hand upon the shoulder of Lucas Kilkenny, who sat to his right.

"Aye, Matthias. We'll fill the armory with everything we can," Lucas chimed in. "There was a fair amount there to begin with, but most of it was used for defense, spears and pikes and broadswords, some cudgels and shields. Good weapons, but not what we're used to, and not what we'll need. I'll take as much hide as you can find, and as much steel as we can lay our hands on. There's a tinker in Ballentrae who should have quite a bit, and he'll know where we can find more. I don't want to draw attention, though."

"Perhaps a trip to Marban might be in order," Bentley suggested. "Let's get things started first, take an inventory, and then decide what's needed. Etienne, you're with me. Let's you and me keep things at a hard pace. Are we all agreed?"

"Aye," Tobe answered for all, after looking about the table.

"What about dinner?" Sybok asked. "Are will still having dinner?"

"Bloody hell, boy." Lucien laughed with the others, his hand swatting lightly at the back of the young man's head. "Pace yourself."

"Plenty of arrows, Lucas, if you please," Orlando requested as he leaned forward to catch his attention. "And no more of your bloody chicken feathers."

Matthias groaned. "Not with the chicken feathers, again, Lando, please."

Orlando's brow went up. "What? What did I say?"

Their laughter filled the room and Hinsa lifted her face into the sunlight.

CHAPTER ELEVEN

Jessa sat up with a start and flipped her curls back.
The fire in the hearth was low, and the air was heavy with darkness as she threw off the covers and pushed from the bed. She grabbed the nearest shirt and shrugged it on, doing up the buttons as she went. A taper had been lit atop one of the bureaus, but not the lamp. "*Akasha?*"

Movement stirred upon the divan and Hinsa stared back at her across the distance, panting beside the stag's hide, her tongue pink in the firelight.

"Biscuit," Jessa said and went to her, kneeling down beside the divan. Hinsa's body was hot as she leaned her heavy head against Jessa's arm, and Jessa kissed the side of her face several times. Hinsa's body vibrated with a rumble of sound that moved along her throat, subdued and almost mournful. "What is it, my sweet?"

"Jess?"

Jessa turned at Darry's voice.

"I didn't mean to wake you."

Jessa kissed Hinsa's forehead and rubbed at her ears briefly before she pushed to her feet and made her way back across the room. Jessa smiled as Darry stood in nothing but a pair of half-buttoned trousers, looking vulnerable and wild at the same time.

"What are you doing, *Akasha?*"

"I was thirsty."

Darry reached out for her as she neared, and Jessa stepped into her lover's arms, her touch delicate as she took Darry's face in her hands. Darry leaned down and Jessa opened her mouth to a hot-blooded kiss of greeting. Her hands slipped into Darry's curls and she pulled closer, her pulse reacting to the heady taste.

Darry ended their kiss in a languid manner. "I had a strange dream," she whispered. "The room behind the stacks in the Queen's Library"—Jessa's heart skipped as a heavy line of blood ran from Darry's right nostril—"was filled with light, and there was—"

Darry looked startled as Jessa wiped at the blood with her thumb. "My love, come back to bed now, yes?" Darry's eyes lifted to hers and Jessa's heart beat oddly yet again. Darry's pupils had eclipsed nearly all of the color in her eyes. She felt the skin of Darry's cheek, and then wiped at Darry's lips as a fresh line of blood slipped down. "Please, *Akasha*."

"Were you missing me?"

Jessa slipped her arm about Darry's waist, her embrace both tender and possessive. "Yes," she whispered. "Since the day I was born, actually."

Darry let herself be led, and without argument she sat upon the edge of the bed. Jessa kissed her cheek and grabbed a handkerchief from the side table. Darry took it and pressed it to her nose as she tipped her head back. Jessa examined the skin about Darry's facial wounds, and though it was swollen and bruised, it was not infected. With a gentle touch she turned Darry at the shoulder and checked her back, her fingers light as they skated along the wounds. The long claw marks would forever mark Darry's smooth skin, but they would not be deep scars and they were not infected.

Darry readjusted the handkerchief. "I've been a bit of trouble lately—I'm sorry, Jess."

Jessa sat beside her and smiled, a potent rush of love filling her chest. "No, my love, you are my greatest adventure." She set a hand upon the center of Darry's chest and Darry's skin was hot to the touch. "You heal faster than I have ever seen, but you have a fever, *Akasha*." Jessa could feel the *Cha-Diah* majik all around her. "Let me see this, please." She took the stained handkerchief with a gentle touch. No new blood flowed, but Darry's eyes had changed, a rim of color bright in her green eye but not her blue. Once again, Darry's majik was uncontained and running an unknown course that she had no way of preparing for. "Lie down," she whispered.

Darry obeyed, her movements slow and somewhat heavy. Jessa brought the sheet over and then the blanket as she sat upon the edge of the bed. Darry lifted her right arm out and Hinsa slid from the divan and padded across the room. She leaped onto the bed and turned in a tight circle before she tucked her powerful body against Darry's.

Jessa could see the faint runes in the air as they came together, and she pulled her hand away in a stilted manner. It was a flash and scattering of light, partial runes caught in her sight that disappeared just as quickly as they had arrived. She pushed through her caution, laid her hand upon Darry's arm, and slid her touch along the strength she loved so well. "What was in the room behind the stacks?"

Darry's smile was lovely. "I'm not sure, but there was laughter," Darry whispered. Jessa waited, and she could feel Hinsa's purr through the feather bed. "Emmalyn was laughing..."

Jessa watched as they fell asleep, and she remembered the words of warning spoken by the Vhaelin. *Her blood is not the blood of the Fox People. There is terrible danger for her.*

"The *Cha-Diah* are the Fox People," Jessa said in understanding. She had never heard their name before, and she realized then that only their majik had retained its identity through the many centuries. The Fox People had died away, but the *Cha-Diah* power had lived on. *Through Hinsa, and those like her, wherever they may be.*

Jessa was most decidedly awake, and her attention was drawn to the divan with a great deal of focus.

She stood and moved, glancing at the fire as she covered the distance. The flames burst with renewed light and energy and the sitting area filled with its glow. She took hold of the stag's hide and let it unroll as she threw her arms out, her grip fierce upon the nearest edge. It dropped to the floor in a solid manner and Jessa spoke softly as she held her right hand out. The small ball of witchlight swirled and formed tightly, floating into the air above the tanned pelt.

The runes were burned into the smooth surface, blackened and clean despite the uneven nature of the coat. She dropped to her knees and bent over the writing, her hand careful as it skated just above the glyphs. They were the runes from Hinsa's portal, and they were the runes that had fallen from Darry's hair. They were the runes of the Fox People.

Jessa's eyes narrowed and her fingers moved beside the nearest symbol, tracing the shadow image that was burned beside it. The witchlight that hovered overhead brightened.

"High Vhaelin," she said aloud, truly startled. Her pulse quickened with excitement and wonder. "This is High Vhaelin," she repeated. "*Shivasa!*"

Each rune had been given a shadow symbol, and as Jessa sat back upon her heels, she took her first true look at the scope of what she had been given, seeing it with a scholar's eyes. There were hundreds of glyphs, perhaps even a thousand, depending upon the translation.

Jessa understood then that her deepest wish had indeed been granted, and that her gods had peered into the most hidden places of her heart. They had given her the means to keep Darry safe. They had given her the power to keep *all* of them safe.

Her mind began to work in earnest as she mapped out her course. She would need a bigger workroom than the one she was using for her herbs and medicines. She would need a proper space, like the one in Sebastian's Tower. She would need fresh air and sunlight and a hearth, perhaps even two if it could be done quickly enough.

She looked to the bed and the voice of her gods came again. *You must help her, or we shall all be lost.*

Darry was still suppressing her majik, or at least she was trying. Darry could no longer hear Hinsa, and though she had not said as much, Jessa knew it was the truth. The thought of such a blessing given and then taken away, Jessa could not even fathom such a unique heartache, for the both of them. And if the Vhaelin were right, if Darry surrendered to her *Cha-Diah* blood without the true heritage to support so much power, it might destroy her and Hinsa both. *Her blood is not the blood of the Fox People. There is terrible danger for her.*

Jessa pushed to her feet as the witchlight flared brightly and then faded from existence. "First I must bring your fever down, my love… And then I shall find you a way."

She grabbed the edge of the hide and dragged it back to the divan, beyond the fire.

When she reached the desk beside the balcony doors she eyed the heavy black bottle beside her papers, remembering their recent celebration. She grabbed the bottle and pulled the cork.

The Pentab Fire poured into a waiting goblet with a gurgle of fluid, and then she lifted her drink as she faced the divan. "I shall make you proud of me, Radha," she declared and then downed the spiced liquor. It burned along the surface of her throat, and she smiled as she set the goblet down, her eyes watering as she recorked the bottle. "Gamar's *balls*."

She grabbed her robe from the back of the chair, and then she was on the move. She would retrieve her medicines from her current workroom and see to her love, and then she would find Bentley. She would need her new work space as soon as possible, and he was just the man to see it done.

❖

The Crown Prince of Arravan poured three measures of Pentab Fire and then set the bottle down. He picked up two of the goblets and held them out as Abel Jefs stepped forward and took them both, handing one to his brother, Mason.

Abel was as tall as Malcolm and dressed in the uniform of the Palace Guard, though his collar was unhooked, and his white tunic was undone by several buttons. His brown hair was cut close along the sides of his head, but he wore a short tail of hair tied behind his head, the ends reaching below his collar in a slight curl. It was the latest fashion at court and Malcolm thought he wore it well. He was lean and a bit lanky, but he was fast with his sword and no one had ever doubted his skills as a soldier. He had been trained by Grissom Longshanks, and as he had risen through the ranks, his brother Mason had followed, at least until he had been called home to lead their father's men.

Mason was huge, and at times, Malcolm had to wonder if the younger son of Lord Jefs had been sired by another. He stood almost seven feet tall, and Malcolm had seen him tilt to the side and duck his head more than once as he entered a doorway. His brown hair was cut as Abel's was, and his blocky but oddly handsome face always held what appeared to be several days' worth of beard growth. His simple uniform held the black and green crest of his family in a patch above his heart, and from a distance, it appeared as if he had dropped part of his dinner upon his jacket, so barrel-like was his chest.

Malcolm picked up his own goblet. "To the annexation of the Humboldt lands into your family's holdings."

Abel smiled as he and Mason put their goblets forth and they clanked against Malcolm's. "Thank you for you generosity, my Prince."

"Yes," Mason said in his deep voice. "Our father has long sought the grazing lands that Humboldt has hoarded all to himself."

They drank, and Malcolm blew a clean breath past his lips in the aftermath.

Abel laughed and then coughed as he set his goblet on the table. "I have never tasted such Pentab, my Prince."

Malcolm smiled. "It's from Madame Dubassant's own cellar."

Mason downed his drink with no apparent effects and set his goblet beside his brother's. He stepped back from the table.

Malcolm picked up the pitcher of wine beside the bottle and poured a fresh drink into a clean goblet. The cool red wine slipped with a familiar and welcome sound, the pitcher beaded with moisture as it fought against the heat of the room. "Help yourselves to the wine," he offered as he walked past the hearth, sat down in his chair, and crossed his legs. He took a welcome sip. "What word from the west?"

Abel topped off a fresh goblet and maneuvered around the table. Mason followed him, and as Abel sat in the chair that had once belonged to Marteen Salish, Mason stood beside it. "We have called up the men from the House of Marston. They will assemble as quickly as possible, and await further instructions from Mason."

"I've placed several of my most trusted men with them," Mason added. "Should we need to move into Greeves's territory, they'll be ready to do whatever is necessary."

"Good." Malcolm's eyes flickered toward the bedroom door and he narrowed his gaze for a moment at the shadows. "If they are hiding the traitor and his bastard friends, we'll know soon enough."

"What of the council?"

Malcolm met Abel's neutral gaze, and he searched for an accusation in Abel's tone, though he found none. He still wasn't sure just how far he could trust the Jefs brothers, though he was in it now and he knew it. "Things are well in hand. With the influx of young lords from the outlying lands, pickings have been surprisingly easy. They chafe beneath the old ways, and they are eager for a chance at their own wealth and power. The idea of choosing their own paths into the future is a novel idea, and one that they like very much."

"And your father?" Abel inquired.

Malcolm peered into his wine for a moment and then looked back up. Abel's expression changed slightly beneath his gaze, and Malcolm felt a rush of tender pleasure in the pit of his stomach at Abel's sudden nervousness.

"I only wish to help, my Prince," Abel added quickly. "If I can."

"He treats with old men and thinks of finer days. His proposed war with the Fakir has brought them out of their warm beds, and stirred talk of old times."

"And the subject of...of your former advisor?" Abel asked in a careful voice.

Malcolm sighed a bit. "They approve of my search for justice."

"Is your sister really dead?" Mason asked in a blunt manner.

Malcolm laughed in surprise but he recovered quickly. "Marteen's shot was off a bit, but I saw the wound, straight through the chest. And if she had lived, she would not have run."

"Retreat would've been advised," Mason countered.

Malcolm's brow went up a bit. "Retreat?" He considered the idea for a brief moment. "No, that was never my sister's way." He took a drink of wine. "She is dead—you needn't worry."

"Her Bastards are a loose end we cannot afford."

"I realize that fact, thank you, Mason," Malcolm said, and his tone was somewhat sharp. He watched as Mason bowed his head and took a small step back. "And the return of Princess Jessa is paramount to my plans."

"I beg your pardon, my Prince."

"I think what Mason is trying to say is that they have gone to ground, and they have stayed there for quite some time," Abel said in a diplomatic tone. He was smarter than his brother and Malcolm was glad of it. Reining in such a beast as Mason was best left to the man he had deferred to his whole life. Malcolm made note of his tone and altered his temper a bit. "They are bastards and drunkards," Abel continued. "And though they are tested in battle, and respected for their skills, they are without their leader now. Mistakes will be made, and soon, if I do not miss my guess. We must be ready to take advantage of that and wipe them out when they step into the sun." He went as if to take a sip of wine, and then paused. "Would they have retreated to your sister's lands?"

Malcolm downed his drink and set the goblet on the table beside his chair. He pushed to his feet in order to accommodate his annoyance. "Darrius held only wild lands, sprawling, useless tracts that served no purpose. These places have been seen to by Melora's men." He walked to the fire and set a hand upon the mantel as he looked into the flames. He could hunt the whole of the Green Hills now, if he so desired. "The Princess would not do well in such wilds."

"Might they return to her people?"

"The people of the Ibarris Plains?" Malcolm asked as he turned and met Abel's gaze.

"Yes."

"Perhaps," Malcolm replied. "But the Singewood Rangers were alerted within a week of the incident. They have reported no such travelers. All have been stopped and searched. They have doubled their patrols, and their numbers have been bolstered by Melora's men."

Mason made a grunting noise. "The Kenton Brigades?"

"Yes."

"Brigands to a man, but good soldiers, as long as her gold doesn't run out."

"It won't." Malcolm smiled. "They bring it to her from the southern Taurus Mountains in large wagons and pile it on her back steps. Lovely bricks with her family's crest pressed right on top for all the world to see."

For the first time Malcolm saw a hint of humor in Mason's eyes. "Then I'm glad she is on our side."

"Then you were absolutely wise in having the Greeves lands under your watch. It is the best place to be looking," Abel replied. "If your sister's lands are uninhabitable, and their route to the Plains has been watched since the start of this, they really have nowhere else to be and still live in relative comfort. And you are right, of course, that the Princess was not made for the wilds. She has powers, it's true, but living in the woods for months on end is not one of them."

Malcolm chuckled at that. "Let us not speak of such indelicate matters where my future bride is concerned, if you please."

"Of course…And your family's lands, my Prince?"

"They are not there, and they continue to be watched." Malcolm's annoyance began to grow. Marteen would never need every little detail spelled out and explained to him. Marteen had always known what he wanted.

"What about your sister's man? Lord Greyson?" Mason inquired.

Malcolm moved slowly from his thoughts. "They are not married, as of yet, and I will put a stop to that as soon as I am able. He is but a third son with little to offer other than his sword and a few minor holdings. The Prince of Senegal has been waiting for a proper bride for years, now. My sister is more than capable of handling a man such as he is and funneling his vast wealth back into Arravan. I am told he is not the wisest heir the Bird of Paradise Throne has ever seen."

"Should we extend the search to include the Greyson holdings?" Abel inquired. "Princess Emmalyn's love for Darrius was a known fact, and she took quite a liking to the Lyoness Princess."

"They were sisters, Abel, it was to be expected."

"Yes, sisters are like that," Mason said in his deep voice, and for a moment he looked as if he pondered the bonds between women.

Malcolm smiled a bit and returned his gaze to the fire, only to have his heart tighten in his chest. He closed his eyes. "Hell and hounds," he whispered. "Evan."

CHAPTER TWELVE

At the soft knock upon the door, Emmalyn set her wine down and picked up the dagger that sat beside it. It fit her hand perfectly, and it had been made to do just that.

Upon the bed across the chamber, the wolfhound lifted her head from the quilt and growled. She was terribly small for a hound of her breed, and her fur was soft and light despite its wiry length. Her coloring was a beautiful brownish red that spoke of a broken bloodline, though the kennel master had been adamant it was not the case. She was the pup that had been meant for Jessa, once upon a spring day, but Emmalyn had gladly claimed her. Her glorious brown eyes were filled with emotion at any given moment, and she was perhaps the most loving dog Emmalyn had yet known. She was a superior guard, as well, and after the Sahwello had attacked, her presence had soothed Emmalyn's sleep as not even Royce could.

"Who is it, Red?" she asked in a whisper.

Emmalyn stood and looked down at the map of Arravan that was spread open across the table. It had been made by a Master Scribe at her private request, and it was the most complete mapping of the land that she had ever seen. It included major land holdings with counts of men-at-arms, Kingsmen, estimates of population, available resources that might be called upon when needed, sites that the Arravan army had used during past conflicts, and even the river currents that were known and that might affect military strategy. It was a work of art, and at the moment it was her most prized possession.

It was a map made for war, and it was sprawled across the table in the hidden alcove room behind the stacks of the Queen's Library, along with two dozen leaves of parchment covered with notes in her own hand.

Emmalyn looked to the bed once more and Red had laid her head upon her front paws, seemingly content. The knock came a second time.

Emmalyn wore a pair of soft trousers and a homespun black shirt that hung past her hips. Her red hair was tied behind her neck, and her curls fell to the small of her back as she walked in her bare feet to the door. She set her hand upon the latch. "Who is there?"

"It's Nina," came her cousin's voice, and Emmalyn pulled the bolt back and opened the door. "I know I'm late, Emma, I'm sorry."

Emmalyn reached out with her free hand and pulled her cousin inside. She gave her a half hug about the shoulders and kissed her cheek. "Hello, love," she greeted and closed the door. She slid the heavy bolt home in a quiet manner.

Nina was dressed much the same as Emmalyn was, though she wore a light coat that fell to the back of her knees. She held out the folded piece of parchment. "Captain Sol sends word."

Emmalyn took the note. "Keep me company."

Nina walked beside her back to the table, and Emmalyn set the dagger down in order to open the note. "Wyatt and several officers of the Seventh have accompanied Malcolm to Madame Dubassant's. Mason Jefs has made a visit to his officers and there's movement in their camp. Half a platoon, maybe more, is gearing up for travel. Kingston says that Mason and Abel are to join Malcolm at Madame Dubassant's at a later hour."

Nina poured herself a glass of wine. "Mason Jefs, the Solstice Champion."

Emmalyn set the note down. "Yes, and he commands five hundred men who would die for him if he but nods his head." Emmalyn picked up her wine once more and surveyed her map. "And beyond that, a regiment of men from their family lands are camped just north of Los Capos."

"An additional three thousand men," Nina added. "Eighty men in a platoon?"

"Give or take, yes," Emmalyn replied. "Malcolm has had himself an idea, and he's sending his own personal army instead of Melora's hired thugs."

"And this will be the first that Mason Jefs has gone to Madame Dubassant's."

"He wishes to drink with Wyatt, the king's chosen champion," Emmalyn mused. "It is said that Mason Jefs prays to Gamar, he fights, he hunts, and not much else."

"What does that mean for us, exactly?"

"It means that my little brother best be on his toes and not in his cups," Emmalyn answered and picked up her dagger as she leaned over the table. She tapped the map just east of the Gonnard Forest with the tip of her blade. "If they skirt the Green Hills here, then they're going north along the Raven's Run, which means Marban, Ballentrae, and the Lanark."

"Which means he's remembered Evan's lands are yours."

Emmalyn met her cousin's gaze as she thought of her first husband, and the lands she had inherited upon his death. That she had gifted those lands to Darry and Jessa had been a brilliant play, but it had always been destined to fail. Someone always remembered, in the end, exactly what you wished they would forget.

Emmalyn had confided in Nina in the days after the Sahwello had attacked, and it was Nina who came to her the night of Malcolm's treachery with the truth of what had happened. That Bentley and Nina had forged a bond did not surprise her in the least. Nina was her blood, but they had become true boon companions, much like Darry and Wyatt had always been. It had been an unexpected gift to Emmalyn, and it was one that she cherished each and every day since her world had fallen apart. It was Nina who provided the rookery and delivered her messages, the ravens at her disposal second to none thanks to a distant Lewellyn cousin that even Emmalyn had not known about. "Darry and Jessa must be warned."

"And if they go west?"

Emmalyn studied the map again. "I don't think they're going west. I think something was said and he remembered," Emmalyn set her dagger down. "He would sooner die than have Melora know of his oversight. They are great allies at the moment, but should Melora's men extract some damning piece of information if prisoners are taken, his house of lies will come crashing down. A small consolation, I suppose, but it took him far longer than I thought it would."

"How long will it take them to reach Ballentrae?"

Emmalyn studied her cousin then, noting that she had lost a bit of weight and her hair was a few inches longer than it had been. It was still short, though, and it suited her. "The Raven's Run flows south, so the river won't help them. A ride like that, depending on how urgent they think it may be, a fortnight and half a week. If they ride hard, we can shave a few days from that. Kingston's man will send word as to their pace. We'll have a better idea in a few days."

"All right then. I'll ride for Gracelin with your message as soon as we hear from Kingston's man." Nina flashed an unexpected smile. "Tobin is making a fine profit this year."

"Lady Nina Lewellyn," Emmalyn said quietly. Nina had changed greatly in some ways, during the past few months, and those changes had chipped away at the wild girl she had been. The woman in her place was steadfast, loyal, and dangerously fierce. "The rightful Lady of Seven Spears and the Ring of Stone Towers. I couldn't do this without you."

Nina held her eyes for a moment longer and then looked down. She gave a casual shrug of her shoulder. "I don't—"

There was a soft knock upon the door and Emmalyn turned before Nina could finish. She glanced at the bed and Red had not moved, nor did she growl, though her eyes were upon the door.

"*Emma…*"

Emmalyn walked quickly to the door, threw the bolt, and pulled.

Jacob tossed back the hood of his black cloak and swept into the room. "I bring good news," he declared as Emmalyn closed and bolted the door yet again. "We have our spy. A maid within Melora's household staff."

Emmalyn's eyes narrowed somewhat. "A woman?"

"Yes," Jacob answered. "Her name is Eleni."

She hadn't thought that Jacob would recruit a woman, but she should have, and she scolded herself for the lapse. "How vulnerable is she?"

Jacob frowned and his shoulders stiffened somewhat at the question. "Now is not the time to become squeamish, Sister."

Emmalyn stood tall as she took a step forward. "Squeamish?" Jacob's right eye gave a twitch. "That was the wrong word, I'm sorry, but our options are limited here. Melora runs her household as she would a small army. Someone always answers to someone else, all the way up the line."

"And so where does this Eleni fall within the chain of command?"

"She's an outlier, hired on as a cook at first. She was demoted to a maid's position within a month or so and has been there since." His expression changed when hers did. "There is danger in this thing by its very nature, Emmalyn. Do not argue with me, please."

"This is just the business of spies, is that it?"

"*Yes*, it is."

"And so we would replace something bitter and careless with more of the same?" She challenged him. "Things must change with *all* decisions, Jacob, or none of this will matter."

Jacob considered her words. "You're right, I see that, Emma... But this particular game has long been established, and there's not much to be done about it, at least not at this point. You have an enemy and you have a spy. If your cause is good, then your enemy is not. There is great risk involved with such an endeavor, for the high ground is only in the cause, not where you must stand and fight. She's vulnerable, yes, but so are we all."

Emmalyn saw something more in his demeanor. Something he did not wish to tell her. "And what else, Jacob? I shall find out anyway, and you know it."

Jacob sighed. "It's not only that she will seek to betray Melora if the opportunity presents itself... She is Romynus."

Emmalyn was truly startled by his words. "In Melora's house?"

"I doubt if Melora even knows her name, much less her lineage. She has a way out, Emma, I've made sure of that. She has several, actually. She is aware of them, and she needs but call on them. I'll not have what happened to Almahdi happen again. You must trust me on that."

Emmalyn held his eyes while she made her decision. "If she is Romynus, then she will not ask for help. We must find another spy, or do without one. A woman in Melora's house is most likely in danger just for showing up." Emmalyn frowned. "And I can tell you now that she was demoted from cook to maid because of her blood. Melora would no more allow a Romyn woman to prepare her food than she would let *me* do it. And if she is found out, a Romyn woman? She would be strung up in an alley before we might get to her."

Jacob's eyes flared with frustration. "There is no one else to be found on such short notice. Please, let us discuss this at another time. Let us see what she might find."

"Discuss what, Jacob? That we have placed an already vulnerable women in an even more precarious position? A position that might get her killed?"

"We could *all* be killed, *Lady* Emmalyn," Jacob said in a fiercely pointed voice. "What we are engaged in is not merely a sibling squabble, nor is it a game of Kings and Jackals while having tea in the afternoon sun. We have not just *discussed* treason, we are actively involved in overthrowing the succession to the throne of Arravan!" He took a step toward her, just as she had done. "If you truly think this will be a bloodless coup of Malcolm's power, you are sorely mistaken, and I shall have to think that I've made a grave mistake in placing my faith in this."

Emmalyn studied his mien and saw to the heart of it. A lifetime of reading his expressions and tone was proving to be an advantage while navigating unknown waters. "I know that you're scared, Jacob," she said with care. "We are *all* scared," she admitted. "I understand full well that compromises will have to be made. But blood has been spilled already, I've not forgotten. I've not forgotten the pool of blood that could not be explained upon the throne room floor, a distance and a bit from the black pool that belonged to Marteen Salish. That blood was our sister's, and it was our own brother who sought to murder her. I understand the full depth of what we are doing, make no mistake."

Jacob's shoulders eased a bit as he listened to her, Nina standing in silence behind him.

"But if the high ground is in our cause, then so must it be in our actions, as well," Emmalyn continued. "Malcolm believes in his objective, and he has let *nothing* sway him from his path. He has committed murder, and attempted the same. How many times has this happened already? I don't know…But a king is dead by his command, bartered for with the lives of children we had sworn to protect. A country is now at war. By that logic, each death that follows may be laid at Malcolm's feet, including how many thousands of Arravan soldiers when we ride to war?" Emmalyn's chest tightened as she spoke. "Those lives are merely pieces on a board to Malcolm. But they are not to me.

"They are husbands and sons, and sweethearts that have yet to know the spirit of their chosen loves. Would-be lovers that have yet to wake in the morning sun with the sweetest of smiles that only passion may bestow. And Darrius, who lay betrayed at the very foot of her father's throne, seeing all that she held dear stolen away, with her lover just beyond reach as the warmth left her body. I see this *every* day, Jacob, and I think, how could we have been so reckless?"

Jacob looked as if he would speak but he did not.

"We must stop being careless. Our power has been parceled off through the years to enrich our family in one way or another. Families join the council, and the court grows deep with second and third sons who want only the power and gold that their brothers have, and so they would treat others unfairly, or unwisely, or they do not care at all but for the heaviness of their purse. Families unite for power and not for love, and so hearts have grown ruthless and cold. And so it is the way of things, that fateful decisions are made that we know nothing about, and our people suffer because we've lost sight of the threads within our own tapestry. We are of the privileged few, Jacob, and we're at the top of the hill at that.

"But who has a care for this Eleni, but a maidservant to Melora Salish? Melora, who has participated in Malcolm's own treason, and Gamar only knows what other crimes. Perhaps Eleni would find the escape that you've prepared for her, though most likely, if caught, her throat would be slit without a thought and, because she is Romynus, her body tossed from the wharf in the dead of night with no one to care or to know. The sins visited upon her people have been great indeed, Jacob, and our own kind have turned a blind eye for generations. Or worse yet, we have shown a callous, bored indifference to their plight. Who is it that waits at home for their beloved Eleni to return from the drudgery of being at Melora's beck and call?"

Emmalyn waited.

"I don't know," Jacob answered softly.

"And though I understand I cannot account for, nor provide for, every broken heart and sadness, or every dishonor that is done in the world, I will *always* remember the twenty-one days and half a night again, I thought our sister was dead, slain by the brother who would be my king. The brother who once danced with me on my sixteenth naming day and told me how dear I was to him. How precious I was to him.

"That man is dead. And in his place is a man who would murder his own family, and force Jessa to bear him a child against her will, so he might lay claim to the throne of a rival country. And he *would* be forcing her, do you understand that, Jacob?"

"Yes."

"Do you? For despite Jessa's power, we have already seen the deadly toll that love might take if leveraged against another. And so I believe the same fate that Darry and Jessa saved me from, at the hands of the Sahwello who was pushing between my legs, even as I screamed against it—I believe *that* is the fate that awaits Jessa, if Malcolm has his way. And so I ask you again, do you understand?"

Jacob's face had turned red but his eyes were steady. "I understand."

"These are hard truths, Jacob, and I don't know how they came to be. I don't know when it was that our brother took that first step down the same sinister road King Bharjah once chose, but take that step he did, and I will not have him drag us down such a dark path without a fight. Everything he has said and done since that moment is suspect. *Everything.*

"And if I must wrest the crown of Arravan from his very hands, I will do so. But I will not do it at so steep a price as your soul, my sweet brother." She looked past him and Nina's eyes were bright with tears. "Nor yours, my darling Nina Llewellyn. I will go on alone and roll the bones, as Royce says, before I will let that happen. And so please, Jacob, pay Eleni a fine sum for her willingness, and her silence. But her services will not be needed."

"Yes, my Lady," Jacob said in a slightly uneven voice.

"Look deeper for your spy, Jacob. I will help you, for my instincts tell me there is a voice there that wishes to sing. We need that *one* piece of evidence that is beyond question, that Malcolm will have no defense against. And if it is not the heirs of Almahdi de Ghalib, then it must be something of equal power in order to sway the King's Council. It must sway them into supporting something that they would otherwise find unthinkable...Though no matter what happens, I swear by Gamar that we are done with being careless."

Emmalyn stepped forward and kissed Jacob's cheek, her arms going about his shoulders and holding tight. His return embrace was strong about her waist and Emmalyn could feel his love, and his solid strength. She was grateful for it as she stepped back a bit and smiled, touching his cheek. He looked older than he had six months ago, and he looked tired, but by the gods he looked cunning and dangerous, as well. It was a new aspect to his personality that she had never thought to see. "Don't be scared, little brother. We will be all right, I promise."

Jacob smiled as a tear slid down his cheek, surprising her. "Alisha is with child."

Emmalyn let out a startled sound and then laughed, taking his face in both of her hands. She kissed his cheeks until he ducked his head with a boyish giggle. "Fucking hell and *hounds!*" Emmalyn cursed happily as Nina stepped close. Still held in Jacob's half embrace, she touched her cousin's smiling face. "I have nothing brilliant to say to that!"

Nina looked at Jacob and they both turned back to her. Jacob's eyes were full of warmth and a fierce look of determination. "You have already said it."

CHAPTER THIRTEEN

Wyatt Durand reached for his wine amidst the laughter, his gaze finding his brother's as he lifted his goblet. Malcolm was dressed in his finest silks, his waistcoat a brilliant deep maroon with gold buttons, the falcon from the shield crest of the Durand family molded upon each surface in fine detail. His cream-colored tunic was high collared and his black hair tipped over the edge of it, longer than was his usual wont. Malcolm lifted his cup and looked back at Wyatt, his dark blue eyes bright with satisfaction at the gold coins he had raked from the center of the table.

He had won his third game of suns which was not an easy thing to do amongst the officers of the Seventh, and Wyatt wondered which man had carefully thrown his hand. There was not much to do on a cold winter's night along the Greymear border, and gambling was certainly among the more acceptable pursuits.

Malcolm was drinking more than Wyatt had ever seen him drink, and though the Crown Prince was in his cups, he seemed to be in control of his faculties, both mind and body. It was disappointing that he would not have the opportunity to see Malcolm beyond his limits, but it was good to learn that his capacity for drink had increased so dramatically.

Madame Dubassant's was twice the size it had been when he had first visited the most renowned house of pleasure in Arravan, many years ago. He and Jacob had ventured through the front doors after his coming of age day, their pockets filled with coin. He hadn't known until years later that Grissom and Armistad Greyson had been there in secret, watching out for them both. He thought of that as his goblet clanked against Malcolm's, and he gave an approving nod. "Your skills have improved, my brother. 'Tis not an easy feat, to best the best of the Seventh."

Malcolm lifted his glass again. "To the Seventh!"

A rousing shout went up around him as their goblets clanked together.

"You have all of my wages, my Prince," Lieutenant Landon Runner said with a grin. "I think I shall call it a night."

Malcolm set his glass down and began to stack his coins in a neat manner. "Fair warning for next time, Lieutenant. It's been a pleasure."

Landon used the table to push to his feet. "By your leave, my Prince? Major?"

"Of course," Malcolm said as he reached for his wine once again.

Wyatt gave him a nod. "Thank you, Landon." Landon's expression was knowing, and as he turned, the other officers of the Seventh pushed from the table.

Malcolm watched them move through the room as he leaned back in his chair. "I seem to have scared away the coin. I no longer play with the likes of Armistad and Grissom, or Father, for that matter. My court is younger and faster."

Wyatt grinned. "I wish you would've been with me in Senegal, Mal—you wouldn't believe the houses there. They are something to behold."

Malcolm's gaze was careful but curious, and Wyatt understood what that meant. Malcolm was no drunker than *he* was, despite that his older brother had downed twice as much. "You were not always so fond of Madame Dubassant's, Wyatt. Have your tastes changed so much?"

Wyatt gave a casual shrug. "I've found they provide a much needed respite from the routine of camp life." Malcolm's gaze had become somewhat intense and Wyatt met it head on. "And it is different, when members of your own court are not there. It's so much better."

"Our renegade sister and her murderous Bastards prefer Madam Salina's," Malcolm replied casually, and then flashed a smile that seemed clever and self-satisfied. "Which seems fitting. Its reputation has always been highly suspect. Not very *clean*. It has fallen upon hard times since they committed their crimes and disappeared into that bloody maze."

Wyatt moved about Malcolm's words with startled laughter. "Salina's? Good Gamar, Mal, you didn't go *with* them, did you?"

Malcolm stared at him, his eyes uncertain. "Of course not," he answered in a hard tone. "Why would you ask such a question?"

Wyatt shrugged. "Seems a peculiar comment, is all. Why should you give a damn where they go?" Wyatt let his gaze drop to the table, and he knew his expression fell, before he could stop it.

His skills were with a sword and dagger, and with the bow. He was a soldier, not a spy.

With each comment Malcolm made about Darrius, whether openly or as a backhanded cut, Wyatt's intentions and tenacity solidified. He believed Nina's words of Bentley's account—he had never questioned that. Bentley and Darry were thick and they fit together in every way but one, they always had. Bentley would die for Darry, and his honor was beyond reproach for that fact alone. And yet Wyatt had to admit that some part of himself, some deep and hopeful corner in his heart, had been holding out against all of it. That somehow, in some way, it could all be made whole again, wishing for a truth that did not exist.

He finally understood that it would never be the same again, in the subtle noise and the bronze fitted lamps of Madame Dubassant's main parlor, in the perfumed air and the smell of the wine.

He had seen the missive sent to Emmalyn by the Princess Jessa-Sirrah of Lyoness. The message itself had been enough, though her words were not quite so convincing as the means she had used to convey them: *Prince Malcolm Durand has murdered Lord Marteen Salish and has attempted murder upon his own sister, the Princess Darrius Lauranna Durand. I write this warning in her blood, spilled in defense of our love. Your king's word has been broken, and my oath to him is no more. Beware my rage, and tell him to mind the stones of his palace.*

"Wyatt?"

Wyatt looked up at Malcolm's voice.

Grissom had told him once, a lifetime ago, that a hearty dose of truth in your bluff could go a long way. He understood Emmalyn's warning to avoid Darry as a topic of conversation, but he also knew that Mal would give him nothing until he gave him this first. Until he had conceded defeat where their sister was concerned. That Malcolm had shown his contempt for Darrius so willingly was giving him little choice. The Crown Prince wanted his victory.

His insides turned with discomfort, and he had not felt so nervous since the first time he had set foot in Madame Dubassant's. He supposed it was fitting that he was here once more, and feeling the same dread of failure in his guts. "You know, I've always had a soft spot for Darry, that's no secret. She makes me laugh like no one else ever has…And I've enjoyed being her protector, I admit that. It always seemed right, somehow, that it should be that way. We both chose the sword, but she made her choice against all odds and favor. Such a thing deserves a champion."

Malcolm made no response, but Wyatt could feel the hairs on the back of his neck stand at attention beneath the quiet scrutiny he received.

"When she told me she was backward, I thought, well, who should care who she likes to fuck?" He gave a shrug. "I never understood why it upset you so much. That *one* thing, more than anything else, has always made me wary of you, Mal. I have had a hard time trusting you."

Malcolm's expression was thrown into a brief, lovely moment of chaos, and Wyatt spied his brother's surprise before he could cover it up.

"Perhaps you would judge me in such a manner, yes?" Wyatt suggested. "Perhaps the girl I would choose for my bride would not be beautiful enough for you, or she would be of a lesser rank, or perhaps she would have no rank at all."

Malcolm was a bit slow to gain complete control over his reaction and Wyatt continued. "I did not understand about Darry, at least, not until I was given command. Not until I went away, and had some distance from it all."

This time Malcolm did respond. "How so?"

"We have responsibilities that are beyond matters of the heart." Wyatt leaned forward and set his wine down. "I saw that in the east. I saw it *every* day. We are needed, and we're not meeting our responsibilities as we should. Our presence is strong, yes, but it should be so much stronger. I don't know, I thought that she would change her ways, perhaps. That she would come to understand that the Durand name comes with power and rights." He tapped his knuckles upon the table in a light manner and then opened his hand. "I don't know," he growled and sat back again. "I'm not sure what I'm trying to say."

"She abused her privilege. She did not fulfill her rightful position," Malcolm offered in a quiet voice. "Is that what you're trying to say?"

Wyatt frowned. "Perhaps, in some ways. I mean, I've always known that she would be a soldier, and why not? She's damn good at it, and being stationed with the Kingsmen at Blackstone, it has always seemed acceptable to me."

Malcolm nodded. "Yes, I've come to agree with that."

Wyatt could see the lie move through the downward turn in Malcolm's lips, on the right side, ever so slight. He had always done it when he was trying to manipulate a situation, when he was uncertain. He had done it at cards less than an hour ago, and he had only won because Landon had allowed it. "But then I saw the great houses of the east, and they are in want of a firm hand. She could have given that."

"And how would she have done that?" Malcolm asked. "By marrying some hapless young lord and fucking the maid?"

Wyatt reacted quickly. "That would be a position of outright weakness. There would be no honor in that, Mal, so no, that would not have been my suggestion," he replied in a somewhat dark tone as he maneuvered about the trap. "But she might have taken command of a new unit of Kingsmen. The Durand name is not to be trifled with, and she could have shown our people that much at least. The east has become somewhat wild, and the Llewellyn forces have a tendency to let resources slip through their fingers in favor of independence. From here to the gates of Senegal, I have seen untapped assets and riches we have yet to take advantage of. She might have put her skills to very good use, and in the name of the crown."

Malcolm started to speak but then closed his mouth, something he rarely did.

"What she did with the Princess from Lyoness, Mal, I'm sorry. Whatever your intentions might have been toward the woman, you should've been allowed your play. I never thought Darry would show such disrespect, despite your feelings toward her. I don't know what to think now, I truly don't."

Once again Malcolm looked genuinely surprised by his words.

"But I feel the need to apologize to you for what she did." A touch of sickness and panic churned in Wyatt's stomach but he held on. He thought of Darry and the bottle of Artanis Gold they were to have shared upon his return. He thought of his closest blood in all the world, and the feel of her shoulders beneath his arm as they walked and talked of whatever struck their fancy. He thought of how he might never know such ease again, for he trusted no one more.

Malcolm smiled in a somewhat guarded manner, but Wyatt thought there was something else beneath it. He saw hope. "Are you not her champion now?"

Wyatt considered his answer carefully. "If she were an officer in my command, if she rode for the Seventh? I would've stripped her of her rank for such dishonor. That is all I know. I'm a soldier, Mal, not a politician. If you ask me what I think, I will tell you, if I know. If you ask me to ride down a hill into the enemy, I ride down the hill. Honor is our standard. Life is short. The rules are pretty simple."

"Then she has betrayed us both," Malcolm said with care.

"She betrayed herself," Wyatt corrected him.

"I would approve of any woman you loved, Wyatt," Malcolm offered in a genuine voice. "If you chose her, then there could be no better match."

Wyatt stared at him and felt the ground beneath him sink away in a slow, horrible manner. He reined in his emotions as tightly as he could. "I must find her first," Wyatt replied and Malcolm smiled. "We are brothers, you and I, and I am home at last. Let us speak of better things. There is much to be done, more than anyone sees."

"Yes, you're right. And perhaps we should have a talk with Uncle Sullidan when he arrives, about the houses of the east."

"I think it should be high on your list."

Malcolm sat forward and reached for the wine bottle as Wyatt extended his cup. "When he arrives, I shall arrange a meeting for us. Let it be *our* list."

"Thank you, Mal. It would be good to be included in such a discussion."

"Has not Father invited you? I don't approve of the way he treats you, still like a boy. He has put you in an awkward place that shows you little respect."

"I don't like it, either," Wyatt said softly. "I am not the man I was when I left Blackstone those years ago."

"I can see that," Malcolm agreed. "Perhaps you should join the Prince's Council."

Wyatt stared at him. He honestly didn't know if he was being toyed with. "Truly?"

"Why not?" Malcolm looked a tad surprised by Wyatt's reaction. "I would value your opinion on all things, truly. Father has a different agenda than I do, and perhaps that's as it should be. He looks to keep things smooth and even, and now he has his impending war with the Fakir to keep him busy." Malcolm picked up his goblet. "It has been left me to look to the future of Arravan. I have great plans, and I could use a seasoned young warrior such as yourself. Not some grizzled old veteran like Longshanks, but someone who has seen what is out there *now*. We need to put our house in order before these opportunities slip away."

Wyatt was about to speak when Captain Abel Jefs approached the table with his brother, who stood beside him like a stone pillar. Abel bowed his head. "Good eve, my Prince."

Malcolm got to his feet as he held his hand out. "Abel, it is good to see you."

"And you, my Prince," Captain Jefs replied as they shook hands.

"And you, Mason. I'm glad you could join us." Malcolm set a hand on Mason Jefs's broad shoulder and turned back to the table. "Wyatt, my dear brother, I don't believe you've met the Solstice Champion."

Wyatt looked up from his seat and a slow smile moved along his lips. Mason Jefs had won the Solstice Tournament, it was true, but his real competition had not yet arrived in Lokey when he had swung his broadsword and taken the laurel of victory. "You have it wrong, Mal," he said smoothly. "The Solstice Champion has not met *me*."

Chapter Fourteen

Darry walked beside Hinsa as they made their way along the edge of the Yellandale.

The weather had turned cool, and it had been a full week since they had run free through the forest. She had been ill since their return, though in the past few days she had made a subtle recovery. Jessa's relief had been profound, and Darry could feel it among her friends—she was on the mend and all would be well again. She had said nothing to Jessa, but she knew that something was still wrong. Her illness was not gone, but changing instead, and what that change might mean for her, and for Hinsa, she had no idea.

There was a menacing ache in her very bones with the suppression of her majik, and she had no idea how long she could keep pushing herself. She could not shake her fatigue, and sooner or later Jessa would see it. She would feel it.

Darry spied the lone oak tree that topped the hill, and it eased her heart. It was a thousand years old if it was a day, and she could feel the years even from a distance. It had become a favorite place, for the light was good, the shade was good, and the grass beneath it was soft. It felt safe, with its sweeping boughs, and heavy roots that arched into the air in curved seats of smooth wood before they returned to the earth. She had never seen its like before, and she had claimed it as her own. The view of the estate was magnificent, and now that it was their home, she wanted to know it as she had known Blackstone.

As they topped the rise, Hinsa padded ahead of her and moved along the nearest arch of root, finding a place and stretching out several feet above the ground. Darry found her spot, as well, and leaned against the wide base of the oak.

The manor house had grown in the past seven days, and she could see the smoke from two chimneys, one upon each end of Jessa's new workroom. Much like Sebastian's Tower, it was filled with tables and bookshelves and all manner of things that a beautiful young priestess might need. Bentley and Arkady had even made drying racks, which now hung from the beams of the ceiling, the smell of pungent spices, herbs, and dried flowers already drifting from the open windows. Its walls of whitewashed stone were a protection against all sorts of mishaps, and they had even moved a bed into one of the far corners, so that Jessa might rest without leaving her studies. They would complete the enclosed walkway that would connect the workroom to the house within the next few weeks.

Raising the structure had gone quickly, and it had been done with smooth efficiency. Having a dozen men concentrating upon a single task had yielded a simple but wonderful result. Darry had helped when she was able, but mostly she had helped Jessa organize the many scrolls and books in their possession. She had bottled dried herbs and labeled them, and she had even managed to make a rather lovely shelf that would hold them. She had received an even lovelier kiss for her efforts, and she knew no better payment.

The opening meal of the Seven Day Feast of Holy Men was to be the next evening, and it was to be a quiet celebration in the dining hall of the main house. She had spent her morning in the kitchen helping with the preparations, and she had been sent packing by Lady Abagail well before noon.

She shifted her back against the oak and pulled her long jacket tighter about her chest as she stretched her legs out and crossed her ankles. She felt a tightness in her throat as she looked down at all they had accomplished in the months since their arrival, and her pride and affection was greater than she had expected.

The leaves would turn soon and wane, and so would her blood, Darry could feel it. Not only did her bones ache, but her flesh, which seemed to diminish somehow with each passing day. Her reasoning and instincts told her there were but three options at this point. Either Jessa would find something in the scrolls she poured over late into each night, or Darry would give in to her *Cha-Diah* blood and disappear into the ferocity of its call. Or, she would not live to see the spring. She knew it as certainly as she knew anything.

Sudden tears slipped free and ran down her cheeks as she closed her eyes and gave in to her exhaustion. She felt the warmth of Hinsa's body move against her own and the safe, familiar weight of Hinsa's head upon her thigh as she fell asleep.

Jessa pulled her dark green cloak tight about her shoulders and made her way up the small rise, her gaze keen as she approached her lover.

The air had turned cold as the afternoon sun fell from its zenith and the clouds rolled in, hinting at rain but unable to deliver on the promise. The spell she had attached to Hinsa after the autumn moon was working well, and she followed the faint splash of runes through the grass. She was fairly certain that Hinsa understood what she had done, and she wondered yet again, what the panther's voice might sound like when spoken deep in the mind.

She could see the runes of their *Cha-Diah* majik and they grew warped and fainter with each day as Darry fought to contain her power. For her part, Hinsa did nothing to stop her child from hiding, and for that, Jessa's love and respect for the great cat could not be measured. It bought them precious time, and no price could be put upon such a gift. Darry's fever and weakness had passed, it was true, but Jessa could feel the ebb of Darry's strength with each passing moment, no matter how hard Darry tried to hide it from her.

She had found something, though, in Radha's many scrolls. She did not know all that it contained, but the hope it gave her was strong, and it was something that Darry needed to be a part of. Something wonderful and altogether amazing.

She stepped close and went to her knees beside them. Darry's cheek was hot beneath her touch. "*Akasha.*" Darry opened her eyes and Jessa smiled at her sleepy gaze. "My love, it grows cold. Come inside with me."

Darry's grin was slow, but it lit in her eyes. "You've found something."

Jessa laughed in her throat and leaned in, kissing Darry's lips. "I'm not sure I like this thing you do, this knowing me so well."

"Why not?"

"I don't know."

"Do you have secrets?"

"Of course." Jessa was unable to keep the tease from her voice. "I am a Priestess of the Vhaelin. What good would that be without a few surprises? That is half the fun." Darry's laughter was wonderful to hear and she leaned in once more for a second, deeper kiss. "Come back to my workroom and see what I've found. I think you will like it."

"Is it pastries?"

Jessa laughed at once, rising to her feet with an easy push and holding out her hand. "Yes. Yes it is. Baked with cream inside and buttered icing on top."

Darry took Jessa's hand. "Splendid."

Darry walked beside the long table with interest, noting a pattern to the scrolls that were laid out, with smooth stones at the corners to hold them open. There were wells of ink, and new sheets of parchment where Jessa had written her translations thus far. The workroom was well lit and warm against the evening air that swept in through the open windows, and all of it, every small part of it, made Darry extremely happy. She didn't know if Jessa had ever had such a place for herself before, but she did now, and it was the best of things in every way.

She watched as Jessa eyed a sprig of dried sweet leaf, her dark curls tied behind her head with the scarlet ribbon Darry herself had worn the night of the autumn moon.

"I just need to put this in the kettle." Jessa pushed onto the tips of her boots. "And then I will show you."

Jessa's elegant fingers bent the sprig of leaves as she walked to the hearth. She grabbed the cast iron hook from where it hung upon the stones and snagged the open kettle. She pulled it out with care and dropped the crushed sweet leaf in the steaming water before she pushed it back above the flames and replaced the hook. She turned with a smile as she wiped her hands upon her homespun skirt.

There were other things that clung to the faded blue material, and her dun colored shirt as well, with its sleeves rolled past her elbows. Ink and a bit of soot, and the dust of other herbs and roots. A few stray curls had escaped her ribbon and hung forward against her right cheek, bringing out the softness of her sable colored eyes.

"What is it?" Jessa asked.

Darry felt her desire stir deep in her belly and a shiver of pleasure spread deep into her thighs. Jessa's smile changed slowly as she stared back at Darry down the length of the table.

"I do not know about other lifetimes, Princess Jessa-Sirrah de Cassey LaMarc de Bharjah, daughter of the Red-Tail Clan and Shaman to your people. Scholar and Priestess of the Vhaelin, and Blooded Princess of Lyoness. Woman within the Shadows, and my own Nightshade Lark..."

Jessa was taken aback as Darry quietly named her titles.

"But as you stand now, in your boots and homespun, with your hair just so and the smell of sweet leaf filling the air as you walk... You are the most joyous love my heart has ever known in any one of them." Darry grinned at the lovely blush that rose in Jessa's cheeks. "I would imagine your face as I lay high up in the crow's nest, sailing upon the Sellen Sea, abandoned to all the world but the blue deep... You would hide among the stars, and my dreams of you would be reflected in the glass of the still night waters. Forever out of reach, but always the very essence of my heart, as you are right now." Darry could feel Jessa's pulse from across the room and though Jessa didn't speak, her eyes wove a spell that caused Darry's heart to skip. "Will you show me what you've found?"

Jessa blinked and moved. "Yes!" she replied. She pushed at her loose curls as she rounded the work table. "Yes, of course." She grabbed several scrolls and then set them on the table before them both. "I think you will..."

Jessa was silent for a moment and then she turned, stepped in Darry's arms, and pushed onto her toes. Her kiss was open and full, and Darry tightened her arms as she returned it with all of the love she felt. She tasted deeply of Jessa's lips and tongue, and Jessa's scent filled her nose.

Jessa's arms were about her neck as she moved her face against Darry's. "*Akasha*," she whispered beside Darry's ear. "I will fix this. I swear it upon my life."

Darry considered the temptation of Jessa's neck. "Give me a quest."

Jessa laughed in her arms, softly but with genuine feeling as she pulled back. Darry did not release her, however, and so she could only go so far. Her touch was like a familiar breeze upon Darry's face, the fingers of her left hand moving along the tenderness of her healing wounds. "Just hold on, my love. I command it."

Jessa had spoken with great effort, and the raw emotion held in her words wrapped about Darry like a warm blanket on a cold night. "Yes, my Lady."

Jessa pushed lightly against her shoulders. "Let me show you, please."

Darry let her go and Jessa returned to the table, pulling Darry with her. She took the first scroll and laid it upon the covered table, grabbing at the stones scattered about and placing them at the corners. "The biggest problem has been my lack of books. But my Radha has always been a trickster," Jessa glanced at Darry with a rueful smile. "She left me her spells, yes, but she would not leave me without the tools I would need to read them, and books are heavy upon the road. She would've been prepared. I've gone through her scrolls and spells hundreds of times, but the new ones she left me? The scrolls we discovered with the truth of Zephyr Wind? I have been breaking them down, one by one."

"And?"

"And they are different."

"How so?"

"She uses proper speech... Look at this, please."

Darry leaned over the table, their shoulders touching.

"Radha never writes more than she has to. Her hands ache, and she would rather be *doing* than playing the part of a scribe." Jessa's fingers moved along a block of text. "But this is High Vhaelin, and

High Vhaelin is nothing if not exact. Each curve and stitch of the pen, the length and the thickness of the ink, it all means something. It is incredibly difficult."

Darry could hear it in her voice. "You like it."

Jessa leaned over and kissed her slowly. "I do. I like it very much. But these are the spells for simple things that I have known since I was a girl. Witchlight." Jessa held out her hand and a small ball of witchlight formed and then popped. It showered her hand with sparks. "Or the fire." The flames in the far hearth behind her flared up briefly and then returned to normal. "There was no need for these to be copied down in High Vhaelin, and yet here they are. She has left me a translation so I might learn."

"And the stag's hide?"

Jessa's eyes were bright. "That is so much more, I cannot even tell you, but I have built upon what Radha has left me and I am now deep into the heart of what I need. I have already begun to translate several spells, though…before I try the next one, what I found, Darry, you must see it." Jessa stepped along the table and gathered up two more scrolls, her expression filled with excitement. "Do you remember the night we spoke of *Senesh Akota*?"

Darry remembered, and then she remembered the darkness of what had followed. The echo of Joaquin's vile words in the Circle of Honor cut through her thoughts and her jaw clenched. She felt a tremble in her muscles that was not exhaustion. It was a memory she had not yet managed to find a place for.

Jessa laid a hand upon the center of Darry's chest. "No, my love, not that," she whispered. "Never that, *Akasha*. It was a lie. His tongue was poison. It was a lie."

Darry felt the heat of Jessa's touch through the soft homespun of her tunic until the echo moved past them both. "Yes, I remember. The spells from Radha's trunk."

Jessa's expression filled instantly with a quiet sort of wonder. "Yes, but I do not think they were ever hers."

Darry reached out and touched the rolled edge of the closest one. It was very old, but it was light and still supple. "Whose were they then?"

"I think they are yours."

Darry stared at her. "*Mine?*"

"In a way, yes," Jessa said gently and turned back to the table. She unrolled the first scroll and set the second one to the side, still closed and tied with a long but thin braid of golden hair. She touched the open scroll with great care, despite that it was empty but for several lines of writing. "This here, it is High Vhaelin, all but for this part…which is written in the runes of Hinsa's portal. It's not a spell and so I set it aside. But I came back to it earlier, for I was tired. I thought it would be good practice. I made it through but the first few words before I came to find you."

Darry pushed the stray curls of Jessa's hair behind her ear. What she really wanted to say did not find her tongue. "You are not sleeping enough, Jess."

Jessa's expression changed in a subtle manner, and Darry could tell that she was searching for the truth of things. "I'm all right, *Akasha*, honestly."

Darry's heart was beating a bit too fast, and though she tried, she could not slow it down.

Jessa touched Darry's face. "*Akasha*, do not be afraid, please. There is nothing here that will hurt you, or Hinsa. I swear it, and if there is, by the Blessed Vhaelin I will not let it."

"I'm not afraid for me, Jess," Darry admitted. "How can scrolls so old they smell of another time altogether, be meant for me? It makes no sense. And if they do not hold what you're hoping to find, I can do nothing."

"If I do not keep looking, are you saying that everything will be all right? That *you* will be all right?" Jessa's tone held sudden challenge.

Darry had no response other than a lie, and so she held her tongue.

"Do you think I cannot feel you slipping away, *Akasha?*" Jessa demanded as she pulled her hand away and turned back to the table. "I will see you run wild through the bloody Yellandale first, and not remember me at all, before I will let such a thing happen. And I will *not* let you run wild through the Yellandale, at the mercy of a majik neither one of us understands yet. And I most certainly will not let you forget me. I will hunt you down and *make* you remember, if it comes to that, and then we shall have a fine mess."

Darry laughed in her throat, unable to stop it.

Jessa smoothed at an edge of the scroll as her frustration turned. "I am more powerful than even *you* might think, Darrius Lauranna."

"If you pull these pretty new walls down with a wayward spell, the Boys will never forgive you for it."

Jessa let out a surprised laugh. "That was *not* a wayward spell."

"Are you going to read the bloody scroll or not?"

Jessa's expression was filled with heat and her eyes with love, and Darry's felt both. "Come closer to me," Jessa whispered. "And I shall do just that."

Chapter Fifteen

Jessa's fingers traced the first words as Darry stepped closer, and Darry followed Jessa's hand as she read aloud in a quiet voice.

"For my beloved, I pray that your gods hold you as close as I do. I have honored my promise to you, though I have held it safe in my heart until the very last. As I will you, my only love, until my last breath. I shall not be long now, Tannen... It has been an endless night without you and I have done what I must. For these sins against our love, I beg your forgiveness. I swear I shall find you, I have seen to it..."

Jessa's voice caught and she stopped reading. Her posture changed in a subtle manner as she pulled within herself, something Darry had not seen her do since they had left Blackstone. Darry's left hand slipped about Jessa's waist and beneath her shirt to the heat of her skin.

"For the spirit who is yet to walk beside her."

Darry's eyes narrowed upon the scroll as the writing seemed to dance free from the ends of Jessa's fingers.

"For the child of my cherished Hashiki, may this serve you well and as it must. I bequeath to you what was hers, for these things have always been yours. I have charged my heirs with the return of Zephyr Wind unto your hands. May all pass through the years unharmed and find you strong. I love you, and I beg you, please, wait for her. She will find you, the yet to be born daughter of my line. You shall be mine once more." Jessa paused and Darry could feel her tense. When she continued, her emotions were thick in her voice. "All you need, is to remember your blood and let it rise…"

Darry stared at the writing and let the words wash through her as Jessa's fingers slid along a single twist and flourish of ink, faded beneath the rest. She settled her fingers atop Jessa's, the scroll beneath their combined touch. Darry closed her hand upon Jessa's and held it tight.

"It is the mark of Neela," Jessa whispered.

The fire popped and fed upon crumbling oak in one hearth and smoldered in the other, the scent of herbs and the must of old scrolls filling Darry's nose. She could smell the sweetened karrem that brewed in Jessa's small kettle, knowing that Jessa made it so for her, for she could no longer drink it unless its bitterness was tempered. The heat of Jessa's skin beneath her hands had moved into her arms and chest, and as Jessa breathed, Darry's heart began to match the cadence of her lover's.

And so here it was at last. Not a bedtime tale to tell a child, nor a story so ancient that the reality of Tannen and Neela might never be untangled from the changes made by time. Not merely a tale to inspire hope in a people beneath the boot heel of Bharjah. There it was, in Neela's own words.

Darry had let it sleep, this tale of time and love and *Senesh Akoata*, the Great Loom and ancient lives. She had let it sleep, and Jessa had let her. But there was little to argue with as she looked at the scroll beneath their hands, for Radha herself, descendant of Neela and High Priestess of Jessa's people, had confronted Serabee El-Khan and fulfilled her oath with the return of Tannen Ahru's stolen sword.

Darry had no proof that Tannen's lost blade was meant for her, but she knew it was the truth. From the moment she had held the blue vale steel it had been a coming home. The warrior within her had known it at once. No blade made so exquisitely for another hand, could have been so perfect for her own, as well. And it was, in fact, perfect. Even the blades fashioned in the past by Masters, for no one else but her, were not so perfect.

And she had been dreaming again, though she could not quite remember them. She would wake up with the smell of a distant land in her nose, and the sense of a presence so near to her, as to be sharing her own shadow. The feeling wouldn't last for very long, but she did not deny it while it was there.

It has been an endless night without you... Darry let her hand slide along the blank portion of the scroll. "What is this?" she asked. "I feel it, like a tremor beneath the ground."

"Yes. There is something else here." Jessa's fingers moved above the scroll. She cleared her throat in a light manner, but her emotions were still thick in her voice. Darry sensed it was more than sadness. "But I have no idea how to free it yet."

She will find you, the yet to be born daughter of my line...

And she had. Jessa had somehow survived Gamar only knew what, in the house of her father, the Butcher of the Plains. Amidst the stampede of endless brothers who had plagued her every moment, and haunted her steps with violence and fear.

Whatever the truth was, in the end, they would face it together. Jessa loved her, and she knew that fact was the only one that mattered. *Jessa* loved her, not Neela, despite Neela's words. Darry had never expected that, to be loved and desired so completely. Of all the things worth fighting for in the world, it was the best thing of all and she knew it. Whether they had come together because it was meant to be, and the Great Loom willed it, Darry might never know, but it was something to be thankful for either way. She could not deny how she had felt in Tristan's Grove, and every day since.

Darry let go of her fear of what *Senesh Akoata* might really mean, and with that acceptance her *Cha-Diah* blood rose in an oddly measured manner. It slipped past her willpower and she let it. It was enough to ease the pain and the aches in her muscles, and lessen the pressure that was always present now, in her neck and shoulders. Perhaps it was a mistake to do it, but she could no longer deny who she was. The time for sleeping was over.

Darry could feel the quickness of Jessa's heartbeat. "Jess?"

"*Akasha...*" Jessa's fear came in a wave of heat that rushed along her spine. She looked at the runes upon the scroll and wondered how they must sound to her lover, to have their love mapped out, at least in part, in a scroll that should have crumbled into nothing centuries ago.

She will find you, the yet to be born daughter of my line. You shall be mine once more...

Jessa had spent her life beneath the exacting tutelage of her Radha, and she had read endless scrolls and tomes. They had argued late into the night, the philosophies and the rules that governed the Great Loom and *Senesh Akoata*. She possessed a lifetime of speculation and learning, and at the very least, she had a fair understanding of what it did and did not mean.

She could feel Neela's grief in the runes like a living thing, and yet Neela's words had caused her a surprising amount of resentment. They were written as if she herself would have no choice in the matter, no voice of her own. As if her love was not hers to give, but merely the echo of another. It was a subject that many had pondered, both scholars and Shamans alike, the path of the thread and the effect it might have through the ages. It was taught that only the strongest of threads might have an influence, and to that end, only in those things that were beyond the control of any given individual. Circumstances, both great and small that might provide opportunity, but never control someone's actions. Free will held sway above all things, always. But Darry had not been privy to those debates, or the sacred laws surrounding the Great Loom.

Her words tumbled out. "I loved you before I knew these things, Akasha. I know *Senesh Akoata* and I believe in its gifts, but this…" Jessa opened her hands upon Neela's scroll as her own words came back to her, and they cut, for she realized she had been careless. *I have only just found you again, Akasha…* They had referenced the deep spirit of *Senesh Akoata's* teachings, but they had meant something else, as well.

"I had no idea that I walked Neela's thread, until I spoke with Radha after the battle in the Great Hall. I had a vision of Neela, just moments before Serabee and the Fakir appeared. The powers of a Vhaelin priestess contain the powers of a Shaman, as well, but…"

Jessa stared down at the scroll and opened her fingers upon the writing before she pulled her hands back along the heavy parchment.

"But what, Jess?"

The tenderness in Darry's voice was too much, and Jessa tipped her head to the side as her temper pushed its way free. She was of Neela's bloodline, it was true, but she had *chosen* Darrius. To have Darry think otherwise, if even for a heartbeat, was utterly unacceptable. Radha had bloody well been right. They were free and no one could tell them otherwise. They were untouched by anyone's need but their own. Radha's theories and her half-truths, her omissions and her many secrets, by the Vhaelin, she had given them the ultimate gift. She would not see Neela's words take that away. "But Neela did not suffer the plagues of the Jade Palace."

The Jade Palace, more than any other place in the world, had been the flame that had forged her steel, and no other could claim such. No other could know what that meant.

"Neela did not suffer his dogs, or the sweet *rotting* stench of his robes… Neela's mother was not murdered." How dare Neela claim Darrius as her own, as if such a reach were even in her power. "Nor her sister," she whispered. "She did not learn the Veil of Shadows in order to *hide* from her own blood." She tried to temper the hatred in her tone, but the effort was of little use. She thought of Sylban-Tenna and what he had done, and she moved her words around it. "Brothers who would've taken what they wanted if they could have. Brothers who are not men of Lyoness, for the true men of Lyoness are fair men and *good* men.

"And she was not a prisoner, nor was she shamed and paraded before the powerful Lords who sought favor of the Butcher." Jessa pushed away from the table and turned her back on her lover. She stared across the room into the flames of the hearth which were a riot of blurred colors. "And she was not sold to the highest bidder who offered the chance at a throne."

Jessa heard Darry's approach and she turned about. She could feel the panther beneath her own majik and though it surprised her, it did not stop her. "We are not merely players in a play, *Akasha*, as those words might make you think. There are sacred rules the Great Loom is built upon, and they are not merely guides, but unbreakable laws. There are certain things that are just not *possible*, and what Neela claims is one of them."

"I know that." Darry's voice was calm and quiet.

"It's said you might travel your thread, in theory, but you may not *change* it and you may not participate. It is only memory. The pattern of the loom itself is what dictates *Senesh Akoata,* and it cannot be changed by a single thread. It would negate free will, and that cannot be undone no matter what god you may believe in. The teachings of Gamar will hold such a tenant."

"They do, actually, you're right," Darry agreed.

"She cannot *claim* you, *Akasha*, please understand that."

"I do, Jess."

"She was not the one who captured your heart." Her voice had eased as she looked in Darry's eyes. "That was *me*, and I *chose* my love, Darrius, it was not chosen for me. And though I am a daughter of her blood, I am most certainly not Neela de Hahvay, nor do I do her bidding."

Darry's expression was quite possibly the most beautiful she had yet seen, and it surprised her into an entirely new turn of emotions. "Neela de Hahvay would not find me pleasing anyway," Darry replied, and her dimple appeared upon the heels of her slow smile.

"Do not be foolish, *Akasha*." Jessa's anger had slipped away completely, and in its place a rebellion of desire pushed through her blood. Darry's face was filled with color and life, and her eyes were true and bright for the first time since her return from the Yellandale. The unrestrained taste of Darry's *Cha-Diah* majik washed over Jessa in a most willful manner. "Why ever not?"

"Because I am Darrius Lauranna Durand, and not Tannen Ahru. I am only who am, as I am now, as *this* life has made me, just as you say. And I am the daughter of wayfaring kings, and the Wild Men of the Taurus Mountains, descendant of the Olden Men who cut their homes from the mountain tops and walked with eagles. And I am in love with *you*, Jessa-Sirrah. I know that you love me, Jess, I *know* it… And whatever we may be in the end?" Darry's smile was almost playful. "In this lifetime? You and I shall be most grand."

Jessa could feel the majik in her blood rising and swirling in a provocative manner, and though its response to the presence of Darry's majik was as potent and as decadent as ever, there was a new fear that came with it. "*Akasha*, what have you done?"

Darry walked to her in silence and reached up with both hands.

Jessa slipped her fingers over the waist of Darry's trousers and held on as Darry pulled at the ribbon in her hair. Her eyes followed the healing wounds along Darry's jaw and neck and the pulse between her legs intensified, the weight of her desire the sweetest of punishments.

Darry's fingers in her hair caused her eyes to close slightly. "This isn't safe."

"I don't care."

The power in Darry's whisper slid along the back of her neck as Darry unfastened the buttons of Jessa's shirt, the backs of her fingers slow as they caressed Jessa's skin before popping each one. Her shirt opened and Darry lifted it, Jessa obliging her as Darry slipped if off and tossed it atop the scrolls.

Darry undid the buttons of her own tunic and Jessa watched as she revealed her breasts, pulling her shirt from her trousers and letting it fall open.

"If you disappear into the wild again, I shall find you," Jessa promised and then caught her breath as Darry grabbed her about the waist and pulled her flush. She opened her mouth to Darry's and grabbed at Darry's shoulders.

Jessa shifted at the pull upon her skirt and Darry leaned to the side. She bit at Darry's lip, her hands delving into Darry's heavy curls. Darry's left arm pulled her up and Jessa reached between them and yanked at her skirt. Darry's hand was between her legs and Jessa grabbed her about the neck as Darry's fingers slid along her sex. She was wet and swollen and she leaned into the touch, straining onto the tips of her toes.

Darry's lips brushed against her own and Jessa smiled as Darry's strong fingers stroked her. "You're so wet," Darry whispered and kissed her. "I've missed you."

Jessa bit at Darry's lip. "Take what is yours," she offered, and she could hear the raw need in her own voice. "Take it, *Akasha*."

Darry's touch became more forceful, more urgent, and Jessa felt her blood let go. "Have you missed me?" Darry asked, her teeth grazing along Jessa's jaw.

"Ye—" Jessa let out a startled gasp. "*Yes*."

Jessa felt as if she were being devoured and it only enflamed her desire. She moaned at the sudden absence of Darry's fingers and then she was lifted up, her legs swinging out as she tipped back. Jessa bit at Darry's neck as she was carried across the room and her hand took possession of Darry's breast, her heart racing at the hard stone of Darry's nipple beneath her touch. She wanted it in her mouth and beneath her tongue, and she would have what she wanted. She would have what was hers, and hers alone.

The covers of the bed were soft beneath her and Darry lay beside her, kissing her, her hand beneath Jessa's skirt once again as Jessa hooked her left leg over Darry's and pulled as close as she could. Her hips pushed and thrust beneath Darry's touch, and when she came, with her lover's touch inside of her flesh, there were but two hearts that beat in unison.

❖

Jessa lay draped along Darry's naked body, the heat they created together beneath the blankets of the bed almost too much. She was propped on her left elbow as she looked down, her hair tumbling along her arm and mingling with Darry's. She traced a lazy finger about the nipple of Darry's left breast and then let her hand rest upon Darry's stomach. "How do you feel?"

Darry smiled. "I feel very satisfied at the moment."

Jessa laughed in her throat, pleased at Darry's answer. Night had fallen and Jessa glanced at the second hearth across from the bed. Hinsa lay sprawled upon the rug and sleeping, despite the lack of true heat from the embers of the fire. "I'm sorry I became angry."

"I did not mind. How old was she, when she died? Do you know?"

Jessa considered what she had read of Neela, but what she knew was less than she would've liked at the moment. It was best that way, though, she understood that now. "She knew several generations of grandchildren, according to one scroll I read," Jessa answered quietly. "Quite old, I would imagine."

"That's a long time to be without the one you love." Darry's expression was thoughtful. "She was old and lonely, and cold at night. What else was there, but the dream of being reunited with her love? It turned her thoughts."

"I know." Jessa moved the palm of her hand between Darry's breasts and to the base of her neck, feeling of her pulse. "It's important that you understand, though, *Akasha*. You are mine and mine alone, and it will only ever be this way."

Darry's expression was pleased and at peace, her eyes sleepy. Jessa could feel that Darry's pulse was not as it should be, slightly erratic and without the strength that was normally hers. "Yes, my Lady."

Jessa's heart ached with love and fear at the same time. Darry was not Darry without her majik, but her power would destroy her if Jessa couldn't find the answer. Her instincts told her that the answers were contained in the concealed portion of Neela's first scroll, but she could not be certain until she had translated both and revealed what was hidden. "Good," she whispered. "Are you hungry? You have not eaten. You must keep up your strength."

"I'm not so hungry."

Jessa leaned down as she turned Darry's face and she kissed her. She tasted deeply of her lips and her tongue as the scent of Darry's musk filled her nose in a heady fashion. "You must eat..." Darry was completely at her mercy, and she could feel it as she ended her attentions with a last touch of Darry's full and willing lips. Her lover had very little strength left at all, now that Jessa was looking for it. "I will get soup from the kitchen, and make tea."

"I can get us food," Darry replied. "I know where she's keeping it for tomorrow night."

Jessa chuckled at that. "Lady Abagail will be displeased to say the least."

"Not really. I think she likes it." Darry's words had become a bit slurred.

"Would it be terrible of me if I asked you to sleep? If I find something more in the scrolls, I will wake you," Jessa said softly. "I like having you here, naked and in my bed." Jessa leaned down and kissed her lips once more. "I have never had a place like this, that was just my own." Her smile was bone deep and she felt it. "And to have my lover sleeping but a few steps away, waiting for me? I will be about my tasks with great anticipation."

Darry eyes were barely open and Jessa watched as a tear slipped back along Darry's right temple. "I love you, Jessa," she whispered. "There will be no endless night for you, I promise."

Jessa swallowed upon a tight throat and then smiled, just a little. "Then I'll not worry, my love...Will you sleep as I bid you?"

Darry's eyes had already closed.

Jessa watched her sleep for a long time, savoring the heat from her body and the softness of the sheets and blankets, the scent of Darry's skin and the curls of her hair. It was a luxury she had not taken advantage of as she should have, and now there was no time.

When the air in her workroom began to turn cold, she slipped from the covers and stepped to the floor, the boards chilly against her bare feet. She found her clothes and dressed before she closed the shutters and locked them. She fed wood into both fires and spoke the spell that was needed, the oak catching fire with a whoosh of heat. Hinsa watched her with a calm expression, and her tail would flick occasionally, as if she had something to say but could not.

She went to the kitchen and Lady Abagail gave her a small kettle of bone broth with meat, greens, and potatoes. It smelled wonderful, and when Jessa returned to her workroom, she set the kettle upon the edge of the hearth where it would simmer. It filled the room with its scent, and as she cleaned out her own small kettle and brewed fresh tea, she was glad she had made the effort.

When all was prepared and only her work awaited her attention, she sat before the hearth and she wept. Her nose became stuffed and her eyes filled and she hugged her knees and buried her face from sight.

The weight and heat against her left shoulder caused her to jump, and as she was pulled from the tide of her emotions, Hinsa leaned forward and grabbed a mouthful of her hair. Jessa let out a startled sound and Hinsa let go, though only to push closer. Hinsa held very still until Jessa wrapped her arms about her powerful neck and shoulders and held on. Her sudden purr rattled the back of Jessa's skull, and Jessa couldn't help but laugh, turning her face against the thickness of Hinsa's fur.

Hinsa sat down in a sideways move, and before Jessa knew what was happening, she had been tumbled over, her back upon the rug. Hinsa leaned her front legs across Jessa's chest and stomach, laid down, and looked in Jessa's eyes. Jessa stared back as her heart raced and she stroked at the hair of Hinsa's face, pushing it back with a loving touch, over and over again until Hinsa's eyes began to droop and her breathing deepened.

"It's quite soothing," Jessa whispered. "I agree." Hinsa turned her head and Jessa smiled at the roughness of her tongue as Hinsa licked her wrist. "If you go and sit by the fire, my pretty Hinsa, I will give you a bowl of soup."

Hinsa looked at her and then pushed with her back legs, rising up. Jessa let Hinsa's fur slide beneath her open hands as she stepped away upon silent paws, and Jessa watched as she walked across the rug and sat beside the kettle of soup.

Jessa pushed slowly to her feet, eying her companion with quiet wonder. "*Sheeva.*"

She immediately made good on her promise, finding a good sized bowl and returning to the hearth. She filled it with soup, careful of the hot kettle. "It's very hot, Biscuit. You must let it cool before you eat," Jessa warned as she set the bowl down and stepped back.

Hinsa sat very still and stared down at the soup, a small huff of expectation leaving her nose. After several endless moments of waiting and a terrible shiver of long whiskers, Hinsa looked up at her.

CHAPTER SIXTEEN

The colors of the setting sun poured through the windows of the great library, painting the tomes and scrolls upon the endless shelves with an opulence that seemed to soak into the leather and soft vellum. Wide rays of light dropped through the heights, landing upon the tables and chairs and splashing upon the stones of the floor, motes of dust thick in the air as they floated downward. The lamps had been lit, and though they were bright, they were not as rich as the remains of the day beyond the library.

Sound traveled differently among the stacks, for the heaviness of the tomes and the oak of the shelves seemed to absorb only certain sounds, the others left to wander in echo through the halls until they came to rest, or there was no one there to hear them. The ceiling was nearly seventy-five feet above, the ribbed vaulting made of polished blackwood. Each carved buttress that lined the main hall led deeper into the building, the lamps that hung from their heights held upon heavy linked chains that were blackened by years of smoke.

The building itself was one of the oldest and largest in the city of Lokey, built by a distant king who had been known in his youth as the Parchment Prince, for his one true love had been the written word. It did not matter the language or the purpose, though the shelves were lined with more scholarly works than not. The art of the pen and parchment had been sacred to him, as well as the scholars that came after, who tended to the great halls of learning.

The High Priestess of Jezara's temple in Artanis walked with a clean stride beneath her homespun brown cloak, her face bathed in shadow beneath the cowl of her hood. Cecelia walked beside her, and they were both dressed in a similar fashion, stout riding clothes and heavy cloaks.

They had not been stopped by the guards at the doors, nor did the apprentice librarians question them as they moved through the entrance alcove. In fact, the librarians had not even looked up from their scrollwork, their pens scratching softly across the vellum as the High King and Queen, with a High Priestess to lead them, made their way beneath the grand archway of carved red granite into the library's main hall.

It had been a week since the death of Master Haba Una, the High Priest of Gamar, and the city was still in mourning for the loss. The streets were not so lively, nor was the music as filled with passion. The people went about their business and their lives with a bit more contemplation, though it was a change that would not last for most. He had been greatly loved, and now that the funeral rites were over, and his body interred in the Tomb of Prophets beneath Gamar's Holy Temple, life went on.

A personal guard of Armistad's men moved among the stacks as they passed, and once again Owen had seen to their security. The guards were nearly triple in number than on their last outing, and there was a touch of nervousness to this venture that Cecelia had not felt before. Owen had not said as much, but she suspected he felt they were being watched, which meant he felt they were in danger. As to who might be a threat to their safety, Cecelia wasn't certain, but she had some idea, and it filled her with a dark sorrow and a sense of dread.

Cecelia felt a touch upon her elbow as they walked and she looked to her left.

"I have always loved this place, Your Majesty," Clare Bellaq said with a smile. "It was here that I met Malcolm. I did not know who he was, and he looked like a young scholar. He would read poetry and carry scrolls about like an acolyte." Her eyes were filled with memories in the shadows of her face. "But he wore more weapons than an acolyte, and there were no ink stains upon his hands, only the calluses of the sword. Turn here, please…"

Cecelia and Owen followed her to the left, Owen falling a step behind them as they moved between two towering shelves. Clare leaned toward her as they walked, her hand still light upon Cecelia's arm. It was not unwelcome, for Cecelia felt a warmth and a genuine kindness in her.

"He liked Eban Parrabas quite a lot."

"My daughter enjoys his words."

"Princess Emmalyn?"

"No," Cecelia answered quietly. "Darrius."

Clare seemed unsurprised. "The mysterious Darrius, yes, of course." She let go of Cecelia's arm and reached into her cloak. "I would very much like to meet her one day." They moved from between the shelves and a set of wrought iron gates came into sight, even in the darkness. Clare pulled a set of keys from within her cloak, the heavy iron keys clanking together before she silenced them. "These were a gift from sweet Haba, so that I might go where I wish when I am here," Clare whispered as she separated one key from the others.

They approached the gates and Clare opened the lock with her chosen key, the mechanism turning and the huge iron padlock popping open. She freed the key with a whisper, and then pulled the door open without a sound, the hinges oddly silent. She motioned them in and then followed.

Armistad Greyson appeared from the shadows and Cecelia jumped a bit.

"My Lord, I must insist," Armistad said quietly, his eyes upon Owen, his hand poised to intercept the gate before Clare could close it.

"Of course," Clare said. "Please come in, Lord Greyson."

Cecelia was impressed, for the two had not been introduced. Clare Bellaq was nothing if not attentive.

"There is a door three stacks down that leads to a courtyard, and from there, you will find an alley that leads to the southern end of Almon Avenue. It is not the safest street at this time of day, for the market vendors have closed and their purses will be full. There is no finer hour for a thief, unless it is the midnight of a new moon. I would suggest posting several of your men there, for it was at one time open to the night and unguarded."

"Thank you, my Lady." Armistad lifted a hand and pointed, and four more men appeared from the shadows in order to follow his command. "The courtyard door. Find it. Lock it. No one in or out. Archers to the second level."

His men obeyed in silence and Armistad stepped through the gate. Clare replaced the lock once the gate was closed and latched it through the bars. When she held out the ring of keys, Armistad was surprised by the courtesy.

Clare smiled in the faint light and shadows. "I will expect them back, Lord Greyson."

Armistad bowed his head and took the keys. "On my honor, my Lady."

Clare turned back into the gated room. "Your Majesty, if—"

"Call me Cecelia, please. We might have been sisters once, and since we are skulking about and having ourselves a bloody fine adventure, let us dispense with the formalities." Cecelia heard the amusement in her voice and she hoped that it would be taken as it was intended. When Clare chuckled in response, it was a relief.

"Have you managed to keep up with her, Owen?" Clare asked as she passed him. She took Cecelia's arm once more.

"Just barely," Owen mumbled and followed as they left Armistad behind.

The stacks behind the gate were smaller and closer together, and as they moved from the light of the main library, Clare whispered and held out her hand. The ball of witchlight swirled in her palm, reddish gold and warm. She gave a flick of her wrist and it rolled down the aisle before them.

"These are some of the holy texts of Gamar, and also, works for the followers of Jezara." Clare's quiet voice was filled with respect. "When I would come here as an acolyte, I found other texts that did not belong, and so I consulted Master Una as to their origins. He told me that some were High Vhaelin and concerned both religion and majik, and that others, no one still alive could remember what they were. Many are in a dead language he knew only as Eeasa, and though many had tried to translate them, no one had yet succeeded. They belonged at one time to an ancient race of people that no longer exists."

They moved about a corner shelf and Clare brought them to a stop, her witchlight hovering high in the air and lighting a small sitting area. There were a long table and several chairs against the west wall, but for the rest of the space, it was open and empty. Clare stepped into the center of the room and turned about as she pushed back her hood.

"It was only by accident that I found what we are about to use, in order to enter the maze and Sebastian's Tower," Clare explained. The witchlight fell upon her dark brown hair and turned her blue eyes violet. "I don't yet know what the words mean, for when I first read from the Eeasa texts, trying to speak words that had no translation, I did not think it would be a spell." There was a sudden vein of humor in her tone. "It was quite foolish, and I'm lucky to still be alive."

"What *do* they do?" Owen put his arm about Cecelia's waist and pulled her to his side in a protective manner. Cecelia set her hand upon his chest and felt better for it.

Clare turned her back on them and lifted her hands into the air. "They open a portal," she answered simply. "A doorway through spans of distance, and perhaps even time itself, though of that I have absolutely no proof. Matters of time fall beneath the sovereignty of the Great Loom, and the laws that govern its pattern do not allow for intrusions of any kind. It's merely a theory."

Clare Bellaq began to speak quietly, and the words held a lyrical quality, a sort of music and melody that only a poem might hold if read aloud in the proper cadence. Cecelia was fluent in four languages and the patois of several others, but never before had she heard such words. The air in the room began to change and thicken, and Cecelia leaned closer against Owen's side as it seemed to pull from the room. His strong arm tightened its hold as she took a deep breath upon instinct.

The air crackled like the flames of a great fire and sparks popped and splattered against the empty wall, as red as blood, before the High Priestess. They began to swirl and spin to the north until they turned in a circle, clinging to the stone of the wall. As Clare whispered her spell the sparks multiplied, and Cecelia narrowed her eyes against the wind that sprang up and swept past them, a sweet hum filling the space like a faraway song.

There was a flash of light and Cecelia turned her face against it, Owen's other hand coming up and shielding her face.

The silence that followed was pure, and as Cecelia opened her eyes, she heard the bell of the barracks watchtower signal the changing of the watch at Blackstone Keep. Within the wall, a circular gate had been cut through the stone, nearly five feet in diameter.

Owen stepped forward, his arm slipping from Cecelia's waist as he took her hand instead. "Sweet Gamar!"

Cecelia stared at the light of the early night sky and she heard the call of a night bird, the heart of the maze but a few dozen feet away. In the distance, rising from the earth, the dark stones of Sebastian's Tower were some thirty yards beyond that.

The Mistress Clare Bellaq smiled, her face flushed. "Bloody brilliant, isn't it?"

Cecelia wanted to weep, but she pulled her hand from Owen's and hurried forward instead.

"*Cece!*"

Clare grabbed her hand and Cecelia met her eyes with a fire she felt in her bones.

"Cecelia," Clare said firmly. "You must wait and follow me." She looked into the maze as fresh air washed gently through the once stale and stuffy confines of the secluded room. "There is majik everywhere, I can *see* it, like the ropes that bound Haba's hand until you released him." Clare's gaze was sharp and quick. "By the gods, it's everywhere." Still holding Cecelia's hand, she stepped closer to the portal door. "I've never seen anything like it. There are wards upon wards, stacked and tangled together...and it's all intertwined with the majik of the maze itself." She cursed beneath her breath. "Amazing."

"Can we get through?" Cecelia asked, her tone somewhat desperate. "I can see the tower, for the love of Gamar."

Clare gave a gentle tug and Cecelia turned back to her. "I know the rumors, and I was told by Haba that your daughter disappeared into the maze with her men and the Princess of Lyoness." She glanced at Owen. "I know that one of her men is said to have murdered Prince Malcolm's advisor, for I have spoken with a friend from the Order here. I know of the attack on Blackstone. I do not recognize these runes on first sight, and the power flowing forth is as great as any I might cast myself, and I am a High Priestess of Jezara. What am I dealing with here?"

Owen searched the depths of the darkening maze. "The Princess Jessa-Sirrah of Lyoness is my daughter's lover and consort. She is also a Vhaelin Priestess."

Clare took in the information and let go of Cecelia's hand as she walked to the edge of the portal. "The Vhaelin," she whispered, her eyes bright. "Of course..."

"Clare, please tell me if—"

Clare turned with a whirl of her cloak. "We're going to make a run for it," she declared boldly. "I will cast as we go. Owen? You lead the charge. If the door to the tower is locked, put your bloody shoulder into it and then get down. If you can crack the wood, I'm fairly certain I can get us inside."

"And if you can't?"

"Then stay close, and I shall get us back out again."

"I'm not leaving that damn maze until I've been inside that rotting tower." Cecelia's statement was calm and matter of fact. She held Owen's gaze. "Put your back into it, my love. There are answers in there that we shall find nowhere else and we both know it."

Clare faced the portal, her gaze intense as she surveyed the stretch of maze they were soon to cross. "Whoever this Princess Jessa-Sirrah *really* is, she is no mere priestess. We shall be protected by the portal for but a few steps, and then we're in for it. I know those bloody needle vines from experience." She laughed unexpectedly. "A fine adventure indeed."

Cecelia smiled, and for the first time in a long time, her blood rushed with excitement.

"Out of the way then, ladies." Owen eyed Cecelia as he took the lead. He paused for a moment at the edge of the portal and then swung his left leg over the stone. He ducked through the opening and ran his hand across the smooth edge as he went, his eyes curious. Once upon the other side he reached back. "Cece."

Cecelia came forward and he took her by the waist as she stepped through.

Her feet touched the soft earth of the garden maze and the night sky spun overhead, the stars turning oddly. "But you cannot see into the maze from the wall above…Not since that night. The vines have buried it all. How is it that we can see the stars?"

Owen set Clare next to her and the High Priestess looked up. "Those are not—"

"The stars of Lokey, nor Arravan either." Cecelia finished Clare's sentence in surprise. She spotted the bright stars of the Southern Cauldron, which could only be seen from the Wei-Jinn Islands, further south upon the Sellen Sea than Artanis.

Clare turned her eyes to the maze, the hedgerows already moving to close off the path. "*Go!*" she hissed and Owen ran.

Cecelia pushed from the shadow of the great library, her boots sinking into the heavy grass as she ran. Owen moved like a much younger man and she smiled as she chased him, her heart racing. The hedgerow upon their right reached out, and he crashed through it, lifting his arm to shield his face.

Cecelia ducked her head as a needle vine lashed out and she felt its sting through the sleeve of her tunic as she raised her arm in defense. There was a flash of light and the vine hissed with a finger of flame as it jerked away in pain. Part of the hedge before her rolled into her path, and she leaped, stumbling a bit as she cleared the height but keeping her feet. She looked back at the smell of burning vegetation, and though Clare had burned through the hedge, her cloak was caught upon a twist of needle vine that stabbed out and pinned the homespun into the ground. Another followed quickly, and then a third as she struggled to unhook the cloak from about her neck.

Cecelia slid to a halt and changed direction as she pulled the dagger from her boot.

Sparks of flames slid from Clare's fingertips as she fought, but the maze had declared her the most imminent threat and she was caught about her ankles by heavy, meaty vines that exploded from the earth and wrapped about her boots.

Cecelia ducked beneath a branch that swung from the closing hedgerow and slid upon her knees, her knife flashing as Clare was taken hard to the ground. Cecelia's blade was true, and as she hacked away she heard Owen yell in the distance.

Clare struggled and twisted as she struck the vine that grabbed her wrist. A rope of flame withered the vine as quickly as it had attacked, Clare's voice filled with strength as she spoke her runes. Waves of red light washed free from her hands and burst into the air as Cecelia found her feet and grabbed Clare's arm, pulling her up even as the High Priestess pushed from the ground.

They ran, the path narrowing much faster than they could cover the remaining distance to the tower, and Clare clapped her hands, a wave of scarlet light bursting outward with a boom of sound that rattled Cecelia's bones. There was an explosion of leaves and branches as they raced ahead, showers of dirt and grass filling the air.

Owen's arms were around her and Clare both, and he spun them, the three of them turning though the open doorway of Sebastian's Tower and tumbling to the floor in a heap.

The ground trembled violently beneath the tower, branches breaking and the earth rolling and heaving as the hedgerows dug through the earth. Owen pushed to his feet and rushed the door. It slammed with a boom of sound and he swung the bar into place, sealing them in. Something deeper in the tower shattered as it hit the floor.

The silence that followed was deafening and they stilled in its sudden presence.

Cecelia pushed onto her knees and then tipped onto her hip, bracing herself with her left arm. Her hair had been pulled free from her clips, and she pushed it back with a shaking hand. She wiped at her right eyebrow, and her hand came away wet with blood. They were bruised and battered, and the sudden thickness in the enclosed tower was filled with a damp, stale heat.

Clare pushed onto her knees, wiped the back of her hand across her mouth and chin, and then smiled. "Perhaps next time, my dear Cecelia," she said as she caught her breath, "might I just come for tea?"

Cecelia stared into the shadows and darkness and then she laughed. It was breathless but it was true, and the High Priestess of Jezara joined her.

"Can you give us light, Clare?" Owen walked to Cecelia, took her by the waist, and lifted her onto her feet. His handsome grin was filled with life. "My wild Lewellyn girl," he whispered. He reached up with the sleeve of his dark jacket and touched gently at the cut beside her eye, and then his hand slid in her hair as he kissed her with passion. She grabbed his arms with fierce hands and returned the sentiment.

Witchlight popped and filled the confines of Sebastian's Tower.

Chapter Seventeen

Darry slipped on her breeches and trousers and buttoned two of the buttons of her tunic before she walked to the hearth. She crouched down and ran her hand along the length of Hinsa's body. Jessa leaned against the table, her hair tied back once more as she studied her scrolls, her quill scratching across the parchment.

Hinsa began to purr beneath the attention and Darry's heart was full. A portion of her strength had returned and she felt their essential connection in a deep part of her soul. It was as it was meant to be and she could not deny it. *Whatever happens, Hinsa, I will not be doing that again. Never again.*

Hinsa shifted beneath her touch and rose in a lazy manner, brushing against Darry's side as she went. Darry smiled as Hinsa's tail dragged against her neck and flicked beneath her nose. She strolled to the now empty bed and leaped onto the covers, finding the underside of the blankets and turning in a tight circle beneath them, her face hidden in the warmth as she lay down.

Darry heard the clink of glass and the tapping of Jessa's pen. "*Akasha*, my love."

Darry stood up as Jessa covered the distance in several quick strides. Jessa took hold of Darry's face and kissed her, Darry delighted by the entire scene as she held Jessa by the waist.

"I was going to wake you." Jessa's eyes were bright. "*Sheeva*, you taste so good."

"So do you."

"I love you," Jessa whispered, and Darry could see how tired she was. "Are you hungry?"

Darry leaned down and kissed her a second time. "Yes, I am hungry."

"I have soup and bread, and I have brewed fresh tea. The kettle is hot, and Hinsa likes the soup." Jessa smiled. "I'll bring you a bit of both."

Darry chuckled. "I feel better. You make me better."

There was a flash of humor in Jessa's sable eyes. "Let us get some food in you, my love, and we'll see how you feel after that."

Darry let her go and walked to the table. She pulled one of the scrolls closer, and though the High Vhaelin was not unfamiliar, she could not read it without Jessa's help.

"I have been looking at Neela's letter," Jessa said over her shoulder. "Looking for clues in her words that might lead to something more."

Darry ran her hand upon the blank portion of the scroll, and once again she felt the tremor of what was hidden. The feel of the parchment had a weight to it that Darry had not encountered before, and she wondered if it was merely age. A thousand years of waiting would most likely take its toll on something, even words. Perhaps especially words, she thought as she let her fingers skate along the texture of the scroll. Forever falling through time, desperate to land before just the right eyes.

"I have moved the runes about, and translated them into three different languages," Jessa continued as she poured two mugs of tea. "I have found nothing that is hidden, or a key of any sort that will unlock what is left. I will tell you, *Akasha*, I am becoming very angry with her."

Darry considered the comment as Jessa moved the kettle. Her sleeves were rolled up and her tunic was untucked, and though Darry could see the determination in Jessa's shoulders, she wondered if they were just too damn tired to figure it all out. She didn't have an answer for that possibility, and she knew that Jessa wouldn't stop. She returned to the parchment. "There has to be something."

"Yes, but what?" Jessa countered. "I am not finding it."

"You need sleep, Jess."

"I need *answers*, not another *fikloche* riddle to solve. I can hear Radha laughing at me from a very great distance."

Darry grinned at that, though she couldn't argue with the need for answers. She let her fingers play upon the last words Neela had written, the ink sunk deep in the parchment: *I would hold my love beneath the skins, when the winter winds would scream beyond the walls of our tent. She would tangle me up and kiss me in her sleep.*

Darry blinked as the words echoed through her thoughts, the voice that spoke them oddly familiar, though she could not place it in her memory. Her fingers trembled upon the runes as she felt the hairs rise upon the back of her neck, her shoulders reacting with a small shiver that tickled over the back of her neck and skull. "All you need," she whispered, "is to remember your blood and let it rise…"

"Yes," Jessa remarked as she turned from the hearth, a mug of tea in each hand. "And that is the worst one of—"

Darry's eyes raked across the table and she stretched out, seizing the dagger beside Jessa's extra quills. She pulled back, absolutely certain of her course.

"*Darry!*" Jessa called her name with true power as Darry pulled the blade and it sliced neatly in her left palm, opening the flesh. "What are you—"

The cut was made beside the scar her palm already carried, a now faded memento of a different life that was not so long ago. A wound that had been made with a better blade, but for a darker purpose. Her blood rose up as she tipped her hand above the parchment.

Darry watched the blood fall and held her breath as it hit.

The parchment swelled upward as Darry's blood soaked its long fibers, and she heard the cups break against the floor as Jessa dropped them. She straightened away from the table with wide eyes as the center of the parchment bulged outward and rose from the wood.

Light exploded from the scroll and Darry twisted away as she felt it burn against her left side, though not for long as Jessa took hold of her tunic and pushed her back. Jessa placed herself between the table and Darry, and her strong voice rang out, her hands above the scroll.

Jessa summoned the Bird in the Hand, runes that had protected them once before in the Great Hall. A second surge of light and power pushed up from the scroll and passed through Jessa's open fingers as she spoke with authority, her hair blowing back and her clothes billowing. The light changed beneath Jessa's counterspell, and Darry heard Hinsa's savage growl of warning as the blinding glow began to soften. It turned gold and then red and finally a vivid blue as it rolled away from the table. It scattered about the room and blew apart in a separate rush of power, a thousand fireflies of brilliance that slowly faded into nothing at all.

Darry took an awkward step back for balance and tried to catch her breath, her chest tight in the aftermath. She could feel her blood rushing oddly and the dizziness that swept over her in the absence of the glare was profound. There was a gust of air from behind her, and her heart gave a terrible push of pain that caused her shoulders to pull inward.

Jessa's hands slid across the surface of the scroll. "It worked," she said in a hushed voice. "Through Sorrow there is freedom. In that freedom, there is life. Sorrow will bring you through, unto the gifts of the Great Loom...My love, do what you must and come back to me."

Darry turned to her right and looked up through the pain.

The bird floated just beyond reach, its neck arched back as its long elegant wings beat in a slow sweeping motion that kept it afloat. Its tail was brilliant with rich feathers, red and black, and a blue that was as deep as the darkest sky. He hovered smoothly, and as his feathers puffed out, his black eyes found hers.

Her memories came back in a terrible flood of power, and her shoulders jerked as she grabbed at her chest, her tunic caught in her closing fist. The mountain and the climb, and the Holy Man from the steps of Gamar's Temple. The warm and loving touch of the scarred woman's hand, and the safety of her laughter. Her tent beneath a sea of stars and the heat of a kiss upon Darry's cheek. All of it came back, and with it, her heart seemed to swell beyond its limits.

Within the slow beat of his wings, Darry heard him speak, and his name was Sorrow.

Sorrow is the only weapon I have left with which to help you. That was my fault, and I'm sorry. When he comes for you, take his hand, or you will lose all that is yours. All that is good and clean and sweet. If you don't, you will lose everything...just as I did.

Darry took a halting step through the pain, and it felt as if the sun were burning through her body. It was the pain of the end and she knew it without question as she stood beneath the gaze of Sorrow's endless black eyes. She saw the stars turn in their depths as she had seen them once before, on a windless mountaintop in the eyes of Gamar's beggar. "*Jess.*"

"It worked!" Jessa spun about, filled with hope. "Darry, you di—"

Jessa stumbled back into the table and grabbed its edge.

She heard Hinsa's terrifying scream, and she heard the voice of her gods in her head as she reached out for Darry's hand. *There is terrible danger for her. Sorrow will come for her. Yes, a bird of sorrow will come for you both, if you're not careful.*

Jessa saw the agony in Darry's expression, and her strong body was twisted as if she could no longer contain the pain. She heard Darry's voice, and their eyes met as Darry reached out, though not for her. The wings of the giant bird swept forward and the air filled with colors, red and black and blue and gold. The long heavy feathers stroked smoothly across the skin of Darry's offered hand.

"You shall have no endless night, my love."

Jessa shoved away from the table and lunged. "Darry, *no!*"

The surge of utter darkness devoured Jessa's hand as she grasped the tips of Darry's fingers, a rush of pure terror crushing through her mind in a single heartbeat. Its weight was infinite as it pushed into her wrist and then farther still, racing up her arm, searching, consuming, a cold swarm of absence, of nothing, of death.

Hinsa's weight slammed into her chest and she was sent spinning away, the great panther knocking her through the air. She hit the floor and slid, tangled in Hinsa's legs and feeling the slash of claws against her arm, though only briefly. They hit the chair beside the hearth and Jessa's head met the floor with a crack of sound that shuddered through her neck and into her shoulders. Her stomach lurched, and she felt Hinsa's strength push against her and pin her to the floor.

The wave of darkness poured over them and Jessa felt her lover go. She felt her leave. She felt Darry move over and through her and then beyond as the nothingness washed across the room and wiped out every trace. She pushed against Hinsa's immovable weight, her arms shaking and her mind dazed as she turned her head.

Everything was still, even the air, for the lamps had gone out and there was but the glow from the burning coals in the grate beyond the fallen chair. Darry lay upon the floor not far from the opposite hearth, her body still as her right arm was bent beneath her at an odd angle, her fingers lax and lifeless. There was no tension in her body, nor the tone and strength of muscle. There was no essence of her at all.

"*Akasha?*" The name caught and broke in the tightness of her throat.

She could smell Darry's heady musk in Hinsa's fur and her chest heaved as she pushed and pulled at the heavy ruff about Hinsa's neck, her hands frantic. She could smell it on her tunic and in her hair when she turned her head. When Hinsa refused to move, Jessa arched beneath her, her scream filled with rage and fear as it lifted in a massive wave of blinding witchlight. Its raw power split and ripped the planks free of the roof, and blew the shutters from their hinges and into the night beyond.

Chapter Eighteen

Cecelia walked about the lower level of the tower and searched beyond the shadows that were cast by Clare's witchlight. The elements had invaded the tower once more, and there was a rope of needle vine that had grown through a split in the shutters of the northernmost window. Something creaked deeper within the structure, and for a moment, she felt a rumble beneath the floor. She reached out for the divan, but Owen was there first, taking her hand and bracing her arm atop his.

"There is majik everywhere." Clare held her hand beside a lamp and tried to coax the flame. There was a pop and a hiss and the glass flue screeched and cracked as she pulled her hand back. "Be careful what you touch. Fire will not burn here."

Cecelia surveyed the divan and the sitting area, noting the chair had been tipped over and the floor before the hearth was…"Owen."

He stepped around her and followed her gaze. "Clare," he said in a voice that was clearly in command. "By the hearth."

Clare brushed past him and stepped beyond them both, though only a few feet.

The floorboards were soaked and stained with the darkness of old blood, blackened and soiled bandages discarded near the raised hearth. The High Priestess stopped at the edge of the blood and crouched down. She wiped a careful hand across the boards at the edge of the dried blood and brought it to her nose. "Goldenseal root and black pepper," she said as if to herself. She stood and walked behind the chair, keeping just beyond the stains. At the hearth she crouched down once more and moved her fingers just above the rough gray stones. "Speaking as a healer, this is an awful lot of blood."

Cecelia swayed awkwardly near the divan and sat down as her knees gave out.

Clare stood up at once. "Cecelia?"

"I'm fine," Cecelia answered as Owen came back to her. "Along the edge, Owen. Do what you must. I am fine."

He stepped back along the blood and used the cushions for balance as he went to a knee. He traced a careful finger along the edge of the paw print, his eyes sharp. He saw a second one a short distance away, and then a third.

Cecelia met Clare's gaze. "Can you tell me if this is my daughter's blood?"

"If I knew your daughter," Clare said with regret, "I believe I could, but I don't know her. I'm sorry."

Owen pushed to his feet as if in challenge to her words. "But you do know who she is."

Clare's expression was filled with sudden caution. "Owen, I don't think you—"

"She is as my brother was, almost to the core. She is wild and deadly, and filled to the brim with laughter and passion. She dances the steps of Honshi and she knows the secrets of steel. She is as my brother would've been, I believe, had the burden of the crown not been his to bear. She does not understand failure, unless she chooses to let you win."

Clare stared at him, and even in the odd glow of witchlight, Cecelia thought that the High Priestess paled at his declaration. They had been the last words she was expecting to hear.

"And she is *Cha-Diah*."

Clare said nothing, and then she laughed in a startled manner. It was followed by silence, though, when Owen did not respond. "I'm sorry, but that's just not possible."

"She was claimed by her *Cha-Diah* mother when she was five years old," Cecelia said, "within this very maze. There are several portals here, I believe, beyond the one we just came through. A golden mountain panther marked her, and they became *Cha-Diah*, I promise you."

Clare stared at her for a time and then smiled a careful smile. "The Golden Panther?"

Cecelia felt her stomach tighten and the light dinner she had eaten some hours ago churned in a dull manner. "Yes."

"And so she has majik," Owen added. "Not like Mal then, in that regard."

"If she is truly *Cha-Diah*, she has always had majik, Owen. There can be no pairing without majik on both sides, or so the ancient texts will tell you. There's not much written, but there is that much." Clare's expression spoke of an inner debate, but it was over rather quickly. "Owen, Mal had majik, as well."

"But he did not," Owen replied.

"Yes, he did. Mistress Antonia felt it in him, the day he spoke for us, and it was no small matter, either. I'm not sure what it might have been, in the end..." She studied the blood and then knelt beside it, sitting back upon her heels. "We were denied the chance to find out. We were denied everything."

Cecelia heard the pain in her comment, and she realized that Jezara's High Priestess, Clare Bellaq, still loved him. After so many years and a lifetime lived, her love still burned hot and bright for the fallen Crown Prince of Arravan.

Clare Bellaq held her hands out, her fingers spread wide above the bloodstains. "It is a deep spell and I have no idea if it will work, but I shall try. If your Darry is truly *Cha-Diah*, I will know if this is her blood."

The air in the room changed almost at once, the witchlight dimming as she whispered her runes. There was a rumble from beyond the walls of the tower, and once again, something fell from a height and shattered, Cecelia's shoulders jerking in response. Owen moved along the divan, and she took his hand as they both stared at the floor, neither one of them knowing what to expect.

There was an odd smell, and when Owen's hand tightened somewhat upon hers, she realized what it was. It was blood, and death, and Cecelia sat forward as the colors upon the floor began to change in a subtle manner.

Clare's hands began to tremble and her voice grew louder as she worked her spell. The floorboards creaked in a heavy manner as if she was pulling a nail against wood that was wet and rotten. The blood rose to the surface and began to move, filled with substance once more after so long.

Clare's shoulders rolled, and she pulled in a sharp gasp as her body jerked and her back arched smoothly before she ducked her head. She tipped to the side and braced herself with her left hand, her right still held out and shaking in earnest. The shutters on the north window which were already split cracked further, the needle vine inching along the stones of the wall toward the hearth. Dust rained down from above, and Cecelia and Owen both looked up, the timbers that braced the upper level shaking in their braces.

Owen took a step. "Clare, you must—"

Witchlight exploded from the mouth of the hearth, shining and bright without the golden hues of Clare's own light. It popped and sang through the tower on a wave of high-pitched sound that knocked Clare to the floor with a violent, brutal shove. Owen turned with the change in his own balance, and he grabbed Cecelia by the shoulders. He pulled her to her feet and embraced her, holding fast.

The witchlight moved upon a turn of deep music, as if a bodhran had been struck far above them and then rained down its echoing, ominous song from the rafters. A second wave hit and rolled in a wash of pure warmth, over and through them all. When it had passed, the tower filled with an eerie silence as if aware of the absence.

Cecelia opened her eyes and took a deep breath, and then she wept.

She leaned against Owen as her knees became weak and she held to his coat, breathing in the glorious scent that lingered upon his clothes. Owen laughed and tightened his embrace as he lowered his face. He kissed her cheek and whispered beside her ear. "There's our girl."

Clare Bellaq used the overturned chair to pull herself up and glanced across the room. "It is her blood," she said in a rough voice. She cleared her throat and leaned against the chair. "And she is alive, or else the spell would not have worked." She wiped at her mouth with a slow touch and then smiled. "Is that her?"

Cecelia nodded as she stepped back a little and wiped at her cheeks. "*Yes*."

Clare's smile deepened as she turned and sat upon her hip, her left arm limp upon the side of the chair. She looked to floor and said something that Cecelia couldn't hear.

"Clare?" Owen asked.

"It's just…nothing," Clare said in a stunned voice and then laughed. The sound was rich and filled with something Cecelia couldn't name, though she would've said it was pleasure, if she were put to the test. "Sweet Jezara's corset…" Clare's voice was still raw and unguarded. "By the hearth, Owen. Beneath the lip of bricks, on the floor."

Owen turned Cecelia and sat her down upon the divan, and then he walked to the hearth. Clare's witchlight brightened and chased at the shadows as he leaned down. When he stood up straight, his hands were full.

Cecelia narrowed her eyes and tried to see. "What is it?"

Owen held out his hands, the better half of a fletched crossbow shaft in his left, and a deadly broad head attached to the remaining shaft in his right, both blackened with blood. He lifted his face and his expression was dark, filled with a seething wrath that altered his demeanor completely. "The truth."

CHAPTER NINETEEN

Darry fell through the darkness, and she kept falling. She fought against it at first, in a panic, unable to breathe or to think, or even to remember. And then she stopped fighting, for she had no air, and she had no thoughts, and she had no memories, either. But she knew something important, just one thing...

She knew but one moment, and it swept through the terrible silence like a sudden summer storm. Within a doorway, within the moonlight, she was kissed by lips that found her through even the absence of time.

She closed her eyes.

The touch upon her mouth was oddly ample for all its lightness, as utterly pleasing as the soft skin that brushed against her face. Her heart was startled, and then it beat in a splendid manner as it swelled with blood to its very limits. Just a breath, in through her nose, and her world was laced with the faraway scent of jasmine.

Darry's back arched as she filled her lungs.

Her entire body absorbed the impact, and though it was not harsh, it pushed her newly acquired breath right back out again. The ground beneath her was bare as she rolled to the side and onto her knees. She tipped back as the air rushed into her lungs yet again, her left arm swinging out for balance.

The hand that grabbed hers had a grip of steel, and as she leaned forward, coughing, she caught a glimpse of blue sky. Darry's lungs rattled and she fell weakly into a firm embrace.

"Breathe, my daughter..."

Darry felt the warmth of skin against her forehead, and a shower of dark blond hair swept across her vision. It was a woman's voice and it was one she recognized.

"I have you."

Darry closed her eyes and did as she was told.

"Can you understand me?"

Darry opened her right hand which was fisted in the rough material of a shirt sleeve. She tapped the arm and tried to stop the world from spinning.

"We are in the Great Loom, and we are trespassing in more ways than one. You may have another minute, but then we must stand. I will help you, but you must find your strength."

Darry opened her eyes and the faded green homespun beneath her hand gave her something to focus on. She tapped the woman's arm again and shifted her legs.

"All right."

Strong arms went beneath hers, and though her legs shook and her stomach rolled in a dangerous manner, she was on her feet.

The scarred woman smiled at her.

She was more beautiful than Darry's memories of her, stronger in her features and yet softer, for her presence was filled with warmth. Darry's muscles trembled, and though she wasn't sure how long they stood there, it was long enough for her to indulge her need and lift her hand. Her touch trembled, but she didn't care as she ran her thumb down the length of the woman's heavy scar, as she had done once before in a dream. But it hadn't really been a dream, not completely, and her knees gave out. Darry grabbed hold and the woman held her up with easy strength, her brown and amber eyes bright with tears.

"You are Tannen Ahru," Darry whispered.

Tannen's smile deepened. "Yes."

Darry wanted to speak but the words wouldn't come.

Tannen pulled her close, and Darry felt a hand in her hair as Tannen kissed her cheek. It was a kiss filled with love, and her lips lingered until Darry was too overwhelmed to do anything other than savor the attention. When Tannen leaned back, her left hand was solid and supportive at the back of Darry's neck. "What is your name, my daughter?"

Darry was startled by the question. "Darrius."

Tannen's expression was filled with interest. "Darrius."

"Yes."

"And who is your *Cha-Diah* mother?"

"She is a golden mountain panther. Her name is Hinsa."

Tannen's smile was replaced by something Darry didn't quite understand. "Hinsa?"

"Yes."

"And you named her this?"

"Yes."

Tannen stared at her with keen eyes. "As it should be, then." She stepped back a bit, though she did not let go. "Do you think you can stand?"

Darry felt her humor rise up. "I think that might be the least of my worries."

Tannen laughed and stepped back another half step. "I am letting go."

Darry took an uneven step to the right but found her balance in a wide stance. Her stomach rolled, and she groaned as she leaned over, grabbed her trousers at the knees, and felt her stomach push toward her throat. Her shoulders jerked, and she pulled it all back before it was too late. She swallowed in a rough manner and her throat burned. "Sweet Gamar."

Tannen stepped close and set a hand upon her back. "It is all right to be sick. I have done the same...I am going to speak, and you will listen very closely, Darrius."

Darry spit the taste from her mouth and made a faint sound of agreement.

"Once you have your strength, we must move. When we do, you must listen to me and do everything I say. If you do not, you will become lost in the nothingness beyond the threads of the Great Loom."

"How much trouble are we in?"

Tannen's quiet laughter seemed to settle Darry's stomach somewhat. "How much trouble are you used to?"

"Quite a bit, actually. You will have to do well, if you wish to impress me."

"I will see what I can do." Tannen's words were laced through with happiness.

"Why am I here?"

"You have become sick, haven't you."

Darry closed her eyes in resignation. It was not a question. "Yes. I've been trying...trying to control Hinsa's majik, but—"

"It is not Hinsa's majik that is making you sick."

Darry opened her eyes at that.

Tannen crouched down and set her elbows upon her knees in an easy manner. "You would not be *Cha-Diah* if you did not have your own majik, Darrius. Hinsa's majik is not the problem." Her expression became somewhat frustrated. "And I am not the one to best explain this to you."

Darry licked her lips. "Then who is?"

"You are going to take my hand and we are going to travel our thread. I am going to try and show you what you need to know." Tannen's sudden smile was brash. "I do not think anyone thought of this complication, a thousand solstice moons ago. No one expects to see the death of their own people." Tannen reached out and pulled gently at a curl of Darry's hair as it hung forward. There was a faraway look of love and sadness in her eyes. "There was only one who was prepared for what your presence could mean to us."

Darry merely thought the question.

"I means that the Fox People might still live, and if the thread is strong enough, like ours...there will be more."

Darry wasn't sure what that meant for her and Hinsa, but her heart beat fast at Tannen's words. "What happens next?"

"Your spirit is going to hitch a ride."

Darry stared at her. "On what?"

"Not a what, but a *who*."

"Who?"

"Me."

Darry gathered her strength and stood up. By the time she got there, Tannen was standing before her.

"We cannot stay long in one place. The Loom has its rules, and there are guardians who walk the threads. They cannot be defeated, but they can be outrun. I will show you what you need to know as quickly as I can, for the longer you stay here, the more dangerous it is for you there. When we are finished, you must find your way home through the darkness beyond. Sorrow's majik brought you here, for Sorrow carries the souls of the *Cha-Diah* to the Great Riverlands beyond this world. He could not keep you for long, though, for you are still alive in the other world. I just had to wait."

"For what?"

Tannen smiled. "For him to drop you."

It sounded about as reasonable as it did not, and Darry had no idea what to make of it. "How do you know this will even work?"

Tannen looked somewhat pleased. "Because it already has."

"How do you know I can get back?"

"I don't," she answered. "But to have her in your arms for always, one chance is better than none, is it not?"

Darry looked her in the eyes. "Yes." She felt her stomach gurgle as she realized where they were, the edges of Tannen's rock dropping away into pure blue sky. The clouds spun about them in a gentle whirl of motion that made her tip to the side. "Oh gods."

Tannen chuckled as her hand landed upon Darry's shoulder and held her steady. "You do not like my mountain very much, but I will not take this to heart."

Darry exhaled and made a face of discontent. "It's not so much that..." Her eyes narrowed across the plateau.

It had been a several years since Darry had last seen the cloaked henchmen of the dark god Amar walking through the streets of Lokey in their procession of lost sins, but the four cloaked figures who faced her across the distance were doing a fair imitation of what she did remember. She did not think they offered the same blessings, however, as the swaying priests who promised punishment and pleasures alike, in their celebration of indulgence. Shadows moved in their wide, deep cowls, and for a moment, Darry thought she saw...something.

Tannen's fist tightened in Darry's tunic and spun her about. "You don't like heights?"

Darry was pulled into motion and they were running in the opposite direction. Her legs were uncertain at first, but as they picked up speed, her muscles began to react as they should. The edge of the mountaintop was getting closer as they ran.

"It's the falling I'm not very fond of," Darry answered in a tight voice as Tannen grabbed her left arm with an iron grip. "Is there going to be falling?"

"I won't let you fall."

They were almost at the edge.

Darry was out of breath and she shouldn't have been. "Are you lying?"

Tannen laughed beside her. "Only a little."

Darry's muscles tightened, and she realized she wasn't wearing her boots, or even socks. In fact, she was still wearing the clothes she'd been wearing when she had reached for Sorrow.

"I won't let go," Tannen promised and her grip tightened even further.

They jumped from the mountaintop into a clear blue sky.

Chapter Twenty

Jessa felt the strong hand wrapped about hers and it was wonderfully warm and gentle. She concentrated upon the skin, rough in some spots and smooth in others. She followed the heat of blood and moved along its path, trying to identify the source.

Her head was filled with pain, but then, there was pain everywhere, and she could feel her majik pulsing beneath it all, barely contained. It was a bottomless ocean of power at her disposal, and churning in it was all of her grief and rage. She felt the tears slip back along her temple, and she felt the softness of the pillow beneath her head.

Darry's scent was still in her hair, and on her skin, and Jessa saw her again, so still and lifeless on the cold boards of the floor.

Bentley.

"Yes," he whispered and Jessa opened her eyes. "And before you destroy the manor house completely, she's alive. Darry is *alive.*"

Jessa stared at him for a moment and then closed her eyes.

"I do not know majik very well, but she is warm, and she is breathing...and she is—"

Sorrow will bring you through, unto the gifts of the Great Loom.

"Somewhere else," Jessa said aloud in sudden understanding. *Radha, what have I done? By all that's holy, she walks the Loom!*

Bentley's hands were firm upon her upper arms as she rushed to get up, her dizziness so sudden and overwhelming that she tipped into his arms as he sat upon the edge of the divan. She pushed against him but her strength was gone. She could destroy them all, though, and she knew it, for her majik stirred with rage, the runes piling up as the spells stacked one upon the other.

Neela's words rose up and slammed through her thoughts. *My love, do what you must and come back to me...*

Jessa's hands fisted in Bentley's shirt, and she held on, the world spinning beneath her. *If this is you, Neela, and you are trying to take what is mine, I swear by the Vhaelin that I shall burn along our thread until I find you and destroy the Great Loom itself with my vengeance. Not even the wind shall find what I leave behind of your black hearted soul.*

In her thoughts, Jessa watched as witchlight traveled along Bentley's arm, and she tried to pull it back as it snaked about his bicep, hissing like blue lighting onto his shoulder.

"It's all right," he told her quietly, unafraid. "Don't. You took a terrible blow to the head, Jessa." Bentley's voice was so kind that it almost made everything worse. "Please don't."

Jessa opened her eyes, her face resting against his arm as she took in her surroundings. The fire burned full and bright in the hearth, and the lamps were lit throughout both rooms. Arkady stood beside the chair next to the hearth, and he looked frightened, although she had never seen him wear such an expression before. She saw Tobe and Etienne beyond, near the bed, and her eyes ached the farther away she tried to focus. "Where is my Hinsa?"

She felt the purr within her bones, even as she heard it, Hinsa suddenly beside them both. The panther pushed her wide face along Bentley's arm until her mouth moved against Jessa's chin, her teeth there for a heartbeat and then gone. "Did I hurt you, Biscuit?" she asked in a whisper.

Hinsa's purr deepened.

"She seems fine, though it took some time to convince her that no one would hurt you."

Jessa closed her eyes, her stomach trembling in a dangerous manner. "She saved my life."

"I beg you, my Lady Jessa"—Bentley pulled her close—"do not scare us so again."

She breathed in his scent, noting that it was clean and safe and not unlike Owen's. She felt her tears come, and she let them fall as Bentley held her in his arms, Jessa hiding her face against his chest as her tenuous strength was swept away.

"You must rest," Bentley whispered.

"Take me to her, Bentley, please. I would lie next to my love, one way or the other."

Bentley shifted and, with only some minor discomfort as her head throbbed, he gathered her up and stood in an easy movement. Hinsa moved at once and pushed against his legs. Her staccato growl echoed in her throat and Bentley stilled at the sudden warning.

"Hinsa." Arkady's voice was gentle. "We mean her no harm."

Jessa could feel the tension in Bentley's body and he tightened his hold, though only a little. "Hinsa," she said softly. "It's all right."

Hinsa's growl changed and she felt Bentley ease as Hinsa stepped away.

"What has happened to Darry?" Arkady's question was tentative, as if he was afraid of the answer she might give him.

"She's been wounded by a spell," Bentley answered, and Jessa was grateful to him. His answer was perhaps not that far from the truth. "We will have to wait and see."

Jessa felt the warmth of Arkady's touch against her arm, and then she felt the ache of her wound, Hinsa's claw marks wrapped in the coolness of damp herbs beneath the bandage on her forearm. "She'll make it through, my Lady. She would never leave you."

Bentley walked to the bed, and as he entered the adjoining room, Jessa turned her face against his chest. "The light by the bed," Bentley said. "Put it out. Pull back the covers, Etienne, and bring Lady Abagail again, and Bette."

"I've made willow bark and ginger tea." Tobe's voice was quiet and soothing.

The light beyond Jessa's eyelids dimmed, and as Bentley moved, she felt as though she were falling a very great distance. When she landed, the softness of the bed and the warmth of Darry's body welcomed her. She lay against her lover and held her, letting her face rest against the crook of Darry's neck. Darry's scent was faint but it was there, and the beat of her pulse was strong and filled with life. Jessa's right arm came to rest upon Darry's chest, her fingertips sitting lightly against the smooth hollow at the base of Darry's throat.

Thank you, sweet Bentley... "My friend."

"You're welcome," Bentley whispered as he pulled the blankets over them both.

He stepped back from the bed and waited, though for what he didn't know. His dearest friend was trapped within a sleep that had pulled her from the world, and though he didn't know much of majik, just as he had said, he knew that much. All of the things except the smallest portion of her essence were gone, and he could feel their absence. Beside her, the woman who had become as dear to him as his own sisters were, perhaps more so for the easy bargain they had struck those long months ago, was wounded deeply and destined to fall should her love not rise again.

He ran a hand over his face and smoothed down his mustache as Arkady set a steady hand upon his shoulder. "It has begun," Bentley whispered and met the warmth of his friend's gaze. "Our idyll here is at an end, and the wheels of the world are turning once more. If we're not already on the move, they will grind us into the road."

"I'll speak with Master Kenna right away. We'll be ready, Bentley. Whatever happens, we're always ready."

"Good. Send Lucas and Matthias to Ballentrae. Have them buy whatever steel and armor they can find, all of it, and tell them to have a care. There is something coming, I can feel it."

Arkady smiled, though his eyes were clear and sharp. "Do you have your mother's gift of sight, my brother?"

Bentley let out a breath of laughter. His beloved mother, the Great Lady Jolie of the House of Greeves, had once been a celebrated seer, her gifts much sought after among the Bloods of Arravan. "Well, I certainly did not inherent her legs."

Arkady stepped closer to him. "Your mother's legs are legend."

"It's true," Bentley responded and then narrowed his eyes. "Careful."

Arkady's hand moved in Bentley's hair for a moment in a gentle show of affection and then he was on his way.

Tobe worked by the hearth where he mixed his herbs and checked the kettle, and Bentley stepped to the nearest chair. He pulled it close to the bed and sat down, leaning forward and bracing his forearms against his knees.

That fateful night before the Blackwood Throne itself, he had seen something he had never thought to see. He had seen hatred and deception of the highest order, and the betrayal of family. He had even seen the betrayal of love. He had seen Malcolm press his boot against Darry's wound and smile as he waited for her to die, mocking her as her life slipped away. Bentley had heard his words, promising death and even rape. He had seen the look of love in Marteen's eyes, and then fear and disbelief as Malcolm had pulled the blade across his throat for the slip of a tongue.

He could not help but think of Aidan McKenna again, since that night, and wonder upon what it was that she had refused to tell him. Her fear of Malcolm had been a wild thing, and now, having seen him at his worst, Bentley wondered what else might have happened.

Bentley hung his head and stared at the pattern of the rug between his boots.

He had understood as the blood poured from Marteen's throat that where he needed to be, and where he suddenly wanted to be, were two very different places.

He had run to her without question, taking the back hallways and the servants' stairs. He had dodged the guards and risked everything. When he saw the sliver of light beneath her door, his heart had nearly burst with need. He could still feel it, an ache in his chest that was quiet most days, and yet always brutal in the dead of night. He closed his eyes and his memories spun backward in time as he relived it yet again, for it was all he really had of her.

He knocked lightly and tried to slow his heart, his eyes fierce upon the light beneath her door, waiting for her shadow, for any sign of her presence. It was taking years from his life and he could feel them slipping away.

"Who is there?"

"It's Bentley, I, ah, I mean..." Bentley cringed. "Lord Greeves, it's Lord Greeves, my lady."

The key turned quickly, and before he could apologize, the door was opened and Lady Nina Llewellyn stood before him.

His eyes took her in before he could speak—he couldn't help it. The pale night shift she wore clung to her body, and as he followed the lovely flow of silk downward, he saw her nipples harden and rise beneath the delicate material.

He felt the coolness of her hand against his chest, and he looked up as she yanked upon his tunic and pulled him into her bedchamber. He slid and stumbled and then stood upright, turning as smoothly as he could as she locked the door and spun around to face him.

Her hair was undone and it fell about her shoulders in turning waves of reddish blond, the darker tones a match to the freckles that covered her face. She must have just brushed it, because it was full and filled with a life all its own, still reaching out for the brush. Her green eyes were wide and surprised, though she smiled. "Are you bloody well *mad*, Bentley?"

Bentley stepped forward and looked down at her.

She did not back away or flinch from his advance, but her eyes widened somewhat and her voice softened. "If the guards catch you here, I mean, they're everywhere now, and you…" She licked her lips and swallowed and it drew his eyes to her mouth. "I'm not sure what my uncle will do to you, but it won't be good."

He stared at her, and he knew right then and there that he would spend the rest of his life chasing down each and every blessed freckle on her lovely body. They were glorious, and he had never seen their like, scattered across the softness of her skin like dusky jewels.

Her expression changed and her eyes filled with something he couldn't name, though he liked it very much. She stepped close and took hold of his shirt. "What's happened?"

"You must listen to me, my Lady, please."

"Nina."

"Nina, please."

"Tell me."

"Malcolm asked to meet with Darry. He sent the message by way of me, for her to meet him in the throne room." He frowned as he remembered. "He'd been told about Darry and Jessa by then, and I knew there'd be trouble, somehow, something, but then I—"

Nina touched his face, and his words faltered. "It's all right," she said with a gentle smile. "Take a breath, Bentley, please."

He did as he was told and his shoulders eased somewhat.

"What has happened?" she asked in a surprisingly calm voice, her hands upon his shoulders as she looked up. "Tell me quickly."

"Malcolm's meeting was a trap. They tried to kill her."

Nina's expression registered her shock, but her eyes were clear. "Who did?"

"Malcolm and Marteen," he answered. "We were there to watch her back, Etienne and I, but it all went wrong. Marteen had a crossbow and he didn't move until he took his shot, I couldn't find him. His bolt took Darry in the chest...and then..."

"What?"

"Malcolm has killed Marteen Salish. He murdered him, right there at the foot of the bloody Blackwood Throne."

"Where is Darry? Is she alive?"

"Etienne took her back to the tower. It's the only place he could go." He was thinking a bit more clearly now and he took her hand as he looked to the balcony. The bells rang out from the walls of the Keep, and Nina followed his gaze. Shouts lifted from within the courtyard beyond and the higher toned bells of the barracks added to the noise. The night beyond the balcony was filled with new light as he turned back to her. "I tried to bargain with him, Marteen for Darry, but—"

Her chamber door rattled, the pounding upon the wood causing them both to jump.

"Lady Llewellyn!"

Nina turned with a jerk and faced the door, her back against Bentley's body as if to shield him. "Yes? What is happening?"

"Stay in your room, my Lady," the guard said through the door. "Lock the door."

"I will!" Nina called out. "I am well. Do your duty."

"Thank you, my Lady. Do not leave your room."

"I won't."

Bentley spun her about at the waist and pulled her against his body. "I lost my dagger," he said softly. "Malcolm will have my dagger."

Nina lifted her hand and it was covered with blood. "Ben, please, let me see." She took hold of his wrist and flinched a bit at the wound. Bentley watched as she examined the cut and her hair slipped forward, hiding her face. Her touch was warm and filled with care.

Ben...

"You must find Emmalyn, sweet Nina," he told her and she met his eyes. "Align yourself with Emmalyn, no matter what occurs."

"I will, I promise."

"Stay away from Malcolm." He grabbed her by the arms and pulled her close once more. "Do you hear me? Do not be alone with him, not *ever*. Do not confront him, do not goad him or prick at his pride. Do nothing, *nothing* that will put you in his path. Promise me, please."

"I promise."

"He makes his move for the Blackwood Throne. Owen must be warned, though he won't believe it. You must find Emmalyn as soon as you can. When the guard comes for you, be ready. Have him take you to her straightaway. Nowhere else, do you hear me?"

Nina stared at him and her eyes raced with thought.

He gave her a gentle shake. "Malcolm has tried to kill Darry, and he has murdered his own advisor, his closest friend and ally. He boasted of forcing Jessa into his bed, with his boot upon Darry's wounds as he did so. If Darry dies, there is no one to speak against him but a son who has fallen so far down the Greeves line, that even my father has forgotten me. Etienne is a bastard and an orphan and has no standing. Go to Emmalyn and nowhere else, do you hear me?"

"Yes," she answered, and he could see fear as well as reason in her deep green eyes. She understood what he had said. "I promise, Ben."

There was shouting in the hallway and the sound of running.

"What is this you're wearing?"

Nina blinked in surprise at the question. "It's...it's for my wedding." Nina's expression was one he couldn't quite name. "For my wedding night."

"Hammond Marsh."

"Yes," Nina confirmed. "It's Hammond's favorite color."

Bentley took a moment despite the situation. "His favorite color is cream?"

"Yes, I know." Her tone was wry and somewhat amused.

Bentley smiled. "It's truly beautiful, my Lady, but not as beautiful as you are wearing it."

"My mother says I'm too fat, and too curvy for a first son."
Bentley stared at her. "What?"

Nina's right hand came up and she held his cheek. Her thumb smoothed at the end of his mustache. "That a first son with a fat wife will take a mistress."

Bentley responded, shocked and offended on her behalf that a mother would say such a cruel thing to her own daughter. "Is your mother...I mean, pardon me for asking, but is she weak in the head?"

Nina smiled and it was in her voice, as well. "Yes, yes she is."

Bentley felt a terrible stab of panic low in his stomach. "I may never see you again."

"Don't say that."

"Don't believe what they'll say about me."

"I won't."

"They aren't true, the things they'll say. They never have been."

"I know that."

"Do these glorious freckles of yours, do they, I mean..." He swallowed at the thought. "Sweet Gamar, my pretty, do you have them everywhere?"

"Yes."

Bentley groaned softly and kissed her.

Her lips were lush and warm and before he could savor their touch completely, he pulled her into his arms, opening her mouth in a hungry manner. Her tongue was sweet and her fingers tightened in his hair, her left arm suddenly strong about his shoulders. He could feel the fullness of her breasts against his chest and the strength in her body, which was in fact curvy and a dream come true for his deepest desires. She moved her lower body against his as she pulled closer and he caught at a breath, slipping from their kiss as he looked in her eyes. His hand moved upward upon the skin of her back and he realized that her nightshift was made of two flowing pieces. Her flesh was hot beneath his touch and the slickness of his blood.

"What," she whispered. "What is it, Ben?"

"Don't do it."

Nina held his eyes as he reached back with his right hand, searching beneath the open collar of his shirt. He grabbed the chain he wore and pulled, several of the links popping free as he broke it from around his neck. He leaned down and opened her mouth in a bold kiss that she returned with passion, her tongue needful against his own. She tasted...she tasted like nothing he had ever encountered before. She tasted like love.

He let go and grabbed her wrist, placing his chain in her hand. The ring that bore the Greeves family crest was covered in blood, but its gold shone through in the lamplight. He closed her fingers over the ring and took a step back, holding her hand between both of his. "Remember your promise. Find Emmalyn. Do not approach Malcolm in any way. I beg you, swear it again."

Her eyes held a touch of fear as he let go of her hand and stepped farther away, backing toward the door. "I swear it."

"I would've asked for green," he told her. "A green that would match your eyes."

Her lips were still wet from their kiss. "But it should be your favorite color." Her voice was filled with heat and he felt it in his loins, her words soaked with intimacy.

His smile was true. "I know."

"*Ben.*"

He stopped at his name, his desire and fear tangled together in one overwhelming emotion that he understood would never come again, borne upon the realization that he was in love.

Nina took a small step, and then she lifted her nightshift, pulling the top piece over her head and free of her body. The breath was pushed from his lungs as if he'd been struck, her breasts revealed to him beneath the thundering rush of his blood. They were perfect and full and slightly heavy, her hardened nipples standing firm and high in the darker skin that encircled them.

Nina came to him with a quick step and took hold of his wounded hand. She wrapped it in the silk and tied a knot with trembling fingers, his ring and chain still held in her grip.

"You didn't lie," he whispered as his eyes followed her freckles across the smooth skin of her breasts. She did not respond. "Look up, my Lady."

Nina lifted her face to his and her skin was dark with the flush of her emotions.

"I bid you do as you must, for your safety and your happiness." The words unraveled upon his tongue with truth and the fierce need to finally be free. "But know that I have waited my whole life to say these words..." He leaned down and kissed her lips before he whispered against her mouth. "I am in love with you, my Lady." His smile came from the deepest depths of his heart. "My own Lady Lewellyn...my sweet Nina."

Her eyes were bright and they filled his vision completely. There was nothing else to see. *"Go. Go, Ben, please, I beg you...before they find you, or you are left behind."*

Bentley opened his eyes and the sweet intensity of Nina's remembered gaze faded in the warmth of the lamplight.

He looked to the bed and considered their next move, and what might be best for them all, if Darry couldn't find her path beyond the majik that held her captive. For if his dearest friend did not return, neither would the Jessa they had all come to love.

He dropped his face into his hands. If Darry did not survive, none of them would.

Chapter Twenty-one

Darry saw light and shadows, and there were voices in the distance. A distance that was a lifetime away and then, suddenly, close to her face as they brushed past her.

"Let go of your thoughts, my daughter, and remember..."

Darry did as she was told and closed her eyes, letting her thoughts slip free as she did when she danced the Dance of Steel. She felt Tannen's touch upon her face, and her rough voice beside her ear. "Remember what the world has forgotten..."

"Sit still, Tannen."

Tannen Ahru looked at her mother and felt less than happy. These things were not important and Enoch would agree with her. Enoch was the holiest of all Holy Men and she felt as he did. Her eyes narrowed as she turned her head, though her gaze stayed upon her mother.

"Do not give me the side of your soul," her mother said, and her voice caused a shiver of fright to move along the back of Tannen's neck. "What good is looking if you do not see what is right in front of you, eh?"

Tannen let the growl rumble along the surface of her throat and Hashiki crawled beneath the low table. She wiggled into Tannen's lap as much as she could. Tannen slipped a hand beneath the table and held on to the soft fur about the neck of the desert lynx.

Be nice, Hashiki told her and Tannen heard the familiar voice in her thoughts. She tipped to the side and looked beneath the table.

Her mother laughed, but it was not very funny. "Do not be planning your escape, you two."

Her mother turned her back as she moved by the hearth, and Pallay moved with grace as she got up from the floor. The red wolf walked to the low table and stepped her front paws onto its surface. Her sleek body lifted up as her hazel and amber eyes stared down her long nose, directly at Tannen.

I told you. Hashiki sighed.

The low growl that Pallay threatened with vibrated at the back of Tannen's skull, and she squinted her eyes against it, her hair falling forward as if to shield herself.

Tannen's mother moved around her and knelt down, setting the wooden plate upon the table. There were flavorful greens, cut apples, and slices of seared beef that made her mouth water. There was enough upon the plate for both Hashiki and herself.

"Tannen, my love."

Tannen looked up at her mother.

Her mother smiled and pushed Tannen's dark blond curls over her shoulder. "I know the joys of the wild," she said quietly. "You think that Pallay and I did not run free for years and years and forever? We did, and I was very late to take my *Shou-ah* in the first place. They had to come and find us, and my father broke his leg in the search." She made a face. "He never let me forget it."

Tannen reached out and touched her mother's cheek. It was warm and plump and lovely.

"Do not be afraid. This will not go away with the *Shou-ah*. You are human, too. That must be honored every bit as much. The *Shou-ah* will only bind your power in balance with all life, yours and Hashiki's. Whatever your place is to be, your power shall find you, and it will be more than up to the task." She held up her left hand and turned it. The light from the oil lamp upon the table caught against the silver vambrace cuff upon her mother's wrist. "This is to protect us both, Palley and me. They must not become too much like us, eh?"

Tannen leaned forward and took in her mother's scent.

Her mother cupped Tannen's chin and lifted her face with a gentle touch. "And so we must not become too wild, either. The essence of *Cha-Diah* is to live in harmony with all things. What good is it to know the language of men and then forget it? This makes no sense. And when you are older, you cannot take the same mate as Hashiki, nor is Hashiki's love the same as yours will be. Each must have a complete life, though together."

Tannen leaned forward and kissed her mother's face, which made her mother smile.

"And it may always be taken off," she said in a quiet voice as she leaned in a bit. "You will see what I am saying, when the time comes. The full power of your wildest blood will always be there should you need it, or should you wish it."

Tannen touched the silver of her mother's brace and felt the raised glyphs upon its surface, smooth but pronounced beneath her fingers.

"This is why we tell the story of Gisa and his great panther, Obo. He would not take the *Shou-ah*, and so when Obo leaped the gap at the green river canyon, Gisa followed. And though we carry the strength of our *Cha-Diah* bloodlines, there are limits to what our bodies can do. And now Obo's spirit walks the river canyon, forever in mourning. For Obo forgot that Gisa was a man, and Gisa forgot that his legs were not the legs of a panther.

"Enoch has told you this. He may be Shaman, but I am the *Loquio* of the Fox People, and as a leader I know things, too. Enoch tends to the spiritual needs and the history of our people, but it has fallen to me to guide our people through each day. To be wise for those who do not take the time to do it themselves, or for those who do not see what is right for everyone. Who decides the hunting ground?"

Tannen set a finger against her mother's chest.

"Yes, and who decides when to lower the walls?"

Tannen tapped her chest again.

"Who sings the songs of the Dog Stars on holy days?"

Tannen smiled and tapped her mother's chest for a third time.

"And who tells your father it is good that you grow in your *Cha-Diah* strength?" Her mother raised an eyebrow. "When it was last Solstice Eve and you were to have the *Shou-ah* sung for you, who was it who said you might have another year, or perhaps two? Even though it will not be long now until your moonblood."

Tannen remembered. "You did, Mamma. You are Adal de Hinsa, *Loquio* of the Fox People, and you are a great woman. One day, Hashiki and I will honor you with our speed and our sword. We shall be great warriors, and all will know that Adal de Hinsa's daughters have come."

Her mother looked at her for a long time and her eyes were very bright. "Yes."

"Thank you, Mamma."

"You are welcome, my wild lynx."

Tannen smiled and her laughter bubbled up.

"But this year will most likely be your time, this is what I am thinking. If your moonblood does not come by the first snow, I shall wonder if something is wrong."

"If this is what you are thinking, then you are right."

Her mother leaned in and kissed her cheek.

"Why have you let me?" Tannen asked quietly. "I do not want trouble for you."

Her mother seemed to consider what she would say. "Do you know, Tannen Ahru, this is the first time you have spoken in many, many weeks?"

Tannen frowned and she returned her hand to Hashiki's fur. "How long is many?"

"Since the Moon of Ashira, which was before the spring rains."

Tannen looked at her and tried to count the days, but it was not possible. She did not think it was so, but her mother would never lie to her. "That is a long time," she replied quietly. "But Enoch told me, what good is speaking, if you have nothing important to say? He said it was best to wait until words are needed."

Adal's face took on a curious expression. "Is that what he said?"

"Yes."

"Well, I cannot argue too much with that. Though you should know, people talk for all sorts of reasons. Sometimes to give comfort, and sometimes to show love. Sometimes it is just to keep someone company, if only yourself. Words have great power, even when they do not have majik. Sometimes, they have the most power of all. A simple word may destroy a kingdom or save it, if spoken at the right moment."

Tannen took hold of her mother's hand and held it firmly. "Is this not the same"—she squeezed her mother's fingers—"as saying I am glad for you? If I kiss your cheek, does that not say I love you? And one day, when I kiss the lips of my beloved, I will use both. It will probably be needed, as I am some bit of trouble at times."

Adal's smile was pure and Tannen's heart filled with warmth. "So you are not losing your words, I see."

"No, Mamma."

"You have your father's tongue, I am happy to say." Adal sat back a bit. "Though your father has no words to say how pleased he is at how fast and cunning you are with the sword. He only praises the Dog Stars and smiles the smile of a river pirate who has stolen many furs." Her mother reached out and took hold of a thick twist of golden hair. She gave it a soft tug. "A strong woman is needed for the future of our people. For the future of *all* people. And"—her mother tilted her head and looked beneath the table—"Hashiki was very small. We did not think she would make it for many weeks. She fought for your lives with the strength of twenty-seven cats!" Her mother spoke with great respect and love, and Tannen could hear the kiss in her words. "She is mighty beyond us all and deserved this time of freedom with you. Even the elders agreed on that."

"She is very brave."

"I know she is," Adal agreed.

"What would happen if I did not take my *Shou-ah*?"

Her mother leaned back. "This is a deep question you ask, and it is not always known until it is known. But I will say this for now… Enoch had no *Shou-ah*, and his powers continue to grow. Tradition says it is only the Shaman who does this, but I am not so sure about that, in the end. For most, the *Cha-Diah* majik overwhelms them and they become sick, and some will die if not taken care of. They fight against their own majik, for most do not really wish to run wild forever, even though they do. The *Cha-Diah* majik is strong, though, and more so for some. But for others? It has not been so. Do you remember Abel?"

"The dark-haired man with the scars on his chest?"

"Yes. He and his great silverback wolf, they went hunting one day and have never come back. They passed beyond the wall and ran wild into the great Killy Mountains. The Fox People have not seen him for many years, though we hear that some have caught a glimpse in the high up lands." She shrugged. "And that was as it should be, I suppose. He was always a good runner, and the silverbacks, they are their own magnificent tribe. If his body could withstand the power of their joining, his path is his own. And though the silverbacks usually want nothing from a man, for they have no need of men in the first place, he has a new tribe now. Abel was always different.

"But many have been different through the long years. He has not been the only one. No one is forced to take the *Shou-ah*, though we have found that to live in the world of men, it is usually wise to have done so. I would see you have a choice in your life, Tannen. I would see you stay with the Fox People, but I would have you go if it is your wish. The *Shou-ah* will make going easier, if you and Hashiki wish to see the wide world.

"Our majik can be too much for those beyond the wall. They do not understand us and they fear us. Or they hate us, like the Fakir. Not the clans upon the plains, for they have always been our friends. It will make it easier for you, and that is my wish."

"I will do as you say, Mamma," Tannen said, certain of her words. "You are very wise and you love me more than anyone, even Hashiki. I want what is best for us. And I want no trouble for you among the elders."

Adal looked at her with the eyes of a hunter. "What do you mean?"

"I see the way Telluk and Tall Brandis look at you. They do not like a woman in charge of our people, when they think they might do better."

Adal's eyes widened slightly and then she laughed, leaning forward and taking Tannen by the face. She kissed her cheek soundly and with plenty of noise. Tannen laughed and fought her off, though before she could return the affection, her mother was up and moving to the hearth. She turned quickly back to her daughter, a second plate in her hand. "And so why have they not spoken against me?"

Tannen started on her plate. "Because they have nothing to complain about."

She ate a strip of tender beef with one hand and slipped a piece beneath the table for Hashiki with the other. After a few moments her mother came and sat beside her with her own plate. Pallay moved around the table and sat close to her. "You and I should talk more, my daughter. We make a good pair."

Tannen's mouth was full when she replied, "Then we will."

Darry reached out at the flare of light and she felt herself turning and sliding, unable to stop herself and go back. Tannen's violent grip was upon her arm once more and held her close. She could feel the security and warmth of her mother's strength slipping away, and Hashiki's heartbeat was fading, as well. She still savored the familiar scent of...the scent of...

Cecelia's quiet laughter echoed in Darry's mind as her own mother leaned down and handed her the fragile orchid, her green eyes bright in the light of a full moon. The warmth of her fingers brushed against Darry's cheek.

"Darrius...for you, my sweet girl."

Darry gasped for air at the sound of her name and opened her eyes.

Chapter Twenty-two

Jessa pulled the fringed black shawl about her shoulders and stared down at the table.

Her Boys had brought her things from the workroom, her medicine bags, her scrolls, and her many quills and papers. They had set up a second table for her, its surface overflowing with everything she could find that even hinted at the Fox People, or Radha's handiwork, for that matter. The scrolls had been unharmed, though she had lost the autumn herbs she had collected thus far, and most of her bottles had shattered altogether. They had fixed the shutters and the window braces in quick order, and the roof had been repaired by the end of the next day. There was damage to one of the hearths, however, which Theroux said would have to wait for a week or so. She did not argue with him.

It had been three days since Darry had disappeared into the Great Loom, if indeed that was where she was, and though Jessa tried, she could only concentrate on her search for a few hours at a time. Bentley had been right about the blow to her head, and though she was healing well, her eyes could only take so much.

She touched the edge of the scroll that had taken her love away, Neela's words in bold letters upon the weathered and ancient vellum. Jessa could still feel the depths of her rage and fear, and it was no more contained than it had been three nights ago. She could not eat, and she could only sleep when she was beyond exhaustion. Bentley had taken to sleeping upon the divan, and it was comforting to have him close. He would give her soup in the dead hours of the night and she would eat, though it was ash in her mouth. Bentley did not force her, though, and so she would eat until his fear diminished.

She walked to the bed and sat, taking Darry's left hand between both of hers, her lover's flesh still warm with life. At times Darry became hot with fever, and Jessa would wipe Darry's brow and pour willow bark tea across her lips. She would take water, and bone broth, though not nearly enough to sustain her for long.

Hinsa prowled their rooms, or she would lie beside Darry. She would not let Jessa out of her sight, and when Jessa would sleep, Hinsa was there to watch over her.

Neela's spell had been made specifically for Darry or, more to the point, for Hinsa's blood. Hinsa's ancestor had lived on after Tannen's death, *for the child of my cherished Hashiki*. It was the only way that such powerful blood majik would work, and though Jessa had only dabbled in the blood arts, she knew the rules.

Jessa had opened the second scroll, and it was a portrait in faded colors, the face of Tannen Ahru staring back at her. It was stained by the years and the punishments of time, but it was the same woman that Jessa had seen upon the piebald stallion in the tall grass of the plains.

She had found something hidden beneath the leather lining of Radha's oldest trunk, and she had hacked at it with her dagger until Bentley had pulled her away. He'd been ruthless with his own blade, and he had ripped apart the entire trunk in no time at all. He seemed more content at having destroyed something, and so she had kissed his cheek and thanked him in a tender voice. He had blushed terribly, and for a brief second, she had felt like laughing.

It had been a small and yet oddly heavy book, written in the runes of the Fox People. It was a book meant for travel, the writing faded and small upon the pages. She would have to translate it, and her eyes would not allow it yet. She had dragged the remains of Radha's trunk onto the balcony, and thrown the pieces over the rail and into the courtyard, cursing as she did so.

She had nowhere to go for information, and if Darry did not return soon, her body would begin to slow, and show the strain. Jessa knew what would come after that, and she had no intention of watching her lover's heart fail and her body waste away.

"*Akasha.*" She leaned down and kissed the back of Darry's hand.

She was fighting against her next move, for she had no idea what the repercussions might be. She was afraid it might damage the fragile hold Darry still had upon the world, though she wasn't sure how. She could think of no other option, in the end, and so the argument in her head was over rather quickly.

She kissed Darry's hand a second time, stood up, and walked to the bureau against the far wall. It had been cleared of everything but Radha's bowl, and the dagger she had earned on that dark day so long ago, its dusted silver blade held tight in its stag bone handle. She tied Radha's scarf about her waist and set her hands upon the top of the bureau. The water began to swirl in response to her presence, and she called upon her powers of sight.

She took a cleansing breath, closed her eyes, and spoke the runes.

It was more of a song, really, as she picked up the knife and held her left arm above the bowl. Her right hand was steady and certain as she pierced the skin upon the inside of her left forearm and drew the deadly blade downward. Her blood ran into the waters and the bowl began to shake as Jessa closed her eyes and capped the spell, the blade stabbed in the smooth wood of the bureau with passion.

Jessa opened her eyes, and the flames of the bonfire raged, the heat they gave off a match to the sound of their hunger as they devoured the great pile of wood.

The night sky was as black as tar, the stars bright and denser than she had seen them in some time. She could smell the earth, and the oak and pine of the wood that burned, and it smelled familiar. There were runes in the flames, and as she walked about the circle of stones that kept the fire from spreading, she found what she was looking for.

Neela de Hahvay stood in the orange and yellow glow and watched her, Neela's dark eyes clear and focused.

Jessa stopped, and the intense heat of the fire moved through her clothes.

"Did you think I would not answer your call?" Neela asked.

Her heavy black hair was tied back and it was streaked with gray. She was older than when Jessa had last seen her, but she was still beautiful and fit. Her skin was dark from the sun and the wrinkles upon the edges of her eyes looked as if they belonged there.

"Was this you?" Jessa demanded, feeling her terrible rage like the weight of a sword in her hand.

Neela's eyes narrowed. "Was what me?"

"Do you seek to take what is mine?"

Neela was silent for a time. "And if you are right, what will you do to stop me?"

Jessa lifted her hands out, just a bit from her sides. Witchlight moved between her fingers, sparks hissing and falling to the dirt at her feet. "Whatever I need to."

"If you kill me, my daughter, you might never be."

"If she is gone, I do not care."

Neela's smile was filled with unexpected pleasure. "So it worked."

Jessa threw her left hand out and a ball of silver witchlight passed through the outer flames and exploded in the heart of the bonfire. Neela turned her head against it as she was showered with streamers of flames and burning debris. "You had your chance," Jessa warned her. "You had years and years with her, if the sages speak the truth. I am sorry it did not end well for you, I truly am. But I will not be you. And I will not allow you to have such power over her."

"What you fear is not possible," Neela said in a careful voice.

"My lover was beside me one moment, and in the next? Her spirit is *gone*. Do not tell me what is and is not possible. I have never known such a spell."

Neela stepped along the stones, coming closer. "What do you know of the *Cha-Diah*, my daughter?" Her tone was somewhat scolding. "You have squandered your time, if you do not see what they truly are. What *she* truly is."

Jessa was about to speak but she pulled her words back, her tongue bitter with silence.

"They are the children of the *gods*."

"That time has passed. Do not burden me with your legends and your stories. She is flesh and blood. I have tended her wounds, and I have held her while she wept," Jessa answered with quiet passion.

"That may well be," Neela replied with conviction. "But the Fox People were born of the Dog Star Gods, enamored of the creatures of the forest. There were those that stepped from their gusty steeds of summer winds and wandered free within the ancient forest of Abatmarle, beyond the northernmost plains. They found fire beneath the cold light of a Winter Solstice, and they sang the songs that have since been lost. And their music drew the creatures from the forest into the warmth of their light." Neela was close enough for Jessa to touch, if she so desired, and Jessa could see the true age of her now. She was perhaps as old as Radha, though she wore it well, and her hair was grayer than Jessa had first thought.

"And so they wove their majik together with that of the forest creatures, for the creatures of the Abatmarle were enamored, as well. And from that union came the *Cha-Diah* majik and the Fox People." Neela's eyes flared like stars in the firelight. "It was not my spell that took your love, my daughter." Tears slipped down Neela's cheeks. "I had my chance, you are right. And I *took* it!" Neela spoke fiercely, her fists grabbing at the air. "And I held on until she was gone. Too soon, she was gone, and I was left with nothing but memories, and my duty to our people."

Jessa backtracked along Neela's words as the witchlight faded from her hands. "If it was not your spell, than whose was it?"

Neela smiled briefly and turned back to the fire. "It was Tannen's spell."

Jessa considered Neela's words, and after a time, she tipped her head back and looked to the stars. The storm of her rage lessened beneath the heat of the bonfire, though it did nothing to ease her fear. "My father murdered my mother," she whispered, looking a bit to the left and finding the stars she sought. "He kept me a prisoner...until he could sell me for the right price. I know nothing of our people, Neela de Havay, save for stories and songs."

Jessa understood as she spoke the words, that aside from her beloved Radha, stories and songs were, in fact, all she really had. Her people were but a dream. When Jessa heard Neela approach, she took a half step back in caution and faced her.

Neela's expression was filled with both compassion and sorrow. "If you think that your words do not fill my heart with pain, then you are wrong. Come home to your blood, my daughter. You must *both* come home. Let us heal what the world beyond the grass has done to you."

"She is not of the Fox People."

"She is now," Neela replied with a knowing smile. "Do you not understand that? She is the descendant of Tannen Ahru. Your love is the progeny of the gods."

It was Jessa's turn to smile. "My love worships the god Gamar, and I would never see her swayed from her faith. The Dog Star gods have no real power, for they have no followers." Jessa remembered Darry's words to her. "She is the daughter of wayfaring kings, and the Wild Men of the Taurus Mountains, the children of the Olden Men... who cut their homes from the mountaintops and walked with eagles."

Neela's eyes brightened and she laughed. "You are as stubborn as I am."

"That does not make me wrong in what I say."

"Perhaps not in everything, but if the Dog Star gods have no power, then who is your lover? Where does her majik come from? Her strength, and the taste of her kiss?"

"Where does yours come from?" Jessa replied in kind. "Does it make you a god?"

Neela's expression was slightly defiant. "No, but my blood cannot be traced back to the Vhaelin. Hers can be traced back, my daughter, to the gods of the stars themselves."

"Tannen's spell." Jessa changed the subject completely, for she could feel her own spell fading. "Where did it take her?"

"Exactly where you think it did," Neela answered without argument. "Your love walks the Great Loom, though for what greater purpose, Tannen would not say...She held her secrets close, and her pain even closer."

Jessa stepped away from her and cast her gaze into the darkness above, the heat of the fire against her back. A star shot across the night sky and Jessa followed its path.

"From the moment I knew she was gone from me," Neela told her in a quiet voice, "I would have given anything to just lie with her, just once more, and to feel the heat and strength of her body against mine."

Jessa glanced over her shoulder and Neela's eyes were closed.

"To taste the wildness of her majik, and the sweetness of her spirit upon my lips. To feel her love pass into my body and make my heart whole again." Neela met her eyes. "I would give up our thread for that, with no regrets."

"Where is *she* in all of this? Tannen Ahru."

"My daughter, who do you think walks the Great Loom with your lover?"

Jessa opened her eyes.

She was sitting on the rug before the bureau, leaning on her left arm. The light was strange as her focus shifted and she looked at the skin of her forearm, which held no wound. The skin was bright and slightly swollen, and though she could see where she had drawn the blade across her flesh, there was no cut.

"Jessa?"

Jessa lifted her face at the quiet voice, only to find Bentley crouched low upon his heels, a fair distance away from her. His eyes were intense, but they held no fear.

"I'm all right," she said softly.

"Did it work?" he asked, his shoulders easing a bit.

Jessa's exhaustion was extreme, and much deeper than she thought it would be. "I was looking for information."

"Did you find it?"

"I'm not sure," she answered. Her eyes drifted to his hands where he held a tightly folded piece of parchment. "It was not…what I thought it would be."

"We have word from Blackstone." Bentley stood up smoothly, walked across the distance between them, and lifted her with an easy strength. He set her on her feet and grinned down at her. "Hello, my friend."

"Hello."

"Come and sit," Bentley ordered, and walked her to the chair beside the bed. Jessa sat down and was grateful, watching as Bentley leaned over the bed and fussed with a curl of Darry's hair before her kissed her forehead. He turned about and handed her the missive. "It bears Emmalyn's seal, not Jacob's. Lucas told me it was hand delivered, in a book."

Jessa looked up sharply, about to break the seal.

"I know," Bentley replied, worried. "This is the first time we've seen him since we arrived. There was a note inside, and it was signed by a man named Alin Sol, a cousin to Kingston."

"Your friend from the Kingsmen, recently married?" Jessa asked. "The archer from the balcony, Captain Sol?"

Bentley nodded. "Good memory, yes. Whatever it is, it is late in getting here."

Jessa broke the seal and unfolded the parchment.

"It's in Emmalyn's hand," Jessa said absently and then read aloud. "As I write this, it is the twenty-fourth eve of the eighth month of Attia's Spear. I believe you are discovered. Depart with all haste." Jessa glanced up as her chest tightened. "A platoon of men has been dispatched by Mason Jefs, allied to Malcolm. They proceed north along the Raven's Run. You have a fortnight at best from this date. Leave no one behind, for I believe no mercy will be shown. Go north to the Sommes Pass and Gillencoe, then east to Cooley's Blue Drink. Within the village of Habishton, upon the northernmost edge, there is a printer of books. You shall be expected and further word will await you." Jessa's shoulders fell as Bentley knelt beside her chair, his hand upon the armrest.

"If you depart for lands unknown…know that I am Emmalyn Jillaine Marget Durand, and I stand for you all. The future throne of Arravan stands for you. I love you both. I love you all. Do not give up hope that you may yet return home."

"It is the fourth day of the ninth," Bentley said beneath his breath. "Bloody hell."

Jessa's eyes went back over the note as Bentley rose up and walked down the length of the bed. The handwriting was bold and clean, and Emmalyn's words were certain. "Bentley?"

"We're not moving Darry, and we cannot leave Master Kenna and his family to face Mason's men on their own. I have seen them, and I have seen *him* in action. And even if we thought it best to run, we're out of time."

"Where is the book?"

Bentley frowned. "Book?"

"The book this was delivered in."

Bentley stepped quickly to the table and grabbed the small book from the top of the nearest stack. He held it out as he neared and she took it. "Why?"

Jessa looked at the title and then back to Emmalyn's letter. She considered all that she knew of Emmalyn, her first true friend and Darry's beloved and trusted sister. The woman who had risked her standing to provide them an escape, and protection. She thought of Jacob's fear and their clandestine meeting in the room behind the stacks in the Queen's Library, and how they shook hands in friendship. He had called her sister, and he had meant it. He had accepted the truth of things, though he had hoped against it all.

"I believe you're right, and this arrived much later than intended," Jessa explained. "But I believe it was meant to arrive in the hands of our messenger."

"Why? Why now?"

Jessa held up the book. "Because the book is part of Emmalyn's message."

"Which is?"

"It is the diary of Prince Janus Anton."

"The old King of Senegal?" Bentley asked. "That was two hundred years ago."

"Yes," Jessa answered. "But before he was the old King of Senegal, he was a second son. When he discovered that his older brother had committed treason, he overthrew him for the crown and changed the line of succession. He became the new heir to the Bird of Paradise Throne." Jessa held up Emmalyn's letter and gave it a shake. "I am Emmalyn Jillaine Marget Durand, and I stand for you all. The future *throne* of Arravan stands for you."

Bentley considered what she said and then took the book, looking at it more closely.

Jessa stood and her hand tightened upon the parchment as she turned to the bed.

Darry still lay sleeping, if indeed that was what it was. Her expression was peaceful and her hair was scattered across the pillow. Her face was soft and young looking, her lashes long with her eyes closed, hiding their brilliance from the world around her. The scars along her right jaw were not yet natural to her, and yet they seemed to belong, and Jessa could almost feel them beneath the touch of her hand, smooth and yet pronounced beneath her fingertips. When she reached out with her senses, Jessa could feel her lover's heartbeat.

"But that would mean..." Bentley's voice trailed off.

"Emmalyn means to overthrow Malcolm for the Blackwood Throne."

Chapter Twenty-three

Darry felt the emotions rush through her, soaking into her chest and bleeding through her body. In a rush of colors, she heard a name called out in a terrible cry of grief. She reached back, but she was too late. The emotion was gone, replaced by others. She felt Tannen's breath against her face. "Listen…"

Tannen looked across the flames of the fire and stared at Enoch.

He was the holiest of the Holy Men, and some of the children had told her that he was nearly a thousand years old. Tannen did not believe it, but he had always been there, and her mother had known Enoch since she was a baby, so who was to say, really, how old he might be. Maybe he was. Maybe he had been sneaking around the woods since the world was born. He'd told her that he talked with the gods on Flat Top Mountain, and when the mornings were cold, they would smoke jumper weed in their pipes and drink karrem. It did not sound like a good idea to smoke jumper weed on the top of a mountain, but maybe they could fly. She didn't know.

His face was wrinkly and he always had whiskers. His hair was white and gray and black, and it was never combed. It looked like it should, she supposed. His robes smelled like pine trees and cabbage, mostly, though once in a while they would smell like soap and rosemary leaves. Sometimes he would have a woman with him for a time, but she never stayed for very long, and she didn't say much. She giggled a lot and she would hum. She was polite, though, and she was a good cook.

Enoch had very skinny ankles. She did not see how he could be climbing to the top of the sacred mountain all the time. He should have fallen and been crushed by now. She was glad he hadn't, though, for she liked him, and Hashiki did, too.

"You should just ask your question," Enoch said and pulled the pipe from his mouth. Smoke swirled about his hair and he squinted his hazel and brown eyes.

"Why did you not take the *Shou-ah?*"

Enoch smiled at her and pointed the mouthpiece of his pipe in her direction. It was dented with teeth marks. He shook it about for a few moments and then put it back in his mouth. "Why do you ask?"

Tannen narrowed her eyes at him. "Does it make you more powerful?"

"Do you wish to be more powerful?"

Tannen thought about his question before she answered. "I don't know what that really means, I guess. But everyone seems to think it is a good thing to have, or to be."

Enoch smiled. "If you are in a fight with many enemies, one sword is good but two swords are better, yes?"

Tannen frowned. "No."

"Two swords are not more powerful than one?"

"I know my sword," Tannen answered simply. "If the second sword belongs to Rookus, the blacksmith's son, then I say that is good. He would make me more powerful. If it is Destry, who tends the goats, I love him like my brother but I do not want his help. I would die trying to protect him. I do not think that is what power is supposed to be. No one would want that."

Enoch chuckled, looking happy. "And so it is the same with majik. There are things that make you strong, and there are things that make you weak. Those things are not always what people think they will to be."

"So not taking the *Shou-ah* will make me stronger?"

"I did not say that. How can you be stronger if you become weak and sick and then die?" Enoch demanded as he puffed his pipe.

"But you did not become weak and sick, and you are not dead," Tannen argued.

"The *Shou-ah* is like a set of clothes. Clothes hold things in and keep them in place. It is a good thing. They remind you that there are rules."

Tannen remembered her mother, and how she had held up her left wrist, showing her the silver cuff she always wore, or at least, most times she did. "Why do some people become sick and die, and others do not?"

"Why is Rookus stronger than Destry?"

"I did not say he was stronger than Destry. I said he is better with a sword."

"But he *is* stronger than Destry."

"Destry can beat him at white stones and black stones. He can beat him every time. He reads twice as fast, and he can read High Vhaelin and Eeasa. That is strong, too. If I had to cross a river and could not figure out how, I would choose Destry over Rookus to be at my side."

Enoch looked at her for a time, and she thought perhaps he was done talking. She thought of dinner, and what it might be. She thought of the day when she would have a dagger to match her sword. She thought of—

"You speak wise words, Tannen Ahru, and it makes my heart glad. You judge a man on who he is and can see that everyone has something of value to offer that is their very own."

"Who does not see like this?" Tannen asked with a downward turn of her mouth. "To see otherwise is foolish."

Enoch made his own face. "More people than you can imagine. It is hard to think with freedom when you live beneath the heavy coat of your own influence. Even when the sun is shining, and they are sweating and confused beneath the weight of their own thoughts, men will still hate what they cannot see and do not understand. They will hide beneath the coat of what they know, even if they are wrong, and snap their teeth at the world."

"This makes no sense."

"I agree." Enoch took up his knife and a heavy block of cherrywood. He began to whittle with the grain. "I am going to tell you two secrets now, that I have only told one other person."

"Why?"

Enoch met her eyes. "Because you are the only person who has asked me about the *Shou-ah*, aside from young Destry. The others, I love them, and they will grow into fine, strong men and women, but they have not thought to ask the man who performs the ceremony. They trust their mothers and fathers and that is good, but they do not question at all. They will not be the same as you and Destry are destined to be. That is not a bad thing, but it makes you different from the pack. I will tell you what I told him." He pointed his knife. "Destry will take his vows on Solstice as my apprentice. His majik is very strong, one of the strongest I have seen since I was a boy. There have been only two others I have seen that hold more majik."

Tannen sat back slightly but said nothing.

"The second thing is that the *Shou-ah* ceremony is but a ritual. It is to celebrate the bracelet that is given to you, and to honor its power. Your cuff is what is important, for it will contain a chain of spells that will bend your *Cha-Diah* majik into a force less overwhelming to your heart, not less powerful. It will channel your combined majik and balance it throughout your body." He tapped the tip of his knife against his chest. "We are a wild people inside, and in our hearts and in our blood, our majik remains untamed. It is the blood of the Dog Star gods. The *Cha-Diah* majik is very pure, and more powerful than all other majik.

"Our *Cha-Diah* brethren choose *us*. They *choose* us, and they make us one with them. We are bound together, and so it was in the beginning with the Dog Star gods. We are still part of the earth and all the elements through this bonding, and our majik is more earthbound than even the Vhaelin. It is why we are compatible with their own particular majik." He tapped his chest again. "We are at the heart of what they worship, and our heart is the home of our *Cha-Diah* power.

"This is why some become sick and others do not. For some, the blood of the stars runs heavy through their veins, for others, not as much. Our gods were wise, though, and saw that love will go where it wants, and so they gave us the *Shou-ah* spells. Your great-great-grandmother of your father's line was born in the cities far to the south. She was not of the Fox People in any way. Her family was killed traveling through the Abatmarle, though she did not die. She was but a slip of a girl when Pallay's bloodline found her and loved her and brought her to us. It was the *Shou-ah* that saved her life.

"It is a lie, that people are different. The clans and the Fox People, and the river pirates. The people from the far brick cities that kill each other over food. Even the Fakir." Enoch spit into the fire and it flared up with his hatred, sparks popping into the air. "Even they were like us once, at one time, long ago. We are all born of the same earth.

"But the soil of the land grows many flowers. The lotus flower that clings to the river, and the yarrow root that lives in the ground. The ferns that curl and shiver when you touch them. All different, and yet all the same." He shook his head. "Even though the stars look different in the sky, they are all stars."

"Why have the Fakir become different?"

Enoch spit into the fire. "Because they have betrayed the path of men. They drink the blood of their dead and of their enemies that fall on the field of battle, hoping to absorb their power and strength. They worship the dark moon and hide from the sun's light. They eat the flesh of their enemies and take their women as slaves. They have broken the sacred laws of man."

Tannen stared at him, and though she tried to be brave, his words caused her eyes to sting and her throat to tighten. She asked her question despite her emotions. "If we are at the heart of what the clans worship, why are they kept beyond the wall?"

"While we are the same, we are the panther lily to their shivering fern," he explained. "They are bound to the earth and so are we, but theirs is a worship and a deep kinship, while ours is the way of our flesh. It is in our blood." He pointed his knife at her. "Though, as I said, it is not required in order to be *Cha-Diah*. But to not have the blood of the Fox People is a hard thing, and they must have their own very powerful majik if they are to survive the final bonding. For most of those not of the Fox blood, it came to pass that their hearts could not withstand so much power. Many died because of this, even with the blessings of the *Shou-ah*. The Fox People drifted into new territories, for the sadness this brought was too great to bear. The *Cha-Diah* brethren choose who they will, though, even if they die for that love."

"Hashiki chose *me*," Tannen said and felt fierce. "I knew her first."

"Yes. You have the heart of a desert lynx," he said with a pleased smile. "And Hashiki's heart might be the greatest of all hearts. She will be legend among our people."

Tannen sat up straighter as pride and love washed through her whole body, and her fingers tightened in Hashiki's fur as she slept beside her.

"Never has a lynx fought so hard to be bound to another. She crawled blind and tapped her tiny claws into you, as you cried in your basket with fever. You will be great warriors, you and your Hashiki."

Tannen had already figured this out, and so she said nothing.

"As for the *Shou-ah*, in the end, if you wish to run free, take it off!" He waved his knife in the air and made a face.

"What about Gisa and Obo?" Tannen asked.

"That is true, actually. Our stories may be old, but we do not lie to our children. There are other ways to scare them, if they are in need of such. Men are weak creatures in general, and they have appetites that grow and grow and never stop. They do not practice discipline or even wisdom when pleasure or power is involved." Enoch tapped at the side of his head. "Do not become a fool and you should be fine."

Enoch was quiet then and went back to his carving.

Tannen waited, but when he did not explain, she whispered, "Gisa?"

Enoch made a startled gesture and let out a grunt. "Gisa did not forget he was a man, but he was arrogant in his strength. He thought he was the most powerful Fox warrior in the history of our people, and to prove it, he jumped the canyon at the green river gap." Enoch let out a bark of laughter. "Or I should say, he did *not* jump the gap, even though he thought he could." Enoch frowned as he dug the tip of his knife beneath a knot in the grain. "We all told him not to, and we tried to wrestle him to the ground, but nothing would stop him."

Tannen narrowed her eyes at him and leaned forward, her arms landing upon her crossed legs. "How old *are* you, Enoch?"

Enoch looked up in surprise. "What?"

"I think you—"

"I think you should take the *Shou-ah*," Enoch said and changed the subject.

Tannen shut her mouth and tried to decide which subject might be more important. Enoch whittled at his carving, the fire crackled with warmth and noise, and Hashiki's legs moved as she slept against Tannen's leg. "Why?"

Enoch did not look up. "Because you are one of the two who holds more majik than Destry, and though you can withstand the final surge of your bonding easily enough, such a trial is not necessary. I would not see you suffer in any way. There will be enough suffering for us all in this life, without choosing it for ourselves."

"Who was the other?" Tannen asked quietly.

"Adal de Hinsa, *Loquio* of the Fox People, and once my apprentice."

Tannen stared at him.

Enoch chuckled. "Close your mouth, my girl."

"Why?" Tannen asked, her hand sinking in Hashiki's fur. "Why was she once your apprentice and not now? "

"She had a vision."

"Of what?"

"She would not say. You must ask Adal de Hinsa that question."

Darry shook free as Enoch looked past the child that Tannen Ahru once was, and the hazel and brown of his eyes slammed into her body like a giant fist. She could hear the echo of his startled shout, and she could smell the cedar that burned in the fire, fading away... She could no longer feel the heat of Hashiki's body against her thigh.

Enoch stabbed his knife into the ground and reached out his hand to her. The child turned with wide eyes as Tannen seized her arm and pulled. The ease of that quiet place, the safety of it and the absolute trust she felt, it all tipped sideways and fell away.

Wyatt's voice fell from a great height and landed within her ears as she looked up. "You are better than I am," he told her in a quiet voice and then smiled, his blue eyes bright with wonder. He held out his hand to her as she lay in the dirt of the practice yard, her wooden sword still in her hand.

"I am on the ground."

"That is because I know more than you," Wyatt answered, his heavy curls of black hair falling forward. "I will show you what I can, until I can show you no more, and then we shall find you a better teacher. We shall find you a proper sword, too, you will need one. If you fall on the battlefield, my sister, I shall fall with you." He gave his hand a shake. "Take my hand, Darry. You must always get back up."

Darry gasped for air at the sound of her name and opened her eyes.

Chapter Twenty-four

"No, Wyatt." Emmalyn's tone was calm and amenable. "The current won't help you at this point. The bulk of the Fourth must take the Green Highland Road. They'll make better time."

Wyatt frowned as he leaned over her map. "But the current moves north."

"It does, but the flooding from the summer storms has not receded, and it will not have the chance to do so before the ground freezes. You will have to slog through a good league of swamped roadside with your equipment and supplies. For every hour you make up using the Taljah, you will spend five more digging your wagons out of the mud. It's the Highland Road or we will lose at least a week. And the men would be exhausted when they reached the Emmerin Gap."

Wyatt looked up, his elbows still on the table. "There was only one incident of flooding in Mal's reports, but they did not say to what extreme. We assumed it was nothing beyond the usual. Where are you getting your information?"

"Where is he getting *his*?" Emmalyn asked with a lift of her eyebrow.

"The Rangers near Tomms Town. And you?"

"The Warden of Sloe Island and his roster of pilots. His reports are being sent every third or fourth day. I thought it wise considering the circumstances in Lyoness."

Wyatt blinked and pushed up as he glanced back down. "A week could make or break the Gap, if they face a full scale assault." The respect in his eyes was a welcome sight. "Well done, Emmalyn, truly."

Emmalyn let her gaze wander down the table and found Nina sitting cross-legged upon its surface. She was dressed much like Emmalyn was, in black clothes that were a much simpler version of the Kingsman uniform. She was staring at the stack of papers not too far from the polished toe of her right boot, her hair hanging forward just a bit.

"Nina?"

Her cousin did not look up.

"Nina, are you well?"

Nina blinked and her eyes focused as she sat back. "Yes."

Emmalyn smiled a bit, hoping to let her cousin know she was not alone in her fears. It had been a fortnight since their message went north to Ballentrae, in search of Darry and Jessa. "You were a thousand leagues away."

"I'm all right, Emma."

"Where in the seven hells is Jacob?" Wyatt grumbled and grabbed a hunk of cheese and some bread from a plate on the table. He stepped to the side and held it out. "Please eat something, water rat, you're wasting away before our eyes."

"Don't call her that."

Wyatt turned back to Emmalyn and Nina's eyes came up.

"Please don't call her that again, Wyatt," Emmalyn told him quietly, and Nina's eyes filled with emotion. "She likes to swim, so what of it? There are no children here anymore. She is the Lady Nina Lewellyn, and she is beyond deserving of the title."

Wyatt's cheeks colored just a bit and he looked down at the food he held. After a still moment he bent the bread over the cheese and stepped close to their cousin. He leaned over, his hand in her hair as he kissed her forehead. He held out the food. "I'm not much of a cook," he whispered. "Please eat, Nina. I won't call you that again—I'm sorry."

She took the food and tipped her face a bit. "Thank you, Wyatt."

There was a soft knock upon the door and Emmalyn turned, stepped, and slid. "It's Jacob." She threw the bolt and he stepped into the room, tossing back his hood as Emmalyn locked the door behind him.

"It's them."

Emmalyn grabbed the edge of his cloak. "Are you certain, Jacob? If you are wrong in this and we go in, we are thrown into the endgame without the evidence we need."

Jacob gave a nod. "Yes, I'm certain of it. The house is owned by Madame Dubassant, past the Circle and the markets, and into the wharf district. She uses it to store her goods, for the most part, but it's been used for other things, as you shall soon see. Most of what she smuggles in from Lyoness is kept there. They are there. My man has seen them."

Emmalyn met Wyatt's gaze. "Your men are ready?"

"More than ready, and at your command. I'll check on Malcolm and keep him occupied."

Emmalyn smiled as Nina dropped to her feet beside the table. "Are you done with your dinner then, cousin?"

"I am more than—"

Emmalyn watched as Nina's eyes became wide and Nina took a step toward the shelves that went back into the room, draped in darkness beyond the spiral stairs. Her hand went to the dagger at her waist, and she walked toward Emmalyn as she drew the blade.

Jacob grabbed Emmalyn by the shoulders and spun her to the side, stepping in front of her in order to shield her with his own body, his own knife coming out. The sound of Wyatt drawing his sword filled the room with the sly echo of steel against steel.

The room was still as Emmalyn saw the cloaked figure in the shadows, just beyond the wrought iron of the staircase. How long they had been there, she had no idea, that was her first thought. Her second thought was recognition.

The High Queen of Arravan walked out from the shadows and let her hood down as she stepped into the lamplight. "Perhaps you should tell me what is going on here," Cecelia said in a quiet voice.

Emmalyn squeezed Jacob's shoulder and moved around him in order to face their mother. Her heart was racing from the fright of the intrusion, but more than that, she felt dread at the words she knew must now be spoken. She touched Nina's shoulders from behind as her cousin sheathed her dagger, then stepped around her, as well. Emmalyn stood before her mother as Wyatt moved about the far end of the table and sheathed his sword.

Cecelia's eyes were shrewd as she looked at Emmalyn, and then beyond her, taking in the others. "You seem very well protected, my daughter."

"I checked the room earlier this evening, and I have not left since," Emmalyn replied. "How did you get in?"

"There's a secret passage behind the last shelf on the east wall. It locks from within. I have the only key that will match the spell that locks it."

Emmalyn glanced into the shadows for an instant and then returned to her mother.

"It is called the Queen's Library for a reason."

Emmalyn smiled just a bit and considered the words she would speak.

"Spit it out, daughter, lest you choke on it."

Emmalyn felt the sting of her mother's tone, though it was not as fierce as it could have been. "Malcolm has committed treason, and worse, in pursuit of his desires. Marteen Salish's death was a murder committed by Malcolm's own hand. He meant to kill Darry, and he tried, and she was gravely wounded in the attempt. The only reason she still lives is due to the presence of Bentley Greeves and Etienne Blue. Perhaps he meant to remove Marteen as a witness, I don't know. I don't know why he did it. Perhaps because Marteen's shot did not do the job."

Cecelia's eyes did not waver beneath her words, and so she went ahead.

"There was a spy in Jacob's employ…Lord Almahdi de Ghalib of Lyoness, once a great man in his country, but since fallen beneath King Bharjah's thumb. Jacob offered protection to Lord Almahdi's family for information on Bharjah and his sons, as and when Lord Almahdi could furnish such details. His family was brought to Arravan for protection, for Bharjah had sold three of Almahdi's granddaughters into marriage, though they had yet to reach their moonblood."

Cecelia's eyes widened slightly. "Almahdi de Ghalib, Bharjah's assassin?"

"Yes."

"Where is his family now?" Cecelia demanded.

"We are about to find out," Emmalyn replied. "His family was stolen from beneath Jacob's protection, and the men charged with watching over them have disappeared. We believe the continued safety of Almahdi's family was offered in exchange for the killing of King Bharjah." Emmalyn paused, and then said what needed to be said. "A deal that was struck by the Crown Prince of Arravan."

Cecelia blinked and her eyes found Jacob. "How certain are you of this?"

"If all goes well tonight, and as planned, we shall have our answer," Jacob told her in his quiet, matter-of-fact voice. "I fear that my men are dead. There were only four people aside from myself, Mother, who knew of the deal that was struck with Lord de Ghalib. Father and Armistad, Grissom Longshanks, and Malcolm."

"And your men?"

"Lewellyn blood to the core."

Cecelia's hand came forward and Emmalyn took it. "Darry?"

"Marteen's shot was to the chest, but she has since healed."

"You know where they are?"

Emmalyn saw no surprise in her mother's expression. "I do."

"Where?"

Emmalyn said nothing and Nina came up beside her. Nina held out a piece of parchment that Emmalyn recognized, and Cecelia took it, reading Jessa's first missive.

"Where?" Cecelia demanded, looking up with fierce eyes.

"I will not tell you that, Mother."

Cecelia's eyes sparked.

"I will not break their trust. As you can read, trust has already been broken." Emmalyn felt her anger slide to the surface. "We are lucky that I was told anything at all. Let us not discuss what happened with Aidan McKenna, or that our father swore an oath and did not defend it."

"But he could not have *known* what...what Malcolm would do."

"No?" Emmalyn countered. "And yet Jessa did. She saw that his lust for the Jade Throne, and his pandering to Joaquin's favor, all spoke of a much larger plan. She knew he would not accept that Darrius is her love. Darry knew it, and she made no secret of it. It's why they were running."

"Jessa warned me, Mother," Jacob said as he came forward. "If there was civil war in Lyoness, Malcolm could make a claim upon the Jade Throne. She predicted this was a possibility."

"How?" Cecelia demanded sharply. "Malcolm has no…" Her eyes changed as her mind moved as quickly as always.

"A grandson of Bharjah's blood would have a claim," Jacob said with care. "And in the chaos and death of a drawn-out civil war, the Jade Throne would be more vulnerable than ever, and it will be so for some years to come."

For the first time, Cecelia's eyes were uncertain.

"She came to me because she was scared," Jacob continued. "She and Darry are in love, and yet the crown had *paid* for her. Malcolm offered Bharjah a chance to claim the Blackwood Throne, with the very same bait that Bharjah used in return, the promise of Jessa's child. A child of the Durand line, a child of the Blackwood and Jade Thrones, with the right to claim either."

"And with a son who held a claim upon the Jade Throne, Malcolm would take the lead in dealing with Lyoness, and thus in the King's Council. He has since packed his own council with second and third sons eager for the taste of something they have not earned," Emmalyn added. "The Prince's Council has already taken on new authority, and Mason Jefs and his men now defer and answer to Malcolm's wishes, his very own personal army. Abel Jefs, his new confidant, has been given a shocking amount of leeway and power to speak in Malcolm's name. Abel Jefs, his stalwart witness against Bentley Greeves in the murder of Marteen Salish."

"And should a son be born of such a union," Jacob said into the pause, "with Lyoness devastated from war and its aftermath, if a vote was put to the council that Arravan might invade and place a Durand upon the Jade Throne? What Lord would not see this as the greatest opportunity of his life, to plunder such riches and land? A hated enemy finally brought to heel."

Wyatt approached. "I've seen it, Mother. They dance around the subject, never saying too much, never actually saying the words…But Malcolm promises more than he has access to, or rights to. Mining claims have recently been spoken of, for the black iron that is only found in the Dark Ridge Mountains beyond the border, when our own operations have yet to produce a viable vein of ore. And does Father know that Malcolm seized Lord Humboldt's lands north of the Blackwood Forest? Humboldt had agreements with the crown for payment of his debts, offering land for the Fourth to use, good land for our soldiers with fresh water and game. We were to build a new outpost there. That land was seized and the deeds given over to Lord Fenton Jefs, lands that he has long sought for his own cattle."

"You sit on the Prince's Council," Cecelia acknowledged quietly. "I was surprised by that."

The room filled with silence and the queen's gaze fell to the missive she still held.

"There is more," Emmalyn told her. "Though perhaps most of all, above all—"

"There is Jessa," Cecelia whispered.

Emmalyn held her mother's eyes. "Yes."

"They must come home," Cecelia stated. "Darry must testify to what happened."

Emmalyn let go of her mother's hand and took a half step back. "Why? Why would they *possibly* do that? This family has broken all faith with one of our own. The man who for now will still be Arravan's king wants her dead. And he has every intention of forcing Jessa into a union that is contrary to the very essence of her heart and desires." Emmalyn's anger resurfaced. "Darry has already lost one woman she loved, through deceit and lies. Would you ask her now to come home, so she might make this a bit easier for us? To the house where her own brother would see her dead, and her lover forced to bear him a child against her will?"

"But it would not *be* that!" Cecelia spoke with certainty, and Emmalyn could see the reality of her words in her mother's eyes, brutal and quite clear. "The truth, the truth would out."

"Perhaps," Emmalyn replied in a softer voice. "But it smells a bit, doesn't it? Like the halls of the Jade Palace must have, on a hot day when tempers were foul and the dogs were hungry."

Cecelia blinked at that and her shoulders went back in reaction.

"I would give almost anything to have Darry back, and for her to take her rightful place in our family once more. The position she has earned over and over again, in acts of love and bravery alike, though it is hers by blood regardless. I would have my sister home." Emmalyn's throat was tight and she could not keep the emotion from her voice. "My sister, who rode for three days and then traded her favorite new horse, so that my lover might take me to a dance."

Cecelia's tears slipped free once again.

"But this burden is not hers to bear, it is ours, and I believe that she waits even now."

"For what?" Wyatt asked.

Emmalyn met his eyes. He sounded like the young man he had once been, before he had gone east, before he had become their spy. Before he had learned to lie with his love. "For us to prove that we will do what is right." She turned back to Cecelia. "I will take my rightful place, Mother, with the support of my brothers. And I will right whatever wrongs I am able to. We did not approach you because you are watched, and Father is under close scrutiny. We would see you subjected to as little pain as possible, though this is ripe with pain no matter how it plays out. When I stand before the King's Council, I will have all the evidence that is needed in order to rain justice upon your son's head, and I will do so with full vengeance…For he stood over my sister while she bled at the foot of our father's throne and boasted of forcing Jessa into his bed."

Cecelia closed her eyes. Her silence lasted but a short time. "You will need to be wed."

"Royce and I were married by Master Haba Una, in the King's Chapel within the Temple of Gamar, but a week after Solstice. Nina stood at my side. All protocol was followed, and with additional witnesses. Our marriage was entered into the Book of Durand by the High Priest of Gamar himself, may blessing be upon Master Una."

Cecelia opened her eyes and her tears slipped free. "Have you forgotten anything?"

"Only that I love you as always, my Queen," Emmalyn replied, the anger gone from her voice. "I love you, Mother, we *all* do. We have all been careless in this, all save Darry." She tightened her fingers about Cecelia's. "And though lovers may be careless, their love itself is never wrong, and it cannot be denied. Darry and Jessa took all precautions. It was we who failed. We saw how he felt, but we did not see what he's become. We did nothing to stop this. Nothing at all. And in the end, promises that are not kept…they become lies."

Cecelia's expression betrayed her.

"This is not your fault. This is Malcolm, lost within his lust for power, and his twisted jealousy and hatred of Darry. Help us make this right. When I stand for my rights, I will need you by my side."

Cecelia's tears had dried. "There has not been a ruling queen in Arravan for over three hundred years."

"Then I would say it is about bloody fucking time."

Cecelia's eyes sparked, and it was a flash of welcome warmth in her expression.

Emmalyn nodded and glanced over her right shoulder. "Wyatt?"

"I'll stay, go ahead. Landon is waiting at the east gate sally port." He smiled and his dimples appeared briefly. "Congratulations, by the way. You might have told us."

Emmalyn smiled in return. "Thank you, brother."

"We need to go," Jacob said.

Emmalyn walked to the door, and Nina stepped ahead of her, pulling down one of the two sword belts that hung upon the wall. Emmalyn unhooked the buckle and swung on her sword, the same weapon Darry had given her years ago. Nina hooked on her own sword and they grabbed their cloaks as Jacob opened the door.

Emmalyn stopped and turned back. "All will be well, Mother."

"Go," Cecelia replied. "And have a care."

Cecelia watched as the door closed, and then looked to her youngest son. "How is it that you are left behind?"

He gave her an easy, charming smile. "I'm the spy, remember?"

Cecelia made a sound of acknowledgment and approached the table, wanting to sit down. Wyatt moved ahead of her, anticipating her need and swinging a chair about for her. Cecelia took hold of its back, though before she sat, she took in the scope of Emmalyn's map. "Sweet Gamar," she commented, her right hand touching the edge of the oiled hide.

Wyatt stood next to her. "I've never seen anything like it. She knows what she's talking about, as well. She's a born tactician, Mother." He set his left hip on the table. "She is a true leader, and she's been learning the sword with Nina, in the practice tent that my men set up. They admire her in a way I've not seen before."

Cecelia was comforted by the warmth of his blue eyes. "None of that will stop this from being violent and ugly."

"No, it won't...What about Father?"

Cecelia felt a shiver of fear, for Owen had not been the same since Sebastian's Tower. "I think it is time that your king was made party to what is happening here, for he is still your king."

Wyatt's brow lifted. "No one has suggested otherwise," he responded in his matter-of-fact soldier's voice. "It is what will happen when he is *not* our king that is in question."

Cecelia studied his familiar handsome face, and how he had aged over the past five years. So much like Owen. "I'm surprised you've not run him through, for what he has done."

Wyatt's frown was intense. "I have thought about it," he replied. "Many times, actually. But justice must be served, and Almahdi's family has always hung in the balance. I could not live with the blood of children on my hands." He took a deep breath and then sighed. "And perhaps it will hurt more if he is publicly shamed and charged for his crimes, and his greed. To be stripped of all that he covets, over his own family and honor. It sounds petty when I say it aloud, I know, but I've thought of that, too."

Cecelia loved him all the more for telling her the truth of his thoughts, despite how deeply they cut.

"In the end, I suppose, it's not really my place. Though if I find he has done anything else that might put Darry and her Jessa in danger, everyone will need to stay out of my way. And please remember I have said that, for I will not stop until I have satisfaction."

Cecelia sat down, her knees feeling weak. She closed her eyes and sat in the stillness, grateful for the warmth of her son beside her. When Wyatt took her hand and held it, the simple gesture eased her heart more than she would've thought possible.

CHAPTER TWENTY-FIVE

A rush of heat pushed through Darry's body in a wanton manner, and she heard laughter that was filled with passion and secrets. Her lips were desperate for the name amidst all of the names that flooded over her tongue and into her lungs.

"No…" Tannen whispered.

There was the cool sway of grass beneath her hands, and the scent of the earth, the absolute calm it brought with it washing the names from her mouth. Her heart was content and she drifted as if in sleep. She felt the warmth of the furs against her skin and a tender kiss upon her lips.

"No…" Tannen whispered.

Darry took in the scent of oranges, and the light scent of rabbit cooking above the fire.

"Here." She felt Tannen's breath against her face. "Do not *ever* forget!"

Adal de Hinsa mumbled as she dug in the large leather trunk, objects falling against each other as she searched in a frantic manner. Pallay ran in a circle about the front table, her tongue hanging from the side of her mouth as her powerful hind legs sought to overtake the rest of her body.

Tannen covered her mouth with both hands at the sight of it, trying to shove her laughter back inside. Pallay tried to stop and one of her back legs slipped to the side, her hip hitting the floor. Pallay slid wildly, and the sound of her claws scrambling upon the worn wood mingled with her mother's shout as she threw a handful of Tannen's clothes over her shoulder. Adal spun upon her knees as Pallay crashed into the cooking pots, on her side as her legs flailed in the air.

Her mother's unrestrained laughter filled the room as Pallay kicked and scrambled and jumped back up. Adal held out the battered rag doll as Pallay's front legs slid out and she ducked her head low, her hindquarters still in the air as her tail swung in a wild fashion.

"You will *never* possess this, it is *mine!*" Adal promised and then laughed as Pallay shot across the room. They tangled together and Pallay licked her mother's face in a frenzied manner, the weight of her body taking Adal to the floor as the red wolf tasted of Adal's mouth and face. Her mother's legs kicked against the floor as she wrestled the red wolf to the side amidst the scrambling of claws and the sound of yips and laughter.

Hashiki slid past Tannen's legs and into the room, the long leather flap of the door swinging behind them as she entered.

Adal looked up, still holding Pallay in her arms, the wolf draped across her body with the rag doll in her jaws. One ear was held straight up, while the other was flopped to the side.

Pallay slipped free as Adal's arms loosened and the wolf sat down in a casual manner. She dropped the toy, her eyes intense upon Hashiki as the lynx slowly lifted a front paw. Pallay leaned down and pushed the doll forward with her long nose.

"You are very far away!" Adal laughed happily.

Hashiki ran forward, grabbing at the toy as she slid into Pallay's front legs. The wolf let her run for a heartbeat or two, and then she gave chase. Hashiki leaped the low table completely and Pallay followed, her back feet knocking a plate to the floor where it broke. Tannen fell into her mother's arms, and the sound and warmth of her mother's laughter filled her body with happiness.

"Where have you *been*, my girl?" Adal demanded and kissed Tannen's face.

Tannen rolled onto her mother's lap and was content as she looked up at her, her mother's arms strong about her upper body. "I was playing white stones and black stones with Destry."

"Uh!" Adal's eyes went wide. "Did you win?"

"No," Tannen answered with a smile. "I tried to break his three rows."

Adal frowned. "This mistake you make, you keep making it."

"But it should work."

"That does not mean it ever will, my daughter...He knows you will try. You fall into his trap every time."

Tannen shrugged. "I do not mind—it makes him happy. And someday he might forget."

Adal's eyes were bright. "I think that we should eat sugared berries and steal some cream from my sister's house," she declared. "And then take a nap in the sun down by the crooked blue creek. This sounds like a good use of our time."

Tannen's eye widened. "There are blackberries in the longhouse."

Adal's eyes became shrewd. "This is a good plan. If we go throu—"

"Adal!"

Her mother looked up sharply at her father's voice, and the flap of the door was thrown to the side. Her father stood tall in his leather breeches, his bare upper body covered with sweat and dust. His feet were bare and dirty. His long blond hair was thick and it curled, his small braids layered through it all. His great sandcat, Letty, came through the door beside him, and Tannen stood as her mother lifted her up and to the side.

"The wall is down."

Adal was on her feet, and Tannen felt the air in the room change, becoming tight upon the letters of her father's words. Pallay leaped into the room and onto the table, and Tannen looked down as Hashiki wound between her legs.

"Where? For how long?"

"Along the green river, by the olden oaks that we brought down from the Abatmarle," her father answered. His eyes fell to Tannen. "It will be all right, little one," he said quietly and smiled just a bit. "No one knows. Betta's Gray Eyes flew over and saw it first. It took us three hours to get there. Adal, Letty could smell them."

Adal took a deep breath and let it out slowly. "Sound the horn," she told him. "Open the main longhouse doors, and gather the children by the forge. I will be along as quick as I can."

Her parents stared at each other across the room.

"You look quite fine in your new leathers, Jace," Adal whispered. "I will know your arms anywhere. I will recognize you."

Her father's eyes were very bright. "As I will know your sweet kiss, Adal."

He walked forward then, and Tannen waited for him as he went to a knee before her. He took hold of her arms. His eyes were green and blue. "I love you, Tannen Ahru." He looked down. "I love you, Hashiki." He kissed Tannen's cheek. "One day soon, we shall catch you a wild stallion near the sacred mountain, and you will feel the gods in your hair as you ride."

"I love you, Pappa," Tannen said, and her heart trembled. She reached up and touched his cheek, and he smiled beneath her hand. "You are the best Pappa in the world, and I am thankful for you. Hashiki is, too."

He smiled and kissed her cheek a second time. "I will see you both at the forge."

He was up and gone before she could respond, the leather door swinging behind him. Letty looked up at her mother, and her whiskers quivered.

"My sweet Letty," Adal said, and Pallay leaped from the table. "Pallay will go with you." Letty twined her neck about Pallay's and then they twisted together as they chased after her father.

"Tannen, my love, my light…"

Tannen turned and watched as her mother went to the hearth and opened the maplewood box upon the stones of the mantel. It had always been there, the box that her mother would stare at sometimes, when her father would sing before the fire on winter nights that seemed to last forever. "Yes, Mamma?"

Adal took something from the box and turned back around, sitting upon the stool beside the hearth. "Come here, my wild lynx… You, too, Hashiki."

Tannen did as she was told and Adal pulled her gently between her legs, Hashiki stepping behind her mother's feet and sitting down. "Who has come through the wall, Mamma?"

"Listen to me very closely, Tannen Ahru." She held up a small leather journal, and Tannen could see that it was bound tightly about cut parchment pages. "In this book, I have written down some stories for you, and a few other things, as well. You must always keep it safe, for you may need it."

"Who came through the wall, Mamma?"

"Take it, Tannen, and feel the weight of it."

Tannen did as she was told.

"It is heavy with my words. Can you feel it?"

"Yes."

"The Fakir have come through the wall."

Tannen remembered what Enoch had said, and she felt her tears rise up in her eyes and then fall down her cheeks.

"There will be a great battle here...right here, where we live. And I must lead our people. But you? You must lead the children. You must lead them to Enoch, who waits even now at the foot of the Maple Tree Hill." Adal smiled. "Because you are my daughter, and I am the *Loquio* of the Fox People, I am entrusting this great responsibility to you." Her mother wiped at the tears and her hands were hot against Tannen's face.

"Is this what you saw?"

Adal frowned, her eyes curious.

"Enoch said you had a vision."

Adal took a deep breath and then nodded. "Yes. This is what I saw."

"Are we going to die?"

Adal smiled, though her expression was heavy with sadness. "Some of us will, yes, though I do not know who. Sorrow will come for many."

"But not you," Tannen stated simply. "And not Pappa."

"I have seen many things in many visions, and that is something Enoch doesn't know," Adal said in a whisper. "I saw a battle with the Fakir, and I saw you, high atop the sacred mountain. I saw you stand before a towering black wall of rock. I saw a girl in a garden with a panther. I saw you standing in a forest of blackened trees, with Hashiki beside you. I saw a chair with jade stones in it, so rich with soft yellow gold that it hurt my eyes to look at it. And I saw the threads of the Great Loom stretched out before me like the hair in a horse's mane, too many to count. I have seen many things, Tannen..."

She held the book up. "It is all here, what I have seen. And I have written down the spells that Enoch taught me, and what they mean. And the spells I have learned over the years, on my own, are inside. I have written down our traditions and our history, for it seemed like a good and wise thing to do. We will read it on Solstice Eve, and talk of the Fox People. Does that sound like something you would like?"

"Yes, Mamma," Tannen answered. "With apple spice cider?"

"Yes," Adal agreed. "We shall have a grand day, and the snow will fall. We will be warm inside, and your Pappa will sing. I want you to keep it safe for me. Will you do me that honor, my daughter?"

"Yes, Mamma," Tannen replied and took the book.

"And this." Adal slipped the silver cuff from her left wrist and held it out. "Today is a day I shall not need this. Will you keep this safe for me, as well?"

Tannen stared at the *Shou-ah* bracelet and then met her mother's gaze.

"Usually, a *Shou-ah* bracelet is made for each person, as you know, their own special cuff. Everyone should have something that is just for them, yes?"

"Yes."

"But I will tell you a secret..." Adal took Tannen's hand and placed the bracelet in it. "They are all the same on the inside." She chuckled and Tannen smiled a bit. "When your Pappa goes hunting? Sometimes for days? He will wear mine, and I will wear his. They work just the same...But that way, you see"—Adal's voice overflowed with feeling, and it caused a painful flutter in Tannen's chest—"we are *always* together, for this is a part of my soul."

"Why do we not take the firefly gate?"

"Because this is our land, in the end," Adal answered. "Over the years, we have been driven from place to place, with few friends. We have nowhere else to go, unless we return to the Abatmarle. Here we have allies close by, for the people of the plains are good friends and would help us. We will send word to them, and they will come. We have our crops that will see us through the winter, and stores that will keep us healthy and strong, though if we must, we will go through the firefly gate and take our chances in the darkness of the Abatmarle. But we must fight for what is ours. If you do not fight for what is yours,

Tannen, it will be taken from you. Or you will be driven away from what you love, by the will of others."

"Yes, Mamma."

"All right then," Adal said and kissed Tannen's cheek. "Go get your boots on, the warm ones. And your coat, just in case. Put on your sword. I will pack a small bag for you."

Tannen hurried about the table and turned at the door to the other room. "But it's not yet cold, Mamma. What if—"

"Put them on, Tannen, do not argue." Adal's voice was firm. "There is room to grow, and should it turn cold, you will have them." Adal smiled at her. "Please, Tannen, then I will not worry until I see you again."

"I will wear them—you are right," Tannen said. "I love you. Thank you for looking out for me. You think of things I can never think of."

Adal looked back at her from across the room. "I love you…You are my heart, Tannen. You and Hashiki, you will be the bravest and strongest of us all. I have seen it." *She picked up Hashiki and kissed her face, the lynx pushing her face against Adal's neck.*

Darry felt the darkness close about her as Adal de Hinsa looked her in the eyes across the distance of a thousand years, Darry falling and spinning away from her. Darry's terrible fear mixed oddly with the comforting smells of home, and then the warmth of being loved beyond all else slipped through her fingers like water…

Darry stood in the shadows beneath the heavy tendrils of the bossa tree and watched as Jessa sat upon the garden bench, bewitching in her dress as the music from the fete played in the distance. Her hair tumbled in dark curls about her shoulders and down her back, Jessa lifting her face to the breeze, and the scent of lilacs in the air. Jessa's right hand smoothed absently against the wide silver cuff upon her left wrist, tracing the pattern upon the bracelet.

I saw a girl in a garden with a panther.

Darry gasped for air in shock and opened her eyes.

"Darrius!"

Darry turned her face and felt the earth against her cheek as she did so. She opened her hands in the dirt and pushed up, rising away from the ground and dropping back upon her heels. Tannen Ahru went to her knees before her and took hold of Darry's shoulders. Tannen's face was streaked with tears, her eyes almost unbearably dark with emotion.

"What happened?" Darry's words barely come out. Her heart hammered in her chest, and the dread she suddenly felt brought an unfamiliar tremble to her body. "We have to go back…" Her voice sounded terribly small beneath the weight of her fear. It was not something she was used to and it shook her to her bones.

Tannen shook her head, her hands lifting and holding Darry's face. "No."

Darry's eyes burned. "Yes, Tannen, *please*!" She grabbed Tannen's shirtfront and pulled in a violent manner, a burst of panic turning her thoughts. "We…we *can*, you and I together…"

"We can do nothing, don't you see?" Tannen said in a pained voice and pulled Darry into her arms. Tannen held her tightly. "That is *my* story, Darrius, not yours," Tannen whispered beside her ear. Darry's forehead slipped and pressed against Tannen's chest. "Though you have soothed my heart."

Darry sucked in her emotions and tried to shove them down. They were long dead, all of them, and she was but a ghost. She had no sword, and worse yet, she had no hand to hold it with.

"I did not mean to cry, I'm sorry," Tannen offered. "I've not been back to that day, not ever. But there were things you needed to see. Forgive me, little one, please."

Darry tried to put her thoughts into order, but it was all too much. She felt terribly small and defeated, and completely, utterly alone. She had reached out for Sorrow because Tannen had told her to, and she had listened because she had everything in the world to lose. Everything, and Tannen had nothing. Though it had not always been so, and it would not be that way forever. She closed her eyes even more tightly. "My head hurts," she whispered.

"Yes," Tannen agreed in a soothing voice. "I know it does."

Darry wanted nothing more than to feel Jessa's lips against hers, and to feel the strength of her arms holding her safe as she fell asleep. *To feel the caress of your majik shudder through my muscles, sweet Jess. To hear you sing, as you braid my hair, and the way you touch my face...To hear you laugh into your pillow.* "I want to go home," Darry said in a strained voice. "I need to go home, Tannen, please. I'm so sorry, but I need time to think, please."

"Yes, you must go now, my daughter. You must go before it's too late." Tannen's face was warm against Darry's as she kissed her. "Come now, on our feet."

Darry wasn't sure how she got there, but she was standing on her feet as Tannen held her shoulders.

"I will tell my *Akasha* of the child who came to me, because she kept her promises. Which means all that you will need should already be yours, Darrius." Her voice was filled with love. She sounded remarkably like Adal de Hinsa, and Darry's heart twisted with sorrow. "And we shall wonder upon your adventures, when the wind blows cold beyond our door. She has been waiting for me, for a very long time"—Tannen smiled—"in the great grass and blue waters of the Riverlands beyond...with my Hashiki."

Darry stepped back, and she felt afraid of what was yet to come.

"Release your majik, Darrius," Tannen told her. "*All* of it, every last drop you have in you, and let it rise to meet your *Cha-Diah* blood. Hold nothing back and embrace who you are. That is the final bonding. Do not fight against it, any of it. It was those who fought against their own truth that did not survive. Those who embrace their gifts, their loves and their sorrows alike, they are the ones who prevail. Be true to yourself, my daughter. You will know what to do after that."

Darry looked at her then, and took her in, all of her. The lean, tall strength of her, and the heaviness of her beautiful hair. Her darkly tanned skin and the white of her scar against her amber and brown eyes. Her simple homespun clothes, and the stitching about her collar, much like the one Tannen had worn as a child. Tannen Ahru, standing before her and looking at her with love. She tried to say the words but she couldn't.

Tannen grinned at her. "You're welcome."

Darry took another step back and then stopped, looking over her shoulder. She began to smile as the edge of Tannen's mountain dropped away from her into nothing but sky. "I'm going to have to climb this bloody rock again, I just know it."

Tannen chuckled happily and set a strong hand upon Darry's left shoulder. "Remember your blood, Darrius, and you shall find your way home. Let them know who you are and why you are there. You are the child of many mothers. You stand for us all."

"Hinsa and I…if they are out there, Tannen Ahru, we will find them," Darry promised.

Tannen nodded. "I know."

Darry felt Tannen's hand tighten in her tunic and her heart leaped with a jolt of renewed fear. She had absolutely no idea what to expect. "Will I see you again?"

"I love you," Tannen whispered, and then smiled sweetly. "Little one."

Darry felt the push against her shoulder and she fell.

Chapter Twenty-six

Bentley moved through the thick of the trees in silence, Arkady some twenty yards ahead of him, and Matthias ten yards beyond that. They had long ago scouted the heavy stretch of trees, both for game trails and to familiarize themselves with the lands surrounding their new home. The brush from fallen trees moved naturally to the bottom of the rise when it rained, and a steady wash of debris cluttered the ground the lower you went. The road to Ballentrae moved through the narrow valley below, and though it was wide enough for most, it had not been forged from the surrounding hills with a large force in mind. Upon the opposite side of the road the rise was not so pronounced, though the trees were thicker and the grass had grown high.

Malcolm's soldiers were camped for the night, and their guards were stationed at regular intervals along the caravan, light in number, though suitable for their circumstances. The wagons were held in the rear, and there were four of them, their supplies full, but not so full as to be a burden. Their horses were picketed along the western edge within the grass, and there were five fires that burned along the length of the column. Bentley could smell the food they had eaten for dinner an hour before, and he could smell the blackgrass tobacco being smoked. Voices could be heard when the breeze moved through the trees, and Bentley understood the relief and contentment they were feeling. Their bellies were finally full and their pipes were lit. Their platoon had ridden nearly forty miles from Ballentrae, and it was a hard pace over some very steep and hilly terrain.

They were two days past Ballentrae, and a day and half's ride from Lanark, though riding hard would cut that in half. And though the caravan stank of sweat and unwashed men, Bentley knew they were fully capable of such a push no matter how tired they were. The soldiers and free riders in Mason Jefs command were hard men and extremely good at what they did.

Bentley crouched behind an oak and narrowed his eyes along the game trail, and though his eyes were adjusted to the darkness, the inky black was formidable. A brief line of blue sparks appeared against the surface of the trail from Arkady's position, and then died just as quickly in the dirt. A moment later, an identical signal from a greater distance.

Bentley returned his attention to the caravan below and rose along the oak, pulling the string upon his bow, his arrow nocked and ready to fly as he picked his target.

Matty the Younger was down there, somewhere, and should he be discovered, he would have a narrow escape at best, if he had one at all. The picket had been set a quarter league farther up the road, but the rear of the caravan had been left with but a light guard. Bentley had counted seventy-five men in total, which included their support staff, all of whom would fight when the time came.

Seventy-five men against a dozen.

And a Priestess of the Vhaelin whom none of them would expect, along with the golden mountain panther who refused to leave her side.

Not the worst odds Bentley had ever seen, but it was damn close, despite the power Jessa had at her disposal. The estate was a stationary target, and though the Yellandale was at their backs, they would have to defend multiple lines of attack, and the estate and its buildings would be in constant jeopardy. It was not something any of them were willing to risk, especially with Darry as she was.

Bentley's eyes narrowed upon one of the wagons, the grass moving slightly near the rear gate. He smiled under the mask that covered his face beneath his eyes.

He looked across the narrow valley to the trees where Orlando, Theroux, Tobe, and Sybok would be holding similar positions. Jemin, Etienne, Lucien, and Lucas would back Jessa's play, and by the grace of Gamar, all seven hells would break loose before the dinner dishes were cleared. All they had to do now was wait for Jessa's entrance.

❖

Jessa walked along the road to Ballentrae, hidden beneath the Veil of Shadows, her boots silent upon the hard-packed earth. Hinsa moved beside her, hidden beneath the reach of Jessa's spell. Hinsa moved differently now, for she could smell what Jessa could not. The hunt had begun.

The night was cool and the stars were out, though the moon was dark. The night birds were silent and Jessa could feel the wind at her back, strong enough so that it turned their smoke to the south. There were fifteen men at two separate fires, and as she approached the small vanguard of Malcolm's men, she lowered her hood and came to a halt, the Veil of Shadows falling away.

They were men of Arravan, not Sahwello warriors of the Fakir, and so she waited.

The first man to see her stood in a rush as he drew his sword. "*Hiyah*," he said in warning.

The men around him reacted quickly and they were all on their feet.

"Spread out." The order came from the largest man there, and the others obeyed. They looked to the grass along the road and lifted their eyes into the trees as they drew their weapons. There were four archers, and they had nocked and drawn their arrows as they searched the darkness for a suitable target.

The large man walked toward her and then stopped, some six or seven feet away, squinting at her in the darkness. The light from the fires did not reach her position and she was still cast in shadow. "And who might you be?"

"I am Princess Jessa-Sirrah of Lyoness," Jessa answered. Hinsa was no longer beside her. "You stand upon my land, uninvited. I will ask you just this once to take your belongings and go. You are sons of Arravan, and it is a place I have come to love. This is not the war you should be willing to give your lives for. That war is yet to come."

He nodded, and then spit as he turned his head. "I'm Martin Ibins," he replied. "And though I thank you for the warning, girl, we've got our orders." He smiled. "You're meant for Mason's dandy of a princeling, and we're to bring you back and kill the rest. Best not to fight it."

"Do not choose this, Martin Ibins." Jessa's tone was one of respect. "Or you will die here. Go home to your family, go home to your children. I am no one's chattel, and I belong to another. The dandy princeling has no rights here."

"That's not really the way things work," Ibins replied, and he gave a tired sigh. "It's not up to me, or you, I suppose. It's up to the likes of them. We have our orders."

"You will never see your family again."

"I ain't seen 'em in near twenty years. These men are my family, that's just how it is," he answered. "And there's five thousand Arravan golds for the men who bring in the head of Bentley Greeves, and another three for Etienne Blue."

"I shall use your own head as a warning to the others then, when I visit them next."

Martin Ibins chuckled as he drew his sword. "As you please, girl."

Jessa pulled upon the fringe of Radha's shawl, tied firmly about her waist. She lifted her hand out, a single piece of black yarn sitting motionless in her open palm.

Martin narrowed his eyes again and leaned forward, trying to see. "Not sure what you're thinkin', girl, but you need to come wi—"

The yarn straightened and flew true as it left her hand, piercing his neck at the base of his throat. He dropped his sword and stumbled back, clawing at his neck. His eyes were wide as he spun to the side and slammed to his knees. The archers fell almost as one, and Jessa watched as the others pulled in their ranks. Daggers moved through the air, and three more men fell as she stood in silent witness, and then another two beneath a second assault of well-placed arrows.

It had taken but a few moments, and Jessa spoke to fire on the left, the flames hissing and then raging high. The five remaining men reacted and fell back, one of them ducking down as an arc of flames reached for the heat of the second fire. One man ran.

Jessa saw Hinsa move in the darkness as she chased him down, and she heard the man's panicked scream, and then she heard nothing, save for the sounds that Hinsa made as she killed her prey.

"Lay down your arms," Jessa told them as the fire behind them sputtered and died back down. "Wait out the night in the grass. Sleep if you can. Find your things with the morning sun and leave this place."

Nothing moved accept Martin Ibins as he pushed awkwardly to his feet, his brothers in arms watching with wide eyes as he rose up. He breathed inward upon air and blood as he turned to face her, drawing his dagger. The front of his tunic was soaked with blood.

A dark shape came out of the night, and the firelight caught in a brilliant flash along the edge of Etienne's blade. He was gone again before Martin Ibins fell a second time, his head rolling toward his comrades. His body hit the dirt of the Ballentrae Road with a dull thud of sound.

"Surrender," Jessa offered again, and those that remained lifted their eyes to her. Hinsa's staccato growl moved in the flowing grass nearby. "You are men of Arravan. Lay down your arms and live. This is not your fight."

Only the sound of the flames could be heard, and then one man stepped forward. "This was my father's sword." His voice sounded terribly young and afraid. "It's all I got of him."

"Then take it with you. I would not see you go unarmed into the night. But leave this place now and never return. Go home. Go east. Seek your fortune elsewhere," Jessa told him. She stepped forward into the light. "War is coming to Arravan, and your swords will be needed. Do not fight again this night or you will die."

They turned from the fire, and one grabbed up a saddlebag, while another took up several skins of water. The third man grabbed their blankets, and then they were gone, running into the night. The young man who had spoken finally sheathed his sword and picked up a cloak. He threw it over his shoulders and moved quickly into the darkness.

Etienne appeared at her side, his touch light upon her elbow. "Lady Jessa?"

"I'm fine." Jessa could see his concern, for he had slipped his mask down about his neck. "He was just a boy, really."

"Old enough to sell his sword, though."

"Let us finish this, Etienne, and go home," she responded and walked to her left. She lifted her skirt above her boots as she stepped about the bodies. She held to the steel that was forged in the halls of the Jade Palace and set her eyes upon the road before them. "Bring his head, if you would, please."

❖

Darry fell through the darkness and she kept falling.

Her thoughts this time were full of images, and though she tried, she could not grab hold and stop her fall. There were colors and heat, and voices too numerous to name or count. It was startling and overwhelming, and she felt as if she were drowning. Like the twisting of time she had experienced along her thread, it was just too much to comprehend so quickly.

She could feel the nothing beyond it all, and it called to her in a different voice. It spoke in a calming whisper that slowed her blood and made her heart sluggish. It made her fingers cold and her legs stiff. It held an influence that could not be denied, and Darry knew she was being hunted.

She tried to focus. *Remember your blood...Remember your blood...Blood...*

She stood strong and waited, knowing what was to come. She could see it, and though her instincts told her to move, it was her heart that told her to stay. The pain of the blow exploded through her mouth so intensely that she barely felt the stones of the floor. It moved like a living thing in her nose, and she felt it blossom behind her eyes. She pulled it inside, all of the pain. She let slide in her chest and swell as she looked up, tasting blood.

She saw the confusion. She saw the fear. She saw all of his strength laid low and crumble to the floor beside her.

Darry...Darry, please, I didn't...

The deep pain in her heart slipped free, and the whispers faded beneath it.

Darry swung over the ledge of the balcony and lowered her body into the air. She stopped at the touch upon her hand and looked up. The glorious sable eyes that met her own were filled with so many things, though mostly they held an invitation. She wasn't sure if it was the invitation she so desperately craved, but it was utterly sweet, nonetheless. She wondered if letting herself fall might be the better option.

If you fall, I will never forgive you.

Darry's heart gave a push, and her fingers tingled with sudden warmth.

She felt the familiar fingers caress her flesh and her body reacted, her blood surging. The heat of Jessa's body against hers was a paradise she had never dreamt might exist.

What do you want, Akasha*? Tell me. Tell me now.*

Darry's heart began to beat again, a fierce rush of blood breathing new life into the stillness.

She hid in the lush wilds of the Green Hills and curled her body beside Hinsa's for warmth. The fallen oak provided both shelter and safety, but Hinsa's body provided both, along with the certainty that she would always be loved. She felt Hinsa's head against her neck and face as she fell asleep, wondering if the purr that moved through her body had actually spoken.

Little one.

Her legs began to loosen, her muscles trembling.

She stood in the Great Hall of Blackstone Keep, her blood rushing with anticipation.

My name is Darrius.

Her legs stretched with strength as she felt the pull of her sword, waiting.

Chapter Twenty-seven

Jessa stood beneath the Veil of Shadows some twenty feet beyond the light of the first campfire, and studied the length of their camp and the surrounding terrain. She could see the wagons near the end of the caravan, and she opened her right hand, the words silent as they passed her lips.

She could feel the tension in each wagon as the heavy threads, tied and bound to each by Matty, strained in answer to her call. Her eyes surveyed the trees, knowing that her Boys were there.

She felt some fear, for they were outnumbered five to one, but it was not the fear of possible defeat. It was the fear of losing a friend. She understood in part, as their talk moved through the night and moments of laughter rose up and then fell away, what it was to lead a man to his possible death. It was not a comfortable feeling, but it was a burden that held weight in either direction. Darry loved her friends, and though she led, they followed. They gave her no say in the matter.

The men in Mason Jefs's command, beneath the lieutenant in charge, had run into the night when given the chance. She did not blame them, but it spoke to a lack of will. Darry's Boys would die for her lover, and Jessa knew that they would die for her, as well. It was not a matter of skill or the rush of combat, for she understood that. She had felt it in the Great Hall, just as she felt it now. It was a matter of love, and knowing what you would give your all for. For Darry's Boys, it was friendship, and she remembered how Bentley had stood over Tobe when he had fallen in the Great Hall, unwilling to leave his friend. He had chosen to make his stand right there, with his brother to the last.

She knew that the men before her would have such feelings, though to what extent, she didn't know. They fought for a man who inspired with the promise of glory and gold, and from what Bentley had told her, Mason Jefs usually delivered on his promises. They enjoyed the reputation of might and brutal strength. Martin Ibins, whose head sat in the dirt beside her, had spoken of family, but before he had died, he must have been aware of the difference.

None of it, however, changed the fact that much like the forward guard, these were men of Arravan. Some would have wives and lovers, some would have children. They all followed the same flag, and that flag belonged to the High King of Arravan. But these men had obeyed the Crown Prince. They were not here upon Owen's orders, but Malcolm's. This spoke to yet another break in the chain of command. *Allied to Malcolm*, Emmalyn had said, *no mercy will be shown.*

Emmalyn.

Jessa smiled beneath the darkness of her hood. An unexpected game was in play, and it changed things in a way she had not expected, nor had she even accounted for such a possibility. The possibility that no matter how difficult the fight, someone sought to make things right.

Jessa twisted at the waist and called forth her witchlight, tossing its energy against the ground behind her and letting it bounce. She stepped forth as the bright white light rose behind her and burst open in the darkness, its brilliance shining down the length of the narrow valley.

The chaos it caused was immense, and men shouted and scrambled for their weapons. The horses shied along their lines and pulled at the ropes that bound them. Jessa watched closely for their leader to reveal himself, and as the men began to form their ranks, one man walked down the center of the camp and beyond the others.

He held up his left hand in order to shield his eyes, his right upon the grip of his sword, though he had yet to pull it free. He was younger than Ibins was, and in better shape, and Jessa understood that due to his responsibility and rank, he was most likely one of their best fighters. She could not say much for his tactical expertise, however.

Jessa wrapped the runes about her voice and then sent it forth, her words amplified in the night. "I am Princess Jessa-Sirrah of Lyoness." Jessa's right hand went back and she pulled at the dirt beneath the head of Martin Ibins. It rose up in a swirl and moved with the push of earth, his head bouncing against the road and rolling to a stop several feet in front of their lieutenant. "I asked Martin Ibins what your orders were, and I did not like his answer. You were sent to retrieve me and bring me back to the Crown Prince of Arravan. This is something that will never happen."

Jessa walked forward. "You are all men of Arravan, a country I love. This is not your fight. Leave now and live! There is a war coming, and your country will need you. This is not where you should die, obeying the orders of a spoiled princeling, who is no equal to even the least among you. Save your swords for the war to come."

"We answer to Mason Jefs, Princess," the Lieutenant responded and lowered his hand as his eyes narrowed. "They're in the trees!" he shouted. "Grab her up!"

Jessa sent the runes through the night and they raced down the column as Malcolm's soldiers spread out, moving toward the trees on each side of the passage.

Two of the wagons at the rear of the caravan exploded in flames, splinters and chunks of flaming wood spraying outward as every man spun about, including their lieutenant.

Jessa's hood came up and the Veil of Shadows with it, the ball of witchlight behind her head spinning into the nearest campfire where it exploded in a fountain of flames. Jessa walked to the side of the road and reached out with both hands, grabbing the tension of the threads that still quivered, waiting for her command.

Arrows rained down from the trees, the guards nearest the edges falling first. The archers were next, and Jessa knew that her Boys raced along their chosen paths, changing their field of fire. The Hawk's Eye spell shook her, its power always unexpected, and she stumbled a bit to the side as she pulled, her arms swinging out behind her.

The wagons shot forward and crashed through the rear of the column, flames exploding anew as they jerked and rolled upon their wheels and rammed through the soldiers in their path. Their screams and shouts filled the night, and Jessa held several perspectives in her mind, watching as the doubletree braces snapped and the wagon tongues rammed the ground and broke apart, splinters flying as the wagons picked up speed.

She saw Etienne, Lucas, and Lucien sprint out of the trees and attack the column, their swords flashing in the light of the flames. She saw Matthias and Tobe move like ghosts through the center of the column, striking fast and then skirting free. Soldiers fell in their wake as they disappeared, arrows pelting the column. A small company of men rushed the bottom of the western rise, and they were cut down as they made their way, slowed by debris.

The horses broke free with their lines cut, and they bolted as Hinsa screamed, running through the long grass beside them. They thundered along the edge of the road, and she saw Matty, dressed in his clothes of earthen colors, as he drove them, low upon the back of a dun-colored mare.

It was complete chaos and the Lieutenant pushed through his men, shouting orders. A good portion of them had gathered at the eastern side of the road as the wagons hurtled through the last of the column. As they neared, Jessa flung her threads away, and the wagons rolled past her, tipping from the road and rolling to a stop in the dirt and long grass. Jessa spoke the Ashes of Earth, and the grass shriveled beneath the wagons and spread along the hillside, stealing its fuel from the flames.

Jessa walked back onto the road and faced them, their companies formed in four blocks, shields out as they faced the trees. Their lieutenant stood between them, roughly two companies upon each side. There were wounded men in the grass, and as Jessa's vision returned to her, she estimated that more than half their numbers were either dead or wounded, their horses gone and their supplies destroyed. The odor of burned flesh hung in the air and it was a vile smell.

Jessa dropped her hood back and stepped forth, letting the Veil of Shadows fall.

"You do not have to die!" she called out as she took a handful of fringe in each hand. "Leave this place and never return!" She had their attention, and in the sudden terrible calm, the lieutenant faced her, standing within the protection his men provided. She stood tall as she looked him in the eyes. "Even I would've known not to camp in such a narrow passage in unknown lands. You should die for that alone."

He pointed his sword at her. "We are in the middle of bloody nowhere, witch!"

"You are in the middle of somewhere now, though, aren't you," Jessa replied in a dry voice and flung her arms forward as she opened her hands.

The lieutenant was the first to fall, a dozen spikes of twisted black yarn, as solid as steel, passing through his body completely. Five other men cried out in pain and fell, their remaining comrades breaking formation.

Jessa clapped her hands and her witchlight swelled and then burst, deep blue as it raced outward. The boom that echoed from her hands was like a giant drum being struck, and it shook the earth as it passed through the soldiers. They were thrown to the ground as if hit by a wave from the sea, the witchlight echoing into the darkness.

Jessa felt a tremble of weakness in her thighs, but she stood where she was as the men before her stumbled to their feet. Her gaze moved past them, and she saw Darry's Boys ride along the destroyed column, their horses stepping high through the grass just beyond the bulk of the destruction. Etienne and Lucien appeared on her left, as did Jemin and Lucas to her right.

"Do I have your surrender?"

One man came forward half a step. "Yes, my Lady. You have it."

"Then leave this place now and never return," Jessa replied, and the soldiers before her stood still as they listened. "Go home. Go east. Seek your fortune elsewhere. Do not fight here again or you will die. Do not return to Lokey," she warned. "For though you have survived this night, your luck will surely fail if you return empty-handed. Clear the road and see to your dead. Take what supplies you may carry on foot and be gone from my lands."

Hinsa moved in a sleek manner about the back of Jessa's legs, and her sudden appearance caused every remaining soldier to back up. When Bentley's Bella snorted in protest and threw her head back, the soldiers closed ranks in a nervous manner. They had nowhere to run.

"For the crime of invading my lands with the sole purpose of killing my family and stealing me from my home..." Hinsa leaned forward and screamed, and there was blood upon her muzzle and down her neck. Even Jessa experienced a chill of fear at the sound. "I will give you three days to ask forgiveness of your gods, and to pray for speed. For if you are still upon my lands by then, my pet and her children will most surely find you."

Hinsa screamed again and prowled into the open space before them.

Etienne stepped forward. "Now would be a good time to start."

They sheathed their weapons and stumbled toward the western rise of land, the man who had voiced their surrender calling out orders.

"My Lady," Jemin said quietly and Jessa turned.

He held to the reins of Vhaelin Star, and the filly stood unaffected by the smoke and the stench of death, though her eyes looked fierce with reflected flames. Jessa stepped close, and Jemin leaned over with his hands cupped. She was surprised as she met his eyes.

"Children," he whispered, and then smiled. Jessa was lifted up and she swung her leg over as she dropped lightly onto the saddle. "Darry will like that."

Bentley maneuvered Bella backward, and the mare obeyed in a rather fancy manner before she sidestepped to the left behind Arkady and the others. Matty rode out of the darkness with their horses in tow, Jessa's party mounting with the jingle of tack and harness.

Bella came close and Jessa pulled the reins to the side. "Etienne, Lucien, you're with us," Bentley ordered. "Lando?"

Orlando came around as he pulled his mask down, his white-maned palomino skidding to a stop. "We'll see that they finish, Bentley, and we'll bring our wagon round." Lando's handsome face held a slight grin. "Looks like we'll have all the weapons and armor we'll ever need. Mason Jefs must pay very well."

"Bring everything that can be salvaged. If we can't find a use for it, than Lanark certainly will." Bentley looked to the right. "The horses, Matty?"

"The second rise over, just like you planned it," Matty answered. "They're bloody fine horses, too."

"Find Theroux and Sybok and drive them home. Be quick about it, too."

"Aye, Bentley...How'd I do?"

Bentley looked at the young man with true respect. "You did a man's job this night, Matty the Younger." Bentley's expression was filled with genuine affection. "If you were my own son, I could not be more proud."

Matty looked startled for a moment, and then he ducked his head as he turned his horse.

Bentley clicked his tongue, and Bella pushed Vhaelin Star down the road toward home. Etienne and Lucien fell in behind, and Jessa felt her exhaustion in an odd wash of relief, her shoulders easing. She layered her cloak over her legs as Hinsa ran ahead.

"Camp is about three miles to the south. We'll leave for home before the sun comes up."

Jessa said nothing as she tried to marshal her feelings. Her heart ached to be home within the hour, but her body was calling out for rest and her head was pounding. She would be no good to Darry without sleep, and she wasn't sure she could make the ride home without it.

"Are you all right?" Bentley asked as quietly as he could and still be heard.

"I threw a man's head in order to make a point that no one listened to," Jessa replied and recognized the tired, acerbic tone as Radha's. It seemed fitting. "Ask me tomorrow, perhaps."

Bentley smiled. "Yes, my Lady. I will do just that."

Chapter Twenty-eight

Darry recognized the softness of their bed beneath her body and she opened her eyes.

She heard the sounds of the fire in the hearth, and she could feel the morning light beyond the drapes that covered the windows. The sheets were smooth and the blankets were warm. She could feel the aches in her muscles and the tension in her shoulders, and she could feel the pain of her isolation from Hinsa. She could feel the absence of her lover against her side.

She felt weak, and hungry, and thirsty.

She turned her head.

The chair beside the bed was empty, and she forced herself to move, wincing as she pulled at the covers and sat up, dropping her legs over the side of the bed. She coughed and her head hurt beneath the force of it, stars floating away from her eyes.

The door opened and she looked up, as Lady Abagail backed into the room and then turned about smoothly. The dishes upon the tray she carried rattled as Abagail's shoulders jerked and she slid to a stop. "Jezara's *bloody* stockings!"

Darry smiled.

Lady Abagail stepped to the nearest table and set the tray atop several piles of books. She grabbed the cup of water and walked quickly to the bed, her eyes wide as she held it out. "Drink it, girl."

Darry's hand trembled as she took the cup, and then she drank, the cold water easing the terrible roughness of her throat. It filled her stomach with cold, and she felt some of the water slip past the edges of her lips and slide down her neck. When she had drained the cup she gave it back. "Thank you, Lady Abagail."

"Blessed be the goddess, sweet girl," the woman whispered, and her free hand touched Darry's cheek for just a moment. "Welcome back."

"Where is Lady Jessa?" Darry glanced toward the fire and the empty sitting room. "Where is my Hinsa?"

"On a bit of a…a bit of an errand, actually," Abagail answered, and her tone was odd. "They'll be back soon enough, don't you worry."

"I would very much like a bath, Lady Abagail," Darry said, and her voice felt odd in her throat. Her words echoed slightly at the back of her skull. "And some food, please."

"Aye," Abagail responded, still startled. "Bone broth with potatoes, I should think, and a bit of green. Nothing too much, so soon."

"That sounds brilliant."

Lady Abagail stared at her, still holding the empty cup.

"How long have I been sick?"

Abagail blinked as her senses caught up. "*Hiyah*, you've been asleep for going on six days now, girl. We weren't sure what would happen. Your Lady has not left your side, but for this one thing."

Darry was truly shocked by Abagail's words, and she turned a bit and looked back at her pillow. It had not been six days in the Loom, it had been…She had no idea what it had been in the Loom, but it had seemed like a day at most, perhaps. Tannen's words whispered through her thoughts. *It bends things. The light and the colors. Time…*

Darry closed her eyes and hung her head a bit. *Oh, Jess, my love, I'm so sorry.* Her insides twisted at the pain she had caused, for she understood how great Jessa's fear would be. "If you would draw me a bath, Lady Abagail, I'll be fine now. I'll have the food when I am done." She looked up. "Will that be all right?"

Lady Abagail smiled, and for a brief second, her eyes held an expression Darry recognized from her own mother. Abagail took a half step forward and touched her cheek again. "Aye, girl," she said in a gentle voice. "That sounds just about right. It's good to have you back. I've gotten used to you and that pretty cat of yours prowling around my kitchen."

Darry's throat was tight. "I'm very sorry for the worry I've caused."

Abagail wrinkled up her nose and then smiled. "Never apologize for a thing such as that. There's plenty of life left for making mistakes that need amends. Getting sick is never one of those things, it just is." Abagail stepped back. "I'll go and get things started. You get yourself right, and we'll have you all fixed up for when your Lady gets home. She'll have quite the lovely surprise."

"Thank you, Abagail."

Abagail nodded and then hurried to the door. When it was closed behind her, Darry heard her call out to Bette upon the other side, her voice filled with emotion as she went down the stairs.

Darry looked about the room again, her eyes sensitive to the light.

It appeared as if everything from Jessa's workroom had been moved into their bedroom, and though it seemed somewhat organized in its mayhem, Darry wasn't sure how Jessa could've been comfortable. Darry knew that Jessa liked her space when writing and taking notes, and between the books and medicines, and the endless piles of scrolls, she would've had no space at all. Darry wiped at her face and tried to remember all that had happened that night, but the last thing she truly recalled before she entered the Loom was reaching out for Sorrow. Anything that happened after that, in this time, in this place, was a blank.

She heard Tannen's certain voice in her head. *Release your majik, Darrius. All of it, every last drop you have in you, and let it rise to meet your Cha-Diah blood. Hold nothing back and embrace who you are...*

Darry wasn't sure how to do that, exactly, but as she sat there, she knew that she wanted it done. She wanted to live her life completely without the weight of so much heartache holding her back, and hounding her thoughts at every turn. She wanted to be well and whole, and the woman that Jessa needed. The woman that Jessa deserved. She wanted to be true to herself, just as Tannen had said. Anything less was a waste of precious life.

She closed her eyes and took a deep cleansing breath, and then... her heart opened wide in response to the furious need of her wish.

She let go of her fear for Hinsa, and the terrible need she had always felt for her father's love. She let go of the chains that held her prisoner, a constant captive to someone else's definition of duty. She let go of her obligation to her country, and the blood of her name that reached back to the Olden Men of the Taurus. The blood that flowed with the salt of the Sellen Sea and beyond, until the green lands of Arravan had called it home. She let go of her hatred for a brother who had turned from his own truth and embraced a lie, sweeping her up in the tide of his arrogance.

She let go of the pain and shame of her first love, and her fear of being less than she was expected to be. She let go of everything that had always held her back, all of it, until she found the child who had once gone searching. Searching for the heart of a maze, only to find, instead, the joy of being chosen over all others. The joy of being found after so many lifetimes lost.

Her majik answered her call, rising in a golden torrent of power and life.

Darry's head tipped back, and she cried out softly as it coursed through her veins, a force that was not altogether unknown to her, but new just the same. She felt the wind upon her face as she looked down from the top of the world, a speck of warmth surrounded by the cold, immovable weight of the endless mountains around her. And she felt the force and heat of her fire as it left her fingertips, smashing into the stone, breaking the bones of the world.

She felt the *Cha-Diah* majik then, separate and apart, the Dog Star gods rising up in Hinsa's blood, swirling and racing to meet her. Darry laughed, the magnificence of it all spilling over the constraints of her flesh in a furious, intimate mating of power.

She was standing when she opened her eyes, and she could see the runes pouring over her body, sliding down her arms and filling her hands with light. She could see the colors splashing to the floor and soaking her feet. She could see them at last, announcing the essence of her majik in a flow of power that was seemingly endless.

She felt it then, what Enoch had said.

We are a wild people inside, and in our hearts and in our blood, our majik remains untamed. It is the blood of the Dog Star gods. The Cha-Diah majik is very pure, and more powerful than all other majik.

Darry reached within her very soul, feeling the wildness of her heart. *Hinsa!*

She felt her call race into the distance, moving through the grass and catching a ride, sliding within the grip of the wind and riding it beneath the sun. It was not so very far, in the end, though it was far enough. Darry laughed as she followed the strength and warmth of their bond, chasing down her *Cha-Diah* mother.

She felt the pressure within her chest, and Enoch spoke again.

They must have their own very powerful majik if they are to survive the final bonding. For most of those not of the Fox blood, it came to pass that their hearts could not withstand so much power.

She could feel it, beneath the joy and wild freedom of it all. She could feel her flesh giving way to the combined power of her *Cha-Diah* blood, and her own ancient majik.

Darry looked to the bureau that stood against the wall beside the balcony doors, the memory she needed floating to the surface. She did not remember moving, but the uppermost drawer opened beneath her touch.

Upon the left, amidst the folds of a long blue silk scarf, Jessa's treasures were hidden. Darry's fingers barely brushed the silk, the material slipping about and opening more to her will than her touch. Her runes spilled like water into the drawer, searching.

Jade and sapphire, and heavy gold. Hair clips and earrings with jewels the size of cherries, and a chain of cut rubies that looked as if the gems had been pulled from the fires of the earth itself. Pearls, as black as tar, strung together on a delicate chain of white gold. A ransom in wealth and beauty, casually held in the folds of a scarf.

"Adal," Darry said aloud, and her voice was not entirely her own. It rose from the depths of her body, from the very heart of her blood, a smooth growl of love and power in a single word. She picked up the silver cuff and held it in her hand, remembering the feel of the glyphs when they were new and pronounced beneath Tannen's fingers. They were worn now, and faded in the silver light, but stronger than all else in the world, molded from a vein of pure Blue Vale silver. "Thank you, my mother."

Darry slipped the *Shou-ah* cuff about her left wrist.

She watched as it changed and moved, closing about her flesh in a soft swell of heat. Darry felt it in her arm at first, a burning that was not entirely unpleasant, and then it raced across her shoulders and spread throughout her chest. The pain in her heart began to ease, and then it spilled outward, Darry grabbing the bureau in order to keep her balance.

She went to her knees and trembled with the change in force, feeling it shift. The power she had held in the very center of her body flowed freely until it filled every part of her, from the tips of her fingers to the ends of her toes. The weight of her hair shifted about her face and shoulders, the few small braids that remained among the rest turning and unwinding of their own accord.

Darry closed her eyes and felt as she had within the Yellandale, utterly free and wild, and yet…she was more, for her own majik, which she had fought so hard to repress, was now at one with her Cha-Diah power.

Little one! We are coming!

Darry laughed and her tears fell instantly, the last of the untamed *Cha-Diah* runes slipping down her cheeks and soaking in the softness of her tunic as Hinsa spoke.

Darry tipped and sat upon the floor, leaning back against the bureau as she covered her face and wept, her tears rising from the most intimate depths of her heart. They could never repay her for the gift of her life. They could never thank her for finally giving Hinsa her voice. Never again would she know the loving kiss of Adal de Hinsa, nor the cold, soft nose of Pallay against the side of her neck. Never again would she look into another's eyes, so like her own, and see such complete understanding of who she truly was.

Jessa ran from the front courtyard, Master Kenna holding the reins of Vhaelin Star.

Hinsa had outpaced her, but she covered the front walkways and the cut grass as fast as she could. She took the front steps in a single leap onto the sweeping porch. She threw her cloak to the floor of the main entrance hall after struggling with her brooch, the material ripping as it came free from about her neck and shoulders. She grabbed the rail, pulling herself as she took the stairs two at a time. Her heart was pounding, and as she ran down the hall, she could feel it in her blood, the Vhaelin rising in answer.

She turned through the open door to their rooms, and her boots slid on the floor until she caught the chair beside the nearest table and her boots hit the rug, a stack of books spilling to the floor in a splash of leather, parchment, and pages.

Darry was on her right knee beside the hearth, holding Hinsa's face, her forehead bowed and resting against Hinsa's in a quiet manner. And then she lifted her face and stood up.

She had bathed and her hair was close to being dry, and though she was still in her bare feet, she wore a clean pair of trousers and a fresh white tunic, the sleeves rolled to her elbows. Hinsa walked about Darry's legs, and Jessa could hear the panther's purr, loud and filled with strength as she claimed her *Cha-Diah* child.

Hinsa moved with an easy push and bounded across the room, lifting her wide face as she neared. Jessa met the panther's eyes and held out her hand, Hinsa pushing her face against it. Jessa felt the roughness of Hinsa's tongue against her fingers, and then she was gone, moving in silence from the room.

Darry walked beneath the arch and into the bedroom as Jessa reached behind her and pushed the door. It swung upon its hinges, and though Jessa knew it was coming, her shoulders jerked when it banged in its frame.

Jessa wanted to say something, but when she opened her mouth, only a small push of sound came out.

"I'm so sorry, Jess," Darry whispered.

Jessa tried again to speak, but she felt its heat throughout her entire body, Darry's majik unbound as it reached across the room and wrapped around her in no uncertain terms. There were no stray runes, however, and her majik was not warping as it once did. There was no blood or pain or sickness—there was only Darry, as she was always meant to be, filled with power and majik, and the sweetness that was her love. Jessa's blood pushed with need as Darry bent her left arm back, and the light caught upon Radha's silver cuff, bright and natural against Darry's tanned skin.

"As it happens, this was actually meant for me."

Jessa let out a trembling breath and pushed away from the chair. She took but two steps before her knees caught oddly and then gave out.

Jessa blinked and lifted her gaze.

Darry's left arm was about her waist and held her close, Jessa startled but not unhappy by her change in circumstances. Darry's eyes were as bright as stars, and her right hand fairly burned against the side of Jessa's neck.

"Please say something, Jess," Darry whispered.

Jessa closed her eyes against the heat of Darry's breath and the scent of her majik. It had never been so pure, not even in the Yellandale. She opened her eyes. "Kiss me."

Darry's dimple pushed within her cheek as she smiled. She lowered her face slowly, and after an endless descent, Darry's mouth covered hers. Her lips were full and touched with warmth, her kiss tender as Jessa slipped her hand beneath the front of Darry's tunic, her fingers sliding over the muscles of Darry's stomach. When her hand closed upon Darry's right breast, Darry opened her mouth, her tongue finding Jessa's. Darry's hand slipped to the back of Jessa's neck and Darry pulled her closer. Jessa moaned and sucked at Darry's tongue for a moment before she opened her mouth farther, an invitation that Darry accepted.

She tasted like all the blessings of the Vhaelin, and Jessa savored the sounds of their joined mouths, her arousal pushing through her stomach and lighting deep between her legs. Her hand tightened upon Darry's breast and Darry gasped and pulled back from their kiss.

Jessa found her feet and pulled her hand from Darry's tunic, finding her will, as well. She pushed Darry's arm away, her hands grabbing Darry's shirt and pulling. The buttons slipped open and Jessa slid her hands upon her lover's flesh, feeling the heat, feeling her breathe, feeling the blood coursing beneath Darry's skin. She ran her hands upon the scars and trailed her fingers along Darry's ribs before she tipped forward.

Her forehead landed between Darry's breasts and she closed her eyes, her hands firm upon Darry's hips. Her tears came against her will and her shoulders trembled.

Darry touched her arms in a careful manner.

"Don't."

Her hands disappeared

"I can't believe you did that. Do not ever do"—Jessa swallowed and tried to control her voice—"anything else like it, not ever again, not *ever*."

"I won't. I promise, Jess."

Jessa's hands tightened upon the waist of Darry's trousers and pulled her close again. She lifted her face and Darry's eyes were filled with fire and all of the glorious emotions that Jessa feared she might never see again. "Six endless nights," Jessa told her. "You have *six* endless nights to make up for."

"Yes, my love." Darry's voice was a caress, and yet Jessa could hear the hunter in it.

"You must tell me what happened, if you can."

"I was—"

"Not *now*, please," Jessa said roughly. Her hands moved about Darry's waist and slid beneath her loose trousers. She felt the firm flesh of Darry's buttocks, letting her hands go where they wanted, and then she pulled free. Her arms went about Darry's neck, and she pushed onto her toes. "Later."

"Command me," Darry whispered. "Let me touch you."

"Tell me you love me."

"I love you, Jessa."

"Again."

"I *love* you," Darry repeated as her face brushed close. Her lips moved against Jessa's as she spoke. "I would die for you...It was the path I was meant to take."

"I know that now." Jessa licked her lips. "I believe you, and yet...by the Vhaelin, I am surprisingly angry with you. I would not have thought that."

"Forgive me, please. I didn't know what would happen, not like that."

Jessa kissed her, savoring the taste of her mouth until Darry pulled back with a low growl of sound and grabbed her, lifting her up. Jessa clung to her as Darry held her in her arms, her face close. Darry was still for several heartbeats, and then she took them deeper into their rooms. She sat down upon the divan and sank into the cushions, Jessa settling upon her lap as Darry leaned back.

Jessa turned her face against Darry's neck, her right hand sliding between Darry's breasts. "Say something, *Akasha*," she commanded.

"My whole life…there has never been anyone like me." Jessa could feel the soft vibration of Darry's voice against her cheek. "When I woke up from my fever, and I felt my connection to Hinsa, I knew it was majik. I could feel the changes in my body, and in my heart. I had no words for it…and I was afraid for Hinsa. I was afraid they would lock us away."

Jessa kissed Darry's neck, her right hand holding Darry's cheek.

"I had a dream of Tannen Ahru, the night of the birch tree grove. And she told me that if I did not take Sorrow's hand, I would lose everything, just as she did."

Jessa sat back from her slightly and Darry met her eyes.

"I didn't understand it then, what she meant, but then my blood called Sorrow, and he came for me…and so I took his hand." Darry's eyes were filled with sadness. "For I could not imagine nor even entertain the thought of living without you, of leaving you to walk alone in the world as Neela was forced to do. I thought, when I reached out, that I would rather die trying to be with you, than let it all slip away. I didn't know what would happen."

"Your majik has changed."

"I'm sorry for the pain my decision caused you, and to my brothers, as well," Darry offered up. Her voice seemed deeper somehow and it was lovely. "Can you—"

"I forgive you, my love, truly," Jessa whispered and smiled at the surprise in Darry's eyes. "What has happened to your majik?"

"I've released it," Darry answered. "I've always thought that my majik *was* Hinsa, though you have told me otherwise. But my own power, I had never freed it completely, not even when the Sahwello came, or in the Yellandale. It has been buried very deep inside, and I do not think that I was the one who put it there, although I can't really explain that feeling. Whatever the truth of that may have been, I have turned it loose once and for all, every drop. It has become one with my *Cha-Diah* blood."

"We shall have to do something about that," Jessa said in a quiet voice and then smiled. She could feel the unexpected blush on her face. "About what that change has done to you."

"What do you mean?" Darry's frown was quite lovely.

"Darry, my love, I do not know what power you had before, or what that has done to your power *now*, but…it is very…"

"It is very *what*?"

Jessa wanted the proper word, but she could only think of one. "Enticing."

Darry considered it. "Enticing?"

"*Akasha*, the scent of your power, the very essence of your majik, the taste of it, to another who has majik, it is…it is now very pure, very…" Jessa's hand slid along Darry's neck, her fingers light as they trailed upon Darry's skin. Jessa remembered Neela's passionate words. *They are the children of the gods.*

Darry frowned slightly. "Very…?"

"Seductive." Jessa felt it then, the subtle wave of Darry's majik as the backs of her fingers rubbed lightly over the hard, sweet flesh of Darry's nipple. "It has always been so, but now it is even *more* so."

Jessa shifted, and Darry lifted Jessa's legs as she turned in order to sit beside her. Jessa lifted her right leg and pulled at her boot, struggling for a moment before it freed her heel. She tossed it aside and then pulled at the other.

"I will apologize now for the dust of the road," Jessa said and took her socks off. She stood up and unbuttoned her shirt, shrugging her shoulders from the homespun and dropping it to the floor. She pulled off her tight homespun undershirt, her hair swishing to the side as she did so. When she turned to face her lover, she had unbuttoned her trousers and was pushing them down, taking her undergarment, too. She kicked from the last of her clothes and stepped without pause to the divan.

"*Jess.*"

Jessa straddled Darry's legs and pulled close, grabbing the back of the divan with both hands. She could hear it in the new depths of Darry's voice, an intimate purr of sound that went straight to the core of her being.

Jessa kissed her, her hands coming back and lifting the shirt from Darry's shoulders. Darry leaned forward and Jessa pushed the tunic down, her hands sliding along the strength of Darry's arms. The taste of Darry's tongue blossomed in Jessa's mouth and raced down her throat, the Vhaelin opening in the heart of her body.

She guided Darry's right hand, and Darry slid her fingers upon Jessa's sex, Jessa pulling back with a hiss of pleasure. Darry's eyes were dark with desire. "That is what it does to me." Jessa kissed her again, Darry's fingers stroking slowly.

Jessa grabbed the back of the divan again and pulled herself closer, opening her legs farther as her own hand reached between them. She leaned, and bit at Darry's jaw. "I am dripping with my need for you." She undid the buttons of Darry's trousers and slipped her fingers beneath them. "Let me in, *Akasha*."

Darry shifted against the back of the divan and spread her legs as much as she could, Jessa's fingers sliding upon her sex and parting her flesh. Jessa pressed her palm as her fingers stroked, Darry's sex distended in a wash of spirit.

Jessa's left hand grabbed the back of the divan as she rolled her hips tightly and her pelvis thrust, her mouth open as she kissed her lover. Darry's breath was quick and hard through her nose as her hips lifted.

Jessa licked at Darry's mouth and pressed her forehead against Darry's, feeling each tease and stroke of Darry's fingers, feeling her spirit slip free and her flesh open further beneath Darry's touch. "Do not *ever*…" she said in a strained, breathless voice. Darry pulled her closer with her left arm and Jessa cried out as Darry's fingers slipped into her flesh. "Leave me…" Jessa kissed her and bit at Darry's lip. "Again."

"Never," Darry replied. Her beautiful eyes closed and she let out a soft bark of sound, her expression filled with something infinitely deeper than pain.

"Yes, *Akasha*." Jessa groaned, losing her control. Her hips thrust faster as Darry's fingers went deeper. "Spend with me," she said and grabbed the back of Darry's neck with a fierce hand. Darry opened her mouth to her, and Jessa kissed her, breathing in her lover's breath, taking in the sounds Darry made. They fed her bliss, and she felt her flesh begin to rise, each quick stoke, each lift of her hips sending a shudder of pleasure through her. She squeezed her fingers about Darry's arousal and quickened her touch, unable to hold back any longer.

Her witchlight pushed through them both in an almost liquid red burst of power, expanding slowly.

Jessa felt her lover come, covering Darry's mouth as she cried out, Darry's flesh changing beneath Jessa's fingers as her spirit covered Jessa's hand. Jessa spent with her in waves of heat, her own majik reacting and sending a second pulse of witchlight into the room. Jessa pulled as close as she could, her legs seizing against Darry's hips and thighs as Darry moved with her. Jessa pulled at Darry's shoulders and cried out against her neck, shudders of satisfaction pushing along her sex until she couldn't breathe, and her muscles let go, exhausted and completely spent.

Jessa turned her face as Darry's fingers slid along her inner thigh, and then she was being moved, letting Darry do as she pleased.

The cushions of the divan welcomed her and she stretched out, feeling a rush of pleasure as she closed her legs and her sex clenched with a supple, sweet decadence, her right side sinking into the cushions. Darry gathered her close, Jessa held between the back of the divan and the warmth of her lover. The heat from the fire was blazing throughout the room, and she opened her mouth to Darry's kiss as her tears slipped free. She took hold of Darry's face, their spent pleasure a heady and provocative scent.

CHAPTER TWENTY-NINE

Jessa wrapped her legs about Darry's waist from behind as the steaming water sloshed in the tub. Darry leaned back against her body, and Jessa hooked her ankles beneath the water, holding her tight.

"I think I shall melt soon."

Jessa laughed happily and moved her hands along the strength of Darry's arms. "You do not like my spell?"

Darry chuckled. "It's very hot, my love."

Jessa clicked her tongue. "Do not be such a girl."

Darry laughed and turned her face to the side.

Jessa pushed aside Darry's wet curls and kissed her cheek. She whispered the runes and the water cooled slightly with a hiss of steam that rose into the air. "How is that?"

Darry dropped her head back. "Perfect."

Jessa let her hands rest upon Darry's chest, her fingers moving with a keen awareness over the scar tissue of Darry's wound. She understood that there was much to be said, but she had felt in Darry a strange and quiet grief that she knew must be honored. She had no idea what secrets the Great Loom had revealed to her lover, but she was certain that Darry needed time to process and understand what she had seen. Darry had stepped beyond the confines of all life and then returned to tell the tale.

Darry's hands moved upon her legs and Jessa savored the caress and kissed Darry's neck. "I love you."

Darry's arms tightened upon Jessa's thighs, and her body tensed with strength, her soldier's hands closing about Jessa's lower legs in a possessive manner. "I love you, as well, my sweet Jess...You should say what you're thinking."

"I just did."

Darry chuckled and Jessa smiled as the vibrations moved through her body.

"We cannot stay here now."

"I know," Jessa replied, and she could hear the regret in her tone. "I have placed wards along the pasturelands, and along the shores of the Lanark. We will not be caught unawares, should we be approached before we're ready."

"I'm sorry I wasn't there, Jess," Darry whispered. "I should've been."

Jessa slid her left hand in Darry's hair and pulled her head back, gently. The side of Darry's face was revealed to her and she had her attention. "You were fighting your own great battle, yes?"

"Yes."

"So do not *ever* apologize for that again," Jessa told her simply. "I did quite well, actually, and we are better off for the fight. We have everything we need, including some rather fine horseflesh, according to Matty."

Darry smiled. "I shall pick one out for you, so you may give Vhaelin Star a rest from time to time. When she is with foal, eventually, you will need a second mount."

Jessa's right hand massaged Darry's breast, and the loveliness of her flesh, combined with the hardness of her nipple, caused Jessa's sex to clench with desire. Her thighs tightened upon Darry's waist as her fingers played, and she wanted the nipple in her mouth. "*Shivasa*, my love. I need to either kiss you now"—Jessa pressed her mouth against Darry's ear and kissed it with wet lips—"or fuck you." When Darry smiled and closed her long legs, her right knee rising from the water as she tightened her thighs together, Jessa was extremely satisfied.

"If you start something, I shall finish it."

Jessa smiled at the threat. "I know. I am counting on it."

Jessa let out a squeal of surprise and her eyes went wide as Darry reacted instantly to her words, moving faster and with more strength than she would've thought possible. Her legs were unhooked and Darry spun tightly, water splashing through the tub as Jessa laughed, her head going back. Darry took her by the waist and she was lifted up. Her legs flowed about Darry's hips again and her arms slid about Darry's neck as she came down, opening Darry's mouth with a kiss and tasting as deeply as she could.

Darry's hands tightened upon her buttocks and pulled her as close as possible, squeezing and pulling at the flesh in a firm rhythm that Jessa knew all too well. Jessa thrust her hips as they kissed, Darry's sweetness and wild nature like a glass of Pentab Fire as it burned through her chest. She dropped her right hand in the water as her left fisted in her lover's hair.

Jessa slid from their kiss, her mouth pressing against Darry's cheek as she came beneath her own touch. She moaned in her throat as her body shuddered with pleasure, and then she laughed in a breathless, intimate manner. "By all that is holy," she whispered and opened her eyes. She kissed Darry's face as her body filled with a flowing warmth and quiet satisfaction. "You are the most desirable woman…" She brought her hand up and took hold of Darry's face. She leaned in and kissed her. "I love you." Darry's lips were full and lush from the attention, and Jessa felt most fine about that. "I love you." Darry's eyes were rich with feeling. "I love you."

Her hands moved along the strength of Darry's shoulders and arms as she pulled back, her heart beating heavy and quick as she surveyed what was hers.

Darry smiled. "That was…" Her left hand slipped to the back of Jessa's neck beneath her hair. Jessa's stomach flipped in a lovely manner at her intense expression. "That one, I shall keep for always," Darry promised. "For *always*, and for when I am missing you, and I close my eyes in the darkness."

"Well, I won't be letting you out of my sight anytime soon, *Akasha*."

Darry swallowed and her expression shifted in a strange wave of unease that Jessa felt in Darry's body. Her eyes were filled with an abundance of color that was beyond what Jessa usually saw, and Jessa caught her breath and held it.

"Within the Great Loom there is a horrible nothing, a dead and vile nothing beyond the threads. And it takes everything away from you." Darry sounded terribly vulnerable as she spoke. "*Everything.* You have no hope, and there is no warmth, and you have no memories. It is filled with *nothing*, this...this ugly *void* of nothing that bleeds into your body." Darry closed her eyes and Jessa swallowed upon a tight throat as the tears slipped from Darry's long lashes. "It is the coldest and most violent thing I have ever known."

Jessa's vision blurred as her own tears fell, her hand coming back up and holding Darry's cheek. She felt the smooth scars beneath her touch, the mark of the wolf slain for love.

Darry opened her eyes, her fingers gentle as she searched, and found a single braid in the depths of Jessa's hair. "But I remembered one thing. There was one thing that it couldn't take from me." Jessa lowered her arm as Darry leaned forward and lifted the braid. "Jasmine."

Jessa felt the tenderness held in a single word, and she swallowed down her emotions as she leaned forward and kissed Darry with gentle lips. She touched the wide silver cuff as she sat back again, feeling the runes. The bracelet looked more at home than it ever had, and it seemed to have been sized specifically for Darry's arm, though it did not restrict the movement of her hand in any way. "This was Tannen's?"

"No," Darry answered her. "It belonged to Adal de Hinsa, Tannen's mother."

Jessa looked in Darry's eyes for a time and then she smiled sweetly. "Hinsa?"

Darry grinned in a charming manner as the darkness of her memory, and the touch of the Great Loom, passed from her eyes and was replaced by warmth. "Yes."

Jessa's eyes skipped away and she frowned, her fingers moving over a discoloration in Darry's skin. Darry's left bicep was marked with white, almost pure in its presentation. "What is this, *Akasha?*" she asked quietly. "Up, please." Darry lifted her arm higher and Jessa turned it, the muscle firm and filled with power. "The pigment is gone," Jessa said in an odd tone, and she raised her gaze as she slid her fingers beneath Darry's arm. She closed her hand.

"Yes," Darry acknowledged.

Jessa's hand was smaller than the tattoo of white upon Darry's arm, but a handprint was exactly what it was. "Who did this to you?" Jessa demanded. Her heart was beating fast as she felt both fear and anger.

"Tannen Ahru. Once she took hold, she did not let go...for fear I would fall into the nothing beyond the Loom."

Hinsa groaned by the door, the lounging panther lifting her head from the floor and blinking toward the tub with narrowed eyes. Jessa was more startled than Darry, and she laughed, the tension of the moment broken and melting away.

Darry smiled. "She likes the smell of your hair, as well."

"Yes, well she has a...she has this way of..." Jessa blinked and then her eyes went wide. "You can hear her!"

"Yes."

Jessa's hands fell beneath the water and she took hold of Darry's, holding them tightly. "*Akasha*, this makes me happier than you can possibly know."

"She took care of you." Darry looked pleased. "She loves you."

"She saved my life." She could see that Darry understood at once what she spoke of, and it was enough.

"I know what I want, Jess."

"Tell me, *Akasha*."

"I would return to Blackstone." Darry's voice held absolute certainty. "I think you were right about Emmalyn's message, and the book. Emmalyn will need a champion, and I owe her that for love alone, much less her generosity, and her help with our escape. I would have Bentley's name cleared, so he may walk in the sun with pride and keep his family's name." Darry's grin appeared briefly. "And so he may woo my lovely cousin from her intended husband, as he so desperately wants, before it's too late."

Darry let go of Jessa's hands and grabbed the edges of the tub. She stood up carefully and stepped over the side, finding the rug. Jessa followed in a push of water, and Darry took her by the waist and lifted her to the floor beside her.

"I want Etienne freed of all suspicion. And I would have you meet my brother, Wyatt."

"The King's Champion," Jessa said with a smile.

"I will have justice, and we will not be driven down a road we did not choose for ourselves." Darry's eyes had darkened and her tone was almost violent.

Jessa's thumb smoothed at the crease upon Darry's brow. "*Shhhhh*…hush, my love. It will be all right. We will make it so."

Darry's eyes slowly softened and Jessa was satisfied.

"You shall have these things you want," Jessa said in promise. "I would not have us run either, nor leave the home we have made in any sort of danger." She smiled with love, hoping to turn the mood. "And if you would like, I shall even let you pick out my dress for dinner, which we are about to be late for."

Darry ginned at her unexpected words, her expression changing completely. "Really?"

Darry listened to the laughter that moved around the table and took a drink of cool ale from her tankard. It tasted good, and though she was on her third mug, she was sober and well aware of the tale she had just been told, as were they all. The Battle of Ballentrae Road.

That she had not been there for Jessa and her brothers caused her a grief she would always carry, but no one had been injured, and it had been a stunning victory. She sat beside Jessa at the head of the table, and Jessa had pulled their chairs as close as they could be. She had felt Jessa's touch in some way almost constantly since her return, and she was glad for it.

Jessa leaned toward her, a slight blush in her cheeks as Darry drank. "I may have left out a few details, I apologize."

Darry swallowed awkwardly and set her drink down, wiping at her lips. "A *few*?"

Jessa gave her a sweet smile and turned back to the table.

Darry cleared her throat and then stood up, her chair pushing back with a scrape of sound. Someone let out a high-pitched whistle and there was more laughter. It was followed by clapping and Darry held her hands up. "Leave off!" she called out and then laughed.

Jessa's left hand slid about the back of her thigh and between her legs slightly, and Darry met Jessa's gaze, startled but smiling at the utter breach of etiquette. Jessa's expression was filled with a playfulness she usually didn't show in front of others, and it made Darry's heart skip. Jessa grinned in a somewhat wicked manner as she looked away, though she did not remove her hand.

"Quiet, please," Jessa said in her normal voice.

The unruly noise in the dining hall died away rather quickly, and Darry cleared her throat instead of laughing. "Well, yes, now that I've lost complete command over everything," she said in a dry voice, "I have a few things to say."

"Do we need more wine for this?" Bentley asked.

Jessa laughed with their chosen family and it made Darry extremely happy. Her right hand played upon the glyphs of her *Shou-ah* cuff, and though the runes were no longer pronounced, for a moment they felt as if they were.

"Please," she said in an almost whisper and sidestepped her grief as best she could.

Silence and complete attention were given in response.

"We have decisions to make, and though I would not spoil the fun, now that I have you all in one place, and reasonably sober…and I am not unconscious"—there was quiet laughter—"I would like to ask your thoughts on what our future should hold."

She cleared her throat, remembering Adal's words. "A wise woman told me, not so very long ago…" Darry frowned at that and looked down. She swallowed, and tipped her head to the side as she realized she could not count the years between then and now, for they were stacked one upon the other until they could not even be numbered. She closed her eyes against it and she felt Jessa's hand move upon her leg.

She looked up. "It does not matter when she said it, I suppose." Darry ducked her face again, searching. Jessa's eyes were bright with love and Darry turned back to the table. "She said that you must fight for what is yours. If you do not fight for what is yours, it will be taken from you, or you will be driven away from what you love by the will of others. And this is what happened to us, in a way. We made our retreat, for many reasons, though mostly for my life. And there are no words that will properly express my thanks to you, for such a stunning sacrifice."

"It was no sacrifice, Darry," Lucien said reasonably.

"Perhaps in some ways, no," Darry agreed. "But the fact remains that we were driven from our home, no matter our circumstances now. And though Lanark has become a home unlike any we've ever had before, and in my heart, it will always be so, nonetheless, we were driven from our lives by another man's crimes. By murder, treachery, and treason. And with this latest attack upon our lives and freedom, we would be driven yet again by the will of another."

Darry reached within her black jacket and pulled out a piece of folded parchment, holding up Emmalyn's last message. "Though as I have just learned, perhaps our fate should be something else entirely." She looked at Bentley and his eyes were bright and filled with hope. "I have learned that the Princess Emmalyn means to overthrow Malcolm for the right to follow the High King and sit upon the Blackwood Throne when the time comes."

She waited for someone to speak, but though there was surprise, no one did.

"I know my sister well," Darry said with a grin. "And she would not make such a move without evidence of Malcolm's guilt. And she would not reveal this to us, unless she was bloody well close upon his heels. I also know that she might have asked for me to return, and she has not done so."

"Why not?" Matty asked, and Lucien reached to his left and set his hand upon the boy's shoulder, giving him a smile.

"Because she would rather make this right than ask any one of us to sacrifice more than we already have."

"So what are you asking us, Darry?" Matthias spoke from the opposite end of the table.

"I would like to return to Blackstone. I would serve as Emmalyn's champion if it is needed. I would not see Royce put in any danger. My sister has already lost one man she loved, and I would not see it happen a second time. Royce is a damn fine swordsman, but I am thinking that Malcolm's champion is better."

"Mason Jefs," Arkady said in a dark tone.

"And though my relationship with my family is, well, not exactly…"

"Smooth?" Bentley suggested, and grinned beneath his mustache.

"Thank you, Bentley. Always a good man in a pinch." There were smiles at that and Darry was glad for it. "We all love Arravan. We fought side by side, every one of us in some way, in the Siege of the Great Hall. We would have given our all if necessary. Honor"—they raised their voices with her—"is our standard. Life is short. The rules are simple."

Darry nodded with pride, and she could feel the heat in her face yet again. "I would return to Blackstone with my brothers by my side and see justice served upon the guilty." She found Etienne's face and held his eyes, and then she turned to her dearest friend. "I would see Bentley and Etienne cleared, and their good names and honor restored. I would see Bentley marry my cousin, if he can convince her of such." Cheers went up as Bentley blushed in surprise, and the dishes shook as fists hit the table.

Darry raised her voice above the din. "I would see justice done, and then *choose* the road ahead, with clear eyes and nothing behind us!"

Chairs were shoved back and Darry's Boys rose to their feet. Jessa stood as they did, and she took hold of Darry's hand in a fierce grip with both hands.

In the sudden silence, Darry smiled and stabbed at the heart of it all. "What say you, my beloved brothers? Shall we see Bentley Greeves properly wed by Solstice Eve?"

Jessa laughed as Bentley stepped back with panicked eyes, Jemin McNeely pushing down the length of the long table. Jemin grabbed Bentley's arm before he could retreat farther and he pulled, bending at the waist. Bentley was hoisted over Jemin's massive shoulder, laughing as Jemin stood up straight.

"Aye, Cap'n." Jemin smiled. "If I have to carry him there myself."

Jessa let go of Darry's hand and moved about the corner of the table amidst the laughter and shouting. Jemin turned and Bentley pushed against Jemin's broad and well-muscled back, his face red as he raised it. Jessa slid close and took his face between her hands, kissing him beside the mouth.

Another cheer went up and the table shook as a plate crashed to the floor.

Darry moved her chair back again and stepped free of the table, grabbing up her sword belt from where it hung upon the back of her chair. Jessa's eyes lit up at the sight of it, and she rushed back, sliding on the floor again until Darry caught her in the circle of her right arm.

"Yes, *Akasha*, now," Jessa said happily.

Darry thought for a heartbeat that she just might die at the joy she saw in Jessa's eyes, and she could think of no better way to go. She leaned down and kissed her, Jessa holding Darry's face and tasting of her tongue.

Darry stepped away from her lover and held Zephyr Wind high above her head, the scabbard familiar in her hand, the light catching upon her *Shou-ah* cuff, gifted to her by the last *Loquio* of the Fox People. Hinsa wound about her legs, and Darry glanced down with a smile. It took a few seconds, but the riot of noise settled into silence, Jemin dropping Bentley to his feet and hugging him before they both turned.

All eyes were upon her.

"There is an old custom which fell out of favor many years ago," Darry said in a strong, steady voice for all to hear. "For the Bloods of Arravan prickled at what it meant for them, and so talked it down through the years until it was no longer practiced. But that which falls out of favor is not outlawed unless it is stricken from the laws of the land. This custom is still written, and so it is still binding by law should any challenge it. It was called the Rite of a Noble Man, and it shall be called so again this night.

"I am Darrius Lauranna Durand," she told them, looking them each in the eyes. "And on this night, I will see you made Lords of Arravan." Darry's chest filled with pride and love at what she saw in their startled expressions. "I have no rank, and I have no title, so I cannot confer upon you that which should already be yours." Darry met Jessa's eyes and lowered her sword. She tipped the scabbard and rested it upon her right arm, its swirling Blue Vale grip an offer to her lover. "But our Lady Jessa-Sirrah, Princess of Lyoness and Priestess of the Vhaelin, has all royal rights and privileges to bestow upon you what you have already earned a thousand times over."

Jessa stared at her in surprise

"Take it, my sweet Jess," Darry said with love. "Custom says that the first you choose shall then be the First Lord among those who are yours."

"*Akasha*," Jessa said, and her heart filled with a rush of love at Darry's choice of words. She wrapped her right hand about the grip of Zephyr Wind, and she felt its ancient power. It slid from its black leather scabbard with a sleek sound, and its deadly tip came free with a *ping* that rang throughout the silent hall.

Jessa looked at the beauty of the blade she held, and then she lifted her sable eyes. "I choose *you*, Darrius Lauranna Durand."

Darry leaned back a bit, as startled as the others had been but moments before.

The dishes upon the table rattled softly, and within a few seconds, the quiet steady beat of sound began to grow. Jessa watched as they rapped their fists against the table, together as one. The beat became louder, and Jessa's heart beat fast and strong in rhythm with their approval.

Darry turned from the room and Jessa saw her lover's wild, generous soul in the green and blue of her eyes. Green for the forests of old, and the mysteries of the ancient and dark Abatmarle that gave birth to the Fox People, and the lost *Cha-Diah* majik that was the very beat of Darry's heart. Blue for the sea, and the wayfaring kings that had sailed it, before they had made Arravan their home, passing their valiant, adventurous blood down through the ages until it ran in the veins of the woman she loved.

Jessa smiled at her, more than pleased that she could actually return the same precious gift that Darry had once given to her. "I choose you, *Akasha*, over all others, always. You shall *always* be my first. Bend a knee, my love, if you would, please."

Darry's hair fell forward as she bowed her head and dropped to her right knee.

Jessa faced her and lowered Zephyr Wind, the flat of Tannen Ahru's sword sitting upon Darry's right shoulder. Jessa swallowed her sudden emotion, though she could hear it in her voice. "I name you my Lady Darrius Lauranna Durand, Princess Consort and First Lord to those who would serve me." Jessa lifted the sword over Darry's head and dropped it upon her left shoulder. "Warrior of the Fox People, and my chosen champion."

Zephyr Wind rose again and tapped Darry's right shoulder before Jessa pulled the sword back, the edge of the blade brushing against a rich golden curl.

Darry touched at the weight of her hair with a quick hand and stood with a smooth, easy push of strength. She took Jessa in her arms, and Jessa's heart leaped at the touch upon her lips. The kiss was hot and sweet, and not the least bit tame.

Darry released her and Jessa caught at her breath as her lover stepped back, placing a heavy lock of hair in the palm of her left hand. "For you, sweet Jess."

It was as soft as a midnight caress, and Jessa closed her hand tightly as she pulled it to her chest. "Bloody hell, *Akasha*," she groaned. "Not the *hair*!"

Darry laughed happily and pulled her close again amidst the laughter and shouting that filled the hall with warmth and joy.

Jessa grinned, feeling a tad wicked in the best sort of way—she couldn't help it. "It's mine now," she declared as her eyes moved in a greedy manner over her lover's mouth, Darry's lips wet and full as she smiled down at her. Hinsa trailed about the back of Jessa's legs until she had circled them both.

Darry's eyes were filled with emotion, and for just an instant, Jessa thought she could see the stars within them, and the constellations as they spun back through time.

CHARACTERS

The House of Durand

Owen Marcus Durand: High King of Arravan. Second son of Niklaus Durand and the Lady Marget of House Winnows. Inherited the throne upon the death of his elder brother *Malcolm*, who was slain in the Sunn Wars (the Lowland War), and left no heir.

His wife, *Cecelia Karina*, High Queen of Arravan. Formerly of House Lewellyn.

Their son, *Malcolm Edmund*, Crown Prince of Arravan. Prince of Ishlere and Duke of Treemont. Liege Lord of Kenton and Barrister to the High Court, and second to the High King in Council

Their daughter, *Emmalyn Jillaine Marget*, Princess of Arravan. Widow of *Evan Kilcullen*, killed in a riding accident. Betrothed to *Royce Greyson*.

Their son, *Jacob Cullidan*, Prince of Arravan. The Prince of Spies and the Bookworm Prince. King's Councillor and Scholar. Liege Lord of Hockley. His wife, *Alisha May*, of House Pfinster.

Their son, *Wyatt Alban*, Prince of Arravan. Major in the King's Army, Commander of the King's Seventh. Liege Lord of Yellow Rock.

Their daughter, *Jacey Rose*, Princess of Arravan. *Deceased. Died at age four.*

Their daughter, *Darrius Lauranna*, Princess of Arravan. The Golden Panther. Captain in the Kingsmen (Renounced Title and Rank). *Cha-Diah*, daughter to the golden panther, *Hinsa.*

DARRY'S BOYS, AND THE LANARK RIVER ESTATE

Bentley Greeves: Blooded Lord; former Kingsman, First Lieutenant. A seventh son of *Lord Treemont Greeves.*

Arkady Winnows: Bastard son of *General Winnows*; former Kingsman, First Lieutenant.

Etienne Blue: Orphan; former Kingsman.

Orlando Davignon: Bastard son of *Lady Jenna Belknip*; former Kingsman.

Lucas Kilkenny: Bastard son of *Lady Sarah Whetston*; former Kingsman.

Jemin McNeely: Orphan of Artanis; former Kingsman. (Sister: *Marlee*)

Lucien Martins: Bastard son of *General Nasha*; former Kingsman.

Tobe Giovanni: Blooded Lord; former Kingsman. A fifth son of *Lord Eaman Giovanni.*

Sybok of the Great Salt: Orphan, washed ashore in Alirra Bay. Found among the remains of the *Lady's Skirt*, a ghost ship spice trader from Wei-Jinn. Youngest of Darry's Boys.

Theroux Cain: Bastard son of *Lord Harper*; former Kingsman.

Matthias Brave: Bastard son of *Lady Tenley Crane*, died in childbirth; former Kingsman.

Matty the Younger: Orphaned son of *Lady Jana Bee*, died in childbirth, given over to the Orphanage in Lokey by his grandfather. Father deceased. Former Kingsman.

Ramon Kenna: Seneschal of the Lanark River Estate. Widower.

Lady Abagail Rourke: Head Cook and Mistress of the Lanark Estate. Widowed.

Bette Kenna: Cook and Lady's Maid of Lanark. Daughter to *Ramon Kenna*.

THE HOUSE OF LEWELLYN

Cullidan Bryce Lewellyn: Lord of the Seven Spears and the Ring of Stone Towers, Lord of Dunbrale, A Lord upon King Niklaus Durand's Council. Family lands held east of the Taurus Mountains to the Escalade River, and west to the Ibaris Plains. Father to the High Queen Cecelia Durand.

His wife, *Jacey Jillaine*, formerly of House Blaylock. *Deceased.*

Their son, *Jacob Cullidan*, lost within the Abatmarle Forest. *Deceased.*

Their son, *Sullidan (Sully) Duncan*, heir to Dunbrale. Acting Lord of the Seven Spears and the Ring of Stone Towers. His wife, *Miriam Miri*, formerly of House McGorhess. Their son, *Thaddeus Culliden*, heir to Dunbrale. *Deceased. Died at age seventeen.* Their daughter, *Nina Lyall*. Betrothed to *Hammond Marsh*. Their daughter, *Melinda Mary*. Their daughter, *Wilhelmina Ash*. Their son, *Brecken James*, heir to Dunbrale. Their son, *Aiden (Pip) Jace*.

Their daughter, *Cecelia Karina*, High Queen of Arravan.

Their daughter, *Tearsa Murdina. Deceased. Died at age twenty.*

THE HOUSE OF BHARJAH

Abdul-Majid de Bharjah: King of Lyoness and Lord of the Dark Ridge Mountains. Monarch of the Black Sands and Butcher of the Plains. The Jade King. Assassinated by Lord Almahdi de Ghalib while in Council. *Deceased.*

His son, *Sylban-Tenna*. Current King of Lyoness.

His son, *Lybinus*, Prince of Lyoness. *Deceased.*

His son, *Qasim*, Prince of Lyoness. Potentate of the Dark Ridge Mountains.

His son, *Malik-Assad*, Prince of Lyoness. Champion of Lyoness.

His son, *Rashid-Warith*, Prince of Lyoness.

His son, *Rasul-Rafiq*, Prince of Lyoness. Commander of the Southern Armies.

His son, *Abdul-Azim*, Prince of Lyoness.

His son, *Trey-Jak Joaquin*, Prince of Lyoness. *Deceased.*

His son, *Kartus-Leh*, Prince of Lyoness.

His daughter, *Jessa-Sirrah*, Princess of Lyoness. The Nightshade Lark, and the Woman Within the Shadows. Priestess of the Vhaelin.

His son, *Kaliq Khaliq*, Prince of Lyoness.

His son, *Ali-Naz*, Prince of Lyoness.

Jhannina de Cassey LaMarc de Bharjah: Shaman and Prophet of the Vhaelin Gods. Daughter to *Radha* and mother of *Jessa-Sirrah*. She of the Sunlit Voice. Stolen from the Plains by *King Bharjah* and made his wife. *Deceased*.

Serabee El-Khan: Lord and High Priest of the Fakir. Slayer of the Stag, and Lord of the Lost Sword. First Councillor and confidant to King *Abdul-Majid de Bharjah*.

THE RED-TAIL CLAN, PLAINSMEN OF THE IBARRIS

Lady Radha de Cassey LaMarc: High Priestess of the Vhaelin. Red-Tail Clan of the Ibarris Plains. Slayer of Secrets, and Mistress of the Black Shawl. Grandmother of *Jessa-Sirrah* and mother to *Jhannina*.

Luka Menden: Leader of the Red-Tail Clan, People of the Plains. Lord of the Long Grass.

Mesa: War Chief of the Red-Tail Clan, People of the Plains

Durasha: Warrior of the Red-Tail Clan, People of the Plains

Enders: Warrior of the Red-Tail Clan, People of the Plains

Alain: Warrior of the Red-Tail Clan, People of the Plains

Tannen Ahru: Ancient War Chief of the Red-Tail Clan. Last known survivor of the Sacred Mountain Massacre. God's Blood Child, and Ghost Rider of the Seven Hills. *Loquio* of the Wind, and warrior of the Fox People. Chosen champion of *Neela Jhannina de Hahvay*. *Cha-Diah*, daughter to the speckled lynx, Hashiki. *Deceased*.

Adal de Hinsa: Ancient Leader (*Loquio*) of the Fox People, or the *Cha-Diah* Tribe. Mother of *Tannen Ahru*. *Cha-Diah*, daughter to the red wolf, Pallay. *Deceased.*

Jace Ahru: Ancient War Chief of the Fox People. The Yellow Haired Knife. Father of Tannen Ahru. *Cha-Diah*, son of the great sandcat, Letty. *Deceased.*

Enoch: Ancient Shaman and Holy Man of the Fox People. Teacher, spiritual leader and Keeper of the History of the People. Sorcerer, and *Cha-Diah* child.

Neela Jhannina de Hahvay: Ancient Vhaelin High Priestess, and Shaman of the Red-Tail Clan. Bringer of the Dark, and the Song Reaver. Direct ancestor to *Radha*, *Jhannina*, and *Jessa-Sirrah*. Taken by the Vhaelin amidst the Blood Fires Ritual. *Deceased.*

The House of Salish

Duncan Salish: Lord of the Kastamon Valley and the Southern Taurus Range. Eldest son of Lord *Winston Salish*, the former Lord of Kastamon Valley. Known for the Kastamon gold mine, named after the matriarch of the Salish family, *Jules Ama*.

His wife, *Deidre Lea*, formerly of House Yarlen.

Their son, *Verl Aman*, heir to the House of Salish.

Their son, *Nigel Merrin*.

Marteen Salish: *Duncan*'s brother, and Prince *Malcolm*'s First Councillor. *Deceased.*

Melora Salish: *Duncan*'s sister, and the Lady of House Salish in the city of Lokey. Salish family representative at the Royal Court. Banished from Court by the High Queen. Her husband, Lord

Jameson Carls Hardt of the House of Hardt. Their daughter, *Kella Ama*.

Anton Salish: *Duncan*'s youngest brother. His wife, *Garwin Jane*, formerly of House Temple.

The House of Greyson

Armistad Greyson: Blooded Lord, first son of the Greyson line. Abdicated from the Greyson line in favor of his younger brother. Sworn man to the High King, and Owen Durand's First Councillor and member of the King's Council.

Davis Greyson: Lord of Hollow Sun, the Greyson lands. Second son, inherited family lands upon the abdication of his elder brother.

Royce Greyson: Blooded Lord and third son of the Greyson line. Betrothed to Princess *Emmalyn Durand*.

Kingsmen, Soldiers, and Blackstone Residents

Grissom Longshanks: Commander of the Kingsmen, General in the King's Army.

Kingston Sol: Captain under command of Longshanks, Kingsman.

Captain Dalaidus: Captain of the City Guard.

Landon Runners: Lieutenant, officer of the King's Seventh.

Danvers (Danny) Giovanni: Lieutenant, officer of the King's Seventh.

Toliver Martis: Lieutenant, officer of the King's Seventh.

Dougal Lewellyn: Master Sergeant, the King's Seventh. Right-hand man to Wyatt Durand.

Abel Jefs: Captain of the Palace Guard, under command of Longshanks. Heir to *Lord Fenton Jefs*. Current First Councillor to the Crown Prince Malcolm Durand.

Mason Jefs: Commander of Fenton's Brigades, hired soldiers and sellswords loyal to Lord Fenton Jefs. Former Kingsman, and current Solstice Champion.

Margery Jaspers: the High Queen's Lady.

Tessa Winjers: Head Cook of Blackstone Keep.

Thomas Silvan: Seneschal of Blackstone Keep.

SERVANTS OF THE GODS

Master Haba Una: The High Priest of Gamar, Lokey Temple.

Master Kaleb Leeds: A Priest of Gamar, Lokey Temple.

Mistress Clare Bellaq: The High Priestess of Jezara, Artanis Temple.

About the Author

Shea Godfrey is an artist and writer working and living in the Midwest. While her education is in journalism and photography, she has spent most of her career in 3-D animation and design.

Books Available from Bold Strokes Books

A Bird of Sorrow by Shea Godfrey. As Darrius and her lover, Princess Jessa, gather their strength for the coming war, a mysterious spell will reveal the truth of an ancient love. (978-1-63555-009-2)

All the Worlds Between Us by Morgan Lee Miller. High school senior Quinn Hughes discovers that a broken friendship is actually a door propped open for an unexpected romance. (978-1-63555-457-1)

An Intimate Deception by CJ Birch. Flynn County Sheriff Elle Ashley has spent her adult life atoning for her wild youth, but when she finds her ex, Jessie, murdered two weeks before the small town's biggest social event, she comes face-to-face with her past and all her well-kept secrets. (978-1-63555-417-5)

Cash and the Sorority Girl by Ashley Bartlett. Cash Braddock doesn't want to deal with morality, drugs, or people. Unfortunately, she's going to have to. (978-1-63555-310-9)

Counting for Thunder by Phillip Irwin Cooper. A struggling actor returns to the Deep South to manage a family crisis, finds love, and ultimately his own voice as his mother is regaining hers for possibly the last time. (978-1-63555-450-2)

Falling by Kris Bryant. Falling in love isn't part of the plan, but will Shaylie Beck put her heart first and stick around, or tell the damaging truth? (978-1-63555-373-4)

Secrets in a Small Town by Nicole Stiling. Deputy Chief Mackenzie Blake has one mission: find the person harassing Savannah Castillo and her daughter before they cause real harm. (978-1-63555-436-6)

Stormy Seas by Ali Vali. The high-octane follow-up to the best-selling action-romance, *Blue Skies*. (978-1-63555-299-7)

The Road to Madison by Elle Spencer. Can two women who fell in love as girls overcome the hurt caused by the father who tore them apart? (978-1-63555-421-2)

Dangerous Curves by Larkin Rose. When love waits at the finish line, dangerous curves are a risk worth taking. (978-1-63555-353-6)

Love to the Rescue by Radclyffe. Can two people who share a past really be strangers? (978-1-62639-973-0)

Love's Portrait by Anna Larner. When museum curator Molly Goode and benefactor Georgina Wright uncover a portrait's secret, public and private truths are exposed, and their deepening love hangs in the balance. (978-1-63555-057-3)

Model Behavior by MJ Williamz. Can one woman's instability shatter a new couple's dreams of happiness? (978-1-63555-379-6)

Pretending in Paradise by M. Ullrich. When travelwisdom.com assigns PR specialist Caroline Beckett and travel blogger Emma Morgan to cover a hot new couples retreat, they're forced to fake a relationship to secure a reservation. (978-1-63555-399-4)

Recipe for Love by Aurora Rey. Hannah Little doesn't have much use for fancy chefs or fancy restaurants, but when New York City chef Drew Davis comes to town, their attraction just might be a recipe for love. (978-1-63555-367-3)

Survivor's Guilt and Other Stories by Greg Herren. Award-winning author Greg Herren's short stories are finally pulled together into a single collection, including the Macavity Award nominated title story and the first-ever Chanse MacLeod short story. (978-1-63555-413-7)

The House by Eden Darry. After a vicious assault, Sadie, Fin, and their family retreat to a house they think is the perfect place to start over, until they realize not all is as it seems. (978-1-63555-395-6)

Uninvited by Jane C. Esther. When Aerin McLeary's body becomes host for an alien intent on invading Earth, she must work with researcher Olivia Ando to uncover the truth and save humankind. (978-1-63555-282-9)

Comrade Cowgirl by Yolanda Wallace. When cattle rancher Laramie Bowman accepts a lucrative job offer far from home, will her heart end up getting lost in translation? (978-1-63555-375-8)

Double Vision by Ellie Hart. When her cell phone rings, Giselle Cutler answers it—and finds herself speaking to a dead woman. (978-1-63555-385-7)

Inheritors of Chaos by Barbara Ann Wright. As factions splinter and reunite, will anyone survive the final showdown between gods and mortals on an alien world? (978-1-63555-294-2)

Love on Lavender Lane by Karis Walsh. Accompanied by the buzz of honeybees and the scent of lavender, Paige and Kassidy must find a way to compromise on their approach to business if they want to save Lavender Lane Farm—and find a way to make room for love along the way. (978-1-63555-286-7)

Spinning Tales by Brey Willows. When the fairy tale begins to unravel and villains are on the loose, will Maggie and Kody be able to spin a new tale? (978-1-63555-314-7)

The Do-Over by Georgia Beers. Bella Hunt has made a good life for herself and put the past behind her. But when the bane of her high school existence shows up for Bella's class on conflict resolution, the last thing they expect is to fall in love. (978-1-63555-393-2)

What Happens When by Samantha Boyette. For Molly Kennan, senior year is already an epic disaster, and falling for mysterious waitress Zia is about to make life a whole lot worse. (978-1-63555-408-3)

Wooing the Farmer by Jenny Frame. When fiercely independent modern socialite Penelope Huntingdon-Stewart and traditional country farmer Sam McQuade meet, trusting their hearts is harder than it looks. (978-1-63555-381-9)

A Chapter on Love by Laney Webber. When Jannika and Lee reunite, their instant connection feels like a gift, but neither is ready for a second chance at love. Will they finally get on the same page when it comes to love? (978-1-63555-366-6)

Drawing Down the Mist by Sheri Lewis Wohl. Everyone thinks Grand Duchess Maria Romanova died in 1918. They were almost right. (978-1-63555-341-3)

Listen by Kris Bryant. Lily Croft is inexplicably drawn to Hope D'Marco but will she have the courage to confront the consequences of her past and present colliding? (978-1-63555-318-5)

Perfect Partners by Maggie Cummings. Elite police dog trainer Sara Wright has no intention of falling in love with a coworker, until Isabel Marquez arrives at Homeland Security's Northeast Regional Training facility and Sara's good intentions start to falter. (978-1-63555-363-5)

Shut Up and Kiss Me by Julie Cannon. What better way to spend two weeks of hell in paradise than in the company of a hot, sexy woman? (978-1-63555-343-7)

Spencer's Cove by Missouri Vaun. When Foster Owen and Abigail Spencer meet they uncover a story of lives adrift, loves lost, and true love found. (978-1-63555-171-6)

Without Pretense by TJ Thomas. After living for decades hiding from the truth, can Ava learn to trust Bianca with her secrets and her heart? (978-1-63555-173-0)

Unexpected Lightning by Cass Sellars. Lightning strikes once more when Sydney and Parker fight a dangerous stranger who threatens the peace they both desperately want. (978-1-163555-276-8)

Emily's Art and Soul by Joy Argento. When Emily meets Andi Marino she thinks she's found a new best friend but Emily doesn't know that Andi is fast falling in love with her. Caught up in exploring her sexuality, will Emily see the only woman she needs is right in front of her? (978-1-63555-355-0)

Escape to Pleasure: Lesbian Travel Erotica edited by Sandy Lowe and Victoria Villasenor. Join these award-winning authors as they explore the sensual side of erotic lesbian travel. (978-1-63555-339-0)

Music City Dreamers by Robyn Nyx. Music can bring lovers together. In Music City, it can tear them apart. (978-1-63555-207-2)

Ordinary is Perfect by D. Jackson Leigh. Atlanta marketing superstar Autumn Swan's life derails when she inherits a country home, a child, and a very interesting neighbor. (978-1-63555-280-5)

Royal Court by Jenny Frame. When royal dresser Holly Weaver's passionate personality begins to melt Royal Marine Captain Quincy's icy heart, will Holly be ready for what she exposes beneath? (978-1-63555-290-4)

Strings Attached by Holly Stratimore. Success. Riches. Music. Passion. It's a life most can only dream of, but stardom comes at a cost. (978-1-63555-347-5)

The Ashford Place by Jean Copeland. When Isabelle Ashford inherits an old house in small-town Connecticut, family secrets, a shocking discovery, and an unexpected romance complicate her plan for a fast profit and a temporary stay. (978-1-63555-316-1)

Treason by Gun Brooke. Zoem Malderyn's existence is a deadly threat to everyone on Gemocon and Commander Neenja KahSandra must find a way to save the woman she loves from having to commit the ultimate sacrifice. (978-1-63555-244-7)